The Chalice and
the Stirrup Cup

The Chalice and the Stirrup Cup

George Baber Atkisson

Copyright © 2018 by George Baber Atkisson.

Library of Congress Control Number: 2018902213
ISBN: Hardcover 978-1-9845-0988-8
Softcover 978-1-9845-0989-5
eBook 978-1-9845-0990-1

All rights reserved. No part of this book may be reproduced or transmitted in any form or by any means, electronic or mechanical, including photocopying, recording, or by any information storage and retrieval system, without permission in writing from the copyright owner.

The black and white cover photo is courtesy of the Fairfax County Public Library Photographic Archive (Virginia).

Any people depicted in stock imagery provided by Getty Images are models, and such images are being used for illustrative purposes only.
Certain stock imagery © Getty Images.

Print information available on the last page.

Rev. date: 02/23/2018

To order additional copies of this book, contact:
Xlibris
1-888-795-4274
www.Xlibris.com
Orders@Xlibris.com
769658

CONTENTS

A Note to the Reader..xi

CHAPTER 1	Homeward Bound 1
CHAPTER 2	The Letter 5
CHAPTER 3	The Redhead 7
CHAPTER 4	Too Shallow 11
CHAPTER 5	Got to Jump 14
CHAPTER 6	Sunday School 19
CHAPTER 7	The Visitors 23
CHAPTER 8	Esquire 27
CHAPTER 9	A Little Whiskey 30
CHAPTER 10	Crazy as a Loon 34
CHAPTER 11	Workhorse 37
CHAPTER 12	Little Bonnie 39
CHAPTER 13	The Davenport 43
CHAPTER 14	Thou Shalt Not Steal 47
CHAPTER 15	Fox Tracks 52
CHAPTER 16	The Angel of Death 59
CHAPTER 17	Grief 62
CHAPTER 18	Hog Killing 64
CHAPTER 19	Those Boys 69
CHAPTER 20	Oysters 73
CHAPTER 21	Pastoral Prospect 76
CHAPTER 22	Daydreams 79
CHAPTER 23	The Story 86
CHAPTER 24	An Innocent Girl 92
CHAPTER 25	Church 94

CHAPTER 26	Billie Slipped In	96
CHAPTER 27	It'll Be Different	100
CHAPTER 28	The Only One	105
CHAPTER 29	A Poem and a Thesis	107
CHAPTER 30	Bell Cow	111
CHAPTER 31	Stirrup Cups	113
CHAPTER 32	The Bit Bet	116
CHAPTER 33	A Deal	121
CHAPTER 34	Boxing Gloves	125
CHAPTER 35	Futile to Fight	132
CHAPTER 36	Scholastic Agenda	134
CHAPTER 37	The Dollar	138
CHAPTER 38	Portly Preacher	141
CHAPTER 39	The Death of Summer	144
CHAPTER 40	Ambush	150
CHAPTER 41	Football	154
CHAPTER 42	Christmas	161
CHAPTER 43	A Right Moment	168
CHAPTER 44	An Unexpected Visitor	170
CHAPTER 45	He's a Ruffian	173
CHAPTER 46	A Clanging Cymbal	176
CHAPTER 47	The Game	182
CHAPTER 48	Philip and the Eunuch	185
CHAPTER 49	Baptism	188
CHAPTER 50	Live by Faith	191
CHAPTER 51	Dr. Price	194
CHAPTER 52	The Moon	199
CHAPTER 53	How to Fell a Tree	205
CHAPTER 54	A Picnic and a Debate	208
CHAPTER 55	The Second Debate	217
CHAPTER 56	The Monthly Stipend	223
CHAPTER 57	Matrimony	227
CHAPTER 58	Jim's Spring	230
CHAPTER 59	Unable to Hear	234
CHAPTER 60	Amos Cloud	238

CHAPTER 61	Dear Diary	241
CHAPTER 62	The Abels	246
CHAPTER 63	A Long Way to Go	251
CHAPTER 64	You My Boy?	255
CHAPTER 65	Apprehension and Fear	261
CHAPTER 66	Birth of Fall	264
CHAPTER 67	Fauquier	267
CHAPTER 68	Poor	270
CHAPTER 69	War	273
CHAPTER 70	Shell-Shocked	279
CHAPTER 71	Patch	284
CHAPTER 72	Illicit Love	289
CHAPTER 73	Your Little Hand	292
CHAPTER 74	Wade Simmons	296
CHAPTER 75	Wade's First Anecdote	304
CHAPTER 76	Wade's Second Anecdote	307
CHAPTER 77	In the Vernacular	311
CHAPTER 78	The Loudoun Limited	315
CHAPTER 79	Home for Good	318
CHAPTER 80	Real Estate	320
CHAPTER 81	Fishing	325
CHAPTER 82	Reacquainted	328
CHAPTER 83	Coming Back Home	331
CHAPTER 84	Give It Time	337
CHAPTER 85	The Call	339
CHAPTER 86	The Businesswoman	342
CHAPTER 87	The Children	346
CHAPTER 88	Respect	348
CHAPTER 89	Secrets	351
CHAPTER 90	Separated	356
CHAPTER 91	The Shenandoah River	359
CHAPTER 92	Go With Maw	370
CHAPTER 93	Prenuptial	372
CHAPTER 94	I Told You So	378
CHAPTER 95	Which Ticket to Buy	381

CHAPTER 96	Judge Not	388
CHAPTER 97	Self-Interest	394
CHAPTER 98	The River Indus	397
CHAPTER 99	Equalizer	404
CHAPTER 100	Family Name	409

Dedication and Gratitude

This book is dedicated to my late wife of nearly sixty-nine years, Carlotta Tuttle Atkisson, originally from Hicksville, Ohio. If time permits, Carlotta will be the subject of my next literary endeavor. In her declining years, I would look at her and remark on what wonderful children and spouses, grandchildren, and great-grandchildren God had given us. Carlotta would smile and nod.

To my late mother, Florence Adams Atkisson, I give my everlasting appreciation and love.

To my mentor, Anna Whiston-Donaldson, I give thanks. I couldn't have done this without her.

Likewise, I thank my editor, Michelle Layer Rahal, whose expertise and demeanor were exceptionally helpful and absolutely required. Her working visits were instructive and enjoyable.

To Emerson Lopez, the 16-year-old son of my caregiver Irma Juarez, I give thanks for his tedious unscrambling and rearranging of my literary efforts on the computer. May he, as I often expressed to him, "Look down, look down, that lonesome road before he travels on."

A Note to the Reader

Sit ye down at the day's darkest hour, just before dawn, and face the east at the big glass window. Turn the wick of your lamp up until it almost smokes. Then begin this book.

Be patient and read on during the darkness as the sun slowly begins to light your world. As you read further, the sun will rise until you feel its warmth in your heart and soul. In the ensuing days of your life, may you likewise warm the hearts of others around you as your being is lifted toward Heaven.

Though the sun will go down each night and the clouds of sadness may touch your soul from time to time, be assured that each day the sun will return and the clouds will pass after nourishing your grain and flowers. And you will find peace and solace in your heart for the rest of your days.

CHAPTER 1

Homeward Bound

And it came to pass in those days that the ravages of man's folly laid waste to much of France, Belgium, the United Kingdom, and others. Trees had been stripped of limbs, their shredded trunks standing impregnated with shrapnel and bullets. Fields lay pockmarked by shells as trenches filled with mud and discarded bedrolls. Body parts were strewn in ditches (worthless waste even to their beleaguered comrades).

And then there were the living. They had endured painful breathing and loss of eyesight—entirely or partially—due to the advent of chemical weapons, like chlorine gas. Few of the afflicted thought these infirmities would follow them to the end of their lives. They hoped against hope, but with little faith, that the war would end before their demise.

The lieutenant stood atop the trench, now devoid of the enemy, and watched gratefully as Sergeant Marcus Dayne directed the activity from the bottom. He saw him stuff an object the size of a mortar shell into his shirt—then another, and another.

The word had spread that at 11:00 a.m. on the eleventh day of the eleventh month of 1918, the war was to end. Cease-fire.

"We must be vigilant," Marcus said. "After all this, we don't want some dastardly Boche picking us off on the last day of the war." Later he cautioned the lieutenant, who was only a boy, "Don't keep looking at your watch; a watched pot never boils." But all glanced intermittently at theirs or someone else's.

As the minutes ticked toward the plodding hour, the soldiers began to stand like children about to greet an angel. With overseas caps, steel helmets doffed and in hand, heavy woolen clothes, trench knives, cartridge belts, muddy leg wraps, well-worn cowhide boots, and rifles—they stood and waited in the cuts of an old wagon trail.

A roar arose just as the hands reached 11 o'clock. Cheers, hats, and even the rifles filled the air. Marcus stood there watching the men who were filled with glee. He knew of the word "glee," but he had never really understood it until now.

"I'm going home to see Momma!!" These were not the cries of men, he thought, but of boys, and Marcus was only twenty-nine himself.

The items that had appeared to be mortar shells turned out to be bottles of cognac. The lieutenant and Marcus sat against the bank in the cut of the wagon trail, each with their own bottle—the lieutenant sipping, and Marcus gulping. He had great respect for Marcus's knowledge of history as well as other aspects of life.

"Damn senseless war," Marcus began. "Most senseless war in history. First one side charging out of a trench into a hail of bullets and shells, and the next day the other side does the same, damn stupid thing."

"More senseless than our Civil War?"

"You're damn right! At least ole Grant could count. He knew that he had far more men than Lee and that if they kept killing each other off, he would eventually win. 'Course, the wasting of men didn't seem to matter a damn to him. Eventually he would be the victor. If he had left ole Burnside in there much longer, he would have come up short. Worse damn general in history, that Burnside. My granddaddy and 'bout three hundred artillerymen killed thousands off at that stone bridge at Antietam. And then there was his little fiasco at Fredericksburg where Burnside produced another blunder. And Lee, as war always does, turned into an inept ole man. But you see, at least he could count and finally knew the jig was up. *That* war had to be fought."

Marcus was on a roll. "The greatest of them all—you probably never even heard of him—was General George Henry Thomas. He wouldn't have put up with this shit. He would have come up with a better tactic that wouldn't have mimicked the senseless damn Mexican standoff. This one is without reason and without fulfillment. This so called "Great War" has settled nothing and will be continued at a later date. By our sons!"

They sat there for what seemed like hours. The lieutenant thought of all the times he had gone into battle with Sergeant Marcus Dayne as their leader. On several occasions, the sergeant had reached out his arm and pushed the lieutenant back, as if protecting his own son. Now as they sat there, sips of cognac lulled the lieutenant into a warm nostalgic glow while Marcus's gulps reduced him to a blubbering pile of inaudible noise—kind and caring of soul, but alcoholic of body. How sad and hopelessly incurable, the lieutenant thought.

The next morning Marcus lay crumpled, dead to the world. "Dayne, Dayne, get up! Hurry up! Get up, the colonel wants to see you."

Marcus rolled his uncooperative body out of his bedroll and headed to the tent.

"You sent for me sir?"

"Yes Dayne. At ease." Looking him over, the colonel added, "You look as if you're hungover."

"I celebrated a little last night, sir."

"How can you call it celebrating when you continually knock yourself out and wake up sick with a splitting headache the next day?"

"I know, colonel," Marcus admitted. "I'm quitting. I am never going to drink again."

"Aw, bullshit. I've heard that before." Motioning to the chair, he said, "Sit down. I want to talk to you. I understand you are to leave for home immediately. Your father works for General March, I understand. What's his rank?"

"Major," Marcus answered.

"What did he do before the war? I assume he's not a regular, is he?"

The line of questioning perplexed Marcus. "No, sir. He was a cadet in college in Georgia. Went to Georgetown law school in D.C., and now practices law in D.C."

"Well, pray tell me how in the hell you wound up over here, the father of three small children? You do have three children, do you not?"

"I was in the guard and was called up."

"Transferred into our division?" the colonel asked.

"Yes, sir."

"Well, we're sending your ass out of here. But look, I want to..." The colonel stopped himself short and reconsidered his remarks. "What are you running from Dayne? Did you join up to get away from your family? Then you drink to get away from the duty? The Army?"

Shaking his head, Marcus said, "I swear colonel, as God is my judge, I'm going home, and I'll never..."

"Oh, bullshit!"

"I swear to you, I'll never..."

"Bullshit," the colonel said forcefully, declaring an end to the subject. "All right, I wish you well. They tell me when you were sober you were a good... well... a good leader. Were you?"

Ignoring the question, Marcus spoke, more to himself than to the colonel. "I'm going back to my family. I can work for my father and perhaps after a while I can take the bar exam or I can always do court reporting."

"At least you fought for your country. But you better lay off the booze and quit running, Dayne. Quit running away from your life."

The colonel rose from his seat and held out his right hand. Marcus shook it as the colonel placed his left hand on Marcus's shoulder. Looking him in the eye he said, "I wish you nothing but the best and, again, thanks for your help."

"Thank you, sir, and good luck to you, too."

Marcus Dayne was homeward bound. The war in Europe had finally ended. But the war within was not fulfilled.

CHAPTER 2

The Letter

A fence in Northern Virginia separated the two cultures living side-by-side yet asunder. It being November, this was the time for toasting bourbon, jumping fences, and chasing to the hounds—all on horseback—on the one side of the fence. On the other side, it was a time for shucking corn, killing hogs, hunting squirrels and rabbits, and gathering chestnuts. By mutual consent, the hunting covered both lands—especially the fox hunting.

Climbing up into the feed box, Billie Blacksheare grabbed both the top of the bridle and the forelock in her right hand and, with her left hand to the horse's mouth, repeated, "Take your bit; take your bit." Once bridled, she crawled down the horse's neck, took her seat and the reins, and steered the animal out the stable.

Her house sat atop a hill about a furlong above Snakeden Station, a toponym derived from a cold creek that ran out of the woods to a clearing where a snake or two often lay waiting for trout minnows to jump up the respectable four-foot waterfall. Certainly, they were not large enough to be spawning. Possibly, they were attempting to swim up the cool Snakeden Creek that emptied into the warmer Difficult Run nearby. Anyone who had observed Snakeden Station itself could see that it was nothing more than a house that served as a dwelling, store, and post office all in one.

Dismounting, Billie stuck her chin over the counter and asked, "Mrs. McKay, do you have any mail for the Daynes or the Browns?"

"Yes, child. One for Bonnie from Europe. I just hope it's good news."

Grabbing the letter, Billie bounced toward the door and squeezed past an incoming patron. Using the fence as a stile, she mounted and galloped down the railroad track to the bridge. Now out of earshot, Mrs. McKay said to the customer, "I have never seen that child where she didn't have her crop stuck in her back—even when she is without a horse."

Adding to Mrs. McKay's assessment, the customer said, "Why, they say she jumps those chicken coops without even being in a saddle! And when the boys tease her, she tells them she's a young Indian squaw and they don't use saddles."

When she reached the bridge, Billie bore off at a left oblique, crossed Difficult Run at a shallow spot, returned to the railroad track, came upon a chicken coop fence—which she jumped—and then continued to the Browns' barn. It was a typical building with three sides underground and the fourth, facing south, at ground level. There was a walk out with a door at each end and a Dutch door on sliding tracks in the middle. The door on the right allowed access to the horse stalls. The one on the left led down an aisle in front of the horse stalls to the cow stanchions. This door had been left open. Billie's horse entered as if it were her own barn.

Tucking her crop into the back of her pants, Billie leaned back, grabbed the track over the door and let the horse walk out from under her. It passed the Browns' tethered horses and entered into a stall. Billie, dangling in the air, pleaded, "Joe Dayne! Joe Dayne! You in there? Joe Dayne, come help me down. I got mail."

The boy who was her same age came out, wrapped his arms around her upper legs, and let her slide to the ground.

Billie took the letter directly to Bonnie's bedroom, as if she were her own mother or at least lived there. Bonnie accepted the letter and eased herself down on the edge of the bed. By some instinct, Billie knew to leave Bonnie to her own thoughts, or dreams; the wife and mother needed to be alone with her letter as if it were her husband himself.

CHAPTER 3

The Redhead

They'd first met about ten years prior.

There was this bottomland that ran along either side of Oak Run that snaked from one side of the railroad track to the other covering a three-mile area. Cattle and other livestock had grazed the fields and surrounding hills to where they resembled well-manicured lawns. It was along this stream that two fields, separated by a barbed wire fence, joined as part of the Carter farm. There were any number of Carters in the county; they owned and occupied much of the farmland, and had so for years. Marcus Dayne's mother was a Carter from Fairfax and related to the Carters who lived on this land. Though it might as well be told that the Carters from Fairfax deemed themselves a social notch above those who lived here, between Vienna and the west.

And so it was, after riding on the train from Washington, D.C. to Vienna to Snakeden that Marcus had arrived at the farm to visit his two Carter cousins, though second cousins they were. Now as the three of them sat in silence along the bank, they spied three girls slowly approaching from up the stream. Marcus's eyes were glued on the one wearing the white blouse and green skirt as if she were the only one there. He whispered to his cousins, "Who's the redhead?"

"That's Bonnie Brown," they both said at the same time.

Lost in their own conversation, the girls were unaware of the boys' presence. When they came within a few feet, Marcus suddenly yelled, "Boo!"

There were screams and squeals of surprise before the girls clasped hands and giggled uncontrollably. Then Bonnie picked up a stick and threw it at the boys. "Don't you ever scare us like that again," she reprimanded, half laughing with eyebrows arched.

Feigning irritation, Bonnie removed herself from the group and went to sit on a tree limb that appeared to have grown parallel to the ground in its early growth before moving in a skyward direction. Positioned only a few feet above the ground, it made for a pleasant seat. The other two girls, along with the two Carter boys, removed their shoes and headed toward the water. Holding their skirts just above their knees, the girls splashed discreetly so as not to wet their clothes.

Finding himself alone, Marcus nonchalantly eased himself down onto the limb beside Bonnie. With a worldly air, Marcus slowly turned his face into hers and said as matter-of-factly as was humanly possible, "I've stayed in New York for great lengths of time; I've been to Florida and ridden the fishing boats out of Gasparilla Island; I've spent time researching at the University of Georgia; I've traveled all over the state from Macon to Atlanta where my people settled, as well as the city of Washington, and I can say without a second thought, and certainly without fear of contradiction, that you are without a doubt the most beautiful girl I have ever seen."

And now Bonnie felt as if she were becoming unseated on the limb—not falling off, but as if she were simply floating upward, suspended. She realized that if she did not regain her senses, she risked being completely swept off the limb. Or worse than that, this stranger might at any moment jump to his feet in laughing ridicule having made fun of her. Bonnie's first thought was to slap the hell out of him and thus render him to his proper groveling position where she understood all unmarried men must reside. Instead, she did the next best thing. She simply turned her attention toward him, slowly moving her head and eyes from his feet to his face, as if measuring his whole body. Though Marcus had felt a certain level of sophistication before, and though he meant every word he had uttered, he was surprised by how this girl's response crushed his feeling of superiority.

"That was a beautiful little lie you just told," Bonnie said. "I suppose I must say I appreciate it even if it is quite farfetched."

"Which part?" Marcus asked. "About my travels or that you are the prettiest girl I've ever seen?"

"I think you know which part," she said, tossing her red hair with a jerk of her head and laughing.

As her locks fell back toward her shoulders, Marcus noticed how the weight of the ends seemed to stretch the curl out of her hair before it recoiled like springs. He concluded that they were natural and not the result of some curling iron that the city girls used. Her hair wasn't kinky and course or unruly like his; it rolled in waves that crisscrossed the sides of her head.

They talked on about their respective families realizing that they both knew of each other's relatives from indirect conversations with other people. She found him to be comical and fun loving at one moment, serious and impetuous the next. She couldn't put her finger on why, but she also considered him to be impulsive.

As Bonnie rose from the limb and started walking away, Marcus whispered, "May I see you sometime?"

"Maybe," she said and strolled off.

"But how will I know how…?"

"I work in the city; you can find me," she said with a wave of her hand.

"Damn it. Why do girls always do that? If she were ugly, she would have given me a dozen damn numbers," he complained. But no one was there to hear him.

Bonnie was sitting at her desk in Washington, D.C., reminiscing of her encounter with the charming boy, when suddenly she heard his voice, and there he was. Smiling. Smiling as if he had just won first prize in something that meant a lot to him.

"How did you find me?"

"My little cousin Ross found you for me."

"You shouldn't have come here."

"Why not?" he asked confidently. "I had to see you! What time do you get off? Let's go for a walk in the park."

"No."

Marcus looked hurt, so Bonnie continued. "You don't realize that there's no way for me to get home if I go for a walk with you after work. The trains don't run that late."

"The last train runs at 7:30, and I will see that you get to the station in time."

"Momma wouldn't like me doing something like that."

Marcus accepted her reasoning. "Alright, then I will come out to your house Saturday at eleven."

"Oh, I don't know. You seem so impatient!"

Deep down in her heart, Bonnie knew it had been a mistake to flirt with him as sure as she knew he would show up.

CHAPTER 4

Too Shallow

As she sat on the bed turning Marcus's letter over in her hands, Bonnie thought of that initial encounter with him. He had always been impatient. One moment he would be full of life and joking, and the next—usually when no one was present—he would be pushing her into making hasty decisions. He wasn't keen on allowing Bonnie to have time to reason through matters of utmost importance that could affect the remainder of her life. Like marriage.

Maw had tried to talk her out of it. She even pleaded with Doctor Leigh to "put some sense into her head." Doctor Leigh had railed assiduously against Bonnie's impending marriage, telling her in no uncertain terms that it would be a mistake to marry Marcus Dayne who everyone knew was a drinker. Bonnie replied that she would tame him. Doctor Leigh scoffed at her answer noting that a million other women had tried the same thing unsuccessfully down through the ages. She would live to regret this nonsense, he had said.

Bonnie held off until one afternoon in Washington when he gave her an ultimatum: "If you don't say 'yes' to me now, I'm never going to ask you again."

While his words should have been soothing, the look on her face manifested impending anguish—not unlike the face of one anticipating removal of an infected tooth. Her hopes for an ameliorative result had been obliterated and replaced with possible pain.

Haunting her now were those words of her brother, Little Joe. One day at the swimming hole when the boys were yelling for her to dive into the water, Little Joe had hollered, "Don't jump Bonnie, it's too shallow!" Then, a couple of years later when she and Marcus sat on the board fence courting and laughing, Little Joe had ridden past her on his horse and said the same thing. "Don't jump Bonnie, it's too shallow."

But soon thereafter, she jumped. She and Marcus settled in Washington, close to his parents and her job. Marcus eventually found permanent employment with the railroad in Hampton Roads, some 100 miles southeast of Richmond. Work kept him away from home, but he would ride the train back to Washington most weekends. Bonnie soon became pregnant and quit her job. Bored with life in the city, she spent much of her time at her parents' home near Snakeden Station.

During one visit, Marcus suggested that Bonnie come to Hampton Roads to stay with him during the week, but Maw rejected the idea saying, "I'm not going to have my baby staying in any far-off place alone all day." She was referring to her daughter, not her unborn grandchild. When Marcus suggested that Bonnie's friend, Prudence, could accompany her, Maw hit the ceiling, saying, "Over my mother's and *my* dead body."

Except for the first few years of their marriage, Marcus was truant, not only at work but at home. He went from job to job with his drinking problem and promises to quit. Bonnie was invariably asked by everyone she spoke to, including her mother, "Why don't you give him up and admit that you made a mistake?"

She would simply lament, "Because I love him."

While she was living with her parents, Bonnie gave birth to Joseph whom they lovingly called JD. In the ensuing years when Marcus would have periods of sobriety, Bonnie gave birth to two more children, William and Mary Ann. Then Marcus joined the National Guard, which he inferred was an act of patriotism in response to the war clouds in Europe. Others suggested it was to escape his family responsibilities and obtain a monetary stipend. Whatever the reason, he was shipped across the Atlantic to the front lines.

To cover expenses, Bonnie took a job at a department store in D.C. where several male colleagues were heard to call Marcus a loser or a ne'er-do-well. A few, including her boss, had variously suggested that she should dump him and go on with her life, perhaps with one of them. At first her response was, "I love him." Later it was, "I've made my bed, and now I must lie in it." Later still, "But you don't understand; I still love the bastard!"

Bonnie hesitantly opened the letter and read it. Marcus was coming home. Sitting on the edge of the bed, she hoped the war might have changed him. Maybe he had seen a different life and would want to be with his family now. On the other hand, she accepted the fact that Marcus was a drinker and had been, even before they were married. She didn't know what had first provoked his drinking, but Bonnie had since learned from her mother-in-law, Nellie, that Marcus had run off to New York City when he was only fourteen years old. The reason why was never divulged.

CHAPTER 5

Got to Jump

Many days of anticipation had passed since Bonnie Brown Dayne had first read the letter and shared the news with her children. The World War had ended, and the troops were coming home—so was their father. Four-year-old Mary Ann, whom everyone called Little Bonnie, and six-year-old Will were elated, but eight-year-old JD was uncertain and apprehensive. He had witnessed marital strife in his family before his father left and now feigned excitement for the sake of his mother and siblings.

Bonnie and her children now lived in a small dwelling on the land owned by her father. Though comfortable, it was less spacious than the main farmhouse where her parents lived. She had declined each of their invitations to come live with them explaining that she wanted a place of her own when her husband came home. Though Bonnie offered Maw rent money each month, she always refused it.

The days passed slowly with no sign of Marcus. Each morning except Sundays, Bonnie caught the 7:30 a.m. train to Rosslyn where she transferred to the streetcar that took her to the department store where she worked in D.C. Taking the same route in reverse each afternoon, she would arrive home at 6:30 p.m. Hazel, the daughter of one of her father's former slaves, kept watch over the children in her absence.

JD happened to be watching the station when the five o'clock train relinquished its passengers and tooted its whistle as a warning to any on the track at the ensuing curve. At first he saw no one and simply stared as if in a trance. Minutes later he was startled by the sight of a man emerging in full view. He moved as if his feet were running to catch pace with his body, neither gaining nor losing ground. It was not until after the man had staggered over the ties in the track for a hundred feet or more and finally fell down the weed-infested bank that JD realized the man was his own father. Concern and compassion for his mother's husband hushed the apprehension in his heart and propelled him down the hill, arms waving, across the foot log that hung over Oak Run.

Before the child could even focus on the face of the gorilla-like man, his body was encircled by hairy arms, brutally squeezing his chest, bending his head backward in suffocation against a stale woolen shirt. For an eternal moment, the hysterical child kicked and scratched loose from the derisive man who heaved vile breath as thick saliva oozed from the corners of his mouth down into his unshaven chin. Once free, JD scampered away through the barbed wire fence and across the creek, taking a shortcut home onto Hazel's lap.

Meanwhile, Marcus Dayne sunk to the ground and keeled over into the weeds in a whiskey stupor. At least an hour passed before the whacking heel of a humiliated Bonnie rudely awakened him as she made her way home. As she stomped off in exasperation and tears, Marcus caught up to her and walked along sideways, much like a dog trotting beside its master. His feet were under his body, but they were dragging along almost in a side step.

"Couldn't you, just once, be sober?" she cried. "Don't you realize how long the children and I have waited?"

"Aw, now wait a minute," Marcus pleaded. "I was just celebrating my homecoming."

"You damn, lame brain! First you celebrated going away, and now…" Bonnie caught herself, and felt ashamed for swearing. "See there, you've made me sin again."

She took off one of her shoes and raised it, but she never hit him.

"What's so bad about me having a couple of drinks?" Marcus asked.

"It makes a cock-eyed idiot out of you!" Bonnie answered. "How do you think I feel when everybody sees you drunk on the train?"

And so they argued as they walked homeward. Marcus did not reconcile his position, which only incensed Bonnie more.

JD was not at the top of the hill to meet her, as was his habit each night. She found him half hidden, though not uncomfortable, behind the kitchen stove. She picked him up and held him close.

Marcus had come home on a Monday. He became reacquainted with his in-laws, Joseph and Lottie Brown, on Tuesday, the same day he made up with his wife. He was able to get a little closer to the children on Wednesday. On Thursday he went into the city with his wife to seek employment and was not heard from again until Saturday when he bumped into Bonnie in the white stucco depot in Rosslyn. He had been drinking but was brazen and confident. His wife refused to discuss his condition or the potential consequences of further drink for fear of a public argument.

Boarding the homebound train, Bonnie went to the regular passenger section while he, with aplomb, went to the smoker section, which was a small, enclosed area in one of the cars where men did just as the word suggests. Marcus had been reared in Washington, D.C. and was considered good company by several of the country boys. Thus, he was insistently invited into their card game called 500. Only a few hands had been dealt and little ground gained toward home before Marcus and three of the men began to steal to the restroom to have drinks, straight from the bottle.

"Go ahead, Brook," Marcus encouraged one of the men, "but not too much. Save us some."

Brook grasped the bottle and took two deep swallows. Ernest, a non-overseas veteran, did likewise. Then Marcus raised the half-filled bottle to eye level, which actually was a toast and measurement together, then drained it with three tremendous, bubbling gulps before casting the impoverished bottle into the trashcan.

"That ought to show you boys who's the man around here," Marcus said.

"Hell!" Ernest yapped.

"I have to say one thing," Brook declared. "That boy will always share his whiskey to the last drop."

Marcus chuckled to himself as he felt the other pint in his shirt that would hold him through the night. It was impressive that he could disembark without falling; however, once off the train, Marcus was unable to keep pace with his wife.

To explain what happened the remainder of the way home, one must have an intimate knowledge of the land. It was as such: the train station was at a road crossing, which immediately forked on the other side. The left fork proceeded due south where it linked to a main road at an intersection where the Beulah Methodist Church was situated. The right fork proceeded parallel with the railroad track for three furlongs over Oak Run before it angled up a steep hill to the closely situated homes. It was common then, because of dust or mud in the case of rain, to walk along the track until one came to within a hundred yards of Oak Run. Then the traveler would transfer to the road in order to cross the run via a foot log rather than the more elevated railroad trestle. Bonnie chose the route by the foot log; Marcus chose the trestle.

Having arrived safely at home, Bonnie went about changing into house clothes. Meanwhile, Marcus staggered along a few feet, sunk down into a squat, and attempted to proceed along again. He repeated the process until he was finally squatting in the middle of the railroad trestle on the very edge, mumbling to himself. When Bonnie heard the seven o'clock train whistle blow for the crossing, she instinctively looked to see where her husband was. Spotting him on the trestle, she screamed to her father who was just then walking back from the barn with JD.

"Paw, Paw, he's on the bridge!" But Paw was too deaf to hear, and JD had to tell him that Bonnie was screaming for help. By this time, the situation was obvious to the boy's grandfather.

"He's got to jump; he's got to jump or he'll be killed. Don't look, son!"

But JD had to look. And as he did, his father fell forward from his squatting position to avoid the crushing wheels bearing down on him. At the very last moment, it appeared to JD as if the train had halted, but it hadn't. He watched as Marcus, with arms flopping, took off from the bridge like a heavy bodied bird, wings begging the body to come on up, but weight winning out. He fell like a heavy sinker taking a fishing hook to the bottom of the stream. Marcus simply disappeared below the trestle as the train clickety-clacked on.

CHAPTER 6

Sunday School

JD stepped over the roughhewn sill and walked along the stone wall in front of the horse manger back to where the cows were in their stanchions. He carried a new sand bucket painted red on the outside and yellow on the inside with a crimp seal running up the side that he thought wouldn't leak milk if Paw Brown let him milk. Walking past two cows, he stood behind Paw who sat on a three-legged stool, his hat pushed back by the cow's flank, alternating teats, jerking squirts of milk into the foaming bucket. JD stood awhile, holding onto the precious moment before he might be denied the chance to milk. After all, his mother wouldn't want him kicked by no cow. But Paw, being Paw, couldn't deny his being grown enough to milk now that JD had his own bucket. He wouldn't ask to milk old Renna or Bossie or old mouse-colored Lady—best cow Paw said he ever had or ever would have—but Paw surely knew he could milk Ole Susie without getting kicked. And he would promise to milk her clean, too, so she wouldn't dry up.

"Yes?" Paw asked without breaking rhythm.

"Paw, kin I milk Ole Susie? I'll be careful, and I'll milk her clean."

"I suppose, son. But you be careful, and don't let that Holstein step on you."

"OK, Paw. I'll be careful."

"Get a feed box to sit on, son."

JD dragged the feed box up in one hand by its cutout handle and, holding the bucket in the other, butted Susie in the flank with his head just like Paw had done, all the while saying, "Back ya leg; back ya leg."

Paw finished the other cows before JD had milked even a quart from Ole Susie, which only half-filled his bucket.

"Whyn't you go strip those other cows while I finish Ole Susie, son? Strip 'em clean. See if I got 'em good'n clean, 'cause they'll dry up if we don't get 'em good'n clean."

And while Paw wasn't looking, JD squirted milk on the cat's whiskers as she stood up on her hind legs trying to grab the liquid with her front paws. She was sort of fighting at the milk but liking it all the while.

"Paw, kin we go fishing tomorrow morning?"

"Aw, son, you got to go to Sunday school tomorrow morning. But after, maybe after we come back from Sunday school and eat dinner, we can go."

"But Paw, you always take a nap after Sunday dinner and fish don't bite in the middle of the day—you say that yourself. Wouldn't hurt none if we missed one Sunday," JD pleaded.

"Nope, son. Young boy like you has got to go to Sunday school. We'll catch some fish, you just wait and see."

Sunday morning when Paw went to fetch JD, Bonnie looked like she was trying to bore a hole in his ear with a washcloth—just like Maw Brown coring apples. As JD tried to escape the cleansing, his mother detained him by bending his other ear back with her left hand.

"Don't hurt the boy," Paw ordered.

Bonnie chided, "I got to get the dirt out of his ears."

JD whined, "Why do I have to go to Sunday school?"

Bonnie answered, "You have to learn 'bout Jesus and God; besides, everybody's got to go to church."

"Why don't you have to go then?"

"'Cause I've got work to do," Bonnie chided.

"Paw says you're not supposed to work on Sunday," JD offered

Refusing to participate, Bonnie ordered her son, "You go 'long now with your grandpa and don't you cut up in Sunday school."

JD, running two steps to keep up with one of Paw's, went down the steep hill to the foot log. As he crossed over in front of Paw, with his hand sliding along the steadying rail, he looked at the sand bar where the two footprints that were made the night before remained. He stopped and peered between both arms, upstretched as if he intended to chin himself on the handrail. Paw stopped behind and watched for a moment as JD's eyes flickered from the trestle to the sand bar below—back and forth. Finally, Paw asked, "You thought he had been killed when he jumped, didn't you?"

"Yes sir."

"What'd you think when you saw him squatting there, grinning, and his feet stuck in the sand?"

JD said, "Nothin'."

"You must've thought somethin'. Weren't you glad to see he wasn't hurt?"

JD sighed, slid his hands along the rail, his body sideways and facing the trestle. "I thought he looked like a turkey buzzard."

"You shouldn't talk like that. He's your father."

"He ain't my father, Paw," JD insisted.

"Yes, he is."

"No, he ain't."

JD sat in the choir loft, which was separated into a classroom by a pull curtain. He peeked out into the sanctuary where Mr. Ferguson, the town carpenter, was telling the congregation how they had all done wrong that week. JD couldn't help but wonder what Paw had done wrong. Mr. Ferguson went on to say that they must ask God's forgiveness and recommit themselves to the principles of Jesus Christ. "It's time we quit worrying 'bout ball playing on Sunday and concern ourselves with how we treat our neighbor."

JD heard Mr. Ferguson tell the congregation that there wasn't going to be any preaching today in light of the fact that the church had no pastor. He also said there probably wasn't going to be any preaching discuss it because he felt a matter such as that should be confidential. Besides, he knew Uncle Cecil would admonish him for doing something that Harley's own father wouldn't do.

Uncle Cecil said, "Joe, your nephews and your neighbors are going to bankrupt you."

"How's that, Cecil?" Paw asked.

"You know how," Uncle Cecil responded. "By borrowing your binder and your horses—your money, too! Why, every time you lend your binder out, it gets broken, and you have to put a new roller and new slats on the canvases. They just don't know how to take care of machinery. You know that."

"I just can't turn my back on my neighbors—even if they bust things up."

"Yeah," Uncle Cecil said disapprovingly. "What about your nephew down there across the track; you think he would return the favor?"

"He's my neighbor and my nephew both. I don't know whether he would or not. You know, brother, it's not as they *would* do unto you, but as you *would have them* do unto you."

"I just hope you get your money back," Uncle Cecil stated.

"I will. Harley is industrious and won't squander the money. If I know him, he'll bring back the same bills the bank gave him."

Aunt Gin and Maw went into the kitchen, which was board and batten on the outside—vertical boards with thinner wood strips called batten nailed over each crack. On the inside, instead of both sand plaster and wallpaper as in the rest of the house, the kitchen walls were covered with a thick brown paper similar to a heavy roofing paper. It was fastened in place to the studding with lathing nails and tin rings about the size of a half dollar.

Maw had an icebox, but no ice to keep it cool, so the iced tea was made palatable on a hot summer day by adding cool well water to concentrated tea. Paw and Uncle Cecil sipped theirs slowly, and after the glasses were removed from their mouths, they almost simultaneously squeezed the moisture out of their mustaches by dragging their lower lips up and out and then down.

Later, while Maw and Aunt Gin discussed housekeeping, Aunt Gin explained how she always put newspaper down on the floors after she mopped on Saturdays and made the children not only walk on the paper but stay out of the parlor entirely unless they had company. Meanwhile, with a boyish twinkle that seemed to sparkle not only from his eyes but also from the twitch of his mouth, Uncle Cecil told Paw how all the young women over at Snakeden had made a fuss over how fine he looked in his black suit and matching black hat. However, he wasn't going to let them turn his head because he already had the prettiest girl.

When Uncle Cecil got up to go, he jokingly jumped up into the air and clicked his heels twice before he hit the ground, saying, "Hot damn, there's a little oil left in the ole lamp." Paw looked at his brother with pleasure.

As one group left, another arrived. Come now the Washington, D.C. Daynes: Charles Lucius Colbert and his wife, Nellie. This Sunday afternoon, the indispensable train had brought them from another hot and humid day in the capital city. Having suffered the unbearable heat of Saturday last in the district, Marcus's parents arrived to invoke relief under the spreading gum trees in the Browns' yard. Untypically, Marcus's father had removed his coat and now carried it hooked on his forefinger over his shoulder. Marcus's mother was not afforded comparable relief from her several petticoats and other underwear too numerous to mention.

Charles Lucius Colbert had originally come to Washington to attend law school. During his early years, he had practiced at a position in the Federal Trade Commission and other government agencies. After the war, he opened his own private law practice. He used his initials as his trademark signature, and thus everyone now referred to him as CLC. All the Daynes, except for CLC were Episcopalians. CLC had been converted by the Catholics at Georgetown or, as it was suggested, joined the denomination or political leverage.

Much to the interest and amusement of those sitting around in the shade, CLC regaled in stories of life in Macon and Athens, the latter the home of his alma mater, the University of Georgia. He could adjust his conversation to keep the interest of all ages. Particularly interested was the young neighbor girl, Billie Blacksheare.

Marcus was present for the gathering and contributed to the conversation by dogmatically stating that a man shouldn't touch whiskey and that the government ought to do something for the veterans. What exactly ought to be done, he didn't say.

Paw, as he was wont, spoke of the value of a clean life where one told the truth, did not steal, and paid his debts on time. Having thusly established such a reputation, Paw had said, any judge in the county would know you and deal with you fairly and reasonably. Billie, having noticed the reference to the court, directed her eyes to CLC and saw him roll his eyes skyward.

CHAPTER 8

Esquire

Within a day or two, Billie decided that she wanted to go to Washington, D.C. and observe CLC in court. She explained as much in a letter, which she asked her father to review.

"Papa, I have written a letter to Mr. Dayne asking him if I could go to court with him. Will you look it over for me?"

Thomas Jackson Blacksheare, or Stonewall as the scattered members of the community called him, was socially prominent by marriage. His smooth talking completely belied the cunning confidence game he was to play in each real estate transaction he made. He had purchased the farm at Snakeden, rendering it into a hunt club showplace of gracious living. The house was colonial with multiple dining rooms, the horse shed boasted a taproom, and the red barn had been trimmed in white like the snaking board fences that separated fields and farms. Stonewall could often be seen sitting astride a horse. Though he might appear regal to an outsider, to the locals he was considered an intruder.

"Well," he said, "it looks okay, except when addressing a letter to a lawyer one must write 'esquire.' Address him as esquire."

Billie wrote "esquire" on the envelope and that was that, until the day she went to Washington and was walking down the street with CLC and started calling him esquire. "Papa says that's what I should call you." Eventually, the rest of the folks picked up on it—some in conformity and some in jest.

"Esquire, why did you roll your eyes when Paw said if everyone was honest the judge would treat them good?"

"Oh, honey! Did I do that?"

Billie nodded.

"Well, in most cases that would be true. But what occurred to me was that people being people, unless the other party to the case were to be a close friend or, worse even, related to the judge, then the judge's interest may be conflicted. Do you know what they call conflict of interest?"

"No, sir."

"That is when you decide in favor of a relative or close friend instead of what is fair and reasonable. In other words, a decision is made on the basis of feelings for one person so it conflicts… I'm trying to think of a word… sway. That's the word! …that sways you toward the person you like most and not the person who is right."

CLC continued, "Say justice is a tree, and standing on either side are the two opposing parties. Now justice is standing straight, tall, and fair. So, the judge looks over at the one who has told the truth and paid his bills and so forth, and then he looks over at the other who may be his kin, a former partner, or a friend. All this kinship and friendship and social connections start blowing the tree of justice just like the wind, and it starts bending or swaying toward the kin or former partner or the friend. So, you can see that the wind or conflict of interest decided the case—not as it should have been in the favor of truth and justice. Do you understand what I mean?"

"I think so. Maybe."

"Well honey, as I have told Nellie a hundred times, Fairfax is a provincial little town. That doesn't mean the people there are bad, but they will sometimes stick together, especially when an outsider is involved. Seems to me that is especially true around little county seats where the courthouse is involved and the stakes are higher or of more consequence.

"The Browns are wonderfully honest people, and you and the others can always go by what they say. You can't go wrong doing what they say. Other than our religion, I believe our laws are of more importance than anything else, and neither has a place for unfairness."

"Do you believe in God, Esquire?"

"Oh yes. Don't you?"

"I don't know. JD does."

Billie's adventure into town did not end with CLC. Afterwards, she spent hours with Aunt Sallie and Aunt Marge who were both sisters of Nellie Dayne and of no relation to Billie herself. Aunt Sallie was a spinster, but Aunt Marge had a daughter named June who was an artist of some repute. She taught in a local school, had exhibited in Paris, and continued to add to her collection of paintings, which were strewn and hung throughout her four-story home. The bottom floor, however, was a walkout basement.

June and her husband were non-believers, yet they were charitable and neighborly and had many of the virtues of which Christians spoke. Billie was intrigued by the many stories June told of Fairfax and the Carter family that were, among other things, critical of the men for their drinking and boisterous speech. June's husband was a frail and quiet man, a lover of music and the piano, which he played well. He also did some painting under the tutelage of June.

In later years, particularly appalling to Billie was June's forays into one picture one day and another the next where she was constantly trying to improve on the paintings—something as simple as a shade that when changed made little difference, or a line here or there. This constant changing not only continued as she grew older, but was exacerbated by her fear that age and time would foreclose before she had finished each picture to perfection. This association was to continue in one degree or another until June's death.

CHAPTER 9

A Little Whiskey

Life changes accompanied the change of season. Marcus, visibly drunk at least twice each week and still jobless, was forced to move in with his parents in Washington because Bonnie had moved in with her parents to establish a marital separation.

As Uncle Cecil had predicted, the binder had to be repaired before Paw could cut his own wheat and pile it into tall pyramid-like stacks, except they were rounded. Later, he thrashed it out with the help of neighbors.

Then there was the third and final plowing of the corn, leaving only the hauling and sawing of the wood into sixteen-inch blocks that created a pile about eight-feet high. Enough blocks were split each night into pieces that looked like a piece of pie at the end. If foul weather was expected, several days' worth would have to be split and stacked on the porch.

The day before Christmas, Uncle Cecil rode up on an unsaddled horse. By the time JD got in from doing chores, Paw and Uncle Cecil were deep into conversation. Uncle Cecil was freshly shaven in a neat white shirt and tie, even though he had had to get the horse out of the barn and ride a mile. He had blanketed the horse to keep the horsehair from getting on his pants.

JD saw Paw turn to Maw and say, "Go and get my safe box." Nodding affirmatively, she started up the stairs to their bedroom.

When she handed Paw the box, JD was watching from the kitchen. Paw opened the little box with a key and took out a pint bottle that JD thought couldn't be, but was, whiskey. JD thought, *Lord, Paw and Uncle Cecil are gonna jump off the damn bridge.* JD didn't even repent to himself for thinking a cuss word at a time like this.

Handing the bottle to his wife, Paw said, "Here Joanna, fix us a couple of drinks."

JD watched in perplexity as Maw entered the kitchen and poured a little whiskey into two glasses. Then she added cold water and a spoonful of sugar to each and, after stirring them repeatedly, marched back into the living room like she hadn't done anything wrong.
Lord, she was crazier than the men, JD thought; she was a woman, and women don't want men drinking.

Now, Maw didn't take any drink herself, but she sure had seen enough drinking that summer to know better than to give Paw, who was crippled up, whiskey. Or even worse, how in the world did she think Uncle Cecil would ever get on ole Tootsie, much less stay on course going home? Horses in those days, at least Paw's and Uncle Cecil's horses, were half draft horse and half standard bred—more of a carriage horse. While not ponderously able to pull real heavy loads, they were, however, able to work in the field and made good carriage horses. Tootsie, as the name implies, was a mare. She was about sixteen-hands high and not mean like some. Nevertheless, she was spirited now by grain and lack of work.

Unbeknownst to the adults inside, JD untied Tootsie's reins from the apple tree and led her out behind the granary where they couldn't be seen. He tried to mount, first by jumping up and grabbing her mane. Unsuccessful at that, he popped up like a chicken jumping up for a bug off a vine, using the horse's spine as a purchase to get his belly up on the animal so he could throw his leg over and come astride like grown folks do. But that, too, was unsuccessful because of the difference in his and the horse's height. Finally, he led Tootsie around the apple trees, using them as cover to keep Paw and Uncle Cecil from seeing him, to the whitewashed board fence. Holding the reins and bringing Tootsie down the lane, he climbed up on the highest board, and just as he was about to throw his right leg over and settle on her back, her head being held close to him and the fence by the reins, she moved her rear around twitching her tail. But he, seeing this, altered his move and jumped astride of her.

Tootsie trotted off, bouncing him not precariously, but uncomfortably. He was unable to slow her to a walk, yet grateful that she did not resort to a downhill gallop that could throw a rider off or, in fear, buck the rider over the head of the horse. When Tootsie had rounded the first hill and started up the next, he felt confident he could stay on and complete his dangerous mission, even if he couldn't regulate the pace of the horse. By the time Tootsie reached the crest of the third hill, JD knew he could ride any darn horse any place.

What seemed like a simple ride was not. A wooden gate to restrain cattle separated each field on both farms. Three of these had been closed by Uncle Cecil and, consequently, had to be opened by JD. He would dismount and remount by way of the gates themselves.

Finally, as Tootsie came to a halt by the well, Aunt Gin shuffled out of her house with apprehension. "Where's Cecil?" she asked as she grabbed the reins.

"Paw and he is getting drunk!"

"Getting drunk! What do you mean?"

"Maw's fixin' whiskey and water and sugar that Paw and Uncle Cecil is drinking."

Aunt Gin pulled JD down off the horse into her arms muttering, "You poor child," while the horse flipped her head and trotted off to her stable in the barn.

As JD walked back through Uncle Cecil's woods, expecting to see him at any moment, he began to realize that Aunt Gin may have been smiling and consoling him at the same time, which meant that maybe he had been wrong about Paw drinking too much. JD relaxed a little thinking about Aunt Gin saying the government was going to prohibit whiskey before long. But as he reached Paw's woods, he was frightened by Uncle Cecil's voice coming up the wooded road in song. *"Oh, Jessie had a wife, to mourn for his life."*

JD slipped over and hid in the huckleberry bushes until Uncle Cecil passed, still extolling Jessie James and damning, *"the dirty little coward who shot Mr. Howard and had laid poor Jessie in his grave."*

Uncle Cecil never questioned how a runaway horse opened and shut the gates until years later when Aunt Gin told him what had happened.

CHAPTER 10

Crazy as a Loon

Paw came home on the three o'clock train, walking slower than normal. As they watched him out the kitchen window, they saw him stop in front of Watson's house as if to see what was going on, but he was just resting. When he finally arrived, almost falling at the kitchen table into his chair, he said he didn't know whether the trip had been worth it, and Maw told him that it served him right for standing around in a large crowd just to see a second term Republican inaugurated. "You could have saved your energy," she said, "by staying home and listening to Coolidge's speech on the radio." It was the first inauguration to be broadcast nationally, so in Maw's opinion there was no reason for Paw to trek all the way into Washington. Paw told her he went mostly to see the parade.

They sat there quietly. Paw displayed an expression of one who had ridicule heaped upon him, which he had. Then his nose slowly rose up into the air as if he were trying to catch the direction and source of an odor that had been prevailing for some time in the kitchen. Because of his stuffed-up nose he had not noticed it before, but now the odor was penetrating even his clogged nasal passages.

"My heavens, what in the name of God are you cooking in that oven?"

This was quite a reach for Paw because he was always on guard not to question Maw's efforts at cooking. It was never a productive thing to do, because they were all aware that such an offense could cause Maw to throw down her ladle or whatever she had in her hand and challenge the one doing the questioning to try their hand at it if they didn't like the way things were being done.

What was in the oven could not be explained with a couple of words. Thus, the story began to unravel as JD, Will, and Little Bonnie took turns telling it. Seems like the three of them had spied several geese paddling around on Black Pond. This was quite rare because wild geese were rarely seen on land or water; they were usually seen flying at a high altitude, well out of shotgun range. Seizing an opportunity for a tasty meal and a chance at an exciting hunting adventure, the children had rushed home, grabbed Paw's *Ole Blanket,* as his shotgun was called because it sprayed shot to where it was said you couldn't miss a target, and rushed back to Black Pond. Fearing that they would spook the geese, they slipped down behind the fill in the railroad bed that served as a sort of dam for the pond. Then they crawled up the bank, and there they were—three of them!

But they being wild were spooked. JD let loose with the *Ole Blanket.* Down the bird came—right back into the pond. But the goose wasn't dead, and each time when the children approached it, the goose would make a dive under the water. Finally, JD seized a long grapevine from the tree, cut off a length and proceeded to try and lasso the goose to shore. After many moments of anxiety and physical torture, JD managed to pull the bird ashore. There he was! All they had to do was pluck him and leave the rest up to Maw to cook him.

Maw, what with her worrying about Paw being out in the cold March weather and other goings on, did not display the mood the children had expected. She observed the goose with great apprehension, and this was of considerable consternation to them because they felt that they had not only pulled off quite a hunting caper but had, by all indications, provided a potentially tasty meal. They expected the bird would be a more than welcome change from the routine pork that they ate at almost every meal. Nevertheless, Maw seemed skeptical. She continued to mutter to herself as she brushed them aside and went about her part of preparing the giant bird for the oven.

Paw wasn't much of a book person, but when he spied the bird coming out of the oven, he immediately jumped to his feet and made his way to the bookcase in the sitting room. With the encyclopedia opened in his hands, he exclaimed like a hellfire and brimstone preacher, "Have any of you ever heard the expression, 'Crazy as a loon?' Well, I'll be damned if that's not what you have there!"

Maw grabbed the book and read it. Then she slammed it shut and proceeded to cast the bird toward the trash. Not in the trash, but close enough to have the option of reclaiming it while at the same time rendering it non-grata. But Paw was not content to let the matter rest there. He castigated the others with the "crazy as a loon" expression the rest of the evening. He even included Little Bonnie. Maw didn't even escape his ridicule. And there were no more complaints of his little excursion into town to see Calvin Coolidge.

"Whoever heard of a goose or a duck having a pointed bill?" he repeated throughout the week. He certainly didn't let them off easy, as they say.

CHAPTER 11

Workhorse

That summer Paw worked nine acres of corn, nine acres of wheat, nine acres of clover, and nine acres of pasture. Bonnie worked six days a week in the city with one week off each year for vacation. But she never left the farm. Marcus would infrequently visit the farm, always drunk and always suggesting reconciliation with his wife. Otherwise, he worked for his lawyer father in Washington.

Prohibition had ended the manufacture of whiskey and closed the dens of iniquity. The saloon had been the prime target for the dries; however, whiskey making began to flourish in the backwoods. The small communities like Great Falls, Clifton, and several places bordering Big Woods (a tract of land covering over 7,000 acres) became the hidden outlets for moonshine. A Sunday did not pass where whiskey drinking and moonshining in general were condemned as an ungodly deteriorate to the temple of men's souls by the ladies. Mr. Cowley, the little man with a hump in the middle of his back, was the women's biggest supporter.

The church remained without a preacher, meaning that Sunday school and the ritual of serving communion constituted the entire church service. JD and the other boys were becoming older and larger now, and he thought that perhaps it was time for them to matriculate to the adult Sunday school class. Then again, he thought, it wasn't any use in giving up their class where they could have their way more often. Besides, they could always listen to what was going on down below anyway.

JD was developing into a build of a plodding draft horse with feet firmly on the ground, though this belied his quickness and strength. As several of the genial parishioners stood outside the church, JD became the subject of their conversation. Farmers, especially those who were getting up in age, were at times inclined to discuss young farm boys in a vein not unlike that of discussing a young colt—*workhorse* of a sort, they said.

Paw stated in a proud but not bragging manner that JD would someday make a fine farmer. "He's so meticulous in what he does. Not like a lot of young boys. He cares and looks after his sister and brother just as if he was the head of the household, which in a manner of figuring, I suppose he is. And don't you know, the other day he was out there sowing wheat, and that drill was setting out in the newly harrowed field. He didn't want to unhook the horses from the drill, and he couldn't pull the drill out of its line and disturb the seed that he had sowed. So, he just walks down across that loose dirt to the wagon that was full of fertilizer and backed up to it to let Will load him up with a 157-pound bag of fertilizer. But when Will tried to shove him off saying, "Go on, I'll bring the other bag," JD told him to put the other bag on his other shoulder, too, and he walked right across that field with both. What would that be? Let's see… three-hundred-and-fourteen pounds on those sloping shoulders in that loose dirt! Then he just turned around and dumped both bags on the top of the drill."

They all shook their heads in amazement, except Mr. Cowley, the little man with the hump in his back. Unnoticed by the others, he turned his head back and forth in a negative way—not toward JD, but toward the comments being made about JD. They were only able to see him as a farmer, but Mr. Cowley saw JD as something more.

CHAPTER 12

Little Bonnie

Marcus's family had been instrumental in naming all three of his children. They were named after ancestors on the Dayne and Carter sides of the family. Coincidentally, Marcus's grandfather and Bonnie's father were both named Joseph. At the time of naming, this did not present a problem when they named their oldest child Joseph Emory Beauchamp Dayne—a name that was identical to that of Esquire's father, the one who, with 349 other Georgians, had held thousands of Yankees at bay at Burnside's Bridge near Sharpsburg, Maryland during the Civil War.

William had been named after one of his grandmother's brothers who was an aid to Confederate General Beauregard and buried next to the general's tomb at Arlington National Cemetery. Caroline Buffington Dayne had been named after Esquire's mother: nee Mary Ann Caroline Boone Buffington.

The Browns had accepted the names, though the name of Mary Ann Caroline Buffington Dayne had been entirely too presumptuous for them. So, while the Daynes had prevailed in the legal naming of the children, the Browns, because of day-to-day proximity, were free to flower nicknames on the children. Hence the reason Joseph was called JD, William was called Will, and Mary Ann was called Little Bonnie.

There came a day when JD sat in the cornfield next to the house shucking corn with his sister who sat on a bundle of neatly tied fodder. She asked, "Why do you all call me Little Bonnie?"

He replied, "Because you remind everyone of mother when she was small."

"Why?"

"Because you have pretty, wavy hair like she has, and you're sweet and pretty like she is."

"You think Billie is prettier than me?"

"No sir, no one's prettier than you are. And honey, it's "prettier than I" not "prettier than me." You can always tell which pronoun to use if you just finish the sentence in your mind with an "am" without actually saying it. For instance, if you say "prettier than me am" to yourself without saying it out loud, you would know that it isn't proper grammar."

"Why do make me say proper grammar 'round you? I'm just your sister."

"No, you're not *just* my sister. You're my *sweet* little sister that I'm supposed to look out for, and grammar is part of that looking out for."

"I bet you think Billie's hair is prettier than mine."

"Don't you believe that for a moment. Billie's hair is black and bluish and it will someday turn to silver. Your hair is the color of gold. Do you know what an ounce of silver is worth compared to an ounce of gold?"

"But I don't have red hair like our mother."

"Well, someday you will. You can bet on that."

"How do you know?"

"'Cause you're a little filly now, but when you grow to be a mare, your hair will turn red just like hers. Don't you 'member that little filly the Blacksheares had that was born black as coal?"

"Yes, I 'member her."

"Well don't you 'member how when she grew into a mare she turned dapple gray?"

"I 'member that. But JD, I'm not a mare."

"Sure, you're not the same thing, but someday when you become a woman, your hair will turn red. You can bet it'll be just like Mother's. Yes, sir, you can bet on that."

"But, I'm sure not gonna get married like she did. Would you let me marry someone like Daddy?"

JD looked startled, as if he had been struck. Almost instantly he dropped the stalk of corn with its ear he was shucking and slowly removed his shucking peg from his right hand. Pointing it at nothing he said, "If someone like that tried to marry you…" He struggled to find the words. "You know what I'd do if a drinker came 'round courting you? I'd hit him with a sledgehammer, like I was cracking a rock. That's what I'd do!"

"S'pose I said I loved him like Mother tells Maw she loves Daddy?"

"Wouldn't make any difference—you'd be loving a cracked rock!"

"Do you think Daddy will ever stop drinking so's we can have a family and a house like other people?"

"'Fraid not, honey."

"But he always says he is going to stop drinking and that we are going to have a little house with a picket fence and be all together like a normal family."

"Yeah, that's what he's always said as long as I can remember. But I hate to tell you this… we just can't depend on him to do something like that. Don't you worry though, when I get out and get a job, I'll see that you and Will both go to college. You have an exceptionally good mind, and you could go through any school you try."

"But girls always have to marry and have children."

"No, that's not going to be true anymore. I'm going to see to it that you have a good education so's you can be independent. You can get married if you meet a nice man, or you can be educated so you can find a job on your own. If there is a nice boy out there for you, Paw will walk you down the aisle. If he's not able, I will do it. Couple more years and I'll be old enough to go to college and be out 'fore you're ready to go. Then I'll see to it that you can go away to a nice girl's school, just like a smart girl like you is meant to do."

"But why do you have to be the one to do all the hard work? Even send everybody to school?"

"'Cause I'm the biggest and the only one here to do it. You ever notice that chain that's hooked from the double tree back to the front of the wagon?"

"You mean the one behind the big horse?"

"That's right. That's called a state chain. And the reason that's there is 'cause that big horse is bigger and stronger than Dick who's also older. Did you ever see us stop a wagonload of hay halfway up the hill to rest the horses? Well, if we didn't have that state chain, the big horse would just pull ole Dick right back into the wagon when we started the wagon again. Just like a seesaw. When that state chain is there, that big horse can almost start and pull that wagon by himself. Besides, the big horse knows he can do it, and he likes helping ole Dick out a little."

"Oh, JD you're so smart and pathetic."

"You mean *prophetic*, don't you?"

"S'pose so. Anyway, you know what I mean."

JD smiled. "You and Will and Mother and I just have to stick in there and hold the fort down for a few more years, and we won't need anyone to help us. We'll make out OK, and we'll have a good life."

CHAPTER 13

The Davenport

The next Sunday, the church service closed with a hymn of invitation. *"Just as I am without one plea, but that Thy blood was shed for me. And that Thou bid'st me come to Thee, O Lamb of God, I come, I come!"*

Mr. Ferguson stopped the singing and called out, "If there be one among you who wishes to declare your belief in Jesus Christ and declare here, before this congregation, that you accept Him as your personal savior, then come now. Don't wait for..."

Before his sentence was complete, Little Bonnie rose, squeezed past her mother's legs around the end of the pew pulling its corner with both hands and started forward. Mother and Maw had known she was going to do it; Little Bonnie knew she was going to do it. That's why they had all gone to church this day, except for Paw who was too overwhelmed. When she had told Paw, he hugged her, teared up, and stammered something inaudibly. But JD and Will hadn't known. For them, Little Bonnie had wanted it to be a secret.

Mr. Ferguson insisted on driving them all home, but the two boys had already cut a beeline through the Ferguson's field, which shortened the trip by half. Mr. Ferguson drove down along the railroad track, and when he started across the ford at Oak Run, he just stopped the car and looked from side to side. Mrs. Ferguson, who had been turned around in the front seat and talking to the ladies, immediately turned back around to face the front and exclaimed, "For heaven's sake, why are you stopping here? Aren't you afraid you'll block the water and it'll wash the car away?"

But Mr. Ferguson just sat there ignoring her. Eventually he said, "I declare Joanna, this is the prettiest ford I have ever seen. I always think about driving back here so's I could just drink in this pretty scene."

"Seems to me you are only scaring me more when you say something about drinking. You know, we might all be drinking more than we want if you don't get us out of here!"

When Mr. Ferguson arrived at the Brown house, he insisted on going inside the house to shake hands with Paw who was sitting on the davenport. "Don't get up; sit where you are," he said.

But Paw insisted on getting up. As they reached for each other's hands, Paw lost his balance and started falling over sideways. Mr. Ferguson tried to break his fall, but instead they both fell onto the davenport, crushing the middle of it to the floor. Mr. Ferguson got up first; then he helped Paw up.

"Darn furniture!" Paw muttered. "They don't make it like they used to."

Maw, embarrassed, apologized profusely to Mr. Ferguson who assured them both that it was his fault for being so clumsy. He insisted that he would be back the next day with his furniture repair tools.

True to his word, Mr. Ferguson came the next day with his tool box and materials and proceeded to work on the sofa for half the day. He told Maw that the material—mainly the wood—was, in fact, not of the best quality. In any event, he declared, he was sure it would hold up under his labor, better now than its original condition. Maw watched him work and wasn't all that impressed with Mr. Ferguson's efforts, but she didn't let on as much.

Sure enough, it was only tested a couple of times in the next few days when the bottom of the davenport was again resting on the floor. JD and Will had steered clear of the sofa, choosing to sit elsewhere for fear their weight might render it a casualty. They were well pleased that when it did collapse again, they were not at fault.

When no one else was around, Maw took JD by the arm and, pointing to the davenport, assured him that she knew he was the only one who could really fix it. JD flipped the sofa up on its back; he felt a wave of apprehension come over him. He thought Maw might as well have asked him to operate on one of the cows. The davenport's innards were hidden by only a thin piece of material, not unlike cotton muslin. After warning Maw that such a job was out of his element, he set out to get tools and material, though he didn't have any idea what he was looking for in either area.

For some reason, instead of going to the granary where Paw kept his tools, he was drawn inexplicably to the barn. He slid the big barn door back on its track far enough for him to enter, and before he had hardly taken a step in, he knew that he had seen his very best hope for success: baling wire. Every time a farmer broke open a bale of straw or hay, two strands of baling wire were carefully loosened and hung over a rafter for safekeeping. Anytime someone wanted to draw two pieces of split wood together, they could wrap a piece of baling wire around them and twist it to draw the two objects toward each other, as if in a vise.

Now with the wire, several sticks, some reclaimed nails, a screwdriver, and a claw hammer in hand, JD approached the davenport with flickering confidence. But after he had removed the tacks and pulled the thin cover off the bottom, he was less confident that there was a way to repair it. With the wire being his only solution, he wrapped a piece around the front leg on one side and the back leg on the other. Pulling the two strands together in the middle, he twisted them until the wire became taut. Fear of pushing his luck, he repeated the process on the other two legs. Miraculously, the davenport seemed to come together, though it was still lying on its back. JD wondered if this was all he needed to do. Then he figured, it wouldn't hurt to use a couple more pieces of wire, so he applied more at every angle he could imagine. Finally, he sat the sofa upright and, to his amazement, it appeared to be in its original shape. When he pressed down on it a couple of times, it seemed as sturdy as if it were brand new.

Realizing there was nothing more he could do, JD replaced the cover on the bottom and set it up right again. He could not fathom what in the world he would do if his efforts failed. Nevertheless, he called for Maw.

They stood there alone looking and looking, saying nothing. All the while Maw moved her head up and down in approval, but she did not ask him how he had done it. Standing there with her arms akimbo, she said, "I knew you were the only one who could do it. I just knew in my mind that when you set out to fix it, it would work. But now, son, I want you to do me one more favor: Let's keep this our little secret. If we tell anyone else it may get back to Mr. Ferguson, and he wouldn't like to hear that you succeeded where he had failed. It would be hard for him to take."

"Okay, Maw," JD agreed. "And if it breaks down again, which it might do, I won't be embarrassed." He said this with a laugh.

Through the ensuing years, people sat on the davenport, they fell on it, and they laid on it, but it never failed. Notwithstanding, JD would look at it from time to time and shake his head in wonderment.

CHAPTER 14

Thou Shalt Not Steal

It was the week after she had been baptized that Little Bonnie came down the stairs and Mother noted the sad expression that covered her face. She said, "Now child, I want you to go in there and pretty yourself up so you can go to the store with Will. I need some things, and I just hope I have enough to pay for them."

When Mother located Will out by the barn, she told him much the same thing. "Now you take Little Bonnie with you and try to cheer her up. Her poor soul just seems to wreak with melancholia."

Will wasn't even sure what melancholia was, but he could tell the way Mother said it—with a frown and not a smile—that it wasn't something someone would want. Could have been some women's disease that men don't know too much about. Hell, the cows might be inclined to get it, too, come to think about it. Seems like that may have been the word the veterinarian used when the old cow got all bloated up and died, he thought.

"She can't be that bad, 'cause she was just baptized last Sunday, and she ain't been nowhere!"

Mother chided, "Did it ever occur to you that *that* may be the problem? That child never has a friend to play with."

"Why does she have to have someone to play with? JD and I don't have anybody to play with!"

"You have each other! She doesn't even have a sister."

As was the custom for the ladies, Little Bonnie wore her old shoes to walk down to the train station. Once there, she changed to a somewhat flimsy pair of patent leather shoes that she had carried with her, and she hid the former under a board behind the Piney Station shelter. She then boarded the train with her brother and, with a giggle, flipped the change collector without actually putting any coins in. The conductor knew her well enough to realize that Will would deposit enough change for them both.

The glass-enclosed collection box was designed for coins to go down a little shoot and lay long enough at the bottom for the conductor to count; then he would flip the floor of the collection box like a trap door and the money would fall through to a holding container. This allowed the conductor to see that Will had first placed Little Bonnie's fare into the box and then done the same thing for himself.

Will had heard tell of people who were able to short-change the procedure, though he had never been able to figure out how someone could fool the conductor. Perhaps, he thought, such behavior had taken place on the streetcars in Washington, not on this train line, though he knew they were both alike. In either event, Will contemplated the possibilities as he made his way down the aisle.

First, he spoke to those sitting on one side and then the other; he was met with laughter and acclaim as if he were a prince, Little Bonnie thought. Even the stately and refined Negro teachers who sat at the very rear of the train smiled, albeit with some apprehension. Then Will opened the door to the very back of the train where only a railing separated him from the railroad track below. Little Bonnie followed him out, holding tightly to her brother and thinking all the while, "He's so much fun." She thought of how JD was always fun, too, though more serious. JD was like a classroom where you had to pay attention while your next step in life was being explained. Will was more like recess, and recess was just as much a part of school as geography or spelling or even history.

Little Bonnie looked first at the fleeting ties and rails as they disappeared from view, then to Will's face where she searched for meaning from his expression. The expression on his face was the one he seemed to save for special occasions. Both eyebrows were drawn up toward each other, with one eye hinting of a squint but not closing. Lots of times he would have turned up his collar with that far-off look, as if he were a sea captain starting off on some exciting journey. But here they were just going to Vienna, and there wasn't much excitement there. Just a stop along the line. Nevertheless, it was fun. Little Bonnie imagined they were racing wildly along the edge of a cliff defying danger, the disappointments of life, and the possible consequences of their future acts.

Their first stop was the Sanitary Grocery Store where one normally read from a list while the clerk went from shelf to shelf in search of each item. Will liked to take for himself the long pole with its trigger that when squeezed would tighten around and hold onto an item. Then it could be gently lowered to nestle in the clerk's arms and finally placed in a bag. Will took free rein at the store. Instead of lowering the round box of oatmeal down to his other hand, he would simply tilt it forward and catch it in midair. He made a game out of it. Sometimes, to the store manager's concern, he would give an item a harder rap, lean his head closer to the shelf, and catch it behind his back. They completed their purchase and exited the store to the manager's relief.

After squirreling the groceries behind Mr. De Faubus's desk at the train station, they went to Frazer's where they each ordered an ice cream cone. Little Bonnie paid with a quarter as she was handed her cone, and Mrs. Frazer gave her back forty-five cents. Little Bonnie disapproved, yet Mrs. Frazer insisted that she had made change enough in her day to know how to do it. But Little Bonnie would not back down. Eventually Mrs. Frazer was forced to see her mistake, though she blamed it all on her optician.

After they were out the door, Will admonished Little Bonnie, "Sometimes you do better by keeping your mouth shut, you know."

Little Bonnie protested, "No that's not right. Thou shalt not steal, thou shall not covert. That's what the Bible says."

"It's *covet*, not *covert*. Besides, it's not Sunday—it's a weekday and we're here in town on business. You think she'd have done the same thing for you?"

"That's not good."

"What do you mean it's not good?" Will inquired.

"JD told me a long time ago."

"Told you what?"

Bonnie put her hands on her hips and said, "JD told me as far back as he could 'member that Paw would set on the horse when it was pulling the drag and without even turning 'round he would say, 'You pay your bills, tell the truth and don't take something that belongs to somebody else; and when you go before the judge, he will know you are true to your word.' And wait a minute! That's not all he said. One time Maw sent him to town to get something, and as he passed by the front of the Sanitary he noticed all these fruits..."

"I don't think you have to put an 's' on that. I think fruit is both singular and plural. Maybe not. Anyway, what were you saying JD said?"

"Well if you would stop interrupting me, I'd tell you!" Little Bonnie blurted out in frustration. "JD said he spied a whole bushel of oranges behind some apples, and 'fore he knew it—and there was nobody in sight—he reached for one. He was so tempted 'cause all he could think about was taking an orange and biting a hole in one end, and holding it up to his mouth and squeezing the juice into his mouth, and then opening it up and eating the rest of it. And just 'fore his hand grabbed that orange, he heard this voice up above him."

"Yeah, I know it was God. Just like Abraham heard the voice."

"No, it wasn't God at all! It was Paw's voice."

Will turned sideways, "What? Where in the hell did he come from? How'd he get there? What did his voice say?"

"If you would quit interrupting me, I could finish. He said the same thing he always said when they were going over in the field and Paw was on the horse and JD and Billie were riding on the drag. He said, 'Don't take something that belongs to somebody else.' JD immediately jerked his hand back, and he said he's never been tempted to steal again. He said he doesn't hear Paw's voice anymore, but he sure 'members what happened that day."

Will and Little Bonnie each took a moment to think about this. Then Little Bonnie added, "'Course I did see JD take that pint of whiskey away from Daddy one night and hide it under the sill in the corn house. And later he poured it out."

"Is that where that went?" Will asked. Feeling vindicated, he added, "Now see, I told you everybody takes something that's not theirs every now and then."

Little Bonnie looked up into her brother's face and asked, "Do you think they have ice cream in Heaven?"

"Why in the world do you ask that?"

"It looks like it wouldn't be Heaven if they didn't have something like ice cream."

CHAPTER 15

Fox Tracks

Will and Little Bonnie sat on a bench eating their ice cream, unconsciously running their hands around the corners of the newly installed armrests. She started to question him about their sudden appearance, to which he replied, "You know there are some things that men can't discuss with women."

How it all came about was just a practical matter on account of Mr. Woggin, a contemporary of Paw's who was working part-time on the railroad. It being too far for him to walk home, he would spend the afternoon in the station where he would nip on a bottle and later lie on the bench. Mr. De Faubus, the station manager, could hear him snoring all the way into his office. That was tolerated for a while, but when he began to wet in his pants and leave puddles in the curve of the seat to be observed by the ladies waiting for a train, Mr. De Faubus remedied the situation by having armrests installed along the bench. This prohibited Mr. Woggin—and anyone else—from lying down.

So there Will and Little Bonnie sat on the armed bench, each counting and recounting their money as if the amount might magically increase. Finally, Will asked, "What'cha gonna do with that?"

"'Gonna start saving so I can buy something for Mother for Christmas."

"Not going to be using it for a while then, huh?"

"I said I was going to save it, 'cept a nickel for the fare back home."

"So, you won't be needing it for a while then. Just so's you get the money back 'fore Christmas. Don't make any difference whether you have it in that piggy bank now or whether you lend it to me for a little while so's I can buy something that's on sale right today and won't be on sale in a couple days? Right?"

"No, that's not right!" Little Bonnie exclaimed.

"Why ain't that right? Tell me now. Why ain't that right?"

"'Cause."

"'Cause why? Tell me now, honey. Why ain't that right?"

"I ain't no fool!" Little Bonnie blurted out.

"Now, listen to me. You know you're my little sweetheart, and I want to let you in on a little secret if you promise not to tell anybody."

"You're just going to try to trick me!" Little Bonnie insisted.

"You just listen to me," Will stated calmly. "You 'member the other day when we were walking up out of the horse branch and I knelt and showed you those fox tracks?"

Little Bonnie nodded, so Will continued. "Well, while I was squatting there an idea came to me. And when I got this idea, I knew right then that I was sure coming into some money. I mean some real money! I didn't say nothing then 'cause I just didn't want to get ahead of the situation. You know how Paw always says, 'Don't go off halfcocked?' Well, what he's telling you when he says that is: if you don't pull that hammer on the gun all the way back before you pull the trigger, it ain't gonna bust the cap. I figured I wanted to check out all the facts and possibilities first. You may have even seen me do it. I went straight to the bookcase and got the almanac out and there, sure enough, I read where we were going to get an early snow. You getting the idea yet?"

"Maybe," Little Bonnie answered. "You're going to set a trap for the fox right where he comes by on the lane?"

"Naw, naw," Will responded. "See there, you go thinking like a woman. Things ain't that simple when you're fooling with a fox. They're smart! He'd just smell your scent and jump over the trap. I can see him now. Just jumping around like he's playing with a field mouse. No, sir. I could tell by the size of his tracks that he's an old, wise one. You'd never catch him in a trap. Now, here's how I'm gonna out-fox the fox himself. I'm just going to keep an eye out for the snow, and soon as it snows, I'm gonna watch for his tracks, and when I find them, I can follow him and get him. And his fur will bring in seven or eight dollars at least in my pocket."

"Oh Will, sometimes when you get to talking, I just think it wouldn't surprise me at all to someday see you sitting right up on a cloud and riding right by. But just tell me, how're you gonna know when to shoot him? And even if you do, he's gonna have holes in his fur from the shot."

"Here's how it's gonna work," Will explained. "Soon's I see his prints, I'm gonna track him to his den. Not going to even need a dog or nothin'. Only a shovel. The weather up to the time of that snow is not going to be cold at all, so we're not going to have to dig into the frozen ground or nothin' like that. Fox dens don't go down that deep, usually just in the side of a bank, so we won't even have to dig that much."

"You keep saying *we*. Who's going to be with you?"

"Well, 'course I wouldn't 'spect you to do no digging 'cause you're a girl, and little at that. But since you're the one who was present when I first discussed it with anyone, and 'course you being my little sister…" Will watched Little Bonnie for a reaction, but she didn't look too pleased.

Will continued, "I been here thinking that you could do me a favor in my time of need. You see, there is something I want really bad from the store, but I don't have quite enough money for it. I'm just a measly twenty cents short, and I'm going to lose out on the sale price. What I'm saying is this: if you lend me your twenty cents, I'll give it back to you double when I skin that fox. And you know for sure, as well as I do, that all I must do is track him to his hole, dig him out, and whack him over the head. I don't even have to shoot him! Just skin him, and the seven or eight dollars are mine. Now, ain't no question that it's gonna snow way b'fore Christmas. Then you'll have your forty cents back in time to buy Mother her present. What ya think about them apples? Makes sense, don't it? How could that plan go wrong?"

Little Bonnie clutched her twenty cents tightly. It was all her savings, including the nickel needed to cover the train ride home. If she gave Will her money, she would have to walk all the way home in her patent leather shoes. "But I've got my good shoes on, and I would scuff them all up walking all the way home. Maw would skin me!" Near tears, Little Bonnie whined, "B'sides, my feet hurt already from these shoes."

Will brushed Little Bonnie's concerns aside. "Naw, that won't be any problem. I'll slap a little polish on them when we get home, and nobody will ever know the difference. Simple as that," he said, snapping his fingers.

Apprehensively, Little Bonnie handed Will her money. He told her to wait for him on the bench while he went shopping. Then he marched down to the tobacco store where he proceeded to select rolling papers and tobacco for purchase. Standing belly up to the counter with a devilish smile on his face, he laid out Little Bonnie's money and his own. The clerk told him that not only was he a little young to be rolling cigarettes, he was ten cents short when totaling up all his items. This fazed Will for just a moment. Then he asked, "Couldn't we just put that ten cents on my account?"

"But you don't have an account with me!" the clerk responded.

"I know, but couldn't we just start one now?"

"I'd love to son, but my wife was just fussing at me this morning saying I had to learn to tell the next customer who asked for credit that we had all we could stand right now. And while I do not like telling someone, especially a fine young man like yourself, that he can't have credit, I was very glad for the way my wife phrased it 'cause it doesn't make me sound like an old Scrooge."

Will pushed a couple of packs of cigarette papers aside and paid his bill with not a cent to spare.

Walking from Vienna back to Piney Station, a distance of about two miles, took its toll on Little Bonnie. Though Will carried all their purchases, Little Bonnie was decrying his judgment in making her walk all that way in her patent leather shoes. When she changed back into her old walking shoes that she had hidden at the station, Will spied blisters on her feet and insisted that he carry her, too, which he did on his back up the hill.

He deposited her on the front porch with the admonition that their plan for the fox was to be kept in the darkest of secrecy—not the deepest, but the darkest. He now projected an air of equity, for in his mind, having carried Little Bonnie up the hill equaled out the walk in the new shoes up the railroad track. When she reminded him that he had a job to do on her shoes, he professed to an emergency that had come up at the chicken house.

After a few moments, Little Bonnie went to the chicken house to see what the emergency was. She found Will puffing on a cigarette he had just rolled, enjoying the comfort of the chicken house sill.

"Is this all a part of the secret, too?" she asked sarcastically.

"Why sure! It was bought with your money wasn't it?"

As for the shoes, they never looked the same. Little Bonnie discovered little cuts and scuffs where the shiny black leather had peeled up and the polish wouldn't keep down.

In due time, it did snow just like the almanac had predicted. It was a wet snow, so it didn't drift. Also, its wetness made for well-defined and firm tracks. Little Bonnie saw the fox's prints when she accompanied Will along the lane, just where they had seen them before. Her feelings of having been tricked were soothed. The tracks led them to a place in the woods near a fence that separated Paw's land from Uncle Cecil's land where the trees were quite close together, growing on a little knoll about ten feet wide. It was unusual because it looked like two trenches on either side had washed out leaving a ridge behind.

As Will surveyed the situation, he wondered how the hill, which wasn't that steep, would wash out with the trees being there and all. He figured it must have happened years ago when the lay of the ground was distorted. You could see by the tracks that the fox had stopped right at the entrance of the den and had turned around several times as if to look to see if he was being watched or followed before entering. There were no tracks leading away, so it was plain to discern that the fox had been off somewhere and didn't get back until the snow was on the ground. Will's plan and prediction seemed to be working perfectly.

Will stood there leaning on the shovel, looking first at the den and then at his sister—and she doing the same thing. They didn't speak a word; he just kept laughing and she giggling. Little Bonnie couldn't help but think what a great general Will was going to be when he grew up. In his thoughts, he wasn't a general at all; he was an admiral dressed in navy blue with a white shirt.

After digging into about a foot of rather soft ground, Will began to hit tree roots. They were far enough apart for the fox, but not far enough apart for Will to reach the fox. Squatting down, he surveyed the situation, snapped his fingers as if a thought had come to him, and then stuffed his coat in the hole so the fox couldn't get out.

"Let's go see if String's home." By String he meant Wally Bean—a real skinny boy of Scottish heritage who lived across the road from Uncle Cecil. Though he was younger than Will, String had grown taller.

They found String at home, and Will informed him of the situation. String agreed to allow Will to lower him into the hole to see if he could pull the fox out. String started to go in head first, but then Will realized that String would need to have his hands above his head in order to grab the fox.

"Go in just like you're diving into the water. Grab hold of his leg or his tail, and shake your leg. Then I'll pull you both out."

String slipped into the hole, his body moving much like that of a snake. In a few seconds, he shook his foot frantically, whereupon Will, in one quick and excited move, yanked him out. As String's hands finally came flying out, all he had was a tuft of reddish brown hair between his thumbs and index fingers.

"You almost got 'em," Will yelled.

"Almost got him, hell!" String screamed back. "That son of a bitch started growling like a dog, and I thought, what the hell is gonna happen if I get stuck in there and that son of a bitch starts eating on me? I ain't going to do something like that again!"

They gave up and went their separate ways. Seeing Will in such a defeated slump of his shoulders, Little Bonnie didn't feel it was a good time to inquire as to how and when, or even if, she would be repaid her twenty cents.

Prior to their excursion, Will had approached Mother requesting an advance of eight dollars to be secured by the fox hide. Now, being empty-handed, and upon hearing the outcome of the venture, Mother turned from the cook stove with a soup ladle in hand, and pointing it toward Will said, "There is an age-old admonition son: Never count your chickens before they hatch."

Little Bonnie and Will both understood the meaning, but Will would never be able in future life to discipline himself to follow this fundamental truth.

CHAPTER 16

The Angel of Death

After having become more and more worthless, Paw's right hand man, Clyde, left right in the middle of summer when Paw needed him most. At the same time, old Uncle Andrew who had lived all his life on the farm, first as a slave and then as a freeman, came down to tell Paw that his daughter Hazel had left her husband and gone into town to live. JD listened in disbelief to all the bad luck.

Before the week was out, while Paw and JD were plowing potatoes and Will was working in the garden, a man was seen approaching the farm with long, striding, and dedicated steps. When he was within speaking distance, Paw said, "Good morning, friend." The man, however, didn't look particularly friendly at all. In fact, he looked both wild-eyed and threatening. JD wondered if Paw had ever laid eyes on the man before, what with Paw being friendly and all. Yet Paw never seemed to fear for himself or for Maw or even for the children.

Dillie Romans was his name, a father of five. With his wife, they were all squatting in the old school house that almost had a complete roof on one room. He begged Paw for a job so he could buy milk for those hungry children. Paw couldn't have said no to him, even if he didn't need the help, which he did. Paw was a marked man and had been for a long time.

The first tramp that came years earlier had asked Paw for permission to sleep in his barn, and Paw had dogmatically denied him that privilege because he never let anyone sleep in the barn for fear of smoking. So he told the man he could make a pallet on the kitchen floor and to keep the fire going all night. This man may have been the one who had cut the sign in the tree down by the foot log that could be seen from then on by every tramp riding the freight cars.

JD had stumbled upon a tramp one hot summer morning cooking breakfast right on the bank under that foot log. The tramp was startled at first, but when JD got to talking to him, he found out about the sign—a mark, really, carved into the foot log. It was a sign that tramps would recognize. It identified Paw as being kind to tramps. JD also learned that there wasn't any sign in front of Uncle Cecil's place nor the Watson's either—just Paw's. Of course, Paw probably knew it was there.

So that's how Dillie arrived, on the same day when Dr. Leigh and the new doctor, Dr. Lytle, had come to see Maw. Things happen that some say are a coincidence while others say it is the will of God. But it's all written up there in Heaven, the same way the hairs on our heads are numbered.

Maw had been sick worse than this many times before, yet Dr. Leigh had not come to see her then. Today, however, he was here with the reputedly brilliant and levelheaded new doctor who had not only graduated at the top of the School of Medicine but excelled at poker, too. Dr. Leigh must have sensed imminent change. Why else would have brought the new doctor?

Maw was sitting up when they arrived, looking quite frail. Maybe, they thought, she was not too long for this world. Dr. Leigh's skinny, white fingers examined her, moving more in frustration than mission. He felt out of place here at the farm and even here on earth. His cheeks were sunken and his hair misplaced. It was hard to tell who the actual patient was.

Paw, JD, and Dillie had picked corn all that morning while Bonnie had prepared a dinner of pork, potatoes, and hot buttered cornbread, which JD ate lustily. After dinner, while Paw melted into the soft chair, JD prepared to haul logs by removing the wagon bed from the wagon frame. Paw had always helped him before, but JD was now big enough to remove the front end up onto the stanchion by himself. Then, going to the rear end and lifting it up over the rear stanchion, he would twist the bed to the ground. Going back to the front, he would complete the move, leaving the wheels and bolsters ready to haul logs.

With a firm right hand, JD shook the bit in the big horse's mouth, moving it up and down until the horse was nodding his accession. With his left hand, JD applied the same method on Dick, a slow stumbling gelding. Unbeknownst to JD, Little Bonnie had climbed astride the back bolster, murmuring to herself about where to sit so she would be close enough behind JD to hold onto him by clasping her arms around his waist.

Suddenly, a twisting gust of wind slammed the corn house door back against the side of the building creating a sound like an exploding shotgun. In one bounding leap, horses, wagon, and Little Bonnie shot out of JD's reach. They went racing down the hill with JD running like the wind after them. Without warning, the horses made a sharp turn and started back toward the barn. JD stood transfixed as he watched Little Bonnie fly over the bolster; her head bounced strangely off the ground, and there she lay lifeless as a rag doll.

JD ran to her, picked her up, and raced her to the house where the hands of Doctors Leigh and Lytle worked on her through the night. JD blamed himself for the mishap through the helpless, frustrating tears of a man, though he was still a boy.

In the morning, Dr. Lytle said sadly, "We've done all God allows us. Now we must just wait and pray for the best."

Dr. Leigh added, "She is resting now, and we shall be back later."

The two men left, but Dr. Leigh seemed to be more with Little Bonnie than with the world.

A few hours later, Dr. Lytle returned unhurried along the dusty road, deep in thought as if to say, "We shall lay the pieces together and access what is reality." For you see, the angel of death had descended on the Leigh household and the Dwayne household. Both Little Bonnie and Dr. Leigh were dead.

CHAPTER 17

Grief

Billie had hair the color of a blued shotgun. An ever-present belt that made her upper and lower torsos appear on the verge of disunion encircled her waist. She was more lean than voluptuous, but she strode gracefully as if each step was a historical link in a chain of important development. Now, however, she walked differently, having forced herself down the track toward the Browns' house only after her mother insisted that words could not dissolve sorrow but that she needed to appear where he could see her.

Up the lane, Billie saw JD bend through the fence. Unable to even call his attention, he disappeared into the grove of huge oaks. Each time she engaged the fence, she backed off as if contemplating the possibility of jumping some great chasm. She allowed her hands to unconsciously strip foul-smelling garlic seeds from their long wheat-like stems only to dash the seeds to the ground in disgust.

Finally, grasping the hem of her dress, Billie bent through the strands of barbed wire. Her back cowered at the prick of the top strand, which on other occasions she would have avoided by wearing different clothes. Instead of her normal determined strides, she now tiptoed like a doe, hesitant as a bride, beneath the giant oaks whose limbs grew in near clasp of unison. She walked and peeked until her eyes finally were drawn up to the top of the trees. There was a gaping hole devoid of limbs that made the grove seem like a giant decapitated dome. There she came within a few steps of JD, the tears of grief's strain running down his face like rain curling down a windowpane. The tears coming close to his mouth were wiped away by his tongue, first one side and then the other, but some managed to escape down his neck.

His grief was the prayer of an abandoned and tortured soul. She fell to her knees beside him, wrapping her right arm around his neck, her breasts confronting his side. With her head at the base of his arm, Billie held onto JD as he quivered with gasping moans.

At the house, Paw was heard to say, "I can go find Marcus if you want."

Bonnie answered through swollen and twisted lips, "No. If he comes, he comes; if he doesn't, you can go for him after she's buried. I just don't care."

The church was full. JD held onto his mother as if he were both husband and son. They followed the casket down the aisle to the front of the church behind the preacher who had come in from town. He read the 23rd Psalm. "Yea, though I walk through the valley of the shadow of death, I shall fear no evil." And then from the gospel of John, "In my Father's house, there are many mansions. If it were not so, I would have told you."

After the "ashes to ashes and dust to dust," Little Bonnie was lowered into the ground outside the chapel. Some stood straight, and some stooped, but all were rigid as if frozen. When it was over, a grief stricken JD embraced his mother and whispered into her ear, "She is not here. HER SPIRIT HAS TRANSCENDED FORTH!"

CHAPTER 18

Hog Killing

JD found Maw and Paw in conversation with Will who had just completed his chores of tending to the horses and carrying in the wood that Dillie has split. Then they all sat down for dinner, except for Mother who would eat alone when she got home from work.

Paw asked, "You think you boys could take off Thursday to kill hogs?"

"YES!" they shouted simultaneously and in like manner, thus displaying their eagerness for hog killing and disdain for school.

Paw raised big white hogs, priding himself on the fact that few people were able to raise 275- to 300-pound grain-fed hogs in the span of nine months.

"Who's gonna help us, Paw?"

"The three of us can do it with Dillie. Your Uncle Cecil is gonna help us some, too."

"You mean, he's gonna open the hogs after we've done all the dirty work," JD suggested.

Paw shot him a look. "Opening a hog is about as messy a job as there is—there's even an official title for it. It's called a Bunghole Reamer."

With that, Maw jumped up with a show of indignation and said, "I declare Joe, must you talk like that at the supper table?"

"Not the way Uncle Cecil does it," Will retorted. "He'll probably wear that black suit over here and not get a speck on it."

"No, son," Paw said. "It takes a good man to open hogs. A man can botch the whole job up if he isn't careful."

Paw had not only prearranged for Uncle Cecil to help, he had also sent for Walter Miller to come and stick the hogs. Paw, desperate, had hired him based on rumor, for there was no actual witness of his ability, and there was no time to waste since the whole operation had to be completed in one day.

A pig-sticker is the heartbeat of hog killing. Failure to deliver the coup de grace accurately and quickly leaves a kicking, squealing, vengeful demon. Paw's rheumatic joints rendered him unable to grip the knife or kneel to administer the coup de grace to an upended hog, so Paw was surely counting on Mr. Miller to do the job, knowing that everything else was brute labor.

Mr. Miller was not physically imposing. In fact, he came dressed in a suit coat with disproportionate sleeves that were determined to slip down and cover his fists. One hand clinched a butcher's knife, begging the question to those observing as to how he intended to run the blade and his hand vertically along the hog's throat and release a fountain of blood without soiling his sleeves.

Paw hobbled back and forth between the meat house and the pole lying in the fork of the locust tree; it was bound and supported at the other end by two poles crossed and chained together. There, too, was the wooden barrel laying at a slant between a wooden platform and the back of the chicken house. Paw called for more hot irons to be taken from the fire and placed in the barrel to heat the water. At the same time he sent JD and Will to fetch the first hog. "R'member what I told you," Paw kept saying.

With a rope tied to one of its hind legs, JD coerced the hog on while Will guided his head with a stick. Will grabbed the rope and choked up on it until he was next to the hog's rear end while JD made his way around the animal, close to its side. First, JD reached under and slightly scratched the hog's chest. The hog didn't purr but did react like a cat being petted. Then he slipped his hand down and grasped the outer leg and, with a simultaneous heave of his shoulder into the hog's side, JD pulled the leg toward him thudding the animal onto its back. Without a second to lose, he pounced astride the hog's chest bending its front legs away from its head and parallel with its body. Will did likewise with the hind legs.

About this time, Paw had to urge Mr. Miller to his station because he stood transfixed watching the boys. With the suddenness of his call to duty, he pulled up his right sleeve, then his left, and grasped the hog's lower jaw forcing it downward, thus exposing a fat layer of meat. He quickly slipped the blade into the hog's neck and sliced toward its chest, his hand disappearing, sleeve and all. The hog responded with nothing more than a grunt. As Mr. Miller released the hog's jaw, he resorted to a bent over squat and authoritatively called out, "Let 'em up."

The hog must have understood the command because he moved with the boys to its feet when he should have gushed blood and sagged to the ground. With a loud, ill tempered, and contemptuous squeal, the hog bolted right toward Mr. Miller's legs and caught its snout in the baggy seat of his pants, which sent him sprawling over its back. The hog then tore off down the hill carrying Mr. Miller—as if he were nothing more than a fly—down into the ravine and flipping him airborne with a violent and indignant upward thrust of its head. Mr. Miller landed on the barbed wire fence as the hog proceeded into the woods and out of sight.

Paw, teeth clinched around his tongue, threw his cane down in disgust. "I knew it; I knew it. He might as well 'uh stuck him in the ass! He might as well 'uh stuck him in the ass!" These were the words he would repeat at each subsequent hog-killing event in later years, until he went to his grave.

At Paw's urging, JD and Will went to catch the hog that, with head and rump alternately bobbing up and down and ears flopping like those of an elephant, had scampered away with industrious kicks despite the ponderous weight of its body. They chased it along in the leaves, down through the ravine, across the back wagon road, down onto a carpet of pine needles with sweet humming pines overhead, and then on through spring branch along the edge of the stream until it, tongue out and floundering, came to an end-over-end halt with Will landing on its chest calling for the rope. By calling for the rope, Will expected to drive the hog back toward the house. However, JD had other plans. He quickly thrust the blade of his pocketknife into the hog's throat until half of his forearm disappeared. Before he could extract it, blood gushed up over his shirtsleeves.

Will jumped up and yelled loud enough to be heard all the way to the house, "Damn it to hell!"

JD pawed Will's head like a mother bear to her cub, saying, "Don't you ever let me hear you cuss like that again." This only made Will madder.

"Now, get him on his feet," JD ordered.

Will raised the hog's head and chest, and the blood life gushed from the hole Mr. Miller had first cut. Finally, the hog sagged in death to the ground, and Will kicked it onto its side. "Now how ya' gonna get him back to the house?" Will asked. "We're gonna have a hell of a time getting 'em back!"

"We're gonna carry him," JD stated

"How in hell we gonna carry him?"

"Didn't I tell you not to swear?"

After about ten minutes of futile grappling, JD stood half bent, grasping one front and one back leg over his shoulders while Will acted to steady and partially lift the hog's rear from behind. Together they walked up the hill and into the backyard amidst the gawking group.

"Whyn't you come get the horse and drag that thing?" Paw asked.

"'Cause."

"'Cause why?"

"Just 'cause, Paw," JD said. And that ended the conversation. As the hog was being placed on the platform to be lowered into the hot water, JD asked, "Where's Mr. Miller?"

"He took off," Dillie said with a thundering sigh of exasperation.

The hog was rolled and wrestled, first one end and then the other, into the hot water. Its hair was pulled and body scraped as clean as a blubbery whale. By the time JD and Dillie had carried the hog to the hanging pole where Will gaveled him, Uncle Cecil had arrived on ole

Tootsie. Knife in hand, he proceeded to open the hog, humming all the while, just like Paw. The knife reamed out around the hog's anus, and with this neatly tied to keep the waste from dirtying the inside of the hog, the intestines began to roll like billowy clouds into the tub below.

"That was a nice thing you did, son."

"What do you mean?"

"You know what I mean," Uncle Cecil said. He knew the hog had met its demise at JD's hand, hidden in the woods, beyond the eyes of Paw. His clandestine action was meant to protect Mr. Miller's reputation.

"You're just like your grandpa," Uncle Cecil added.

As the last bit of guts rolled out into the tub, JD reached into the hot belly of the hog and helped Uncle Cecil extract the liver and heart, making sure blood didn't get on the guts. With one heave, JD swung the tub up onto his shoulder as Uncle Cecil watched in disbelief. JD took a few quick steps around the house, kicked the door ajar with his foot while standing on one leg, and deposited the intestines right on the kitchen table. Before he could turn the tub lose, he was nudged aside by the ladies who were waiting to strip the little pieces of fat off the intestines that would later be melted down to use as lard.

The process continued. From then on, Dillie helped Will hold the hogs while JD administered the coup de grace with thrust and speed. Uncle Cecil would open the hog, and JD would carry the intestines into the kitchen. Paw, leaning on his cane, would shake his head in approval, all the while lamenting, "He might as well 'uh stuck him in the ass!"

CHAPTER 19

Those Boys

They rode the lumbering electric train to and from school together each morning and afternoon. Billie walked by JD's side, never holding his hand or running her arm through his, though she could easily have done it for his hands were constantly sunk in his pockets. His once straight back was now slightly stooped; often her hand would rest lightly on his forearm as if she were trying to turn his face to hers.

After a brief stop at their respective homes, Billie would gallop into the barnyard almost by the time JD had changed his clothes and devoured several of Maw's biscuits on the sly. Maw didn't like him eating between meals, though she didn't have to worry about watermelon preserves and biscuits spoiling his appetite.

After customarily lowering Billie from the door track on which she would hang, JD would stand beside her, the two of them talking low so Paw could not hear. She would stroke a cow's back, occasionally grabbing the teat and squirting warm milk into her mouth as JD had taught her to do. JD and Paw didn't sing anymore to make the cows give their milk; however, Paw was still apt to lather the cat's whiskers from a distance. The milk was taken to the pantry that was adjacent to the new kitchen and poured into the huge steel bowl of the separator. Billie watched in awe as the massive boy coerced the handle faster and faster until the separating mechanism whirled in speed sufficient to perform its task. The spigot was turned on the big bowl, sending warm milk down into the whirling discs where a huge stream of thin blue milk emasculated of the thick golden cream streamed through into the crock.

Each evening, JD would carry the cream to the cream house, which was dug into the earth about ten inches deep and eight feet square, accessible through a cellar door. Cool spring water kept the cream from spoiling. Once the milk was deposited, JD would turn toward home as Billie galloped off. It was a well-rehearsed scene.

But on hog killing day, things were different. As JD dropped the tub back under the next hog to be opened, he saw the train stop at the station to let the schoolchildren off, and he was reminded of Billie. He had been so busy all day that he hadn't had time to think of her or school or even, now he realized, go out behind the barn to relieve himself. By now she would be running into the house to change her clothes, pounce on the horse, and ride out the gate with her mother hollering after her, "Where are you going?"

JD was pulled from his thoughts when he heard Uncle Cecil ask, "Who're those boys?" JD turned to find them at his back.

"What's your name?" the bigger boy asked.

"JD."

"Zat one name or two names?"

"That's two names," JD answered politely. "What's your all's names?"

The six-foot-two, stoop-shouldered one with fuzzy cheeks and real green eyes said his name was Sidney. The other one, just an inch shorter and a little heavier, was named Ruben. They lived in Vienna and had come to visit their grandfather, Mr. Cowley—the man with the hump in his back.

"Who's she?" Sidney asked.

And with that, JD turned around and saw Billie sitting on her horse as if she had been sitting there for some time. At the same time, Paw called for him from across the yard, and rather than answering Sidney's question, JD turned his back on Billie and headed toward home. He felt uneasy about it and regretted leaving her there with them, but he felt too embarrassed to do otherwise.

Billie let her horse graze on around behind the meat house, trying all the while not to look like she was following JD, when suddenly Sidney reached up and grabbed her by the boot.

"You know, at first I thought you was a boy."

"Let go!" she said, trying to shake her leg free.

"Now, what's the matter with the little country girl?"

"Let go!" Though she tried to kick his hand away, he held her fast.

"Well, I always heard country girls was shy, but I never knew they was this bad."

Billie didn't wait for him to make another move. She parted his straight, black, greasy hair right in the middle with her crop, putting a nice, red whelp down the part line. Sidney squealed in humility, just like those hogs would have done if they had been lowered into the steaming water alive.

While Sidney was screaming and rubbing his head, Billie turned the horse around to face him; all the while it pranced as if it were waiting to be turned loose to trample the boy. Ruben crouched and said, "Let's get her," though his manner in saying it suggested that he didn't care to lead the charge.

Sidney finally let go of Billie's foot. "Naw, let the little bitch go."

Whereupon Billie broke the horse at Sidney, but Ruben joined in almost as if he wanted to be chased too. Uncle Cecil heard some of the commotion, and as Billie raced the horse through the boys like chickens, he slapped both his hands down on his thighs laughing. "Hot damn! She's given 'em what for!"

The boys escaped through the fence, but even with that obvious protection putting some distance between them, Billie stuck out her tongue and yelled, "Sissies! Sissies!"

Like whipped dogs, the two walked sideways to see whether she would sneak up behind them. On they went, over the little knoll and down toward their grandfather's place.

Billie didn't come by the Browns' place the next day after school. JD thought maybe the boys had hurt her somehow after she rode after them, hungry for hell and conquest. Or maybe she was just mad—maybe she was worse than mad because he hadn't been there for her. But he hadn't wanted to stay and talk to those boys. There was something wrong with them.

CHAPTER 20

Oysters

Dillie had harbored a stick in his craw for some time. It started when Paw had been quietly milking the cows and saw Dillie hit the gelding horse across the nose with a board. Paw, red in the face, teeth trying to sever his tongue, and cane flailing the air, chased Dillie around the barn. Dillie was able to keep at least twenty feet between them, though Paw kept yelling as if he were hitting him.

So this Saturday, Dillie had walked up the track somewhere for whiskey—not one bottle for the night, but what looked like a gallon jug. JD, meanwhile, had ridden over to Uncle Cecil's on an errand and was on his way home, tired and hungry. He had worked long after Dillie had quit, and he was without enough clothes on him to keep from getting chilled by the evening air while riding on a horse.

Dillie saw JD coming long before they met, right where the two roads came together. With a vengeance toward Paw, Dillie grabbed the horse's reins as JD went to pass. JD's attempt to push Dillie's hand free with his foot was unsuccessful, and they went around like a couple of dogs sniffing each other's rear ends, hair all up on their backs. JD did finally make the first offensive move by jumping off the horse and giving Dillie a push. When he did this, Dillie punched him.

JD was stunned not only by the pain but also from the surprise of the attack. He had never been hit like that before and could tell that his cheek was cracked. As he stood there stunned, Dillie hit him again, right in the nose.

By this time, Dillie's body and passion were riding on a wave of heated emotion and confidence spurred on by alcohol. Likewise, JD was suddenly transformed into a snarling and wild animal defending its lair. With his upper lip curled and his teeth grinding, JD hit Dillie right between his eyes, sending him staggering backward into the old oak tree that grew at a bowed angle. A low limb caught Dillie in the small of his back. As he leaned backwards, JD struck him again—first on the head, which brought Dillie's hands up, and then in the stomach, which brought his hands down. This left his head unprotected and wide open for the next blow. The force of these blows twisted Dillie like a wrung washcloth over the tree limb, his head hanging out of reach.

Then, with a kick into his rear end, JD sent Dillie sprawling to the ground whereupon he started to hit him some more. Luckily, he stopped himself short, significantly aware of a strange chill and sadistic pleasure going up his spine, just like an electric charge. JD looked around for something else on which to vent his anger and spotted the whiskey jug setting on the ground. With one frenzied leap, he grabbed it and slammed it against the black oak tree, sending the whiskey flying into a thin spray.

JD shuddered and stopped. There was music, something like church music except it was sad and lamenting. The dusk began to light up like dawn, and JD began walking along with an unexplainable lightness, like a high moon in movement. But he was unable to walk away from the music, which seemed to be following him.

All of a sudden, she appeared—covered in white, though there didn't appear to be any hem or sleeves in her garments. Her hands weren't clasped together or hanging at her sides either; rather, they were motioning in front of her as if they were speaking. JD followed while Little Bonnie talked to him with her hands all the way home. When they got under the big gum trees, she disappeared. Then everything went dark.

The next thing JD remembered was his mother grabbing him as he entered the kitchen door, faintly aware of the blood that had dried in streams down his face. JD heard voices coming from the dining room. There was company.

Mother led JD to the washbasin in the little pantry. She begged him to tell her what had happened, but she kept interrupting his story to tell him not to talk too loud because the prospective preacher was in the other room dining with Paw and Maw.

Once clean, Bonnie led JD out the kitchen door and around the porch to the hall door and on up the stairs where he fell backwards on the bed, the lower part of his legs dangling to the floor. Now JD began to feel the aching bones in his face, not like a toothache, but rather one solid pain all over his face. His nose was swelling, forcing the end to turn upward as if an invisible hand was pushing it. He felt sick and nauseated at his mother's offer to bring him oysters to eat. Breathing anguish, frustration, and wonderment, she cried and wiped her tears on the end of her skirt with one hand and patted his face with a cool, wet washcloth with the other. Finally, she eased out of the room and down the steps to rejoin the company.

In the dining room, Paw watched in amazement as the preacher, having devoured a dozen oysters, continued to reach over and scrape more oysters onto his plate all the while extolling the message of "love thy neighbor" until there was only one soggy oyster left lying there. All told, the preacher had eaten either three or four oysters shy of five dozen.

JD, with his face all black and swollen, didn't make it to church that Sunday to hear the preacher. Of course, no one else heard him either because he wasn't there. It was never clear as to whether the parishioners didn't like his preaching style or his gluttonous eating habits. Perhaps both.

CHAPTER 21

Pastoral Prospect

Two weeks later, a wet blanket of snow greeted the next pastoral prospect. Paw had offered to pick them up at the station in the two-horse wagon—that is, just the regular wagon with a one-by-ten board across it for a seat. The plan was to drop them off at Mr. Cowley's place, for he had agreed to sup them. However, because the wet weather made his rheumatism act up, Paw sent JD with the wagon instead. JD hadn't wanted anybody to see him, what with his face still swollen, but he did as his grandfather instructed.

The Reverend Parman had black hair and a lean, six-foot body. His face was neither round or square but had the appearance of both. His wife was slender and attractive. Their daughter had the best features of both parents. Katie, whose posture seemed to defy and challenge the heavy snow, held her head erect—not haughtily, but with courage and purpose.

JD was glad that he had cleaned the wagon body as much as he could with the snow. It wasn't immaculate, but at least it hadn't been used for hauling manure lately. Though he had slid the seat back about halfway on the wagon, there still wasn't room for all three of them to sit. So the Reverend Parman stood beside JD, balancing himself by laying his hand on JD's shoulder.

Reverend Parman asked him, "Your grandfather is one of the leaders in the church?"

"No, sir, I don't think Paw's a leader."

"Well, he does attend?"

After JD thought for a moment, he decided not to answer directly. "I guess Mr. Cowley and Mr. Ferguson are mostly the leaders."

Reverend Parman started to ask another question when he was interrupted by Mrs. Parman who managed to get the words, "What happened to the last…" out before she was nudged into silence by her husband. JD felt relieved that he could ignore the question that wasn't fully asked.

Reverend Parman continued the previous conversation. "Your grandfather, he is a praying man?"

"Oh, yes sir, yes sir! He prays every morning. I hear him every morning; he doesn't miss a morning. 'Course, Paw is the only one at the house that prays in the morning, everyone else prays at night. And Paw prays out loud. He's deaf and probably don't… I mean *doesn't* think anybody else can hear him."

"What does your father do?" Reverend Parman asked.

"He lives in town," JD answered flatly.

The perceptive preacher noticed the sudden chill unrelated to the snow and ceased his inquiry. While he realized that the question hadn't been answered directly, it had been answered fully.

After dropping the Parmans off at Mr. Cowley's place, JD traced his path home all the while thinking about Katie's face—the red blush of her cheeks from the cold wet snow, her bright eyes and full lips. He also appreciated the way she held her head high and had patted the side of the wagon body as she thanked him for the ride. It seemed to infer that she did not consider him the country help; in other words, she did not view him as being beneath her.

JD looked down on the path every now and then, trying to keep the wheels in the previous ruts—not necessarily because he had to, but to make a game of it. And he felt good, despite the bruises covering his face and memories of Dr. Lytle sticking things up his nose like he was trying to push both his eyeballs into the top of his head! Something about that girl coming made him feel the way he had on the day that Doll birthed her colt, which was more of an occasion than a litter of puppies since it just didn't happen very often. The tingle was all over him, even as he twitched his face that was made sorer from the wet snow.

No one had asked about his face. So as far as JD knew, no one suspected that he had had a fight with Dillie, though Dillie had gotten the worst of it. But something about the fight didn't seem fair. JD had worked hard that day, and though he never went anywhere, whiskey always seemed to follow him like a thick fog. He hadn't meant to break Dillie's ribs and all those teeth; he hadn't wanted to fight at all! But he couldn't have gotten out of it.

He knew Paw had been in fights when he was young, even though he hadn't wanted to. Yet Paw had never told JD to turn the other cheek. Instead, he had said that if you see a fight coming, it wasn't any use backing off or running away because the guy would just come and get you. Or worse, he'd be after you all the time.

The Parmans seemed like nice people, but they weren't anything like him and Paw. Come to think of it, he and Paw weren't anything like Mr. Cowley or Mr. Ferguson either. Considering the facts, JD figured he and Paw probably weren't Christians.

CHAPTER 22

Daydreams

JD got up early on Sunday thinking about her as he milked the cows before church. He also thought about how different it would be to have a preacher actually preach. This would probably encourage more people to attend church, too. Of course, Katie would be there since her father was the preacher.

While he and Will washed up, JD got the impression that his mother—and maybe Paw and Maw, too—didn't think too much of his going to church with his face black and blue, even though it wasn't quite as bad as it had been. JD told himself that it didn't matter what they thought since they weren't going.

The boys put their overshoes on and started walking to the barn in the snow. It was one of those snows that didn't require shoveling a path because it was wet and packed having been walked on a couple of times already. As soon as they started out of the barn on the horses, they saw a car coming up the road. It slipped some but made its way along the level road down through the branch. When it started up the hill, it immediately spun to a halt. They'd never seen the car before and couldn't figure out who might be inside. Curious, they rode right up to it. Then the doors flew open, and their father emerged with that curse of a smile on his face. Drunk. It was evident that he and the other man had been that way all night.

Marcus asked his sons where they were going, as if he didn't know. Then he saw JD's face. "Did you let some kid beat you up?"

JD didn't answer. Marcus repeated the question to Will, but he didn't answer either. With a flick of the reins, the boys began their ride down the hill. Marcus mumbled something after them, but not in protest. Then he got back in the car and started up the hill. A solemn pale came over JD—so unlike Will who was mad. When the horses stopped in the branch for a drank, the brothers agreed not to go to church and turned up the track heading west instead.

JD had never been to the Blacksheares' house on a Sunday, mainly because he usually went to church while Billie and her folks never did. They were probably the only people who had a fireplace, or at least they were the only ones he knew that did, and JD was cold.

Billie hadn't seen JD since the hog killing. She opened the door with a pretentious feminine motion of her body and without making eye contact. "There's ole handsome," she said with an air. "Ya' all come on in."

She always kidded JD when they were around other people, even if it was only Will. But when they were alone, she never teased him. They didn't argue either. They talked serious—academic serious—at least that's how it appeared to her.

Stonewall approached the boys, took one look at JD and said, "My God, son! Who... what happened to your face?"

Billie's head spun around like a top, her eyes now focusing on JD's bruises.

"I got in a fight," JD responded.

"You sure did," Stonewall confirmed. "I didn't think there was a boy in this neighborhood that could handle you."

Will spoke up. "It was Dillie. But JD beat the devil out of him."

It was then that JD realized that Billie was staring at him, frozen in place. She hadn't known. And why should she? She hadn't come back to school since the day they had killed the hogs.

"Why haven't you been to school?" he asked her.

"Momma's making me go to school in the city," she answered.

"For good?" JD asked.

"Well," she responded, "as far as I'm concerned, it isn't for good. But they say if I want to go to college, I've got to go to school in D.C."

"I'll be going to college, too," JD stated matter-of-factly.

Stonewall seemed surprised when JD mentioned college—not surprised necessarily from a financial standpoint, but otherwise. JD said nothing more about it, for talk of college just made the world seem further complicated, as if that were possible.

Billie's mother soon entered the room to see who had come calling. Displeased, she told Billie and Stonewall that they would have to leave before long for their Sunday outing. Not one to be told what to do, Billie stated that she wasn't going to leave. With a slight inference, she indicated that she was going to study. Her mother threw up her hands and let her have her way.

Billie went to fix herself and the boys something to eat, and JD immediately started to feel better. At least he wasn't thinking about his father or church or Katie. Food in hand, the three of them gathered around the fireplace and began kidding around, with JD slapping her backside as Billie bent over to stir the fire up.

"So, what is the real reason why your parents pulled you out of school?" JD asked.

"You 'member that book, *The Little Shepherd of Kingdom Come*? The one about Chad Beauford who bought the mare with the filly named Dixie, and when he joined the Yankees they tried to make him rename her, but he wouldn't?"

JD and Will nodded.

"Well, I remember looking forward to that story every morning. But as soon as the teacher finished reading, my mind would traipse off into fantasyland. It was then that I started keeping an eye on myself, and I noticed that sometimes I was not only daydreaming, sometimes I would just stare into space and my mind was blank. Nothing was happening. My eyes weren't even recording what was out there. I would just stare off in a stupor and start to laugh to myself.

"Then there was a day when teacher scolded me for inattention. I told her that school is supposed to teach students how to think, but just as soon as I go off thinking, someone hollers at me and wakes me up.

Everyone started laughing when I said this, and it looked like teacher was having trouble not doing the same. She admonished me, and I told her I was truly sorry for what I had said.

"Later, teacher took me outside and started asking all these questions about my health. Then she started prying into my parents' relations with each other. Almost every day after that she would take me aside and tell me I was daydreaming all the time. I told her I had gathered more wool in her class than an Australian sheep herder."

JD and Will exchanged confused glances.

"Most of the time when I'm having these moments of daydreaming, I am thinking of something in particular. Quite often it would be something mean someone had said to me or something they had done that was disagreeable, like being overbearing or picking on someone smaller or poorer. I don't know whether one would say that I was holding a grudge or not. You told me the Bible says to forgive, but if the thoughts keep coming up in your daydreams, have you really forgiven the other person? Are you listening to me JD?"

"Yeah, of course!" he answered.

"Well, I wondered because you look so far off."

JD shrugged, and Billie took it as a sign to continue.

"I understand the Christian teaching of forgiving seven times seven, but if you know the bastard is just going to keep on doing mean stuff until the time he dies, what then?"

"Let me give you a short answer to that," JD offered. "First, you give him the benefit of the doubt and you try to persuade him to change his ways. You even pray for him to change his ways. Now he may or he may not. Other than the praying for him, you have no control over him. Second—and this is the most important part and the hardest to do—is you stop allowing these thoughts to keep coming up in your mind. It's like having a splinter in your hand and never picking it out. The splinter of unforgiveness hurts you. It doesn't hurt the other fella. It hurts *you*. Tell the guy you've suffered from the splinter and, if he's real mean, he might just laugh."

Billie started to squirm in her chair, pulling her legs up under her and waving her hands in the air. "Okay, okay! Let me go back to my original and most important concern. Momma finally ran into my teacher in the store, and she told her I was not doing well—and that's putting it mildly. As you know, I had been riding my horse after school, then going to my room to write—first in my diary and then some story. These two activities occupied my mind all the time. It was a matter of my mind being elsewhere—in my stories. I just couldn't pay attention in the classes I didn't like. It felt like I was tied to a stake and couldn't get away. It was torture! So Momma moved me to Wilson Prep. But it's like I have no freedom or friends there, and certainly no one to talk to like we used to talk."

By now Will had finished eating and saw no reason to stay. He said his goodbye, unhitched one of the horses, and went home leaving JD and Billie alone.

They both became quiet. They didn't say a thing or look each other in the eye, but glanced first at the fire and then at the floor. Suddenly, Billie fell to her knees in front of JD, placing her elbows on his knees, her eyes dragging his down into hers, which were floating in tears that began to leak down her face. "Oh, I've missed you so. It wouldn't be so bad if I could see you just to talk to you. Have you missed me?"

"Sure, you know I have," JD said, cutting her off.

"Oh, if I could just talk to you when I feel like that. I try to talk to Momma, but she says I'm a dreamer, and Daddy just agrees. And moving me to a new school has worked out for Momma and Daddy 'cause you and I are separated. They're such snobs!"

"I wouldn't say that," JD interjected. "I suppose if it were my little girl with some boy from poor farming stock with a father like mine, I'd probably try to steer her up the social ladder, too, or at least up the intellectual ladder a little. All parents want that, don't you suppose?"

"Oh, JD, I love you," Billie blurted out. "Do you love me?"

"Sure," he answered with a shrug.

"Do you really? I mean, do you suppose we are in love and don't know it?"

"Well, now wait a minute. Don't talk like that." JD said, standing up. "I mean, let's just do like we have always done before. We can still see each other. Haven't you still got a horse? Can't you still ride down to the house even if we don't go to the same school? Even if your folks aren't crazy 'bout me, we can still see each other."

"Yeah," Billie agreed standing, "but you don't miss me like I miss you."

"You're crazy," JD told her, walking nervously around the room. "Look, I'd leave here, too, if it weren't for you, and maybe Momma, and I guess Little Bonnie. If I could, I'd get so darn far away from this place that…"

Billie cut him off. "JD, you know Little Bonnie's not here, right?"

"I tell you, she *is*," he insisted. "She came right out of the grove."

Billie burst into tears.

"Here wipe your eyes!" JD told her. He sat down and changed the subject. "What do you write about?"

Sniffling, Billie answered, "Lots of things. I want to be a writer someday. Do you think I will? I mean, after I finish college and all?"

"Sure, you will!" JD assured her. "You sure gonna try, aren't you? Not gonna let somebody else tell you what you can or can't do, are you?"

"Oh, JD," Billie gushed. He was the only one who truly understood her. "Mr. King made me stay after English class to discuss a paper I had written about the most impressive thing that had ever happened to me. It changed my philosophy of life."

JD encouraged her to go on.

"It took me a couple of days to decide what to write, but only a short time to write it. It had not come to me out of the blue, but when it did come to me, I knew it was the very thing that created a wedge between our beliefs—yours and mine, which continues to this day."

JD didn't say anything because he didn't know what to say.

Billie continued. "Mr. King sat me down after class one day; he stood in front of me with his rear end up against the chemistry table in a very intimidating manner. He was holding my paper and shaking it in my face with a lot of jabbering. Although we were not that close, I could see that he was mad as hell and puffed up like an old rooster ready to fight. But I puffed up right back at him, yet I didn't make a move or say anything.

"Now b'fore I go any further, I want to tell you that I was riding down to your house to let you read the story before I turned it in, just to see what your reaction would be since it involved you—to some extent anyway. However, when I arrived down at the bridge, there was your father. Knowing he had had a lot of experience in writing and editing in New York, I immediately asked him to critique my story for me—more to share it and have his praise or acceptance than to critique it really.

"Anyway, he read it over twice, the second time just shaking his head. Then to my surprise, he said, 'You are the most genuine, controversial—in the good sense—interesting, intriguing, anomaly of a girl I have ever come across! You'll certainly receive high acclaim for this paper.' And I think he meant it 'cause I saw tears welling up in his eyes.

"After hearing this, I didn't think any more about having you read it, so I just jumped on my horse and rode for home, never thinking of showing it to anyone else either. So, you can imagine when Mr. King confronted me in such a ridiculing manner, I was completely thrown off pace and confused. He said I was a silly girl who, among many other things, should never have written something like this in such explicit terms and handed it into class as my presentation of an important subject.

"As he was ranting on, he dropped my paper and it fell to the floor behind him. He turned and backed away to pick it up, not even stopping his ranting. As he did, his pants became very tight across his behind. Before I knew it, I jumped up and struck him right across his buttocks. He raised up, screaming and hitting his head on the table. I grabbed my paper and ran out of the room and on over to the train station."

Wide-eyed, JD said, "B'fore you go on…"

"I have it right here," Billie announced, jumping to her feet to get her story.

CHAPTER 23

The Story

My Best Friend's Grandfather's Best Cow

My best friend's grandfather's best cow was a fully gray cow, described as mouse-colored, which aptly described her color considering there are many shades of gray. She was of mixed breed: half Guernsey and half Holstein, or so they said. But I always wondered about that because they never kept breeding records on cows as we did for our thoroughbred horses. Yet I never saw fit to question any of their oral history.

Her name was Lady, which likewise aptly described her manner. I would often watch Lady as she chewed her cud in the barnyard at evening time, displaying a sweet countenance that one often sees in kindhearted fat ladies, especially colored ladies like Hazel. Lady would never switch her tail and hit someone in the face like some of the other cows did, particularly when they were wet from inclement weather. Nor would she dirty the trough behind her, whereas the other cows deposited their waste without a second thought to where it was going. Some even had it caked on their behind when they laid down for the night. Lady just didn't do things like that.

Toady townies who have never lived on a farm would not know it, even if they were at the top of their academic classes, but generally speaking, and almost without exception, Guernsey cows give richer milk than Holsteins, although not as much in quantity. However, Lady's was richer by far than the Holsteins and just as much in quantity. Somehow the size of her bag seemed to belie the amount she gave. That is not to say her bag was not full-size.

Reflecting in time, it seems Paw displayed a certain affection for Lady because one could see that he even patted her differently on the back than the other cows. And when he sat down to milk her, he never hollered at her or butted her in the flank to back her leg where he could reach her teats. All the above is not to indicate that Paw was the only one who felt love and affection for Lady. My best friend and I felt and treated her as if she were a human being and, thus, one of the family. Perhaps some of my affection for her was a spiritual radiation of my feelings. Lady was treated like family, though she was not like a cherished member of the family because she ate cow feed and slept in the barn.

While my best friend and I, being young children, wondered about many things that transpired in the day-to-day scheme of things, we never had particularly wondered or asked about the source of babies of any species entering unto the world. So, as it were, there came a time when Lady dried up. This was a normal cycle of things when a cow is to bear a calf, which was all explained to us and, thus, anticipated by us.

Sure enough, in due course, when I rode into the barnyard one morning, there laying next to Lady was a beautiful, mouse-colored bull calf. I silently lamented the fact that it was a bull calf and would never be kept because bull calves never give milk and, consequently, are only several weeks from being loaded on the mail car (of all places) to be sent to Baltimore as veal. Paw would just send the bulls to market and raise the female calves, not having to buy milk cows like Lady, Susie, and Crook, the latter of which always had calves backward and stillborn but gave an abundance of milk. (As an aside, it might be of interest that last year I overheard someone saying that my best friend saved one of these calves by reaching up into the cow and assisting her by either turning the calf around or something otherwise.)

While I was mulling over the bull calf's fate, out stepped my best friend, beaming and pointing to an almost identical calf, which I could see was a heifer. Lady had bore twins! It was then that I surmised that Lady, and no one else, would ever top this feat.

Later, here came the neighbor Harvey inquiring, as he always did without fail, "By golly, what's going on here?" We never answered his questions before because he seemed to be always nosing around for gossip or money. But for some inexplicable reason (by 'inexplicable' I mean something that can't be explained, like the existence of God), we both asked Harvey at the same moment where baby calves came from. At first, he didn't seem to know or want to answer the question, but then he blurted out the whole secret. He said, "You just dig them up out of the ground." When asked where in the ground one would dig, he said "Just go where the last cow dug up her calf."

Harvey had hardly left before we ran to find a shovel. Then my best friend started jabbing the shovel into the hard ground and even jumping up on it with both feet at one time. This didn't work because there was a layer of rock coming out of the ground. In the dictionary, it is called outcropping, although this was not the flint rock that sparks when one clicks them together, nor was it the gray rock that looks like tombstones. This rock seemed to be more in sheets or layers. When my friend couldn't penetrate the rock with the shovel, he ran for a pick. Even though he was a small boy then, he choked up on the handle and started swinging that pick like a wheel going around. There was none of that slow hitting or grunting like all the other men would do. His blows just seemed to go in a never ending circle. However, the stone soon wore him out, or at least he saw the futility in it.

Then my best friend fetched the crow bar and started pounding it into the immovable rock as if it were a pile driver. He told me later, as he sat down exhausted, that he had imagined all those calves down there yearning to get out. But when the crow bar yielded to the stubborn rock, his dream went up like smoke in the sky.

We went out to the barn again after supper. I hadn't even gone home yet. His mother followed us out, sat down right there on the rock, and told us the truth about babies. It had seemed from the beginning all too easy to both of us that one could simply dig up calves from the ground; however, we wanted so much to have it happen that way.

Though disappointed in learning that calves were made by the mating of animals and the cow having to suffer the agony of passing a whole calf out of her private parts—all at God's design—I did wonder why God had not made it more pain free and possibly less embarrassing for the cow. As I contemplated the situation now with two beautiful calves and Lady literally dripping with milk, I became more reconciled to reality. And, as my best friend had said, "God had not only blessed us with a nice little heifer, which perhaps would some day give milk like Lady, but also with a veal calf."

The next day as I rode to put my horse in the stall where my best friend would help me down from the barn door, I spied the family all standing around Lady. She was laying, all swollen up in her stomach, right where we had dug for the calves. With my new awareness of calves coming from the cow's stomach, I immediately thought that she was going to have more babies. Perhaps, I thought, she would just keep having more until Paw was a rich, or at least a prosperous man. But then, when I detected the stern frown on everyone's faces, I feared for the worst.

I overheard the men say that a veterinarian had been called, but to no avail. Someone, I don't recall who, suggested that the veterinarian was more inclined to be recuperating from his weekly poker game than tending to his normal duties. Repairing to the house, I learned that the women were equally concerned, since Lady was cherished by all, even the neighbors.

Later that afternoon the veterinarian showed up. It was revealed that Lady had died, probably of milk fever after getting into the green clover field overnight. I ran to the barn and observed this grotesque cow laying on her side with all four legs sticking straight out as if she were a wooden model. I remember at the time, I wanted to put a blanket over her but had none. I wondered why God, who was to have had a hand in all this, never even afforded Lady the dignity of letting her top legs rest down to the ground in a more peaceful and natural position.

I stood there beside my best friend as he cried. I did not console him or Paw because I equally felt the loss. And then, as a further assault on her dignity, the veterinarian walked up, opened his pocketknife, and without any warning or permission, stuck it in Lady's stomach. Not only did this foul-smelling gas come charging into our faces, a hissing noise like someone passing gas continued for an embarrassingly long time. Then he said, as if he were observing the demise of a fish, "Maybe if you had done that when you first noticed her swelling, it would have saved her." Then he said—and I still hate him for this—"Doctors have knowledge of simple rules or acts *that other men do not possess."* He capped it off by suggesting that even if the knife did not save her life, it did mean they wouldn't have had to dig as large a hole in the dry hard ground to bury her in. Then Paw sent my best friend to the house for money to pay the bill.

My best friend and his little brother were always quick to point out how they dug her a nice deep grave—deep enough to prevent animals from digging at her. When they put her in the ground, they discovered there was no place for her four legs, which of course continued to stick out. To accommodate this (perish the thought of cutting off her legs or even trying to break them, which they could not have done), they discussed digging four postholes at the bottom of the grave and standing Lady upright in a death defying position. But seeing the futility in that, they dug a trench next to the grave and laid her on her side.

While the lament of the loss of Lady continued over the kitchen table for months, thanks was always given for her little heifer, now named Duty, for it was assumed when one viewed her conformation and demeanor that she would be an apt replacement for Lady. Though our hearts mourned for Lady, there were also my best friend's grandmother's lamentations when she sat pressing the butter destined for market into the wooden form that left a flower-topped imprint. It seemed that each Friday as she performed her chore, her assessment of the decrease in the amount of butter for market increased, all due to Lady's void.

As the months passed, Duty grew into a beautiful mouse-colored heifer. She developed a small bag, but one that was comparable to what one would have expected. For months—probably sooner than I should have—I watched to see if she was ever bulling. Of course, 'bulling' was a term that was used by farm men to indicate a cow was ready to be bred. They never used terms like 'in season' or 'in heat,' as one might when referring to other animals. This was probably because a cow in this condition would stand perfectly still and allow a bull to mount her. I believe this act is unexplained by people of science and only happens to cows. One other question that is raised by this phenomenon is, why is the cow who is standing still said to be 'bulling' when the bull is doing the mounting?

For months, I had heard Paw and the boys discussing, not in so many words, whether they had observed Duty bulling. Then there came a day when I rode into the barnyard and saw my best friend crying as if his heart was broken as he led Duty into Mr. Myer's truck, which was headed for Baltimore. I know Paw couldn't walk much, but it didn't seem right that my best friend had to lead his much-loved heifer to slaughter.

And then I started crying, maybe even more so than when Lady died. It just seemed to me at that moment, and still to this day, that some force was responsible for this sinister chain of events. First, my best friend and his family were blessed with the twin calves. Then, Lady was taken from them, which was followed by the cruelest event of all: the months of hope and anticipation of Duty coming fresh with a calf didn't happen. Instead, she was shipped off to a degrading fate.

From that time on, my best friend and I have wrestled with the existence of God. Despite this whole series of events, he still believes in God, whereas I contend that while there might be a God, if there is, he is displeased with the Browns, or at least with their cow. In either case, God is not always righteous.

I went home crying all the way, and I told my parents that I didn't believe there was a God, and if there was, I was mad at him. So, this experience—or group of experiences—changed my philosophy far more than any other—even more than when my best friend's little sister was killed for no reason at all.

Billie Blacksheare
English III

CHAPTER 24

An Innocent Girl

JD sort of smiled and furrowed his forehead into a perplexed expression. Then he said in jest, though it didn't come off that way entirely, "You are kind of explicit with great detail, but that's good in telling the story. You being a high school girl, I wonder why in the devil that teacher couldn't just consider your story the writing of… you know… an innocent girl."

"Well, Momma and Daddy put me in the car, and Daddy said, 'Now, don't either one of you say a word until he gives us his explanation and I respond to his explanation.' So, Daddy just sat there and, don't you know, ole King thought he was going to rule the roost! The more he explained about my improper choice of words and the meaninglessness of my subject—the demise of a cow!—the more angry Daddy got. And, he said I used a horrible word: bulling."

JD said, "We would never use that term in front of a woman or girl, but we use it among farmers. And words like *tits*. I guess it's one of those things where you must be careful how you say it; but you spelled it right! 'Teats' and not 'tits.' And bulling isn't that bad anyway. It was, after all, a writing class and not a class about social manners or something else."

Billie nodded in agreement. "Then Daddy lit into him, and called him a damn sissy cad. And he asked him where he thought the milk he drank came from. But Daddy never let ole King reply. He finally told him, 'My daughter is not suspended; she's going to transfer out of your little school. You have backward teachers here anyway!'

"Now here's the best part: Right out of Mr. King's office window, we could see a bunch of girls and boys playing in the auditorium. They were quite loud. Ole King finally asked Daddy to excuse him so he could stop the ruckus. He swung the door open wide and placed his hands on his hips like he was a big shot and bellowed out, 'You children stop that horsing around.'

"Well, he might just as well have put a sword in Daddy's hand. Daddy jumped up, grabbed King's shirt and spun him around and said, 'Now where in hell do you think the word *horsing* comes from? That's what they call a mare's action when she is in heat.'

"Then he pushed him off and said, 'If I hear one word of this around this provincial little town, I'll walk down the street with your head on a platter.'

"As we left, ole King kept repeating, 'Why, I had no idea! Why, I had no idea!'"

CHAPTER 25

Church

They hired Reverend Parman, who seemed pleased with the small house he was provided. He was also pleased that the Cowleys invited him and his family to dinner every Sunday. Mrs. Cowley sure must've cooked something good since the reverend always made mention of it each Sunday, and that was a full week after he had eaten it! Or maybe he was thinking about the meal he would get later that day.

Reverend Parman preached well, digressing every time to tell some little story about his boyhood and associating it with how he came to believe in Jesus, which he said freed a man and made him happy. He said a man didn't know what being happy was until he was free.

Mr. Ferguson still taught Sunday school. Mr. Cowley and Reverend Parman both talked freely, but Mr. Ferguson did all the teaching. There was a kindness between the three of them that bound them together, though they didn't ever sit close to each other. Mr. Cowley always seemed to cheer Mr. Ferguson on, even if it was nothing more than a head nodding smile, and he was always doling out compliments to Reverend Parman, but inconspicuously. There was no rivalry amongst the three.

Sunday nights, the children, including JD, Will, and Katie Parman, would sing at the urging of the reverend. *This little light of mine, I'm gonna let it shine ...* Then, *We shall come rejoicing, bringing in the sheaves* ... and *When the roll is called up yonder, I'll be there* ... followed by more of *This little light of mine.*

JD had a hard time keeping his eyes and his mind off Katie. She, likewise, was attracted to him.

One Sunday morning, Sidney and Ruben accompanied their grandfather, Mr. Cowley, to church. They sat behind him and flipped their finger against his ear, which caused him pain and startled him from his hypnotic trance in the word and the music. He would put up with them until he got outside, and when he did, he tore after them. But they, being younger, would just run down the hill laughing at their grandfather. The only way he could have had a go with them would have been in the church where they couldn't run away, but he would never do that to Reverend Parman.

Paw and Maw came to church often then, as did JD's mother. She could get light-hearted at times, but once church was over it was back to the ironing board—literally speaking. Sundays were her only day off and used to iron the boys' shirts for the next week at school.

CHAPTER 26

Billie Slipped In

That winter and spring JD rode the train to school in Herndon while sitting beside Katie. She never touched him on the shoulder like Billie did, but he always carried Katie's books though he had never carried Billie's. He thought about Billie whenever the train went by her house, but he never saw her anymore. He knew that one day she would go away, whereas Katie seemed stationary, like a light stuck in a lighthouse. He imagined himself as a ship going in and out to sea, but his heart always yearned to come back to the lighthouse.

Katie seemed to have the Bible all figured out. Not that she pretended to know everything, just the opposite. She wasn't impatient with JD either, even though he hadn't joined the church yet and been baptized. He talked to her about everything except Billie and his father.

The quiet and gentle spring died, thus giving birth to a hot and impetuous summer. When Katie left for Lynchburg to spend the summer with her grandparents, a void seemed to rest over the farm.

Paw hadn't planted anything in the new ground that was next to the oak grove. The corn had been planted in the field next to the house from which JD could not escape Paw's eyes, the house being set from a panoramic vantage looking down on the field. Not that Paw wouldn't have let him rest. JD could cause the horse to turn around right at the edge of the yard and stop at that end of the corn row; a few steps in and he'd be under one of the gum trees, their cool green leaves mitigating the heat of the sun. A few steps farther, and he would be at the well. This day was hot, and even the ground, plowed up by the cultivator, seemed warm.

JD had just come out of the stable through the windbreak fence when he heard her yell, not at him, but at her horse. And there she came, galloping across that twenty-acre field Harvey had bought from the estate of his father. She jumped one chicken coop and then the next. He had first caught sight of Billie when she jumped the fence right where the train had peeked out of its hole like a snake. She must have yelled, he wouldn't have had any other reason to look in that direction much less down in that corner of the field where she was almost out of sight.

Billie finally ran out of jumps, unless she was to try the bars between Watson's and Paw's place. The fox hunters hadn't put a jump that close to a house, which was most considerate of them. A horse can jump higher, more in stride and less inclined to refuse, if he comes to a jump fast. Of course the rider takes the risk of being thrown harder if the horse does refuse. In one of those fast charges, Billie steered her horse right toward the bars in full gallop—up and over, right to where JD was.

They never even spoke. Their eyes said everything. His hand clasped her forearm as he helped her dismount. Together they came into the yard, passing under the gum tree and continuing into the big kitchen where the egg-shaped table stood extending plates and food. Billie slipped in like she had never left, and after dinner she and JD took to the swing, rocking back and forth by the flection of the muscles in their legs. Paw sat in a white lawn chair rasping the ground with his cane as if he were trying to awaken someone or something below. He could neither see them or hear them.

"Have you seen *her* lately?" Billie asked, referring to Little Bonnie, not Katie.

"No," JD answered. "I been plowing corn, and we been turning the horses out right there in that field. So, I haven't been over to the grove lately."

"Let's go tonight. I mean, you could turn the horses loose over by the horse branch. You know, you could tell Paw that you are going to water them there instead of oak branch."

"You'll have'ta make sure your folks don't know where you're going," JD warned. "They'd never let you go out of the house again."

"You come right up the lane and go in right at the big oak tree. I'll come in up at the other end by the new ground; we can meet in the middle, and nobody will see us—at least not together."

"No, I'm not gonna come in that end. I've never come in from that end 'cept a long time ago when Paw and I were squirrel hunting."

"Okay," Billie conceded. "I'll meet you right there at the new ground."

"About seven?"

"About seven."

While he stood there looking down the lane for Billie, she came out of the woods down at the other end, her horse walking as softly as a doe, as if it knew to be quiet. They dismounted. Then he, stepping on the lower strand of the barbed wire fence while lifting up the next, allowed Billie to gather her skirt tight to her lower torso and slip through. He passed through quickly. Normally he would have half straddled and half jumped, balancing himself by lightly touching the top strand of barbed wire. But it was more reverent this way.

Now their hands were unconsciously clasped in union as if they were one, as if they were looking for someone but expecting no one. They passed under the decapitated dome of the grove, their eyes searching upward and then down to the front. The light glanced off the tops of the branches, not entering the space below, and yet darkness was dispelled.

The whippoorwill's shrill, as if from aloft, rang in the woodland sanctuary like a lone voice in a giant cathedral. It could be heard in the field but never seen, never there. Yet how could anyone doubt its presence? The whippoorwill, such a loner that he mates at night, is a spirit bird that disappears in the day. Artists lie because they've never seen the whippoorwill. It never sings in the same place twice, but always sings from somewhere else and never when you're there. Tonight, it sang its praise—not for long, but for long enough.

And then JD saw her.

She began to turn, and a thick, soft voice sang out, which only JD could hear. *"I'm with you always my sweet. Life may heave and death may sigh, but I shall lift thy spirit to my breast and tilt my head upon it. I shall not leave without thee, not until thou taketh my hand in bond and leave with me. Don't wait so long, for I wait alone."*

"Oh, JD, I wish you wouldn't hold your breath like that," Billie cried, breaking his trance. "I'm afraid when you hold your breath like that!"

And just like that, Little Bonnie disappeared. Billie kept on talking. "I don't care 'bout whatever happens; I wouldn't have missed meeting you tonight for anything. Do you feel the same way 'bout me?"

"Yes," JD answered listlessly.

"I miss you! It just feels like I'm dying of thirst. I know we'll never marry, I know. But I hope I always have you to talk to. I couldn't ever marry you; it'd be like marrying God."

"I thought you didn't believe in God."

"I don't," Billie quipped. "And just because you see *her* doesn't mean there is a God."

Disturbed, JD blurted out, "Don't ever say that to me again." He turned his back on Billie and began to walk away.

"Oh, I didn't mean to make you mad," Billie apologized. "Don't get mad, please!"

JD stopped and turned to her. "I'm not mad; I just wish you wouldn't say that. God and me have never exactly shaken hands. Especially over *her*."

CHAPTER 27

It'll Be Different

In his naivety, JD never expected trouble, though unpleasantness seemed to haunt him. He had a habit of grinding of his teeth, not in anger but more like a cow chewing her cud softly like she's contented when suddenly she is struck by a painful object. If one can envision that, then one can imagine the look on JD's face when Marcus came back. The air he breathed became stale and hot, and the food became tasteless and unappetizing. The future itself seemed futile, for all was tainted by his gibbering and drunken presence.

For several days, Marcus commuted from the house to his source of whiskey. Not once was he seen eating, just transitioning from one drunken sleep to a rousing and nervous search for more alcohol. Back to the former again and so on and so forth.

Finally, the day came when Maw knew that both he and the time were ripe. She sat him down to feed him. At first she fed him broth. Later that night and over the next couple of days, more stable food was introduced.

"Maw, as God is my judge," Marcus stammered, "I'll never drink another drop of whiskey. Honestly, I hope God strikes me dead if I ever even touch a bottle."

"You've said that before," Maw said firmly.

"I know, but this time I mean it. I've never been like this. No, I hope God strikes me dead if I even go near a bottle."

"So, what are you going to do with yourself?" Maw asked.

"I don't know," Marcus said, shaking his head. "There's nothing to do in this town."

"Marcus, you'll keep drinking until it's too late. Then you won't be able to stop. You'll let the days go past, and then it'll be too late."

"No, not this time. I've finally learned my lesson."

"You keep this up, and your boys won't ever accept you. They barely know you now. They've grown up without really knowing you. They've never had a father. And though they've got each other, they've never been the same since what happened to our little girl. Especially JD. I don't know what he'll do, but he's going to do something with his life. Whatever it is, he'll do it and nothing or no one will stop him."

When Marcus didn't say anything, Maw went on. "Only one thing I suppose: those boys have seen enough whiskey to last them the rest of their lives. You can be sure of that! I remember the day JD got in a fight with Dillie. A boy being beaten up in the woods after he had worked all day—by a drunken brute no less! And where were you? Then you and that cursed friend of yours made fun of him that morning when he was going to church with his face bruised like that. Good heavens, his spirit must have been in his shoes. I'm afraid for them boys. You've waited too long. Maybe too long for yourself also."

"How about Bonnie?" Marcus inquired slowly. "Don't you think... Don't you think we can still make a go if it?"

"I hate to say."

"I'm sure gonna try. This time it'll be different. I'm gonna show her that I can do it. I'm not going off this place. I'm not going near a bottle or even near anyone who has one. I'm just going to prove to her this time that I can stay sober."

He ate silently, then asked, "Did you hear 'bout Louie?"

"You mean 'bout him losing his job?"

"Lord no, Maw. He's been locked up in Occoquan for ninety days. He got drunk and started breaking things and hadn't paid his rent, and the lady he roomed with called the cops."

"What'd they send him down there for?"

"'Cause nobody would pay his fine. He called his brother, but he told Louie he wasn't going to pay a fine again for him."

"Again! You mean he's been locked up before?"

"Lord, yes."

"That poor boy, ruining his life. I've always felt so sorry for him."

"Why?"

"Oh, I don't know. You boys always teased him so much and he looked up to you all so much."

"We never hurt him!"

"How 'bout that time you threw his gold watch off the train?"

"Well, the darn fool trumped my ace!" Marcus griped.

"Yes, but that wasn't anything for you to get mad about. It was only a card game."

"I paid him for it."

"Yes, but you didn't pay him for the humiliation you caused him in front of everyone. You know, while we're on it; you must admit that while you display considerable humor and friendliness in general, you seem to be completely without concern, sympathy, or generosity for others, including your own children and, indeed, your wife."

"Now, come on Maw! How can you possibly say that when you know how much I have always loved her?"

"Oh yes, you persuaded her to marry you, and you love her also, but only for your own selfish desires. You've done nothing but break her heart. And to tell you the truth, I don't even know why in the world I even speak to you!"

The talk with Maw had its effect. Marcus stayed in the other house at night and didn't touch a drop of whiskey. Dillie, on the other hand, didn't miss a weekend of drink. However, there wasn't a brand of whiskey strong enough to induce him to bother JD again.

Marcus plowed corn with JD every day while Will and Dillie fixed the fence. Paw mostly directed. Marcus and JD weren't far apart as they worked, so they could plow and talk at the same time. JD got closer to his father during this time, attentive to his city stories and kidding about things like how Dick the workhorse walked fast when Marcus was plowing up the hill toward the barn but hardly moved when they went the other way. Their concerted efforts glowed; not only was there fresh corn, the garden didn't produce a single weed—even the fence rows and corners in the fields were clean of weeds and briars. It looked like a well-kept park.

Weeks later, on one of those ideal summer evenings when the heat had dissipated, Marcus and Will were returning from the field near Uncle Cecil's, right near the fork in the road where JD and Dillie had had their fight, when Marcus reached his arm out, stopping Will in both walk and talk. Then he directed Will's eyes down the road to the new ground where they saw JD and Billie entering the fence, just like they had done several times before. Through the fence they went, clasping hands, and then they disappeared from sight.

"Where in hell are they going?" Marcus asked.

Will replied, "Leave them alone."

"Leave them alone? What in the hell are they thinking? Her old man would shoot the hell out of him if he saw that. I'm gonna follow 'em!"

Will stepped in front of his father as if to restrain him, saying, "No, you're not."

Marcus butted up against Will's outstretched and restraining hands. "What do you mean I'm not?"

Will, talking low so they wouldn't hear him, replied, "It's none of your business."

"Who in the hell do you think you're talking to boy? I'm your father, and don't you forget that!"

But Will stood up to Marcus. "You're not going to bother them. It's none of your business. Besides, they aren't going to do anything."

"I'm telling you for the last time to get out of my way."

"Look, I don't want to have to fight you, but I will if I have to."

Marcus thought a moment before responding. "It's a damn good thing you're my kid or I'd whip the hell out of you."

So they continued toward home, but not without Marcus mumbling to himself and looking over toward the grove to see if he could see anything. Will wondered just exactly what would have happened if he had had to fight his father. Even if he wasn't around much until lately, he was his father nonetheless.

Marcus had been in plenty of fights—anyone who drinks and gets drunk can't escape fighting. But how in hell do you fight a teenage kid like he was a man—especially if he's your kid and all? Marcus had to wonder this: suppose Will was like JD and couldn't be whipped?

CHAPTER 28

The Only One

Fathers consider discretion in their daughters a sacred enticement, but where a son is concerned, a girl in trouble has no one but herself to blame. Mothers, on the other hand, fear some dirty little hussy will get their innocent little boy in a jam, thus creating a shotgun situation. Perhaps for this reason, Marcus didn't feel inclined to chastise Bonnie for something he thought her son apparently had been doing with the full knowledge of his younger brother.

Marcus didn't even bother to tell Bonnie that he had seen JD and Billie heading into the grove, but seeing them gave him the feeling of having superior knowledge. He silently gloated as he dwelt on the matter; the case probably was not closed, as they say. His furtive glances at Will throughout the rest of the evening surely made Will feel like an unindicted co-conspirator—that is, if Will had been familiar with such legal terms.

Their foreheads were now beaded with sweat as chills and goose pimples raced up their forearms and down their backs. JD repeated the words aloud that he had heard from Little Bonnie. *"For as the sun sinks in a deep and downward sway; they come to my bosom as a resting place to pray. They seek the small mist form to speak. Oh, move away; move away you treacherous fog."*

"Oh, Jesus, JD!" Billie screeched. "No matter what, my whole life will be a bore if I lose contact with you! Don't you ever forget that," Billie insisted. "You are the only one!"

"If you ever tell a soul I'll kill… well, I won't kill you. I don't have anything to blame you for—you've never told. But you know how I feel. I don't even talk to Will or anybody about this!"

"Oh, Jesus, I love you," Billie wailed. "I mean it. I don't care if you don't ever marry me. I'm still gonna love you. You're always gonna be mine. But what did she mean about the treacherous fog? What did she mean?"

"I don't know," JD answered with a shake of his head.

"Oh, please tell me," Billie begged. "I'll give you anything if you'll just tell me."

"I tell you, I don't know!" JD insisted. "You better go on home now."

"I'm not going home 'til you kiss me goodbye."

"You're crazy. I'm not kissing you g'bye. Get the devil on that horse."

"No," Billie stated, holding her ground. "You've got to let me kiss you just on the cheek. I don't care. I love you."

JD stood still as a fence post while Billie eased up to him, stretched up, and kissed him on the cheek. She stole a hug from him, too. He was seventeen going on eighteen. He had coarse, curly hair and unblemished skin, the roughness of a tanned hide.

Billie mounted her horse and rode home like the wind. JD turned his horse loose in the grove for the night. Then, with the bridles hung over his shoulder, he raced in downhill momentum after her with a burst of speed. This was accentuated by the final flexion of his Achilles tendon that seemed to propel him further in stride. He ran so fast that he fairly coasted up the next steep hill, which was every bit of a hundred yards or more. Quite unbelievable for a boy of his physical stature.

CHAPTER 29

A Poem and a Thesis

Billie usually wore her jodhpurs and boots. Each day she would come to the field where the men were working; this day they were plowing corn. Tying her horse in the shade, she climbed up on one of the boy's horses and rode backward while talking to them. Sometimes she sat on the horse's rear end with her legs hanging down so it looked somewhat like the horse had three tails; and sometimes she sat on the hames with her feet on the traces.

This day she sat on the brass-topped hames of Will's horse, which were not as sharp as those on JD's and, thus, were less intrusive to her hands as she placed them palms down between the hames and her buttocks. It seemed as if when she wanted to play and joke, she liked Will; and when she was serious—perhaps even woolgathering—she gravitated to JD. More often, she was serious. Her general demeanor suggested that she was about to perform her normal gymnastics, even doing handstands and the like while the horses plodded down the rows of corn. But today she was different—she had a dress on, which made her seem more of a girl.

Billie said to Will, "Charlene says she loves you and when she becomes older she is going to marry you."

Will laughed, "What does she want to wait for? I'm old enough. Tell her to get her dowry from her father now."

"You're not even out of school, and ya don't have a job."

"We can live on her dowry 'til I get old enough to git a job."

Bonnie shook her head. "Will, you say 'git,' 'get,' and 'got' too much. They are bastard words."

Will glanced up just in time to see Billie perform a handstand on the horse, with the skirt of her dress draping down over her head and arms. Soon as he took his eyes off the plow and the row, the plow tilted, sending the outside shovel into the cornstalks. He'd seen Billie do this trick before, but not while wearing such a revealing outfit.

All this caught JD's eyes, and though he was several rows away, he could see the plow laying the row of corn over as if it were being mowed down on purpose. He hollered, and they both resumed their previous positions. Though JD was inwardly laughing, he put up a false front and admonished them both when they gathered in the shade at the end of the field.

"Quite a show, Miss Blacksheare. I thought my little brother was going to plow up the whole field."

"Oh, I am so sorry. I forgot I had a dress on."

"If Paw sees that corn, you're gonna catch it," he warned.

"Well, Paw doesn't have to know about it," Will stated.

"Unless I tell on you," JD threatened. "Maybe if you went down to Jim's spring and brought us a jug of water, I might be able to forget about it."

At the suggestion, Will began to saunter off toward the spring.

"What's with the dress?" JD asked once Will was out of earshot. "You shouldn't be riding around on a horse with a dress on."

"Don't try to fool me JD. You know boys like to see girls wearing more erotic…"

"Whoa!" JD interjected. "Where do come up with the *erotic* bit?"

"Never mind," Billie brushed him off. "Listen, I wanted to tell you something special today, which is why I wore a dress."

"Go on," JD said.

"I've a poem here somewhere in my dress that I wrote for you, and I wanted to tell you of my new discernment and thesis."

"Wow! That sounds very formal and convoluted."

"Now you're making fun of me!"

"I'm sorry, I was just kidding," JD apologized.

"First, here is the poem," Billie said. Then she began to recite.

> *"The lonely hours I have spent*
> *But not a stranger I have meant—to be.*
> *Hours plodding with a pen,*
> *Where else would I have rightly been?*
> *For 'tis the search I struggle for,*
> *Not to entertain and certainly not to bore,*
> *But find the end forevermore.*
> *He says he knows; he's sure he knows he knows.*
> *But not for me, though I wish it were,*
> *If only for him who dreamed so long in his repose.*
> *He says I walk the lonely Cimmerian.*
> *If this be true, while in this thicket,*
> *I shall try to paint the Rose.*
> *If it's born in me where else do I belong?"*

"It's not much," Billie confessed, "but I wrote it just to put you in the mood to listen to my thesis."

"Okay," JD stated. "Go ahead."

"First, just let me say that I love dreaming and writing. I know some say it's daydreaming but, to me, writing is just as pleasant and intoxicating as drinking Daddy's scotch."

Shocked, JD retorted, "Drinking Daddy's scotch? When have you been drinking your Daddy's scotch?"

"Oh, you know," Billie responded nonchalantly, "Will and I have a couple of nips now and then."

JD's eyes widened. "No, I didn't know! And I'll beat the pants off Will if I ever catch him."

"Oh, now don't digress me from what…"

"*Digress* you! You can't use digress like that."

"Oh, you know what I mean," Billie said with a flip of her hand.

"Okay, go ahead with whatever you want, but I'll find out about the scotch sooner or later," JD warned.

"Now, please don't tell Will," Billie pleaded. "I've inadvertently betrayed a confidence, and you would be taking advantage of my slip."

"Well, hurry up then. I have to get back to plowing."

"Okay. Here's my thesis," Billie began. "The prophets wrote of God—a God they had not seen, trying to describe God to those who also have not seen. And they wrote of God's will, of His commandments, and even of a Messiah who was to come to save the world. But this was all being done without context, and certainly, without visual sight, even though they professed to hear Him speak.

"So where does all this leave me? I liken this to a situation where a seeing person is trying to describe a rose to a blind person who has never had eyesight. So, the task that I have prescribed for myself is to write—or as I am wont to say—paint the rose in words so that the blind person can see the flower. Of course, the blind one can feel the softness of the petal, maybe even its shape, and perhaps the lone dew drop that neither runs nor seeps into the petal, but the blind cannot feel its color and beauty."

JD stared at Billie as if seeing her for the first time. She returned his gaze and then asked, "What do you think of that?"

JD nodded approvingly. "I think it's great honey."

"You've never called me honey before."

"You've never touched me in this way before."

Billie tingled all over. "Do you think I can do it?"

"Paint the rose," JD commanded.

CHAPTER 30

Bell Cow

The row of corn Will plowed out while Billie did her handstand died, even though he had replaced it with his foot; Paw cursed the cutworm that he assumed had eaten it.

When the wheat was full grown, JD set to cutting and binding it with the binder being pulled by three horses. Billie rode and guided the inside horse while JD manned the controls of the binder. It would have been nearly impossible for even an experienced man to guide the horses around the undulating hilly field and handle the controls at the same time. Billie proved indispensable since Will had to shock the bundles in case it rained before the wheat could be thrashed. Wheat thrashing, which was done with the help of neighbors, and hog killing were the two most eventful days of farm life.

Next, the potatoes were dug and stored in the cellar and the corn plowed again. Billie spent each day with the boys. She would arrive by horse, grab the overhead track at the barn door while kicking the horse out from under her, and yell for JD to help her down. He'd come, wrap his arms around her, and let her slide to the ground. Each time he would ask, "A little big for this, aren't you?"

Billie would answer, "No. I might twist my ankle."

Later in the kitchen, Maw said to Billie, "Child, you have a lovely complexion, but I'm afraid if you don't stay out of the sun, those pretty freckles are going to take over. Now, don't misunderstand—I know you're a great help but I hate to see…"

"Don't worry Maw, I'm no beauty queen," Billie responded, "and besides, I want the experience so someday I can write about it."

Maw said, "I hope you do. I'd just love to be around to read it when you do."

"Oh, you'll be around," Billie speculated. "You know, I could have gone to see Grandma Blacksheare, but I feel closer and more at home here with you."

Maw smiled. "And I think of you as if you were my own child."

"Do you think I will ever amount to anything, Maw?"

"I most certainly do! I've always thought that you were a bell cow."

"Oh, goodness!" Billie responded appreciatively but bewildered. "What's a bell cow?"

As she stirred the pot on the hot kitchen stove, Maw explained. "Well, if you can, imagine a herd of cows walking up and across a hill in a line as they always do. If you watch them each day, they usually stay on the same path—one that's not too taxing, slopes gently. Anyway, there'll always be the same cow in the lead, and that's the one you always put the bell on."

"Why the bell?"

"That's if they become lost you can find them all. 'Cause when you find the bell cow, the rest will be around since you've found the leader. And I know that you are going to be a leader, Billie. JD's a bell cow, too."

"Oh, that's great Maw! You should be a writer."

Maw blushed. "Doctor Leigh told me the same thing back when he was my teacher, 'fore he went to medical school."

CHAPTER 31

Stirrup Cups

The stirrup cups were on trays to be served by butlers. Some were ceramic and some were made of pewter, but all had handles. Those who were to participate in the foxhunt were served a cup filled with spirits while mounted on their horses in order to drink a toast at the start of the hunt. The rims of the stirrup cups were curved inward so the drink would not spill if the horse moved and jostled the rider.

On this beautiful October day, Billie had arranged for the boys—Will and JD—to work for pay. They assured Paw that they would make up the lost time shucking corn. JD was to remain on the ground and not participate in the hunt while Will mounted and dressed in borrowed foxhunt attire.

The stirrup cups were passed to each person—even to JD, who did not know what it contained. Being preoccupied with protocol, he took one not realizing it contained liquor. Everyone raised a cup. Billie, who was mounted on her horse right next to JD, watched intently and with an air of delight as he joined in the toast. But when the liquor bit his throat, he gasped and spit it out. Then he emptied the remainder upon the ground. Will, on the other hand, drank his cup heartily, and all of it.

"Oh, JD, don't be a prude," Billie said in a harsh but somewhat muffled voice.

Billie and Will rode together chasing the yelping hounds while JD tended to the roasting of the pigs. They would be delicious, but he roasted them with mixed feelings about the stirrup cup. It even crossed his mind as to its juxtaposition with the Last Supper. It also crossed his mind that Billie had scolded him.

Not long after the stirrup cup incident, JD sat with his mother and explained how he thought drinking would have offended Billie, to say nothing of her mocking response, which he knew was a bit farfetched. In any event, it was one of the few times he had sought his mother's guidance.

"Ya' know," he said, "there's always been two things that have baffled me."

"Only two, JD?"

"Well, two in particular," he clarified. "I used to talk to Paw—still do for that matter—about things that only men can understand. Things that women just don't seem to have a part in."

"I think I'm about to disagree with your premise before I hear what you're about to say," Bonnie cut in.

"I'm talkin' 'bout fighting, war, turning the other cheek, and things like that. But I guess the other thing I'm referring to you would deserve to have a say in, though you might be inclined to go overboard in light of your own personal experiences."

She turned around from her work to face him directly, and looking askance asked, "Now what in the world might that be?"

"It's about liquor," he answered whereupon, Bonnie jumped in with, "You don't have to go a bit further; I know what you're getting at. And just let me tell you 'bout what you did and what you did not do also. Had you drunk from the stirrup cup, or even held the drink without acting, you would have thereby spared Billie's feelings. However, you also would have been setting a bad example for Will. And while we're on it, let me say that I know Will. Will has—it's sad to say, but it is the truth nevertheless—some of his father's ways."

JD tried to say something, but his mother held up her hand in protest. "Now let me finish. Just ask yourself this question: Which would have been the worse offense? To temporarily hurt the feelings of your friend, or to have led your little brother to sin and toward a life of destruction? And do not consider the fact that one is your friend and a girl, and the other is your brother. Forget all that!"

JD considered his mother's question but did not answer.

"Just think about it," Bonnie said. "Will is of his father's ways and you're of mine. After the mistake I made in marrying your father and the broken heart I've carried around since, I can tell you now, if Jesus himself offered me a stirrup cup of liquor, I would have done as you did. Cast it to the ground. Yes, I know, Paw would have drunk it, and perhaps Maw would have touched it to her lips and maybe even taken a sip, but I'll be damned if I would. Some will say I'm principled to a fault, I suppose. But the only criticism I ever heard said about Jesus was that he was too good!"

CHAPTER 32

The Bit Bet

JD and Will rode the train into Vienna to do some shopping for Maw with the intent of running back home and using the return fare on candy. Maw didn't care. On their way past the station, they walked right into a bunch of boys who were wrestling with a steel bit used for drilling wells. A couple of them looked strong, but they weren't able to lift the bit—at least both ends—off the ground at the same time. The bit was about 10 feet long and five to six inches in diameter. The boys were being smart-alecky when, right there before their eyes, JD squatted down—and with a heave not unlike the thrust of a draft house—proceeded to lift one end of the bit about a foot off the ground.

JD heard one of the boys whisper, "Isn't that the guy who carried that dead hog all that way?"

The other said, "Yeah, but I didn't believe it."

JD motioned a "let's go" to Will, whereupon Mr. Cowley's grandson, Sidney, stepped forward and started kidding him. His brother Ruben joined in, and the two circled around JD like a couple of hounds. Before Will realized what was going on, JD had bragged to the boys that he could shoulder the bit. Sidney then offered him ten dollars to prove it. He could try as many times as he wanted, but he had to do it by himself. If he couldn't do it, Sidney said, JD would have to pay them.

About that time, JD looked up to see that the big sliding door, which was used to store freight, was half ajar and Mr. De Faubus, the station agent, was standing there looking for something. JD knew he was biting off more than he could chew, but he agreed to Sidney's challenge by ordering the boys to put up their ten dollars with Mr. De Faubus. They, in turn, asked him for his ten. When JD said he would pay later, they said they would, too. JD was just getting himself in deeper and deeper.

Both parties agreed to meet again the next night with their money in hand. At that time, JD would try to shoulder the bit. As he walked away, Will could hear the other boys arguing as to who was going to have the opportunity to cover the bet, which by now looked like a stupid bet on the part of JD, and they all knew it.

Walking home gave Will more time to admonish JD in terms of superiority. Finally, JD told him to shut up and, in no uncertain terms, not to mention the bet to anyone.

When they reached home, the family was sitting in the yard in the white lawn chairs under the gum trees as usual; Marcus was among them. He had been just as sober as any of the women and, therefore, of equal stature and no longer doing penance. Will watched as JD looked first at one face and then the next. He could tell, even though JD wasn't saying a word, that he had one question on his mind: Whom could he borrow the ten dollars from?

If JD couldn't come up with the ten dollars, he would lose the bet without even getting a chance to lose it properly when he couldn't shoulder the bit. Finally, JD's eyes rested on Maw, and then Will knew she was the most likely one. Even if she didn't have ten dollars of her own, she had every bit of Paw's money that she could nibble on without Paw even knowing about it.

The next day dragged on as JD and Will, with soap and towels in hand, watered the horses and took a bath in Oak Run, which they often did every summer. Marcus had agreed to milk the cows so JD and Will could go into Vienna and get back before dark—that's when "sin broke loose and ran amok in that town" according to Bonnie and Maw.

Vienna was so unlike Herndon, where a two-hundred-fifty-pound peace officer prevailed. JD had managed to finagle the ten dollars from Maw, but he obviously hadn't told her the truth about its purpose.

JD seemed anxious to get down to the station to show the other boys that he could lift that bit. But Will knew that any fool should know it couldn't be done, and if JD wasn't his brother, he wouldn't even bother to go with him and watch him make a fool of himself. His concerns worsened when he saw JD put on a blue cotton shirt without an undershirt and stuff a handkerchief in his hip pocket. However, he was sure that JD was insane when he saw him stick the bottle of Vaseline in his pocket rather than use it on his hair to make it lay flat. Nobody but an insane person would think of touching grease before lifting something like that bit. It would be worse than climbing a greased pole. Perhaps his poor judgment was due to the lick in the head that Dillie had given him.

Will began to reflect on how JD had been changing even before his fight with Dillie—actually, ever since Little Bonnie had died. He suddenly realized that JD had been acting funny lately, too. Not funny like funny ha-ha, but funny like fruitcake, like a horse turned loose in the field after eating too much gram where he kicks up and shows his ass.

Well, it was no matter; Will knew he had to go along with his brother even though he knew he was going to be humiliated. Maybe some of the boys would take pity on JD and allow him to keep his ten dollars. Sidney wouldn't, but maybe some of the others would make him do it.

In later years when Will retold the story, he would describe JD as ostensibly stoic and at the same time paradoxically mean—almost as bad as Marcus when he was drunk.

Will and JD arrived at the station to find the boys sitting there laughing—all except Mr. De Faubus who liked JD. The boys were fooling around with the bit, more confident now about winning the bet than the night before. JD walked right up to Mr. De Faubus, who was sitting in the doorway of the freight room, and handed him his ten dollars. One ten-dollar bill. This kind of surprised the boys for a minute, but then Ruben walked over with ten one-dollar bills. He apparently didn't trust Sidney to do it.

Mr. De Faubus then announced the conditions of the bet, much like a circus announcer. The bit had to be suspended in its entirety from the ground and sit on JD's shoulders for a period of five seconds. JD could have as long and as many tries as he wanted, at which point the boys envisioned him working well into the night and growing weaker and weaker.

JD reached down to his belt buckle as if to unbuckle it, but instead, he pulled out his shirttails, unbuttoned his shirt to take it off, and threw it to Mr. De Faubus. Reaching around to his hip pocket, he pulled out the Vaseline, at which point Will felt a sudden hard place developing in his own stomach. JD motioned Will to put the Vaseline right on the top of his shoulder, "Right on that hunk of muscle that runs down from my neck to my arm."

Will didn't move. "Go on," JD ordered.

Now here was JD's shoulder, already slipping at a forty-five degree angle to the ground, covered with grease. Will knew he was insane. The rest of those boys looked more than surprised, as if they couldn't believe what they were seeing.

JD then walked to one end of the bit, and using his shoe as a measuring stick, marked off the middle by drawing a line with the side of his shoe in the dirt. Then he proceeded to the back end of the bit and started to squat. But before he did, he winked and insanely smiled at his brother. Will immediately felt tingling goose pimples running up the back of his legs. JD hunkered down, not unlike a heavy draft horse about to restart a heavy wagonload up a steep hill, and with a tremendous heave while expelling a grunt with air from his lungs, he lifted the end of the bit up to his groin. With another heave, he was under it with the bit resting on his shoulder, right where Will had put the grease. His body was almost completely straight now, except that he was leaning a little forward into the bit. Then JD inched his way little by little down toward the center mark in the ground.

Meanwhile, all the boys were ready to scream, but they didn't. Either because they couldn't believe what they were seeing or they were afraid JD might still drop the bit. Yet, there was a look of protest on all their faces, but not Will's and Mr. De Faubus's. Their faces revealed a look of *"I'll be damned,"* as if they were saying it out loud.

JD inched himself on down the bit, taking care that he didn't pass the line, which would have allowed the bit to flip back down from the original end. The far end slowly inched up from the ground, and the whole bit became suspended on JD's shoulders. Mr. De Faubus started counting with as much pleasure as the devil himself. "… three… four… five."

JD half heaved and half stepped out from underneath the bit as it fell to the ground. He extended his hand for the twenty dollars, which Mr. De Faubus eagerly turned over to him. JD grabbed his shirt, not even attempting to put it on, motioned to Will with a nod of his head, and stalked up the track as unconcerned as if he had just stopped to pick up a can of beans for an old lady. He strode off with determinedly quick strides, skipping every other railroad tie. Will could hear the boys jabbering away as they departed—nobody listening, but everyone talking at the same time.

Every few steps Will would look up into the side of JD's face searching for some morsel of information that would reveal to him what his brother's next move in life might be. It had to be something momentous, for he could feel it in the air. It was as if his pleasant and seriously caring self had suddenly changed from a boy into a man of formidable possibilities. What really worried him though was that he sensed that the change in JD might not go in the right direction. It was as if JD was no longer in the family picture. Without him, Will would be placed in an oxen yoke with only one ox. It just wouldn't work if the other ox were not there, if for nothing else than to hold the yoke level.

After witnessing JD's strength and comparing it to the story of the state chain he had heard from Little Bonnie, Will doubted whether he was in a position to replace the big horse. For a fleeting moment, he thought of Marcus. Would his father be able to fill the void if and when JD left? The thought dissipated like a puff of smoke.

CHAPTER 33

A Deal

That Sunday at church the congregation sang the song it always did during the altar call. *"Just as I am without one plea, but that Thy blood was shed for me. And that Thou bid'st me come to Thee. Oh Lamb of God, I come, I come."*

Without forewarning to his mother or his brother or anyone, he came right out of the pew. Reverend Parman had said, "If you're not for Jesus, then you're against Him. Christ died for you that His spirit might dwell in you, and you thereby have eternal life. Are you willing to take God as your father and Jesus at his word as your savior? Let him set you free."

Many times in the past when they were singing the hymn of invitation, Reverend Parman would invite anyone to come to the altar, but no one would. And always, just before they started the last stanza, he would stop the pianist and urge anyone to come up and accept Christ as their personal savior.

Will didn't wait that long. It was during the very first verse that he walked up the aisle to the outstretched hand of Reverend Parman without ever looking back to see if his brother was following him. The congregation smiled discretely and approvingly at each other before making side-glances to see whether Will's brother, who hadn't gone up, was still standing there. JD was still in his row, looking quite perplexed.

After the service, everyone gathered around Will to congratulate him, saying that he had done the right thing. JD, still standing where he stood in the pew when Will went forward, was rallied from shock by a light tug on his coat sleeve from Mr. Cowley.

"Why don't you let Will walk home with the folks, and you come on with me? What they say to him will sound better to him if he's alone with them."

It struck JD that this was the right thing to do because he didn't want to be part of that discussion, at least he didn't want to be asked when he was going to join the church. It wasn't that he wasn't glad for Will, but he hadn't set it in his mind yet to go forward. A true act of acceptance must be free of coercion.

As they walked down along the path in the woods, Mr. Cowley spoke freely and sincerely, without apology or reprimand. "I heard about the bit. It's a wonder you didn't kill yourself. I suppose you know that the other horses in the neighborhood know you are the only one who can lift that thing."

JD turned to look at Mr. Cowley who was smiling. JD smiled back, acknowledging the fact that knew that Mr. Cowley truly knew him. He didn't know whether Paw knew him or not, or even his mother. But he knew Maw knew him well enough to know that he would not steal based on that one time when Marcus had placed two dollars and sixty-five cents on the table and it had disappeared.

Marcus had kept trying to make JD admit that he had taken it. After all, it had disappeared right off the table while Marcus was pouring coffee at the stove, Maw was in the pantry, and 12-year-old JD was sitting there at the table. Marcus kept insisting JD took it and threatening him with a good beating when Maw suddenly turned around and said, "He didn't take that money, and he doesn't steal." And almost within the next breath, a puff of wind through the window flipped the tablecloth over and there was the money beneath. JD never did figure out, as long as he lived, and he thought about it often, how Maw had been so sure of him.

JD and Mr. Cowley walked on through the woods to the railroad track where they normally would have parted ways with Mr. Cowley going directly south to his house and JD turning right and west up the track. But instead of separating, they sat down on the end of the ties.

"JD," Mr. Cowley began, "there are many forms of conquest. A cat plays with a mouse, not only for food but also for some other tantalizing reason unknown to man, as if she were filled with the indignity of man. She's not provoked into it, neither is she in a vicious mood. But why she flips a mouse from one paw to the other—in vindication? in arrogance?—not one of us knows.

"Then there's the man who feigns affection for a girl for what he may take in pleasure; whereas a girl might set wine and candlelight on the table to conquer her man. And then there's the man who lowers himself by performing feats of strength or one who casts meaningless arguments into the mire of swine. Why? We don't know.

"Then there's the man who seeks to gain the throne by accumulating enough riches for a thousand men. Why? Perhaps it's personal motivation or, more specifically, because he wants to play the part of God himself and not a servant of God.

"And what is man's destiny? Is it to be a king, or president, or scavenge the earth for all he can snare to put in his nest, which he must vacate in a short time? No. We've seen this happen time and again without avail. Man's destiny is not that of a king, or a millionaire, or a fighting dog, and certainly not a slave—for those things that man self-inflicts. Man's destiny was revealed many years ago in the words of Christ who died for us, and through this act we might see what our true purpose is: to be, simply, a servant of God. We are to serve man in the name of Christ for God. God—that is Christ on His behalf—asks for nothing for himself but only for man.

"Now son, you think about what I've said. I've not rebuked or criticized, but spoken truth from one who sees in you the strength of a giant. You're different than the rest, and that is no criticism of them. My advice is this: Don't lower yourself in undignified acts and words. Rise above this."

JD understood but made no sign of acknowledgement.

"I've waited a long time to talk to you," Mr. Cowley continued, "and I'm glad it happened today. I want to make a deal with you. Next year, when you are ready to go to college, you will find that your folks will be hard pressed to give you the money. But if you register for college without fear of money and without a feeling of indebtedness, I shall send you as much as I can. You will owe me nothing in return. What I seek is to lead you to God in the name of Christ."

Mr. Cowley, quietly and meditatively scratched a line in the cinders with his walking stick. "Think it over," he said. "Take as long as you wish, but let me know what you decide."

There was nothing more to say. They both stood now, brushing their tears away with the backs of their hands.

CHAPTER 34

Boxing Gloves

With his usual long strides, skipping every other tie, and his eyes to the sky that by now was clear, JD eventually reached the kitchen table. Even though the meal satisfied his hunger, and afterwards the cool gum tree shaded the white lawn chairs from which they talked and read the newspaper, there was still something missing. Even to Will, time lagged.

Sometimes they had company on a Sunday, but it was usually someone like Uncle Cecil or the Watsons—no one who could complete a ball team for baseball. So, the folk sat in imponderable conversation, which often seeped into a fruitless discussion on the irrelevant question of age. Maw always had the last say on this because she was the obvious authority, able to link one's age with that of someone's they all knew.

"Who is that coming down by the schoolhouse?"

That question didn't invite an immediate reply; it was just a way of drawing everyone's attention to the fact that there was a car coming. It created quite a spectacle because rare was the occasion of seeing an automobile. You could see it a mile away due to the trail of dust it bore. But, at this point, no one was sure it was coming up to the Browns' house. It could still be going to the Watsons or maybe on over to the Beulah Church, so they didn't even speculate as to who it might be. That wouldn't be necessary until they were sure the car would turn onto their road.

As it crossed over the track, the car disappeared out of sight. Suddenly Maw exclaimed, "Good Lord, it's as long as a box car!"

Now the vehicle appeared coming up the little knoll before descending the hill that led down to the branch and the railroad bridge from which Marcus had tried his wings some years previous. No one got up; no one even looked at the car as its radiator came over the crest of the hill as if it were oozing right up out of the ground. It then drove downhill a short distance to the edge of the yard at the end of the sidewalk right in front of their house.

Country people who are well-reared never look or run to a window to see who's coming, nor do they even let on that they notice a car as it moves into their yard. But when the car doors open and the occupants descend, then one will stand as if a lady just entered the sitting area. Only then are they sure that the car is not on the wrong road and that they won't be embarrassed by standing up to greet their company.

Marcus was the first to recognize the occupants. Noticeably, his ego picked up, something not unlike the appearance of a hound that finds himself confronted in a strange yard when his pack suddenly appears with great influence. Marcus's relations had arrived, and thus he started the introductions.

"You all know Toby's husband," he delivered casually, as if he would have you believe that Morton Moore was just a plain old shoe salesman rather than a successful realtor who sold out just in time and now lived with his wife in Florida. Morton was married to Marcus's sister, Toby, who was self-exalted by reason of the obvious affluence of her husband.

Also in the car were Marcus's father, CLC, an intellectual, and his mother Nellie, an incessant talker. Nellie spoke continuously of her ancestors, even though she must have known that everyone was already aware how much the men in her family had suffered the social and economic upheaval of the Civil War. One would think she would have felt better about the whole thing had she never brought the subject up again.

"Mr. Dayne has been a very busy man," Nellie stated in reference to her husband. She didn't use the title in any juxtaposition to the Browns' social standing, but as a maneuver of respect. She had always called her husband Mr. Dayne, even at the kitchen table. It began when he first came to Washington to go to law school. At that time, CLC boarded with Nellie's mother, and though Nellie was considerably older than he, she apparently started calling him Mr. Dayne and never stopped.

"We had planned to come see you folks sooner," Nellie continued, "and, bless your little hearts, we wanted to see our lovely grandsons, too. I just can't decide who is growing up to look more like their papa. Such wonderful boys; don't you think, Mrs. Brown?"

The question kind of caught Maw a little off guard. It was a question that an outsider might ask if she didn't think your son was a good fellow. Maw swallowed hard before simply answering, "Yes."

Nellie was good for an hour if someone didn't stop her, flitting from one subject to the next with barely a breath. "We had been planning to pack a little picnic lunch and just take a leisurely ride out on the train, but we came by way of Morton's car instead. Marcus, you look so well. This wholesome country air certainly agrees with you. Oh, Mr. Brown, these are lovely gum trees."

"Ah, Granny," Will chimed in, "we got millions of 'em out in the woods."

Maw immediately realized that Will's English was a reflection on her. She reminded him that his sentence was rather clumsy, and both of the city grandparents nodded their approval. Marcus nodded as well, though he seemed to want to dismiss it as a joke, whereupon Nellie started talking baby talk to him as if he was still a little boy. Without saying so directly, she suggested that Bonnie was wanting as a wife, more socially than otherwise. And she couldn't help herself from coming right out and saying that she knew that Marcus was completely through with drinking and that there was nothing more to worry about. Most everyone there, including CLC, had been crossing their fingers all summer that Marcus would not depart from the wagon.

At this point, CLC snatched the conversation from his wife. Changing the subject, he launched into a story about two brothers, young men and law partners in the office next to his. When this storyline ended, Paw talked about the purpose of holding hands during introductions. He said American women shook hands like men with their thumbs pointing skyward while French ladies always presented their hands palm down. The French had it right, he thought. In case the man bent forward to kiss the lady's hand, he would not run the risk of a thumb in the eye. Paw had a sense of humor, matchless in many ways, and he enjoyed this type of small talk. He did not know law, and CLC had no interest in farming; consequently, their talk was of a general nature—except for politics on which they nearly agreed.

While the elders conversed, Marcus and Morton took turns driving the two boys back and forth in the big convertible behind the house. It was a thing of beauty, even though it was driven gently for fear of breaking a spring as it rolled over the rough dirt. Eventually, Morton stopped the car and pulled out a pair of boxing gloves. When both boys declined to spar, Morton thought they were afraid, which was not the case. Will was unwilling to engage because he had joined the church only a couple of hours ago, and JD didn't want to participate because the talk with Mr. Cowley was still on his mind. But Marcus, acceding to the prestigious Morton, finally needled Will into putting the gloves. What else could Will do when his father sided—even in banter—with an outsider, his brother-in-law?

While Will was pulling on the gloves, Morton was promising that he wouldn't hurt him; he would only give him some of the finer points of art, which he proceeded to dispense. For example, if a punch was to be aimed below the nipples on a man's chest, the fist must be delivered palm upward; whereas, if the blow was to be delivered above that region, the palm must be facing the ground. JD wanted to take the gloves away from Will and do the boxing for his little brother, but he assumed Morton would not punish a boy of fourteen.

Will didn't bother to tie the laces, which Morton did not notice. One should always notice such a trivial thing because it suggests that the one so doing does not anticipate a battle of long duration.

They circled. Will slightly bent, both hands near his chest, while Morton pared out with a left jab and at the same time circled. Each time he stuck his left hand out, he made a funny motion of pulling his right hand back and chin in, somewhat like pulling on a bow and arrow. As the jabs became more effective, Morton got daintier until he hesitated, wavering only slightly as he pulled his hands up to protect his chin. The two were standing close now when, suddenly, Will tucked his shoulder down and brought his left fist up, his left hip was into it with a push off his right foot. The punch was executed in one smooth, rhythmic motion. His fist dug into Morton's stomach, right below his last rib as if Will meant to smash his kidney. Morton's mouth went open like a balloon turned loose with air trampling to get out the exit. Both his gloves grasped his sides without pretense. He was done for.

As Morton eased down to the ground on his knees, JD nodded a 'serves you right' response. With similar beckoning, he motioned to Will to take the gloves off because it was over. Marcus, who was holding his sides, managed a smile.

When Morton rose to his feet, he said lightly, "You boys ought to think about playing football; except you can't play around here unless you go to college."

"I plan to go to college," JD answered just as lightly, "and if Will wants to go, I'll be out in time to help him."

For just a moment, JD thought he was about to get another endowment, but then he sensed the strain in the air. Everyone had advice when it came to college, but no one offered money—no one except the little man with the hump in his back. Mr. Cowley.

Returning to the shade of the gum trees, CLC said to JD and Will, "Your mother tells me you can come down for a week."

Had CLC said, *"You boys are sentenced to one week at hard labor on the state farm,"* he wouldn't have caused more anguish. The dilemma? The hot sweaty corn and hay fields mitigated by the shade of the gum trees and a swim in Oak Run versus the hot and humid streets and apartment in Washington, D.C.

Each summer, without fail, JD and Will were invited to spend a week with their city grandparents, mostly for philosophy. Nellie's cooking wasn't an attraction nor was the city in July, which was not unlike the heat and monotony of the Sahara Desert, or so they thought. And a big-league ball game and a movie were monetarily out of their reach, except on rare occasions. There was nothing to do except walk around the block in a square circle, go to the market, or visit the park. The market didn't hold any secrets for farm boys nor did the park with its pools of gushing water that held nothing more vital than red carp, which were called goldfish in the city. But this was the ordeal the boys had to suffer for their mother. It was her annual sign of love and fairness to her in-laws—if not to her husband.

CLC and Nellie stood, insisting they must go. In response, Paw insisted that they needn't rush off, to which CLC explained that it would be dark before they arrived home. Not wanting to send them off empty handed, Paw beckoned JD and Will to do some picking in the garden while he went to the meat house to cut from a pork shoulder.

Saying their goodbyes, Toby admonished JD to stay in school. "You'll need a high school diploma, even if you intend to be a farmer. Try to finish as much as you can."

Astonished, JD immediately replied, "I'm going to go to college."

"Oh, fine," Toby commented. "Remarkable, really. Even if you only go for one year, that would be most excellent."

The subject was then dismissed as Toby simply moved over to Maw to kiss her goodbye. Morton, with Marcus at his side like that of an aide, reached out to shake JD's hand. Once clasped, he preceded to calmly, but persistently, squeeze it, as if to slowly tighten the vise until JD conceded. However, that which was caught in the vise suddenly began to squeeze the vise in a frightening manner. Morton then realized he could not extricate his hand without some doing. But this was no longer feasible for the eyes of the others were boring down on his duel, which he hadn't planned as anything more than a push over and physical admonishment of the boy. With all eyes on him, Morton's face began to redden like that of a blushing young girl. This was followed by beads of perspiration. But JD, his nostrils bulging with just a trace of smile on his innocent face, continued to extend pressure. Paw and CLC, unembarrassed, began to root for JD.

For only a moment, Morton thought he would be able to stand it. But the pain won out, and Morton slumped to the ground.

"JD! JD cut that out," his mother reprimanded. She wasn't close enough to tug at him and thus save Morton from falling to his knees as he yelled, "Uncle! Uncle!"

After a little moment of victory, JD turned him loose with, "I was just kidding, Uncle Morton. You're the uncle, not me." Then he helped him to his feet.

Morton rubbed the circulation back into his hand as the city dwellers piled into the car. As it drove away, JD noted that Marcus had undergone a change. He was displaying a fit of nervousness, as evidenced by the clawing at his fingernails. JD was reminded of the slight overture he had witnessed earlier between Marcus and Toby, which the latter had immediately quashed. Even Nellie didn't intercede on his behalf. Marcus had asked to go back with them to the city, and they had wanted no part of it. That was obviously what was bothering Marcus now.

The world seemed strange to JD and Will, doubly so when they had swapped perspectives when no one was around. They were often perplexed and anguished over the age-old lessons: Turn the other cheek; when hit below the belt, do not do likewise; and do not hit a man while he is down. In the ultimate case of guns and warfare, it wasn't a distinction between CLC's common law and Paw's countryside ethics. It was the distinction between the world's teachings and Jesus's.

CHAPTER 35

Futile to Fight

The day after the visit, Marcus was still distant, somber, and quiet. Then, around 11:00 in the morning on Tuesday, JD and Will were startled by the vision of their father approaching the yard nervously. They knew he had been somewhere, but up to this moment, they had not missed him. Now he came as if he was carrying the Hope Diamond amidst a colony of thieves.

Marcus made his way around the porch, which was encircled by barberry bushes. JD took a flying leap off the porch and over the bushes blocking Marcus's path. He could see by the bulge in his coat that what he carried was a big bottle. However, Marcus hadn't yet taken a drink from it.

JD grasped his father's right arm and reached into his coat to snatch the bottle. But Marcus was desperate and would have none of it. "I'm just gonna have one drink and that's all," he pleaded.

But JD knew better. There was no middle ground between sober and drunk for Marcus; he either didn't have a drink and was sober or he drank at least half a pint—usually more—and was drunk. JD also knew that it was futile to fight his father. He stood perplexed and frustrated as he watched hope and reason spiral down into a puddled gutter. Within minutes Marcus was drunk, sitting on the porch sideways, head down as if asleep, but talking incessantly in inaudible tones.

Around dinner time, he awoke and tried to pull himself together. After borrowing money from Maw for the train, he stumbled to the station with the bottle concealed in a brown bag beneath his clothes. Once on, he and the conductor shared the bottle until the train arrived at Rosslyn. There he transferred to the city street car, rocking and swaying with its every move that threatened to put him on the floor.

That evening, Toby and Morton found him languishing near the top of the stairs where Nellie and CLC lived. They dragged him to the sofa, all the while Toby frothed curse words severe as blows themselves causing Marcus to become belligerent a few moments later and insult Morton. When Toby and Morton retired to their bedroom, Marcus beat on the door till he broke the lock, which sent him flailing over their bed. Toby then mauled him with a hair brush. Seeing that her vented anger was of no avail, she stormed out of the house with audible screams.

Within moments, she was back with two policemen. Thus Marcus spent the rest of the night talking to himself and cursing her from the city jail. In the morning, Nellie borrowed fifteen dollars from Morton to bail Marcus out. Then she spent the afternoon with her sister Sallie, and where Marcus went, she did not know.

When Nellie arrived home later that afternoon, she found Marcus waiting at the door and cursing Toby because she had locked him out. The police were called again, and the above act was repeated. This time, however, Nellie borrowed fifteen dollars from Aunt Sallie to bail him out.

When Marcus didn't come back to the house the next evening, Nellie blamed Toby for his disappearance. Toby and Morton cut their visit short and soon returned to Florida.

CHAPTER 36

Scholastic Agenda

The boys arrived at their grandparent's place in the city in the late afternoon, and other than the fact that Nellie's string beans had not been cooked in fatback and the milk was cold, they enjoyed discovering that two of her brothers were buried under the statue of Confederate General Beauregard in Arlington National Cemetery. However, they did wonder why the Yankees had not removed them when they took over the cemetery. CLC added to the discussion by telling of his father, Joseph Emory Beauchamp Dayne, who served in Colonel Troup's troop at Burnside's Bridge. While thousands of General Burnside's Yankees had tried to cross the bridge, 350 loyal Georgian soldiers successfully held them off until Confederate reinforcements arrived.

Changing focus, CLC said his father was a Shakespearean scholar—even as a teenager—and loved poetry. His mother had wanted him to follow her family tradition and become a doctor; the doctor lineage extended all the way back to Charles II of England. Wounded after the war, CLC'S father had returned to school to become a doctor, but soon gave it up in favor of establishing a private school that lasted until his demise.

JD was awakened that first morning by the wrath of car horns on the city streets, a beastly thing at 6:00 a.m. He lay there for what seemed like a half a day before Will stirred. Then they talked awhile, expecting Nellie at any minute to assume her responsibilities at the kitchen stove. She and CLC, however, slept on.

When Nellie and CLC finally did get up, she appeared in a disheveled robe and he in BVDs with suspenders flopped down. Shaving mug in hand, he pumped the lather with the bristled brush, indignant to the fact that there was business to attend to in this stuffy, humid city heat.

JD and Will found the milk cold again. The eggs, which one could easily gather at the hen house and barn, were nonexistent. Nor was there any cornbread or pork—only cornflakes. But they lied in deference to Nellie's feelings, telling her it was good. The biggest lie of all JD told when he said that he had had enough to eat.

Other than going to the market or crawling out onto the portico where one could look down from an exciting height, the boys did nothing all day but listen to Nellie talk of her side of the family. She embellished less when CLC was home, but when he wasn't, she got carried away to frightening heights of glory about her brothers who were aides to General Beauregard in the Civil War. She also told about Hog Carter, an uncle, who was summarily promoted to a judge from his meager beginnings as a paper shaver, which was a legal specialist who lent money to near bankrupt farmers at interest with payment rates that guaranteed foreclosure. And she spoke of former Governor "Extra Billy" Smith, a brigadier general in the Civil War, who always stayed at their home when visiting the area. He had acquired his nickname by taking advantage of the affluent postal route to Richmond by going the extra mile to deliver mail to outlying areas for extra pay. Then there was Little Tommie, the dog that had been lost for two days. He was small and white, part Scottie. Though he made a nice pet for the city, he couldn't chase rabbits or stand birds or tree a raccoon. "Maybe a car ran over the little fellow," Nellie speculated.

Soon the boys jokingly dramatized the excitement of returning to the portico in order to escape Nellie's claptrap on ancestral lineage. The portico, however, felt like a pen five stories up and soon became as monotonous as Nellie's conversation.

Around three in the afternoon each day, CLC would come into the hall wearing a dark blue pinstriped suit and a dapper black homburg—a formal hat with a dent running down the center—and carrying an ivory-handled cane. The cane was more for vogue than purpose. Paw needed his cane to take the weight off his legs. CLC did not.

CLC was learned; no one could deny this. It was true that he held two degrees and could write a brief that many lawyers admired. It was true that he wrote on such subjects as federal trade practices and the Constitutional Sources of the Laws of War for members of Congress at the behest of President Wilson. It was also true that he learned to read Latin when he was six. Yet, to the boys, he wasn't any smarter than Paw and Maw—the comparison being made in practical matters like farming and moral precepts. Paw and Maw had spirit as their common denominator whereas, CLC, Nellie, and all the rest of the Daynes revered money, rank, and station.

One day Nellie came forth from the kitchen with the ice water, though it was not sweet tasting like that from Jim's spring. She also emerged with bacon so modest as to suggest that it was put there as some traditional emblem from the kitchen where hot cornbread and biscuits were strangers.

"Boys! Boys!" Nellie yelled out to the portico. "Come get yourselves ready 'cause Mr. Dayne's going to take you all for a walk in the park."

CLC had no intention of taking the boys for a nice walk in the park. Certainly, he knew that for boys who did little without walking—to school, to the barn, down the corn rows, to the train station—walking through Meridian Park would not be much of a walk. What he really planned was an oratory on the hoof: their complete scholastic agenda.

As they walked along the sidewalk toward the park, CLC continually poked the air with his cane in pretense of drawing a line, yet his cane rarely ever touched the ground. He was sure of himself. He had the air of a man about to bequeath a verbal and significant gift.

With his head up, CLC stated, "I've been watching you boys grow each year thinking all the time about your future. Your grandmother talks about the Carters, but you two are not like them—and thank goodness! JD, you must come first of consideration, for no other reason than you are the elder and at a point where you must decide upon your educational direction. You *must* go to college. You have the Dayne intellect, and it should be continued toward development. All of the Daynes have gone to college. In years gone by, one was even a personal doctor to King Charles II himself. And above all, don't pay any attention to that patronizing prattle I heard Toby expounding. You, JD, must go to William and Mary first, and then you must study law here at Georgetown. That would mean you could stay at home while you are going to law school or, hopefully, you could come live with us. I, of course, would be on the scene to help you with any legal questions."

JD responded respectfully, "I'm not sure I want to go to law school."

In a matter-of-fact tone, CLC responded, "I think once you have thought about it for a while, you will change your favor."

JD thought it best not to object for fear there might be something going on between his city grandfather and his mother that he was not privy to—like money—which at this point seemed to be elusive. As the three walked back and forth across the park, CLC tapped the sidewalk to emphasize his talking points. The boys, meanwhile, played silent games with the cracks in the concrete. Every now and then they would jump up and walk along the edge of the cemented pools of water. It was while Will was walking along one of these, maintaining a precarious balance, that CLC began to discuss Will's future at the United States Naval Academy. Will protested, which made him lose his balance and fall knee deep into the water. It seemed everyone in the park was watching.

CLC declared, "You might as well forget about the Navy because you would fall off the damn ship and drown in the ocean."

With that, he briskly strode toward the exit of the park toward home. The unspoken air of frustration in CLC was not a manifestation of his disdain for what Will had done, but rather a voice within. He wanted so much for his grandsons' education yet the distance between the boys and the Daynes was vast. He made no further mention of their schooling, which JD and Will found to be a relief.

CHAPTER 37

The Dollar

The guest and the host are never more affable than when they are parting. They grope for some small favor to equal out and make amends for any shortcoming they feel guilty of having perpetrated during their visit. This explains JD's and Will's hugs for CLC and Nellie, though they withheld their affection from their father who was inclined to camp out in the upstairs rooms.

"Now you, JD, take this dollar bill and divide it up between the two of you."

"Aw, you don't have to…"

"I want to," Nellie insisted.

With that, JD and Will departed down the stairs to meet Harvey Watson who was to give them a ride home. Harvey pointed the boys to the car and told them to wait; he wanted to say hello to their grandmother and grandfather. The boys did as they were told and crawled into the backseat, windows rolled down on account of the heat.

The minute Harvey was gone, Marcus came down and engaged his sons in a solicitous way. JD should have expected it. He had seen his father clawing at his fingernails in the doorway when Nellie had handed him the dollar and hugged them goodbye.

Finally, Marcus said, "If you will lend me that dollar, I'll pay it back to you tomorrow night when I come out to the farm."

JD said, "No. She gave it to us. I knew you were going to ask for it just as soon as I saw you come down."

Marcus looked at his hands, "Look, you're not going to spend it before tomorrow night, are you?"

JD answered, "That don't make any difference."

"Now, why can you not do me a favor? I'm your father. You know I wouldn't ask you if I didn't need it badly, don't you?"

"Look, I know you're gonna go right straight and buy whiskey."

Marcus placed his foot upon the running board of the car, but JD kept his elbow stuck out the window and continued looking straight ahead

Marcus said again, "I said, I'll give it back to you tomorrow."

JD knew the only thing that would keep him from giving in would be if Harvey came back. Marcus wouldn't nag him in front of Harvey. But Harvey didn't come back for he was prisoner to Nellie's rhetoric and unable to interject his goodbye.

So the nagging over the dollar went on and on in a frustratingly repetitive verbal feud. Marcus pleaded as if his life depended on it, and JD became increasingly inflamed, all the while knowing that the madder he became the closer Marcus was to getting the dollar. JD criticized Marcus by reminding him of the times he had let him down—like the time he and his parents had ridden on the train together and his mother was to go to work while Marcus took JD to the hospital in a cab due to a pulled ligament in his ankle. But when JD hobbled off the train, instead of hailing a cab, Marcus insisted that they walk to the hospital. JD had hopped on one leg for a couple of blocks before he couldn't go any further. Marcus still refused to spend the half dollar Bonnie had given him for transportation. After a few minutes, a boy came by on his bicycle and agreed to push JD on it to the hospital. That night, when Marcus came home drunk, JD naturally figured he had purchased the whiskey with the half dollar Bonnie had given him for the cab fare. JD hadn't forgotten that day, even though it had happened a long time ago. Strangely, his ridicule of Marcus didn't make him lose his calm.

And now, as Marcus persisted in his incessant nagging, and Harvey persisted in staying inside, JD became more and more frustrated and eventually handed his father the dollar. Then Marcus departed across the street, and Harvey emerged from the house.

The dollar meant nothing to JD—perhaps candy, but nothing more. It was the way Marcus had attached himself like a bloodsucking leech without care for his sons that spoke to JD. By giving in, he was able to purchase a moment of his father's love and respect for a dollar.

CHAPTER 38

Portly Preacher

At church that Sunday, the Reverend Parman announced that he had unexpectedly been called by God to go to a church in Lynchburg. Hopefully, he was to be replaced by a preacher by the name of Jones who also worked during the week for the Treasury Department. Thus, the Reverend Parman, whose soul did now seem to JD to feed humbly and contentedly on the word of Christ, departed in sweet sorrow whilst big tears flowed from his eyes. JD was sincerely saddened by the news, not because he felt a connection to the reverend, but because he felt an attraction to his daughter.

There was something about Katie that JD would never forget, though she did not have the audacity that Billie possessed nor did she reach beyond the realm of the church. JD surmised that there seemed no way to maintain the good things in life, like the sober father who was dangled in front of him all summer only to be snatched away in drunken frustration. Now he would never see Katie again; it would have been better if he had never met her.

Surprisingly, the Reverend Jones was built like JD, except he wasn't as strong and he had more belly, which was emphasized by the long watch chain he carried. The Reverend Jones's sermons were religiously oriented, but his lessons were half Bible and half anti-New Deal. This portly preacher began each Sunday school class with the jocular, "Now, when I become czar of this country, I'm gonna… "

That was a strange way to begin, JD thought. Equally astonishing was the fact that he was a republican. And lord, so was Mr. Ferguson! JD had been sitting there all this time and didn't know that Mr. Ferguson was a republican. Paw and Maw must really like him, JD thought, because neither of them had ever mentioned his affiliation, even at election time when they discussed politics. Their forbearers had voted against secession.

In between the Sunday school lesson and the sermon, Reverend Jones would sing a solo. He wasn't one to sing just to hear himself. In fact, he never would have crooned one note if they hadn't all insisted every Sunday. His singing was deeply melodious and resonated strongly with the overhead woodwork. Not that the rafters rang, but the strength of his voice bounced in vibration from the corners of the ceiling. Both boys liked the pastor's singing, yet they would have been delighted to hear him sing some other music, but they never did.

This autumnal Sunday, the leaves were blowing down to the ground and covering the earth when Reverend Jones taught the Sunday school lesson. Sam Parsley had just explained the subject of brotherly love rather emotionally and dogmatically. Church people can be dogmatic when they get emotional, JD thought. Sam claimed that the Bible said that every man was a brother to all men.

Reverend Jones, solemnly and impatiently, replied that he had not interpreted the said passage that way, partly because he couldn't make himself believe that he was a brother to Snake Mouck, a parishioner of questionable character. He said he had always felt that Christ meant that we should overlook the shortcomings of others and be aware of their needs and desires, much in the same manner that we were inclined to be charitable to our close kin. Nothing more was said on the topic, yet the reverend seemed tired and weary. He did insist, however, that the word 'equal' pertained to inalienable rights and not necessarily to physical or intellectual abilities.

It was as if the Reverend Jones had been there for ten years, his rapport with the congregation was that strong. Of course, Mr. Cowley had met him somewhere before and was probably instrumental in bringing him to this church.

CHAPTER 39

The Death of Summer

From their position on the porch, Stonewall, Mrs. Blacksheare, and Billie watched as JD approached. Stonewall couldn't accept JD's jumping style, which he viewed as unorthodox and effortless. JD's method was to keep his left hand free from the horse's reins at all times so he could hit the horse with the crop at the slightest hesitation as it neared a jump. He would take both reins in his right hand, reach out in front of his groin near the horse's neck, and form a tripod simply by leaning forward. This prevented him from falling back at the takeoff, and the hand on the horse's neck precluded his becoming off balance when the horse touched down after the jump.

Stonewall started mumbling something about horsemanship while Billie laughed, saying over and over again, "Nobody can keep up with my man!"

"I don't want to hear any more of that 'my man' stuff," Stonewall chided. Whereupon Mrs. Blacksheare echoed her husband's sentiments as she sipped on a cocktail, though she would have preferred to smoke.

"I'm going to marry him and live on a hog farm and have nine kids," Billie stated without reservation.

"Is that what we send you to a finishing school for?"

"Oh, Momma," Billie breathed, "you know I'm just kidding. 'Course you know he's the best man you ever saw!"

Exasperated, Mrs. Blacksheare shook her head, saying, "Lillian someday..."

"Momma, don't call me Lillian!" Billie exclaimed. "I don't know why you all ever named me that anyway! I would rather have been named William."

Billie stepped out to meet JD as he dismounted, seeking a separate audience with him. But Mrs. Blacksheare quickly suggested that they come and share their conversation with her and Stonewall on the porch.

"JD, that's a nice horse," Mrs. Blacksheare commented, "but isn't she one of your workhorses?"

Billie shot her mother a disapproving glance, forcing her to change course. "You both will be starting a new phase in your life now, and you will meet new friends, and you will probably have different tastes as you grow older anyway."

"We already do," Billie interjected. "JD believes in God."

"Well, I think that's very nice," Mrs. Blacksheare said. "And how is the new preacher?"

"He didn't look too well this morning," JD answered. "I think he's worried 'bout something."

"JD," Mrs. Blacksheare probed, "what do you want to be?"

Billie broke in. "He wants to be czar, Momma."

"Czar!" Stonewall said in surprise. "Where'd you hear that from?" Then he relaxed back into his chair chuckling, "That's pretty good, boy. Better than being president."

"What's your church like, JD?" Mrs. Blacksheare asked.

He could see that she was serious now, so he thought he had better not come up with another smart-alecky answer or it would reflect poorly on the church.

"Well, I suppose I wouldn't describe it like anyone else would."

Once again, Billie interjected. "JD talks in the subjective, Momma."

"You keep quiet, Billie, and let him talk any way he wishes."

JD continued. "Well, the people are alike yet, on the other hand, they're all different. Mr. Ferguson and Mr. Cowley, they don't meet socially, but when they're in church talking 'bout the Bible—that is, talking 'bout Christ—they act like they've been talking about it forever and they agree with each other. They call themselves deacons or elders. Paw looks up to them both at church with respect; that doesn't mean he doesn't respect them out of church.

"And then there's Mr. Cowley. He acts as if money is paint or fertilizer, like he just uses it to improve someone else. Then having done so, he steps back and looks at that person like he was a rose bush that he's growing. And Mr. Ferguson's brother and sister… you know Mrs. Welsh?" JD asked.

When Mrs. Blacksheare nodded, JD continued. "That's Mr. Ferguson's sister. Anyway, they never say a thing but "hello." They're always doing something for the church, like fixing it up and everything. The way they talk 'bout the Bible and Christ, it's as if Christ's way of unlocking the secrets of life were so simple that man can't bring himself to believe it, much less do it. It isn't that any of you are going to Hell if you don't repent—it's just that, every time someone moves in 'round the church, Mr. Ferguson has them there the next Sunday. I don't care what church they come from or even if they don't come from a church, he makes them feel like they belong. You know, Mr. Ferguson and Paw both lost sons in the war, but it seems that Mr. Ferguson is closer to God as a result of it. He's sad, but reconciled in a manner that seems hard to understand."

JD shook his head as if he'd come to the end. But then he decided to share one more thing. "I've always thought that Reverend Jones was a beautiful singer, but this morning he sang that song, you know, *When They Ring the Golden Bells?* He started singing, *"In that far off sweet forever, just beyond the shining river…"* and 'fore I knew it, I could see Heaven!

"You probably think that's crazy, but in my head I was standing right at the bottom of a hill with this stream of water. Reverend Jones walked right down to it, and he looked like he was in it, but he didn't make a ripple. Yet, he didn't look like he was walking on it either—and I'm not suggesting that he was. Fact is, I'm not suggesting anything! I'm just telling you what I saw.

"Then he continues on across the flat bottomland, walking in what looked like grass up to his waist. But I could still see his heels as he lifted him off the ground. And then he was lost from sight. But I could hear his voice, though I couldn't make out the song. And all the while this is going on, where I was standing was like I was in the shade, but there wasn't any trees or clouds to make the shade. Over across the water where Reverend Jones was walking, it looked like the sun was shining brightly, and the sun's rays looked like transparent gold.

"Next thing I knew, everyone was getting up and walking out of the church. I don't remember hearing a sermon. I don't know if he preached one or not—he was supposed to, and everyone acted like he had, so I didn't ask anyone if he had or not.

"All the way home I got this thing in my mind and I couldn't get it out, so I sat down and wrote it out to give to Billie. I figured she would fuss at me if I told her 'bout it later or if I forgot it altogether."

No one knew what to say. They were speechless.

"I'm not going to read the last two lines," JD explained. "I know she will ask me to later if she can't figure it out, and I wanted to give it to her 'fore I left."

JD took the piece of paper out of his pocket, unfolded it, and began to read.

> *"He takes so long a 'coming. We wait, oh, so long in discomfort and seclusion. Then suddenly with bees humming at buds, he stifles us with heat and dust and thirst. His heart includes no dearth of day or night or ancestral melancholy memory. He's green with vibrant growth and sweet to warm the egg yolk life. Pleasant though he is, by now assume he makes his move away from me. And I observe his pleasant air, and life reminds me he'll go, but I know not where. But still, even before his hair begins to turn to colorful array and each day crawls too early to sleep, somewhere the new birth stirs. Why can he not linger with me? For his touch to my face is now like a strong and glorious—but too soon over—embrace. While his hair turns color, it begins to fall and seep into the earth in slow decay. I know his time is short and earth's halo will*

> *fall to dust, but these last gasps represent the culmination of beauty to behold at its best. Though death seeps in, the beauty of it all transcends, and the final coup cannot arrive 'til birth seeps out as death seeps in."*

Mrs. Blacksheare spoke first. "That's very nice JD—something rhythmic about it. But it's not poetry, is it?"

"I reckon not. I just wrote it."

"Do you all know what it means?" Billie asked her father.

"I'm not sure, but I like it."

"That's nice of you to say," JD acknowledged, "but it's kinda dumb, too, and I may just have written it that way as a riddle. Sometimes we do things like that and don't even realize it—nothing but a stream of consciousness."

Stonewall commented, "I never cared a damn about poetry. If you have something to say, why not just say it like normal speech?"

Mrs. Blacksheare agreed, adding, "I can't think of one poem worth anything."

"How 'bout the 23rd Psalm?" JD asked.

"Yeah, Momma," Billie piggybacked. "How about the 23rd Psalm?"

Stonewall took his opportunity to change the course of the conversation. "What do you think you want to be JD?"

"I don't know," He answered thoughtfully. "Reckon I want to go to college to find out."

"You ought to do well in college," Stonewall said. "They say your father, and certainly your grandfather, are very smart."

"Which grandfather?" JD inquired.

Somewhat flustered, Stonewall responded, "Well, your grandfather Brown is smart, too. I just meant the others were… shall we say… scholastically inclined?"

JD responded defensively. "Looks to me like it depends on what we call *smart*."

There was an awkward silence before JD said, "I'm glad I'm going away to school. I think outside influences can be better than being around your folks too much after you grow up, though I hate to leave them alone."

Billie said, "Read it again, JD."

He obliged and read it again.

When he was done, Billie speculated on its interpretation. "I think it means the death of summer. What you're saying is that death is not final but that it's beautiful, and that death and birth happen together, contingent upon one another. Birth is birth, and death becomes the afterbirth. They are both painful, but beautiful."

"Lillian, for heaven's sake, do you have to talk like that?" Mrs. Blacksheare admonished.

"I was just trying to explain it to you! We're all grown people, you know."

Billie sat with her shoulders slumped, her face upward, and her eyes closed like a child in a guessing game, waiting for someone to open the box to reveal the secret item inside. "Read the rest of it JD. Read the rest of it."

> *"Then, one morning I awoke to a cold wind with a northern head and geese flying south and all. T'is then I knew for sure: summer is dead and 'tis the birth of fall."*

"See I told you!" Billie proclaimed. "Now that's real poetic."

Her parents said they liked it and told JD how much they had enjoyed the conversation.

As he untied the reins from the board fence, Billie bid JD goodbye with a futile tear in her eye. He started to say something, like it was going to be all right, but then he became unsure, not knowing what would really happen when they each left for college.

CHAPTER 40

Ambush

JD rode his horse along the car track, deep in thought and feeling melancholy. His left leg was thrown up over the top as if he was riding in a sidesaddle, and the mare was drifting slowly along as if she were likewise in deep concentration. As they approached the culvert high above Difficult Run, the horse came to an uninstructed halt. JD not did object as he stared down at the movement of the stream.

All of a sudden his eyes caught sight of a head sticking up out of the sand. Of course he knew it couldn't be a head, but it looked just like one. He sat there staring without dismounting. The bank was steep and covered with weed; it would be silly to walk down into that mess only to find an optical illusion. But still, he wondered.

JD looked and looked. He couldn't be sure from where he was, and he couldn't go home until he found out. Cautiously, he slid off his horse without once letting his eyes leave the object. He knew it would turn into something else, and he wanted to see how that happened. Even as he half slid down the bank, he kept his eyes riveted on the object, expecting it to change at any minute.

The sand was deep and wet. JD refrained from jumping down because he had his good shoes on. He looked at the object sideways thinking he could make out an eye, wide open as if lifeless. Suddenly, good Lord, the eye blinked at him! JD was shocked into stillness, frozen hard as a rock. How in the devil could it be alive without a body? Even if it were attached to a body, how in the devil did it get buried in the sand?

For the first time since he saw it, his eyes began to wander. There, a few feet away, was another head. There was no question about it now. There were two of them, and the other one was blinking, too.

JD was just about to jump down onto the sand when they got up and came out of the bushes with their heads firmly attached to their bodies. This was an ambush!

JD instinctively stood erect, and in one motion swung a short punch that sent Sidney sprawling onto his face. JD slipped on the wet ground and landed on his knees, his back facing skyward. Ruben took advantage of the position by hitting JD across the small of his back with a stick and then pouncing on him. The two began rolling around on the ground. First JD was on top, then Ruben. Then JD; then Ruben. Suddenly, crazy Sidney jumped onto Ruben's back and attempted to take a swing at JD, his face protected by Ruben's body. But JD, whose arms were under Ruben's armpits, managed to get his hands around Sidney's neck. Thus, Sidney's face was now firmly pressed into Ruben's back, and Ruben's' chest was pressed into JD's face, and JD was on his back with both boys of top of him, which made it hard for him to breathe. JD squeezed them both with all his strength, but each time he did, he had to hold his own breath.

This went on for quite awhile, as if they were children content to be holding each other indefinitely, although there was no joy on any of their faces. Finally, JD knew he had to do something different or he would be at their mercy, maybe smothered to death by the weight. With short jerks like those a dog makes when he's tearing meat off a bone, JD began to rip Ruben's shirt open with his teeth, then his thin undershirt. Now his mouth was pressed against Ruben's hot, salty chest, very close to the nipple. The first bite sent Ruben into a state of perplexity, but he did not scream from the pain. The next bite was administered in such a way that Ruben felt as if he were being eaten alive. He screamed and screamed for Sidney to get off, but Sidney himself was finding it hard to move because JD still had ahold of his neck, which he gripped tighter with each bite.

And then the blood began to trickle down into JD's mouth. He felt suffocated, but he couldn't stop. Sidney could not break the hold either, feeling as if his own neck would snap if he tried. Ruben, also, could do nothing because he couldn't get a grip on JD. Finally, they simply came apart like a pack of sleeping dogs after being kicked.

JD scrambled to his feet in preparation for a fight, but Ruben and Sidney took off, running up the track along the bottom of the embankment, their legs thrashing in the weeds. JD crawled up the bank slowly, not because it was steep and he had to rest his hands on the ground like a gorilla, but because his back ached as if a roll of barbed wire was being blown back and forth across it like tumbleweed. JD eventually pulled himself up onto his horse, feeling frustrated and perplexed, mostly because of Ruben and Sidney's connection to Mr. Cowley.

His horse, as if impatient to reach the barn, now strode in quick steps bordering on a trot down the cow path, her feet sinking into the soft mud. Suddenly, she made a half U-turn and stopped short, dipping her head under the foot log to take a drink. That's when JD's eyes caught sight of her. She hadn't descended as a dove or as a parachutist or anything like that. Little Bonnie just appeared like a fog, soft and billowy white. She had no body, but swayed like a negligee with slightly rippling ruffles. Her hair and her face were beautiful, but traced with pain.

Though her lips did not move, he heard, *"How long, how long shall clouds abound around thy heart and stifle thee from Godly deed? The red door waits, but the white door abounds; yet, you choose the former and run with the hounds. Come away! Come away as I have pleaded and see the western mountainside. My love for you withers and grows cold. Thy ceaseless trampling about in search of the path thou know'st as sure as I. Why then thy race with wrath?"*

"Good evening, son."

Mr. Cowley's voice pulled JD from his trance. He had appeared as quickly as Little Bonnie had disappeared. At the old man's urging, JD pulled his horse out of the ford so he could dismount. JD then hunkered down beside the water, splashing it on his face in an effort to wash away the dried, gory mess. But it would not come off easily. JD reached down into the water and scooped up a handful of soft mud like he had seen Paw do after helping to deliver a calf. Whereupon Mr. Cowley said, "Don't do that, son, you'll get it in the cut."

"I'm not cut," JD countered.

"Oh, it came from your nose then?"

"No sir. It isn't my blood."

"Isn't your blood? Then whose blood is it?"

This was the moment JD had dreaded, though he knew it would come nevertheless.

"It's Ruben's; I got in a fight with him and Sidney."

And while JD cleaned his face with mud and water, he unburdened himself of the whole story.

"As soon as I see your grandfather, I'll go get them boys," Mr. Cowley promised. "Don't you worry 'bout it; it's time they were punished. They can't go on this way. I shall contact the authorities, and they shall be punished by the court."

Nothing more was said about the horror of their deed, nor did they talk at all as they climbed the hill with JD riding and Mr. Cowley walking along beside him.

Mr. Cowley had been on his way to the Brown house before being sidetracked by his talk with JD. He waited for everyone to assemble so he would only have to say what he had come say once, though it had nothing to do with any of the boys. The preacher, Reverend Jones, was dead.

Upon hearing this, JD recalled the vision he had experienced at church. He couldn't help but repeat silently over and over to himself: *"There's a land beyond the river that we call the sweet forever, and we only reach that shore by faith's decree…"*

CHAPTER 41

Football

Fall came and he told Paw good-bye. Just told him—didn't shake hands or anything. Paw had sat there with his hands piled on top of his cane, his chin resting on his hands.

While he was kissing Maw goodbye, she repeated over and over, "You got it in you, son. You got it in you. You'll make out all right, but you study hard."

His mother had preferred that he go to school in the city and live at home, but she had not insisted. For that, he was grateful. This was the venture he had been waiting for. He wasn't in search of material gain, just the secret that would explain life—the secret locked inside college doors. JD wanted that something that would at last free him of whatever he wasn't free of.

He started walking away from the house with his arm around his mother, thinking all the while that there simply was not another one like her. Only the day before she had come home with her red hair wrapped in a green turban wearing a matching green dress, the contrast of which exuded a beauty that he had rarely seen in any woman. Her every effort and move and desire was for her sons—never for herself. Nor did she have the time of day for another man.

Bonnie had never told JD how to behave himself or to study hard; the only thing she told him was not to start drinking. And when he had scoffed at the possibility, she reminded him that many a boy, now drunkards, had said those same words. "It's something that gets into a man and brings him to his knees. It will ruin the best of them." JD didn't doubt it.

After kissing his mother goodbye, JD and Will started down the hill. Will had only intended to walk as far as the foot log, but when they arrived there, he acted like a boy wanting another piece of cake not due him. Will asked if he could go on to the station, and JD said, "Yes. I want to talk to you anyway."

With tender brotherly love, JD said to Will, "I'm sorry you're not going, too. It'll be the first time we haven't been together. Paw's growing older, and now you'll have to take over. You'll have three or four more cows to milk each day, and I hate to leave you with that work. But if you study, I'll see to it that you have the money to go to college when you graduate."

JD stood on the steps at the station for a last look until the conductor pulled the rope signaling the motorman to go. As the Washington train passed through Alexandria, JD thought about how Paw used to come all the way down here in a horse and wagon to bring butter and chickens—and sometimes rabbits—to market. On the return trip, JD would hold onto one rein, Paw the other. As they neared home, Paw would let him have both reins because now he was feeling more secure.

Paw would sometimes sneak a pint of whiskey to nip on the way home, but he never got tipsy and always hid the bottle in the hay. Nonetheless, Maw and Bonnie could always tell when Paw had taken a nip or two by the fact that he could be heard singing from half a mile away.

The train's solemn and melancholic whistle blew for Manassas junction, the prize of the Battle of Manassas. When Paw was a small boy, he had heard those guns boom like constant thunder. The history books said Bull Run ran red with blood, but Paw said it was mostly that old, red clay dirt that they have up around northern Virginia.

JD sat humming the words of the *Wreck of The Old 97* to himself. *"It's a mighty rough road from Lynchburg to Dansville."* Not because the train was racing along at a dangerous speed, but just because JD was on his way south to Lynchburg.

The train was half full when a young woman jostling her baby up toward the neck of her dress boarded. It looked like she was about to shove the child down her dress when she suddenly pulled out one of her breasts and stuffed it in the baby's mouth. JD knew he shouldn't be looking, but it didn't make any difference how far he turned his head, his eyes would wander back to that women with her breast hanging out right there in the car. He'd heard talk of a woman's breast, but he had never seen one before. It was beautiful.

JD had seen hills back home, but the seven hills of Lynchburg were something else. Arriving on the college campus, he was directed to a small room not much larger than the one he and Will had shared. They had always slept in the room together, but now there were two strangers to bunk with. He suspected they knew he was country folk; however, it was not in him to divulge it. Not that he was ashamed of his upbringing. He knew how to eat properly, and his suit was as expensive as any he'd seen. He and Will had always worn suits whenever they went into town, even when most of the boys didn't have them. So it wasn't that. He just wanted to be given a few days to find his way around on his own.

Each day when he headed to class with books tucked under his arm, there was rampant anticipation in his heart, like the feeling one gets when you go see what's caught in a trap. The weeks went by; the lessons didn't come easy, nor did the food. Sometimes it was like taking your first bite of a meal only to have it ripped away from you. The only constant was Mr. Cowley's check, which came faithfully as promised.

Every Sunday, JD went to the big church where Reverend Parman preached. One of the reasons JD had selected Lynchburg College was to rekindle his friendship with Katie, but she was not there; she was at Sweet Briar College, about 20 miles away. Sometimes JD would go to the Parmans' home to eat; it was usually Mrs. Parman who invited him, but it was the reverend who would engage him in conversation. They didn't talk often about religion, but mostly about things that happened back home. Whenever JD mentioned Katie's name, the discussion was quickly broken off—even by Mrs. Parman.

There was something about JD that Mr. Parman didn't like—something more than the fact that JD hadn't joined the church. Maybe it wasn't a true dislike, but more of a chilled air of misunderstanding brought about by those days when JD used to sit by Katie in church. JD knew it and considered it a small price to pay for the pleasure he had experienced. Not once though had he let it deter him from keeping her company, nor had she submitted to her father's will.

Reverend Parman liked JD's mother well enough along with the rest of the family, including Will. Will's carefree and happy disposition seemed more of an attraction to Reverend Parman than JD's. JD was serious, like his mother; Will was more like his father. Yet Reverend Parman had no time for the likes of Marcus who was as carefree as they came.

Other than the fact that the Lynchburg's football team had had a disastrously winless season, the school year was uneventful. Then the summer came, and JD returned home to work. With Billie and her parents spending the summer at Virginia Beach, JD saw very little of her. She attended Radford Briar College where she quickly established herself scholastically by gaining attention through the brief articles she wrote for the school paper, although some critics considered them quite radical.

The second year of college marked a major turning point in JD's life. At the beginning of the second year of college, CLC died. It was while JD was home for the funeral that his mother told him that her pay had been cut and she could not continue to send him as much money. This, she thought, would bring JD back to the farm, but it did not. He alone knew that Mr. Cowley would send him the money he needed when he returned to Lynchburg. Unfortunately, within the first month, JD was devastated to learn that a streetcar had fatally injured Mr. Cowley. JD's ability to remain in school appeared precarious.

In one last gesture to stay in college, JD approached the athletic director on the possibility of obtaining a football scholarship, though he knew nothing about the game. Probably because the team's future looked no better than the previous year, JD was directed to speak to the coach.

The coach, Babe Lunsford himself, had only graduated from Georgia Tech the year before. He saw JD walk down to the field to where the players were scrimmaging. His size caught Babe's attention, and he turned the team over to an assistant.

"You play any football before?"

JD answered, "No."

"What makes you think you can?"

"I need to. I need the scholarship. If you'll give me a chance, I know I can play."

"Where do you want to play, on the line?"

JD shook his head no. "I'd like to run with the ball."

"Hell, boy," the coach exclaimed, "You're too fat and slue-footed for that."

"I haven't ever had anyone beat me running yet."

Babe decided to test him. They agreed that the team wouldn't even take time to put on shoulder pads, just helmets. Babe lined them all up with JD standing in the fullback position. As he stood there thinking about what he was going to do, the ball came toward him. It all happened so fast. He got his hands on the ball and headed down the field. There was not an overabundance of blocking, so JD was quick to cut a swath through the center of the line even though two men stood stiff-armed in an attempt to block his way. JD barreled right through them. When he was about 25 yards past, Babe hollered, "Alright, let's see you come through again."

By this he meant for JD to come back, get set, and run in the same direction again. Do the play over. But JD didn't understand it that way. He turned and tore off running right toward the players as if daring them to tackle him again. As they look up and saw his thundering feet churning toward them, panic set in, and they scattered like chickens.

Babe clapped his hands down on his thighs yelling, "Look at that bull go!" That's when Babe called for his stopwatch. He lined JD up on the goal line and made him run the length of the field. Each time JD passed him, he shook his head in disbelief.

The first game they played was against Washington and Lee University. Lynchburg made the first touchdown, but W&L came right back and made the next one. The opposing team made their gains by passing long, whereas Lynchburg was relegated to grinding out a few yards at a time—five yards or eight yards, and so on. Not once did they stack JD up at the scrimmage line.

With about one minute left in the game, W&L was leading by six points. It was the first down when JD got the ball and started around the end. It looked like he was going to go on in when a would-be tackler punched the ball right out from underneath his arm. The game ended as Washington and Lee recovered.

In the locker room, Babe yelled at JD. "Damn it, boy! You had the game right in your hands! The whole damn thing, right there in your grip! You gotta carry that ball just like a loaf of bread; let them tear at you. Let 'em do anything, but don't let 'em get that damn ball!"

"I'm sorry," JD apologized. "I guess I learned my lesson. It won't happen again. The end was coming in on me, and I was stiff-arming the other man and trying to hold the end off."

"Okay. I know you haven't played much, but this is a game of the head, too."

At each subsequent game, JD barreled time after time into the line while the crowd yelled in unison, "Oyez, oyez, tote the ball." The nickname of Bull had now been discarded in favor of Tote.

Later, when a player by the name of Iver Wayne began to share in the ball carrying, the two became known as Big Tote and Little Tote. At first, Little Tote would clench his fist and shake it at the opposition. As time wore on, he began to notice how JD would get up smiling, sometimes even helping the man who tackled him get up or patting him on the head. Little Tote began doing the same thing. This didn't set too well with Babe who could be heard yelling after each play, "Damn! He hits 'em, and then he pats 'em!"

When JD and Little Tote would come to the sidelines, Babe would stand there with his fist clinched and paw up. "You gotta get mean! You ain't playing badminton! If you don't get 'em, they'll get you."

They would respond by smiling like a couple of frolicking puppies. However, sitting in the stands at a distance one would assume they were as mean as Babe wanted. JD and Little Tote ran over every football team that season and never lost another game.

CHAPTER 42

Christmas

As Thanksgiving approached, the campus became lonely. There wasn't much going on, except football. JD borrowed a shotgun and hiked off into the mountains to hunt. Toward evening, he spied a little boy driving cows up from the pasture. Every time the boy got the herd near the barn, this one cow would sidle off and run back down into the field. All the other cows followed.

Upon seeing the boy's frustration, JD grabbed a couple of pieces of loose corn fodder and walked toward the cows. He showed them what he had, then turned away from them and started walking toward the barn. The cows followed. Once in the barn, the boy set to milking while JD explained the purpose of the fodder. His message was simple: it is better to lead than to push.

A few minutes later, the boy's mother appeared. She proceeded to tell JD that her husband had killed three hogs the day before, but he got drunk before he could cut them up. She was one of those skinny mountain women who could probably grow corn on a rock if she had to. Nonetheless, she did not feel up to butchering those hogs and wondered if JD would be willing to tackle the job.

JD slept that night on the floor by the kitchen stove. By noon the next day, the hogs had been cut. As a thank you, the little boy invited JD into the house where he produced some shelled corn for popping.

Together, they popped the corn, salted it, and buttered it. Then they sat around eating and talking. JD had never seen corn popped before. He felt sorry for all the years he had missed growing popping corn back home and had to wonder why nobody had ever thought of growing it.

Babe had been a good football player himself, as well as a golfer. However, he was amazed at JD's mode of existence and looked up to him as if he were the older and more experienced one. There had been some confusion about Babe's trip home to Georgia for the Christmas holiday (something about a girl), so in the end he came home with JD.

Bonnie treated the football coach as if he were a prodigal son. It's hard to say why—maybe it was because he liked her so and charmed her, or maybe it was because his carcass was stuffed in a pretty hide.

One morning while sitting at the kitchen table drinking coffee and eating eggs and corn bread, JD asked Babe, "Have you ever ridden a horse?"

Babe responded, "A couple of times, but I like cars better." That got him a laugh.

JD said, "The reason I asked is, I thought you might want to go for a ride with me."

Babe said he wasn't particularly interested, but he would go. "We'll just head up the track a bit to see Billie Blacksheare," JD told him. Naturally, Babe assumed Billie was another boy.

Mrs. Blacksheare answered the door when JD knocked. After introductions, she asked JD to follow her to the kitchen and beckoned Babe to take a seat in the living room. Not knowing anyone was in there, Babe sauntered in and came face-to-face with two piercing eyes. He couldn't have been more frightened than if he had met a man with a gun. She didn't make a move or change the expression on her face, which was not mean nor unpleasant. So Babe just stood there, transfixed, unsure of what to do next. He'd never had a woman scare him like that before, even when he was a little boy.

Babe was still standing there staring when JD came in. A trace of amusement was on Billie's face. "Babe, this is Billie Blacksheare," JD said. "Billie, I'd like you to meet Jerome Lunsford, but everybody calls him Babe."

Without saying a word or taking her eyes off Babe, Billie walked over to JD and put her arm around his back. Then she grabbed his arm and threw it across her shoulder, drawing herself in tight, as if she were pulling a fur piece around her neck. This sent Babe into a silent frenzy of emotions. He wondered to himself about JD. *First this big clown walks over every football player he meets, and then this goddess walks right up to him and hugs herself with his arms. And he doesn't even pretend to be interested. What the hell has he got?*

Babe's arms suddenly felt awkward to him hanging down by his sides, so he put his hands in his pockets, which he realized made him look worse. He decided to lean up against the wall and immediately recognized that he was physically stammering. With Billie still looking at him, Babe felt like an embarrassed six-year-old boy.

Finally, by the grace of Mrs. Blackshear, Babe was offered a chair. As he took a seat, Babe thought to himself: *Just like women, the prettier they are, the uglier men get.* Babe made a note that Billie was not delicately pretty, but handsomely pretty. She wasn't too big or too tall, but she had a damn big presence. Then, as if representing the Chamber of Commerce, Billie finally spoke, which made Babe feel better.

"Nice of you all to come see us."

Babe responded cordially. "JD has told me so much about you. I have been looking forward to meeting you folks." It was a lie, but a good one.

"Babe's our football coach," JD said.

"Oh," Billie grunted with some surprise. "I thought you two went to school together."

Stonewall now entered the room and shook Babe's hand. Upon hearing that he was from Georgia, he asked, "You're not related to Harvey Lunsford from Savannah, are you? He was a member of the House for some years."

"As a matter of fact, Mr. Blackshear," Babe responded, "we are first cousins once removed."

"Wonderful old man," Stonewall acknowledged while rolling his head from side to side. This normally indicated a negative response, but in this case indicated that the old man's record was quite impressive.

"I've always felt that the bulk of the prudent legislators have been men like Congressman Lunsford. And most of them, if you check the record, have come from the south."

"Mr. Lunsford…" Billie interrupted, her eyes boring into him.

"Just call me Babe."

Billie smiled. "Do you intend to continue to coach?"

With a half laugh, Babe said, "I hadn't intended to coach at all—until I picked up that boy over there." He tipped his head toward JD.

"You don't mean to tell me you're going to quit coaching as soon as JD graduates?"

"As a matter of fact, Billie, I intend to go to law school."

"My, my. For a church-related institution, Lynchburg certainly places an unusual amount of emphasis on football.

"As a matter of fact, I've considered that same thing on a number of occasions; yet I see merit in the intent."

"Which is what?" Billie inquired.

"I suppose one might call it building a certain pride or *esprit*, if you will. There's something to be said for general esprit de school."

"Oh my, Mr. Lunsford," Billie exclaimed, using his formal name. "I believe you have just coined a new phrase."

"Well, it's not entirely original," Babe admitted.

"Yes," Stonewall acknowledged, "I'm aware of hearing something like that before."

Babe continued, "Basically, we have a fine group of boys on our football team. Probably as fine a group as you'll ever come in contact with."

"All good Christian boys, I suppose," Billie expressed with a sigh.

Babe nodded. "Yes, I would certainly agree."

"Which kind are they?" Billie taunted. "Like the Crusaders, maybe? From what I hear, JD has turned into quite a battler. Do all the boys take a beating or are there just certain ones?"

Babe was mulling this over when JD changed the subject. "Why don't we talk about Radford for a while?"

"I think perhaps that's a good idea," Mrs. Blacksheare said. She and her husband were most grateful for the suggestion, but then they just prattled on about politics and politicians they had known. The topic of Billie's college was never addressed.

Billie walked JD and Babe to the horses. JD said in a laughing manner, "Well, Miss Blacksheare, maybe sometime when you're not in such a hostile mood, we'll come back."

Feigning a pout, Billie turned and said, "I'm sorry. Babe, you'll come back, won't you?"

"Sure," Babe responded, pleased by the invitation.

They rode off down the track, JD riding without a saddle and Babe holding tightly to the reins, his feet and rear end planted firmly in JD's saddle.

When there was enough space between them and the Blacksheare house, Babe said, "Damn! She's a hellcat."

JD shook his head and said, "Nah, coach. She just liked you."

Billie's parents were not as pleased.

"Lillian," her mother asked, "Why in the world were you so rude to that young man? Your father and I were just saying that you seem to resent people of any consequence."

"Lillian," her father chimed in, "you could see that that young man was well reared, and you know how that other boy was raised, yet you seem to place…"

Billie cut him off. "JD was *reared* Poppa! If ever anyone was *reared*, it was JD."

"Now look, honey," Stonewall said unapologetically, "both your mother and I like the boy; it's just that we want you to be aware of people who are cultured."

"What's culture, Poppa?" She waited a moment, then said, "No, don't answer that. I know what you'll say. But you all just wait until JD finishes school and has his chance. He won't be used."

"That is not the point," Mrs. Blacksheare stated. "What we are saying is, there was no reason for you to be rude to that young man—especially in front of your father and me."

"If it will make you feel any better," Billie said, "I apologized to him outside, and I invited him back. It's just that I think the people at that school are mercenary and have no feelings for a person who really loves school for school's sake. They're not interested in *him*. No one down there has ever mentioned church to JD. Why, even the Parmans don't think he's good enough to sit in their church with their daughter!"

"I don't suppose they make him play football," said Stonewall. "He must want to."

"Oh, no," Billie responded with a bit of arrogance. "They don't *make* him play. They just tell him that they'll board him and pay his tuition if he *does* play. There's nothing subtle about that."

Stonewall and his wife had no response.

"Mr. Cowley died, Momma," Billie reminded her. "Those men over there at the church and his own family are the only ones he's got in the world."

"All right, honey," Mrs. Blacksheare conceded. "We just want you to be interested in someone who'll... you know. JD's father was a good boy, too, when he was young. Then he took to drinking."

Christmas Eve fell on a Sunday. JD and Will attended church with their mother and felt the poverty of spirit created by the absence of both Mr. Cowley and a preacher. The entire congregation could have fit comfortably in the modest choir loft. Though a few like Mr. Ferguson continued to attend, there was no man present to stand up in the pulpit for God. God had no advocate here, save this small band of helpless people.

JD was filled with anxiety and despair. He reeked of it. It was as if a malignancy taunted the church, neither taking its life nor letting it repose with dignity. At least the sun shone through the stain glass windows, coloring the wainscoting in rainbow-colored light. The Fergusons had built some of the church; of course, Mr. Cowley had helped with the financial backing, but a certain Mr. Foster had done most of the actual carpentry. There was never an illusion on anyone's part to equate the work he did with that of another carpenter. As a matter of fact, there was no reference to Jesus being a carpenter at all.

CHAPTER 43

A Right Moment

Billie, of all people, did not want to return to school at the beginning of her junior year. Her mother and father—unable to influence her otherwise—finally in desperation, called JD to persuade her. They were not present when he talked to her, just as they had not been present during the times the two had talked quietly over the years.

He came on horseback, and they immediately rode off together on separate mares. They jumped each chicken coop, but her style was different. She raced in a wild manner, which JD viewed in wonderment and concern. On they went, directly to the oak grove, as had been their custom. Dismounting, they slipped through the fence and sat in their usual places.

"Make her appear, JD."

"No," he said.

"Please?"

"No."

"Just this one time," Billie pleaded. "We'll never have a chance again."

"Now, why in the world would you say something like that?"

"I will not be here to come again," Billie stated with conviction.

"Why do you say that?"

"I'm going to kill myself."

JD shook his head. "Billie, I thought you had some sense."

"They want me to go back to that nunnery, and I don't want to! Yet if I don't, they will nag me to death until I do."

"Radford is a good school. Why don't you want to go back?" JD asked.

"Because I know what I want to do, and I want to do it now!"

Billie had a mind of her own. JD knew her all too well. Tenacious. Unyielding.

"You're too anxious. I've told you that you have to wait until the right moment."

"There'll never be a right moment."

JD sighed. "There will. There'll be a moment for you. In fact, there'll be lots of moments."

"How do you know?" Billie asked, desperate for an answer.

"Have I ever told you wrong?" She shook her head. "That's right! Then I want you to remember the promise we made—and have *remade* ever since we have known each other."

Billie looked at him longingly. "I suppose I just wanted you to tell me again."

JD understood. "So, we're not going to have any more of this, you hear? This year or next. Right?"

Billie nodded. She went back home alone; JD had done what he had been asked to do and now wanted to be spared of the burden of telling her parents goodbye.

His horse stepped and slouched, stepped and slouched, in a slow abiding gait. JD also slouched in accord, sitting sideways without a saddle, watching the ground pass beneath. So many things had changed, but some things had stayed the same: stinkpots sunning on logs in the swamp, creaking bugs, summer dying to autumn, honey colored sunsets, and slow moving trains whose whistles screamed bleak oaths. In these, JD took comfort.

CHAPTER 44

An Unexpected Visitor

JD's third year of college and the football season kicked off with equal emphasis. The bigger, experienced team members had graduated and were replaced by small, inexperienced ones. The quarterback and Little Tote were both back, but running the ball was more difficult, perhaps because the schedule included more impressive teams.

JD had become more interested in his studies each year, and it showed in his grades. He wasn't above arguing; however, he never pushed an instructor too far. No statement could be made in his presence where he did not angle to hear both sides of the argument. To JD, learning and believing could bring freedom from text or instructional position only if it were turned over and observed from all sides.

Lynchburg won the first game of the season, though it was a close score. In the third quarter of the second game, Lynchburg was behind, but each team appeared at a standstill as far as moving the ball forward. Then the band struck up *Dixie*, though they had never played it before. A chill came over JD's body and—without his even knowing it—he executed one plunge after another until he made a touchdown, the last run being about fifteen yards. Hysteria swept the crowd.

When the other team caught the ball on the fifty-yard line, JD broke through the line, falling into the quarterback who released the ball. It flew high into the air like a basketball, whereupon JD grabbed it and ran a few yards before being tackled. Then *Dixie* resounded again. There was no trace of a smile on his face as he barreled head-on into the line—defiant, not even trying to run the ends.

In the last waning moments of the game, JD managed to make two touchdowns, both from gaining possession of the ball by fumbles of the opposition. This set the pattern for each succeeding game that year. The band would wait to play *Dixie* at the last possible moment, like a cat teasing a mouse. When the song played in the last quarters, JD would barrel down the field, his feet beating the ground like drumsticks on a bass drum. It was later said that an Indian with his ear tuned to the ground could have heard his steps a mile off.

Katie had come home for a visit. Upon hearing this, JD went to see her. He stepped up onto the Parman's porch to where he could see into the living room by looking through the glass in the front door. At the moment when his fist was poised to knock, JD saw a tall, good-looking man with black hair holding Katie's hand and swinging her arm back and forth. The man smiled down on her, and they both were caught up in laughter. Before he could look away, JD saw the man touch Katie's face in adoration.

An old adage popped into JD's mind: *Hell hath no fury like a woman scorned*. JD reworked the saying to apply it to his situation: *Hell hath no fury like a man unexpectedly dumped*. Katie hadn't even given him the courtesy of letting him down gently. He guessed her parents were relieved and happy about the turn of events. Surely, a preacher and a preacher's wife wanted something better for their daughter, yet he wondered just how long the events had been turning. It didn't matter; he was not in a position to make a commitment to Katie. He still had school to finish, and then he had to fulfill his promise to Will when he left home.

JD could not see a ring on Katie's finger. It was impossible to tell whether one was there with her being squeezed up under the man's armpit as if there had never been anything between JD and her. Even if there hadn't been any commitment or promises between the two of them, he thought they had an understanding.

There was no question that the man was good looking—tall, too, and round-faced, like Reverend Parman. As if on cue, the reverend suddenly appeared and put his arm around the other man's shoulder. *So,* JD thought to himself, *this was the reason ole man Parman didn't like him.*

Just then, the reverend noticed JD standing at the door, his fist still suspended in the air prepared to knock. For a fleeting second JD felt like he had committed a sin for peering through the glass, but then it occurred to him that there was no way for them to know how long he had been standing there.

Reverend Parman's smile disappeared as soon as he saw JD. Even his lips pursed to express imposition. But it was too late for JD to slip away and too late for the reverend to not welcome him in. To JD, it seemed like he had been standing on the porch for hours instead of a few moments.

Upon entering the house, the first thing JD noticed about the other man was that he was quite a bit older than Katie. The second thing he noticed was that Katie was squeezing the jerk a little tighter than before. JD braced himself for the coup de grace.

"Clark," she began, while looking adoringly at the man, "this is JD. JD, this is Clark Parman, my brother."

Relief swept through JD's body in one huge surge. So, this was the Doctor Parman he had heard about for years but had never seen! Extending his hand, JD said, "Doctor Parman, I thought for a moment that I was going to have to run you out of town because you were trying to steal my girl."

Katie giggled. Displaying a sense of loyalty, she left her brother's side and slipped her warm, thin hand into JD's, whereupon Reverend Parman stalked out of the room.

CHAPTER 45

He's a Ruffian

The homecoming game was the third game of the season. Katie hadn't particularly wanted to go to the football game, but she didn't want to think of it as something worthless or out of the bounds of her liking. In any regard, it was time to make it clear to all that she was wholeheartedly in support of JD.

Concrete and an iron railing buttressed her seat near the ramp. Her eyes were drawn to ground, which smoked of dust from the players' cleats. They trotted like steers to the arena in uniforms padded with conglomerate stuffing—especially around their shoulders. The crowd became hysterical in anticipation of the brawling, frothing, and wrenching of college boys converging in play acts around a ball. They swelled to their feet with their fists clinched and raised in roaring demand for action. Blood was what they desired, though despair set in at its sight. Katie assessed the crowd as one frenzied mob. She looked from one person to the next, taking note of their jabbering predictions about who would do what to whom.

JD trampled into the line like the draft horse he was. His smile was gone; his warm heart was a singeing fire with the devil fanning the flame. Early in the game, Little Tote took a hit and had to be carried from the field, the victim of a mountainous wedge of human flesh converging upon his body in lethal battle called a game. JD could later be seen with blood trickling from his mouth like tobacco juice. Each time he hit the line, he would grit his teeth and turn his face toward the ground as if to say, "I'm coming at you."

From the sidelines Babe would yell, "You gotta get mean boy! This ain't no picnic! You gotta get them, or they'll get you."

Though it was a cold day, the hot sweat trickled down JD's calves, which were stiff and aching. He knew, come hell or high water, he could mash them all into the ground, if necessary. JD wasn't running for fun or to win; it was in vindication for what they had done to Little Tote. He didn't care about himself, but they had ganged up on Little Tote who was not any bigger than his little brother. They hadn't done it to win; they had done it because they were mean and overbearing.

In the fourth quarter, the band launched into a spirited rendition of *Dixie*. The words to the familiar tune played through JD's mind. *I wish I was in the land of cotton. Old times there are not forgotten. Dixie*, some boasted, was the best rallying and marching song ever played. It certainly inspired hell and chills in all the Lynchburg players, especially JD.

The game came to an end with Lynchburg winning with a score of 20 to 17. Everyone in the stands started marching—not toward the exits, but back and forth like members of a drill team. *Dixie* played on as the drums boomed. No matter how one listened to that song, the boom-boom of the drum demanded steps in drill-like precision.

JD, clearly the hero of the game, was exuberantly carried off the field on the shoulders of his teammates. He begged for them to put him down so he could find Katie, but they did not do so until they were inside the clubhouse. Extricating himself, JD rushed back to where she had promised to meet him, but she was not there. Katie had gone home disappointed, seeking some solace from her father, but the opposite occurred.

"Katie, you know I wouldn't do anything to hurt you. You know you're my baby, honey."

"It's time you realized that I'm a grown woman, Daddy."

"Baby, it's just that I've seen what other people have gone through. That boy's father was just as fine a lad as you'd want, until he got to drinking."

Mrs. Parman added, "I remember them saying what a fine and interesting boy his father was. But even Mrs. Dayne's folks tried to stop her from marrying Marcus. Why, I even heard that Dr. Leigh begged her not to go through with it. He told her he was a drinker."

"You don't know JD," Katie chided. "You never have known him. You've never tried to give him a chance to communicate with you. You and Momma have just never liked him from the day you saw him with his face all swollen up."

"Honey, he's a ruffian," the Reverend Parman stated with conviction. "Why can't you see that? I like the boy—and his family, too. It's just that I can't stand to see my little girl mixed up with someone like him. We've reared you better than that."

"No Daddy, you haven't. You haven't reared me to make my own decisions about who I want to marry."

"Good Lord, honey! Don't tell me you're going to talk about him in that vein! Even his brother is more genteel."

CHAPTER 46

A Clanging Cymbal

About three weeks later on a Thursday night, JD received a telegram from Billie.

> *Have a few days off STOP Want to see you STOP Am taking the prerogative to invite myself STOP Will be on eight o'clock train in need of shelter for two nights STOP*

She didn't say what day or whether the train would arrive in the morning or evening. When she didn't arrive on the 8:00 a.m. train, JD, Katie, and Babe stood on the platform at 8:00 p.m. in hopeful expectation. The crisp November night was chilling as they peered up at the sky. A visible ring around the moon meant snow was on the way.

Billie was startled to see all three of them at the train station. Something told her that Katie was not with Babe. In one cringing motion, she drew her shoulders up toward her chin, pushing her back up and letting the air escape from her lungs, much like that of a hissing cat being surprised by a dog. Babe grabbed Billie's bags and with a motion of his head suggested that she follow him. Katie saw it all, whereas JD's expression never divulged his feelings.

JD, with solicitous mumbling, began to circle Billie; his feet chased each other, end over end like a barrel rolling around its rim suggesting collapse. His obsession with Billie rendered her into a frozen but regal state, as if it were her duty to let him froth at her side so she could be queen.

"Did your folks know you were coming down here?" JD asked.

"Now, why would I worry them with trivia like that?" Billie responded. Babe chuckled at the devilment and secretiveness suggested by her remarks.

"When I'm home, they worry about me. When I'm in school, they can't worry because they don't know where I go. What they don't know, they can't worry about."

"Well, it's always nice to see you," Katie said sincerely.

"I'm glad you're happy to see me, even if no one else is."

JD drove Babe's car, playing the role of a chauffeur with Katie beside him. Each time they passed under a streetlight, Babe stole a glance at Billie, pretending there was more between them than the seat they shared. He was in awe of the blue shadows in her black hair as it draped near her high cheeks. The bronze of her freckles seemed to float on her rich, milk-colored skin. There was slender strength in her bones upon which her elegant blue suit draped. But it was the determination in her countenance that made him swoon. He knew he loved her. He—the ultimate lady's man had met Her—the queen bee. Babe had courted plenty of girls, but not one was like Billie.

While she talked on and on to JD and Katie, Babe continued to stare, transfixed in astonishment. He was possessed by one thought: he must have her. Unfortunately, he suspected Billie was obsessed with JD, and he was such a clod, sitting in the front seat with the preacher's skinny daughter. Billie could be JD's for the asking, but he didn't ask. And she had come all the way down to Lynchburg to see him!

Oh, to be selected, he thought.

The car's floodlights exposed the frostbitten chrysanthemums, the naked trees, and the locust tree butts measuring four feet at least, which appeared like many hands and forearms with knurled fingers reaching up out of the ground.

"Looks like the mums are dead," Billie noted. "I'll bet they were pretty."

"Mums are perennials," JD stated, as if that were enough.

He pulled the car in front of a house that boasted huge double doors and windows, replete with gingerbread molding. White columns sustained the porch where a chandelier blinked from the ceiling, its faint light shimmering as if the propane gas were near exhaustion. It dangled in majestic pretense by a silver chain, but it was dissuaded from swinging in the cold wind by four chains at opposing positions.

Babe had suggested this place; neither JD nor Katie had ever been there. The brick mansion had been converted into a restaurant with a fireplace in every room, except in the basement where it had been replaced by a gas stove. Though the wallpaper seemed tired of hanging and insecure, its chandeliers, staircase, and delicate window frames—as well as the antique furniture that had been there since the original construction—conveyed a spirit of elegance. It was as if the year had been turned back tenfold times tenfold.

They climbed the staircase, half in search of privacy and half in search of secrets, before settling into four captain's chairs by the fireplace in an upper room. JD drew them into dialogue.

"We'll be playing in the snow tomorrow."

Billie responded, "Football is an accredited subject here, I assume. Does it supplant English or Philosophy?"

"All right *William*," JD said, teasing her. "I'm just saying, tomorrow will be a fun day."

Billie shook her head. "Let's all agree that football has tremendous sociological value, providing you agree not to discuss it anymore tonight. You know, we'll have to sit through an hour of it tomorrow. Good heavens, maybe in the snow."

Now getting serious, JD said to Billie, "Obviously there's something on your mind. You didn't come all the way down here to see football."

Katie reprimanded JD for his boldness. "JD, don't be so serious; let's eat and then talk."

Billie unapologetically stated, "I don't know Mr. Lunsford well."

"Just call me Babe."

Then, as if the thought occurred to them both at the same time, Billie and Katie looked at each other as Billie blurted out, "We don't really know each other either. We have only met once or twice ourselves."

"That's right," Katie agreed.

It promised to be a long night, so Babe announced that he would be ordering a bottle of wine. "That's why I had us seated up here." Despite the passage of the Eighteenth Amendment several years earlier, many establishments continued to sell alcohol to their customers, albeit discreetly.

The waiter pranced up the steps like a Tennessee walking horse, defying gravity. Reaching the room, he backhanded the lights from bright to dim, then glided to the table carrying an old bottle covered with wax drippings with a nearly spent candle protruding from its neck. As the candle was lit, Babe commented, "This'll lighten up the atmosphere 'round here." Then he ordered a bottle of red.

"I thought there was a law against that," JD stated. But he was ignored.

Billie and Babe drank wine while JD bristled. For himself and Katie, he ordered tea. Nothing more was said about prohibition as they sipped their beverages from teacups.

Their conversation centered on the house and millionaire horse farms in Warrenton and Middleburg. These were pompous circumstances to JD and Katie, the residual of culture to Billie and Babe. Billie, however, was not without sympathy for JD's arguments.

A waitress appeared to refill the tea. She poured the hot beverage into Katie's cup first, then JD's. Billie allowed her to pour tea into her cup as well, as it had already been drained of wine. But Babe tried to dissuade the waitress from pouring anything into his teacup by placing his hand over the top. Not seeing his hand, the waitress poured the scalding liquid right onto the top of it. The hot tea splattered off the back of his hand like the proverbial cow peeing on a flat rock. It took precious seconds before his nerves told him he was being burned. Finally, he clutched his hand and contorted his face suggesting he was about to backhand the girl when Billie gave him a dissuading kick. She managed to do this while maintaining a smile and a dignified pose, as if there were no relation between the prohibitive foot and the upper part of her body. Babe accepted the kick graciously noting that she had kicked him like a wife.

Sometime later, after a pound of butter had been applied to Babe's hand and apologies from the waitress had been accepted, the conversation returned to the old house. JD first compared it to the aristocracy of the South being reduced to common dirt farmers. Sticking his jaw out with conviction, he said, "The mode of splendor stands here still, lonely and useless as a poor departed man's will. Steeped in tradition, mortared and mortised to make lesser men tremble, but now empty of spirit, reminiscent of biblical cymbal."

"What do you mean?" Billie asked, intrigued as if it were a riddle. "Don't tell me; let me guess."

Babe showed his confusion. "What are you talking about, Big Tote? This house?"

Billie came to JD's defense. "Didn't you know that JD likes to speak subjectively? Like Christ."

Babe shook his head. "We've never discussed that much. Never had time. Just football."

"Perhaps you've missed something," Billie noted

Katie agreed as she looked upon JD in adoration that served only to depress Billie.

JD continued. "Why does a man with a small family build a house large enough to house five families? Because he needs the room? Of course, not! He does it to attract attention—thus the house is a cymbal."

"A symbol of what?" Babe asked.

"Not a symbol: s-y-m-b-o-l," JD explained spelling it out, "a cymbal: c-y-m-b-a-l."

More confused than ever, Babe clamored, "What's a cymbal? Hell, I thought those were metal disks that band bangs together!"

Once more, Billie came to JD's rescue. "It has to do with the biblical passage about a clanging cymbal. Imagine the sound and fury of an idiot child running through the street yelling a fallacious or imagined statement as if it were the truth."

"How do you know what he means?" Babe asked skeptically.

With a territorial look of superiority, Billie said, "JD has used that analogy on me before to describe the rich man's way. He has preached subjectivism to me up and down the corn rows of his farm for over ten years now."

Katie turned to Billie and asked, "You're an objectivist?"

"No," Billie answered. "I believe him in some ways. I just don't believe in a life hereafter. I wish I could, but I don't."

Uncomfortable with her comment, Babe laughed and said, "Big Tote, don't you get too enmeshed in your rhetoric and forget the signals for tomorrow."

JD, his jaw jutting under a twinkling smile, said, "Let's Indian arm-wrestle to see who pays the bill."

"JD, don't you dare," Katie scolded.

Babe paid the bill, blew out the candle, and they all departed.

CHAPTER 47

The Game

The next day the girls sat together by the iron railing near the ramp. Billie twisted and grimaced in pain from the hard seat as she contemplated the following story: *The gladiators thunder out from the ramp below unto the field like a herd of steers, their cleats whirling dust and cleat-sized clods into the air. Reminiscent of Roman warriors, they gather to fight an unpaid performance in controversy. Down they squat, like so many felines ready to pounce on their quarry; then they charge in unison toward an imaginary prey.*

On the sidelines, the band drums started thumping and the horns started tooting while the cheerleaders strutted in unfettered kicks, their hair and skirts whirling with each diverting move. Something seemed to suggest that she should arise in a fist-clenching yell, but Billie's steeple-chasing upbringing won out.

On the first two plays, the runner from the other team broke through the line of scrimmage only to be powerfully greeted by JD's tackle. From the sidelines the coach, completely devoid of last night's equality with one of his players, yelled, "Hit 'em! Hit 'em!"

On a subsequent play, the ball went spiraling toward the intended receiver until JD raced in front of him, caught it, and charged into the line with dead seriousness. Billie found herself intrigued as she watched JD run and pummel and then help those he knocked down to the ground back to their feet. It's a boy's game to him, she thought. Fun to watch, but certainly not as enjoyable as fox hunting.

Late in the game, JD plunged over the goal line to tie the score. He then cantered to the bench for respite in reward for his efforts. Even at that distance Billie saw his faint, pleasant smile that belied the blood. His uniform and face were stained with it, and he sniffed it back up into his nose while half wiping it with the back of his hand—like a small boy with a runny nose and no handkerchief.

Virginia Tech now had the ball in the middle of the field. The moments were ticking away toward a stalemate when Babe turned and yelled to the bandleader, "Hit it up! Hit it up! Dixie, Dixie, Dixie!"

"*I wish I was in the land of cotton, old times there and not forgotten. Look away! Look away. Look away Dixieland.*" The crowd rose to its feet with screams and rebel yells that pierced the air like a pack of wildcats. For a fleeting moment, tears welled into Billie's eyes. Without thought, she began to rise like the rest of them before catching herself. A wave of remorse settled her to her seat as the stadium fans towered over her, screaming, hollering, and laughing.

Billie stared at JD thinking of his head, that beautiful mind, that compassionate brain from which emerged eternal wit and magnificent, meter-less poetry like routine conversation. He is so precious to her. That is why she cannot keep herself from feeling and fearing that something was about to happen to him—something reminiscent of the sister he lost, of *Her* whom he had mourned. Billie was the only one who had experienced those moments with him and with Little Bonnie in the grove. What if something were to cut him down? And to come to an end at his own choosing! These were Billie's thoughts as she gazed out across the field.

There was no attempt on the part of the quarterback to throw the ball or hand it off to the halfback. Babe had directed him long before the game started to just throw the ball to JD when *Dixie* was played. Regardless of progress, injury, or fatigue, JD was to get the ball every time.

Now, as the screaming frenzy mounted, Babe yelled loud enough to be heard in the stands, "BIG TOTE." At the line there was nothing but deafening noise. Nonetheless, the center hiked the ball when he saw the quarterback flinch his hands. He made the pass to JD who caught the ball, ran to five yards, back to eight, then to two, swerving but never stopping until he was swept across the goal line by the vibration of the crowd and the band. The game was over except for the inconsequential kick after touchdown.

Excitement swelled and the crescendo of *Dixie* continued to shatter the air as if it would finally explode into boundless devastation. Meanwhile, the players retreated under the ramp.

Eventually the crowd began to exit the stadium. But Billie and Katie remained where they were, alone and spent. Whipped, actually. It was as if they had played the game instead of JD.

CHAPTER 48

Philip and the Eunuch

That night, the four of them went out again—this time in a cold, dry snow, just as JD had predicted. It had started snowing soon after the game, right when each was approaching their lodgings. Katie had gone home to her parent's house. Billie was staying in the girl's dormitory. Babe had a place in town. And JD lived in the boy's dorm. The snow, now about two inches deep, swirled at the slightest breath of wind, though it had not begun to collect on the road. Instead, it seemed to be drifting, but not by any discernible measure.

JD had yet to undress when he heard the knock on his door. He was shocked to see Billie standing there. How she had managed to sneak into his dormitory and find his room was a mystery to him. But he didn't ask for an explanation. Had she not come—uninvited as it were—he would have gone alone. Johnny was on his mind, and it was as if the motivation in his heart had aroused Billie to come to be with him when he sought the boy out.

They walked up the road together and through the woods. The road, cut by wagon wheels, had probably never been traveled by an auto. Billie held tight to JD's arm but kept her eyes on her feet as they mustered a fine snow to flip in front of her shoes with each step. At that moment, Billie Blacksheare felt removed from the world. The warmth in her body tingled against the cold snow as she imagined that they were the only two human beings left in existence.

Billie winced when the back of JD's fist beat on the door. Had it been daylight, it would have been different. But now, it was well past three in the morning. The mother came to the door quickly, as if she had been waiting in the darkened house for their appearance. With the coal oil lamp raised to the level of her head, she gave vent to a passive, "Oh!"

JD stated, "I've come to see the boy."

The mother turned sideways, suggesting that they enter. "He's in the back room, to the left. But don't you think it's awful late?"

JD did not answer but went straightaway to the back room. He sat on the corner of the bed and cupped his hands under the boy's jaw. Johnny awoke immediately, his hands grasping JD's wrist.

They didn't say a word. They just looked at each other. JD pulled his hands back slowly, and the boy sat up in a lotus position, pressing his back against the wall. There was no headboard, only a small pillow made of duck feathers. Looking around, Johnny sensed that it was late and that something important was about to happen. Why else would JD be there at this time of night?

"How's the hunting?" JD whispered.

"I killed some squirrels, but I used up all my shells."

"Do you know why I have come?"

The boy nodded with some uncertainty. "We gonna do like Philip and the eunuch?" Johnny asked, referring to a Bible story JD had shared with him about coming to faith.

JD smiled. "Yes. I plan to go tomorrow, and you remember what I promised you."

"I must meet you in the morning," Johnny stated.

"Why don't you just come with me now?" JD offered. "I will make you a pallet, and you can sleep the rest of the night in my room."

Johnny got up and started to dress. Listening from the doorway, his mother asked, "Johnny, are you sure?"

He buttoned the final button on his jacket and answered with conviction, though he could not look her in the eyes, "I'm gonna confess, Momma!"

With her palms extended in surrender, the boy's mother turned to JD. "But he's so young."

"I'm a man now," Johnny said, his eyes finally meeting hers. "I've put away childish things."

His younger sister, awakened by the noise, clutched her mother's skirt and buried her head in the folds. "Who's gonna stay with us, Momma?"

She shook her head, unsure of the answer. "But he's just a little boy!" she said, as if she were trying to convince herself and not JD.

With a wisdom that belied his age, Johnny said, "Poppa's passed, so I'm head of the household. I'll be back tomorrow."

"Oh, he doesn't even know what he's saying!" These were the last words spoken as Johnny left the house and headed out into the cold, snowy night with JD and Billie.

CHAPTER 49

Baptism

That Sunday morning, as the organ hummed in deep bass the prelude to the hymn of invitation, the Reverend Parman asked like he did every week, "And now, if there be one among you who wishes to confess that Jesus is his personal savior and be baptized, come forward as we sing together our hymn of invitation, number 295 in your hymnals. Let us stand."

"Just as I am without one plea, but that Thy blood was shed for me, and that Thou bidst me come to Thee, O Lamb of God, I come. I come."

At the end of the first verse, JD sidestepped into the aisle, pausing to wait for Johnny to do likewise. Together, they walked toward Reverend Parman. As they neared the front of the church with its awesome ceiling echoing the singing back to the congregation, the little boy—without realizing what he was doing—reached up and clasped the hand of his friend who plodded down the aisle in slow cadence.

Reverend Parman's mouth fell agape as the music played on. *"Just as I am, though tossed about with many a conflict, many a doubt..."* JD and Johnny stood before the altar while the congregation sang on. *"Fightings and fears within, without, O Lamb of God, I come. I come."*

JD handed the reverend two green cards as the music and singing ceased. Reverend Parman whispered to the boy, "How old are you, son?"

"I'm the head of the household."

"Where is your father?"

"He's gone to his eternal reward."

With all eyes on him, the Reverend Parman began to read from the card, exactly as JD had written it. Though no one would have guessed, he did it with reluctance in his heart.

"John Alton Abel, do you believe that Jesus is the Christ, the Son of the living God, and do you accept him as your personal savior?"

"Yes, sir," Johnny replied.

The reverend opened his mouth to ask JD the same question, but before he could speak, Johnny added, "I confess that I'm a Christian."

Reverend Parman nodded and moved on. "And do you, Joseph Emery Beauchamp Dayne, believe that Jesus is the Christ, the son of the living God, and do you take him now as your personal savior?"

Katie, who was sitting about halfway back, noted that this was the first time she had ever heard her father call JD anything but "that boy."

"I do," JD answered.

"I shall ask the members of the congregation to remain seated for a moment while we prepare for the baptism of these two individuals who have come forward." With that, he turned his back, wringing his hands nervously and departing to the baptismal pool that stood about four feet high and was set in tile above and behind the altar. JD and Johnny followed behind him.

Johnny went in first. His body, rigid as a log, was quickly immersed and released. JD stood on the side, unsure of his next move. The reverend offered him no outstretched hand. With some bewilderment, but showing no sign of a grudge, JD entered the water while Reverend Parman appeared confused. Meanwhile, Katie sat up in her seat, peering above the heads in front of her as tears of happiness curled down her face and dropped into her lap.

The elder began to read scripture from the Bible. "And as they were going along the road, they came to some water; and the eunuch said, 'Look, here is water! What is to prevent me from being baptized?' He commanded the chariot to stop, and both of them, Philip and the eunuch, went down into the water and Philip baptized him. When they came up out of the water, the Spirit of the Lord snatched Philip away; the eunuch saw him no more, and went on his way rejoicing."

Reverend Parman placed his left hand at the back of JD's head and his right hand over his mouth. JD clasped the reverend's arm with both hands as he was laid back into the water. Katie stretched her head higher, trying to see down into the pool. Apprehensive of his rising from the water, she stuffed a finger into her mouth.

The water rushed over JD's face and, after a slight pause, the reverend attempted to lift him up. But JD was so close and heavy, the reverend became unsteady on his feet. JD tried to pull himself up using Reverend Parman's right arm as leverage, but the reverend wasn't strong enough to balance him and had to reach out his left arm to prevent himself from falling forward over JD.

Katie was now gnawing at both of her hands. Finally, JD placed his right hand on the bottom of the pool and pushed his face above the water, but not enough to keep the ripples from splashing into his mouth. Notwithstanding, he appeared relaxed. Reverend Parman, however, felt a heated wave of frustration and helplessness wash over him, which he credited to JD. After what seemed like minutes, JD swung his left hand over the side of the pool, turned himself over, and stood up, back first. The reverend's constant feeling of insufficiency in JD's presence now reached its summit. He tried to say something, but could only muster outstretched palms. JD shook it off, saying, "It's alright. Could have happened to anyone."

"I thought I was strong enough to lift you up," the reverend explained. "I've never had that happen before."

"You really shouldn't worry about it," JD said, cutting the reverend some grace. "The pool should've been built wider, or perhaps I should have been baptized sooner, when I was a little less unwieldy."

When the service was over, Reverend Parman signed the Certificates of Baptism for both boys. His hand was shaking so much that his signature looked as if an aged person had written it. He handed Johnny his certificate while placing his hand on the boy's shoulder. Then, for some unexplainable reason, the reverend spontaneously embraced him. Johnny, without a second thought, hugged him back in an affectionate and appreciative manner.

CHAPTER 50

Live by Faith

When the sun ducked behind the clouds, the fickle air blew cold. Then, as the orb began to peek out, warms breaths of air emerged from the heat reflected off the white snow. JD breathed it all in with a jovial manner. Johnny was much more serious.

"Shall we stop and get something to eat?" JD asked.

"Where?"

JD shrugged. "There's a little lady down the street who serves dinner after church. Maybe we could get something there that you would like. You aren't embarrassed to eat out, are you?"

Johnny looked at his feet making tracks in the snow. "You don't have to buy me nothin'."

JD chuckled. "I would like to."

The room was crowded when they entered, but there was a secluded corner table available. JD ordered for them both, but Johnny didn't eat much. JD figured he probably didn't have much more than milk, bread, and corn mush at home each morning. Johnny's behavior, however, didn't inhibit JD's appetite. He shoveled it all in. Johnny watched with an expression of bewilderment wondering whether each mouthful would be the last.

"You sure can eat a lot," Johnny said. "Is that why you're so big?"

JD smiled. "You'll eat more when you grow a little more. Didn't you like your food?"

"Oh, good Lord! This stuff is awful!" Johnny exclaimed. "I wouldn't feed it to my dog! Guess I was just trying to be big."

The two laughed. Then Johnny said, "I thought I was going to have to walk home alone."

"Oh, for gosh sakes," JD responded. "Why did you think that?"

"Well, 'cause Philip was taken up by the Holy Spirit and I thought maybe you'd be taken away."

"No, no," JD cut him off. "Now, you know, Reverend Parman baptized you. I didn't."

"Yes, but I went to the body of water with you. The preacher didn't tell me 'bout being baptized. You did."

JD thought a moment. "There will always be parts in the Bible that are hard to understand, like the part where Philip is gathered up by the Holy Spirit. However, you must live by the faith of Christ and trust the rest to him. Know what I mean?"

Johnny nodded with sincerity.

The conversation at the Parman's house was not as genial. Katie had accused her father of trying to drown JD, "right in front of the whole congregation." Her comments were prodded by tears and excitement but were stated with little justification. Reverend Parman felt miserable about the situation when he arrived home, but now Katie was making it even worse.

With her eyeballs bulging, Katie said with exasperation, "You all just don't understand JD. It's as if he's done something wrong, like he just got out of jail and you're waiting for him to commit another crime."

"Has he committed a crime?" Reverend Parman asked. As soon as he said it, he knew it was the wrong thing. So, he sucked in a deep breath of air as if he were trying to suck the question back in.

"Oh, Daddy," Katie sobbed. "You are impossible!"

"I'm sorry, I'm sorry. I don't hold a thing against the boy."

"Why then do you not want me to go with him?" Katie asked. It was a valid question. "I'll bet he never comes 'round here this afternoon. He'll go to Billie all because of yours and Momma's attitude."

Though that would have pleased the reverend, he said, "No, honey, that's not so."

Katie could not be consoled. She no longer tried to wipe away the tears that were streaming down her cheeks. Weeping, Katie took a stand. "I want your permission to marry JD."

"Has he asked you?" Reverend Parman inquired with trepidation.

"No," Katie answered, "but I want you to tell me it's alright if he does."

It was now the reverend's turn to take his stand. "We've been through this before. Under no circumstances will I permit you to marry that boy."

Keeping a stiff upper lip, Katie asked, "Is that final Daddy?"

He turned his back to her, indicating that the discussion was over. Katie looked to her mother who had been sitting by quietly, but nervously, listening. "Momma?"

"I agree with your father," she said.

CHAPTER 51

Dr. Price

By the lateness of the hour and the discerning plea in the boy's muffled voice, JD knew it was a matter of urgency. It was after midnight when Johnny arrived, having been sent by his mother to bring the doctor for little Peggy.

After considerable rapping on the doctor's door, they could hear his slippers slapping the back of his heels as he made his way in the dark. But before he unlatched the door, he called out, "Who's there at this ungodly hour?"

Without revealing his name, JD simply said, "We need you, Doctor Price. We have a very sick little girl."

"Well, bring her in," he answered, unlocking the door. "You shouldn't be carrying her around at this hour of night!"

"No, no we don't have her here," JD said, which was now plain for the doctor to see. "You've got to go see her."

Scrutinizing JD's face, Dr. Price asked, "And who are you?"

But before JD could answer, the doctor answered his own question. "Why, I know you. You're that football player."

JD reflected the attention to the boy standing beside him. "This is Johnny Abel."

"Yes, I know him," Dr. Price stated, "but who is the little girl?"

JD never answered; he could see by the expression on the doctor's face that he had figured it out. After making mention of the fact that he had not been paid for the last couple of times he had seen the children (stated in an offhand mode as if he were speaking in code for JD's ears only), they came to an understanding that the bill would be paid, even if JD had to pay for it. JD managed to work a few Latin words into their conversation, which all doctors and lawyers understood, like pro bono and pro se and others—words he had acquired by listening to his city grandfather, CLC.

The doctor continued his attempts to extract even clearer terms of their oral agreement, but JD had had enough. Fearing Johnny might become embarrassed or dissuaded from ever turning again to a doctor for help, JD assured the physician that they could discuss payment more openly on their way back to town. The three then piled into Dr. Price's car. However, in one last negotiating ploy, the doctor glanced down and made mention of the gas gauge being sucked dry by the thrust of the two-mile journey.

When they arrived at the Abel's house, they found Peggy talking as if she were out of her head. First, the clock on the wall seemed to bother her; she complained that it was ticking too loud. Then she railed on about the moon not being visible. It had been cloudy for several days, but in the dark of night one would not expect her to notice that. JD promised Peggy that he would quiet the clock and make the moon appear if only she would let Dr. Price examine her.

With her mother holding the coal oil lamp, Dr. Price peered into Peggy's throat. He remarked that her throat was almost closed shut; yet he didn't seem to have a medical term for her condition. One could easily surmise from his grim facial expression and the shaking of his head that things were not encouraging.

Dr. Price turned to JD and said, "Well, I have come all the way out there in the middle of the night, and I'm probably not going to get a cent for it."

JD turned the tables. "Well, I have come all the way out here in the middle of the night, and I'm probably going to fumble the ball on the one-yard line tomorrow and lose the game 'cause I'd been weakened by being up all night without anything to eat."

Dr. Price started to laugh. "Okay, okay, I give up. I give up!"

JD smiled. "I'll see to it that you're rewarded for all this. It's mighty kind of you to help these poor people out in their time of need."

"By the way, what are you studying down there at the college?" the doctor asked. "Wait, don't tell me—you're studying for the ministry, right?"

"Yes, I am," JD answered proudly. "That's exactly what I'm doing. I may need more schooling after I finish here, but eventually that's what I intend to do."

Dr. Price nodded in understanding. "The way you talked me into caring for these people, I knew right away what you were going to do with your life. All that pro bono talk had me confused for moment, but I knew they didn't teach law at Lynchburg."

It promised to be a long night. Dr. Price attended to Peggy, and JD kept him company. "How'd you run into this family? How'd you come to know them?"

"Well, it's a long story," JD offered.

"We aren't going anywhere," Dr. Price confirmed. "Tell me!"

JD told him how he had first met Johnny when he saw him rounding up the cows. Then he told how he had cut up the hogs when the father had gotten drunk. He explained that he didn't know why, but Johnny seemed to latch on to every word he said, in thirst of being led to something. During one of their talks, JD said he brought up the Bible story of Philip and the eunuch who was in search of something more. And that was that.

Dr. Price nodded and asked, "You being in school and everything, how do you plan to help them?"

Thoughtfully, JD responded, "In the first place, when they ask me for help or seem to be in need, I just can't turn and walk away. And in the second place, I know of a family back home who lives on a horse farm, and the daughter—even though she's in school and an agnostic or atheist—is kind and good-hearted. I thought I might convince her of the merits of an arrangement. You know, work out a deal or something."

"Like the way you worked out an arrangement with me?" Dr. Price asked tongue-in-cheek.

"No, not quite," JD said. "It would be more of a mutual relationship. The Blacksheares have a need for someone, and I think Johnny's mother could fulfill that role. It could be a quid pro quo arrangement. And there's a little house on the property, like a tenant house, where they could live."

"Well, how about the eunuch part?" Dr. Price asked. "How does that fit into the equation?"

The question was asked in a challenging manner, JD thought, as if Dr. Price were trying to attach a label of welfare to it under the guise of religion. JD set his jaw and leaned back, which indicated to the doctor that he was in for a long explanation. The doctor was up for it though, for by now he was intrigued with all JD had to say.

JD began, "As you have suggested, there are two parts to this. If the Blacksheares need someone to do the cooking and cleaning, I think Johnny's mother would do, 'cause none of the Blacksheare women take to that. And then there are the stables to look after, and Johnny can do that to their satisfaction. The Abels need the work and the income. If both parties are reasonable, it'll benefit everyone; all they need is someone such as myself to put them in touch. Now, that covers the simple material needs of the two families. And I emphasize the word 'material,' which is one part of the dichotomy."

"I do hope you're going to get to the eunuch part before long," Dr. Price said.

"Right now," JD said. "The eunuch is the other element in the dichotomy. When Jesus said to Peter, "Simon son of John, do you love me?" he asked him the same thing more than once. When Peter acclaimed that he did, Jesus said, "Feed my sheep." By that, as you know, he was saying to teach and serve your fellow man. So, I think in the scheme of things, my helping the Abels out with their materiel needs is just an aside to my real calling, which is to feed Jesus's sheep spiritually.

"Johnny is like the eunuch in search of God, and I am like the apostle Philip who led him to Christ. I should in all honesty point out to you that at the time I was doing the leading, I was not a baptized Christian. I was merely pointing Johnny to the altar. Some may take exception to that, but when you think about it, Jesus rarely spoke or described things in objective terms. He usually spoke subjectively, in parables. For example, the emblems at communion symbolically represent food for the spirit."

"Well, that's all very nice," the doctor said with little conviction, thus bringing an end to their conversation, "and I wish you luck in your chosen field."

CHAPTER 52

The Moon

Having agreed to return to see Peggy the next night, Dr. Price and JD met to do just that. On the ride there, the doctor said affably, "Didn't I hear you say that you were going to make the little girl a moon?"

"Yes," JD answered. "I'm gonna try."

"Well, Copernicus! Tell me how you're going to do that?"

JD laughed. "You're just going to have to wait and see."

Although Peggy was a bit better, she was not completely without fever. She showed great respect for Dr. Price—as, of course, they all did—however, she was waiting for JD to perform a miracle.

When the time came, they pushed Peggy's bed up to the window; then JD and Johnny went out behind the shed with a lantern and a paper bag while the doctor sat waiting for failure or scam. A few moments had passed when a yellow light slowly rose above the shed. Like a yellow moon, it went up, up, and up into the sky until it finally halted. There was no denying it. Even Dr. Price yielded to his surprise and emotion, exclaiming, "I'll be darned."

And Peggy, lying on her side facing the window, nodded off to sleep as the moon prevailed almost motionless in the sky.

Later, on the way home, Dr. Price couldn't help but ask, "How'd you get that damn lantern up into the sky like that?"

"I didn't," JD answered humbly. "I brought it back into the house."

"So how did you do it?"

"I reckon I could explain it to someone—that is, all the technicalities of it. I suppose I could tell you if I had a cup of coffee and a piece of pie." Dr. Price started to laugh and shake his head. JD was working him again.

"However," JD continued, "this little incident should never go beyond the two of us."

As they entered the all-night establishment and made their way to a booth, the burly owner in a white apron and a chef's hat (proceeded by a considerable stomach), rushed from the kitchen with a glowing smile on his face. His right hand was outstretched to shake, and the left was poised for a slap on the back.

"Big Tote," he greeted, not even noticing the doctor.

"Big Cheese," JD, responded, "how you been? You have a piece of apple pie for a hungry traveler?"

"Of course, of course. Coffee for everyone?" He asked, finally acknowledging Dr. Price. "What'll you have doctor?"

"I'll just have a piece of that lemon meringue pie and a coffee, please.

Big Cheese, as JD had nicknamed him, was not about to let some common waitress serve these two special guests. In short notice, he brought the doctor a quadrant-sized piece of newly cut lemon meringue pie and JD a half a pie, still in the pan. As he passed the apple pie, he said, "This is nice and juicy even though it might look like it's burnt and sticking 'round the edges, so I just brought you what was left. No use trying to scrape it out and mess it all up."

Big Cheese placed the desserts on the table and nodded his head affirmatively. He gave the men a generous smile and waited for a comparably responsive look of delight.

Then JD gave the old trite cliché. "Big Cheese, your generosity is exceeded only by your good looks!"

The doctor put in, "I should certainly like to echo that remark!"

Big Cheese walked away as if his favorite maiden had just kissed him. Dr. Price shook his head in wild disbelief at the size of JD's serving.

"What you got is exactly what he would normally serve to a group of four!"

"He's probably placed a little bet on that one-yard line scenario. Just protecting his venture," JD explained. "Underpinning the foundation of his odds."

"The way you talk, you must place a little wager on yourself, too."

"Never in your life, Doc," JD said. "Closest I ever came to making a bet down here was when I offered to arm-wrestle Big Cheese for some pie. He tried once, but that was it."

Long after they had finished eating, they sat talking. It became obvious to JD that the doctor, though he did not say as much specifically, was of a fundamentalist bent. Their conversation was as wide as it was deep.

Dr. Price asked, "Why did you pick this small school when you seem to have an intellect for Princeton or Yale? I certainly don't mean to belittle this wonderful school—you know what I mean. But there is a vast difference in the scholastic standards in colleges."

JD pondered the question while looking down into his coffee cup. Eventually he responded. "I know what you're referring to. It's just that... at the time I left, there were questions in my mind: tuition, the assurance that I was worthy to be a preacher, things like that. It's worked out for me. I found a way to pay the tuition with a few bloody noses and bent fingers from someone stepping on my hands. Besides, to tell you the truth, I like football and the running. I guess I have a lot of kid in me. I'm serious about things though, especially when it comes to the underdog or people in desperate circumstances, but I still like to kid and have fun."

The doctor asked, "Do you follow the Ten Commandments?"

"Not exactly. I think more toward the Beatitudes. The Ten Commandments are all: *Thou shall not*, whereas the Beatitudes are: *Thou shall*. I should say more accurately, Jesus began each Beatitude with, *'Blessed are they that...'* and so on. And when Jesus said he came not to destroy the Law but to fulfill it, I believe he did refine or acutely sensitize the word of God that heretofore had come down through the prophets. The Jews, being clannish and astute, were always having their very existence come into question. The remoteness of the various peoples of that time to have closer social discourse is like all of us today—self-serving. There are those in all societies who are divided in their beliefs. Some have egalitarian or liberal views as our would-be president Roosevelt would claim; and there are those with more individualistic or conservative views, such as the present incumbent. People create their own agendas based on their needs or desires. For instance, am I taking advantage of your graciousness and patience here? Tell me if I'm keeping you.

"No, not at all," Dr. Price said. "With all the coffee I've had, I couldn't sleep anyway."

"You know, certain admonitions in the Old Testament are nothing more than dietary restrictions or social prohibitions regarding a man and wife. They are codified in our modern day common law and local ordinances within the county. To put it quite simply, the prophets, inspired by God, provided their depiction of the word God, which was later refined by Jesus. Now if you were to ask me if some of the restrictions were canceled or superseded by Jesus's teachings, then I would have to beg for time and ask you to itemize your points. As someone said to me some time ago, the prophets were trying to paint a picture of God whom they had not seen; whereas, Jesus was perfect in his understanding and knowledge of God because he had seen him.

"Therefore, as I have learned from readings other than the Judeo-Christian ethics, faith based on an understanding of Jesus—indeed the lifelong search for this understanding that only Jesus brought forth to perfect exclusion—is paramount over any other rule or prophesy invoked through oral or written decrees. It is even more important than the demand for allegiance through obedience."

JD took a breath. "Having heaped all this spiritual dialog on you, I want to make clear that I have no answers concerning the questions that revolve around God's plans for conveying land or his administration of storms, plagues, and the like. I intend to save that for my graduate school studies. And I suppose I should add that we have Jesus's teachings to live by, as well as his hope—a sure and steadfast anchor of the soul—with respect to eternity."

"So, what you're saying," Dr. Price ventured, "is he, Jesus, deliberately did not explain what he meant."

"Yes!" JD acknowledged. "It's a mystery! And above that, it's presumptuous—if not sinful—for us to speculate what he meant. If he had wanted us to know, he would have told us. Perhaps some may think that's a little strong."

The doctor found himself drawn to JD. "I wish to talk with you more regarding your studies. Perhaps we will be called to the Abel house again in the next day or two."

When they departed and went their separate ways, the doctor went with an expression on his face that was somewhere between grim and perplexed. In any case, he was deep in thought.

It was well after midnight when the doctor arrived home. Mrs. Price was waiting for him. "Where in the world have you been," she asked?

"First, I went to see the Abel child." Suddenly, Dr. Price remembered. "Damn it, damn it! He never did tell me how he did it!"

"Who didn't tell you how he did what?" his wife asked.

"That boy—that football runner—you know, down at the college. He never told me how he made the moon come up!"

Bewildered, Mrs. Price asked, "Are you out of your mind? What are you talking about?"

"He's the one I told you about—the one who befriended that deprived women and her two children out on the mountain. After seeing him run like he does, I thought him to be a rough, brawling brute. But I was wrong. He's always smiling and good-natured. You could probably see that if you were up close to him when he was smacking the opponent on the field. Anyway, we rode out to see that little girl together. I told you I had an appointment out there."

"No," his wife responded somewhat sarcastically. "As a matter of fact, you told me you had an appointment, but you didn't say where."

"Alright, let's not get into all that. Yesterday I heard him tell the little girl that he would make her a moon. So, soon after we arrived and I attended to her, she asked for the moon. Well, I knew damn well he couldn't produce it. Nonetheless, he and that little boy went out behind the shed with a lantern and a paper bag—and there wasn't any damn tree or anything for him to tie it up in the air. But I'll be damned if he didn't do it! Not just a few feet; it went way up in the air a couple of hundred feet. But sitting with the little girl lying in the bed, it looked just like a yellow moon floating way up into in the sky.

"On the way home I asked him how he did it. He admitted he hadn't put the lantern up there. He brought the lantern back with him. Now, he told me he thought he could explain all the technicalities if he had a cup of coffee and a piece of pie, but he never did. And the owner brought him over half of a pie! Before I knew it, he surprised me by telling me he was studying for the ministry. Then he changed direction from the moon to religion, and I forgot all about the moon. And that was the only reason why I took him out for pie!"

Mrs. Price looked more confused than ever.

"Don't misunderstand," Dr. Price continued. "That boy was very abstract, yet clear and assuring in explaining his thesis. All in all, he seems to be a person of contradiction, though clear and perceptive. He's an anomaly. His talk is simple and concise, yet forthcoming. It is moving not only in the sense that it is persuasive, but in such a prompt cadence that one has to race to keep up. He does all this with clear diction, syntax, and metaphor, with simplicity and confidence, but certainly not with so much as an ounce of condescension.

"Also, his thoughts are noted for attribution if they are not his originally. Much of what he said was not new, but his thoughts sounded new when hearing them from him. As I said, he's a contradiction—an anomaly, if there ever was one!"

The doctor sat back, staring out the window into the black night as if he could see clearly. He thought he could make out the moon, but he couldn't. Had he been in the chair near Peggy's bed, however, he would have seen that it was going down and would soon diminish from view.

CHAPTER 53

How to Fell a Tree

By mutual arrangement, Doctor Price agreed that JD and Johnny could cut down two locust trees near his house as payment for the visits he had made to attend to Peggy. So on this day, Johnny arrived with a crosscut saw slung over his shoulder, its end flopping up and down with each step he took.

When the doctor warned them that he could not have trees falling onto his house, Johnny directed him to the peg he had placed in the ground to mark where the tree would fall. JD stood behind the tree and lined it up with the peg as Johnny began to notch the tree. JD grabbed the ax from him with good-natured admonition, stated, "Better let a man do that."

Having been instructed by the doctor to saw the trees off level so he could set a couple tubs of flowers on the stumps, they began to saw on the opposite side of the notch, which was on the side next to the stake. Although they both felt that the doctor had patronized them by inferring that they didn't know how to fell a tree properly, they merely exchanged quizzical expressions and ignored the remark. JD chalked the doctor's attitude up to "townie inexperience."

The first tree hit the peg a little off-center, splintering a piece off the side. The next tree fell as intended, right on top of the first. JD and Johnny then sawed the felled trees into lengths to be used as fence posts, which was the normal use for locust trees. Since the posts were expected to last fifty years, this created a kind of statute of limitation guarantee, as noted by the doctor. If God permitted, Johnny would be the only one still around when, and if, the posts rotted out.

JD claimed the lone ax during the trimming, working at a feverish pace. The boy, having nothing to do for the moment, ambled into the kitchen to fetch some water. There was Mrs. Price, and she took it upon herself to find out about the Peggy's moon. In the proverbial sense, she had asked for the time of day but Johnny proceeded to tell her how to make a watch. In other words, Johnny provided more than what Mrs. Price had asked for by relaying the following story, which JD had shared with him:

Many years ago, Harvey Watson had, in somewhat of a ridiculing tone, questioned the validity of Santa Claus, the virgin birth, and the appearance of the North Star. This took place way back when JD and Will were still small boys, though not small enough to believe in Santa anymore. Harvey had stood nearby and hollered his challenge up to the boys who were working on a Christmas tree. "I'll believe in the virgin birth the day I see the North Star in the sky and hear shepherds singing in the field."

When the boys informed Paw of what Harvey said, his jaw became set and locked for a moment. As JD had told it, "a coal oil lamp lit up in Paw's head." (He didn't call it a light bulb because they hadn't ever had electricity.) Paw then said, "We'll show him. Come with me."

Paw sent the boys to the barn to gather a couple pieces of baling wire and some string while he pulled out a large paper bag and a handful of small candles from the pantry. Then he tied the candles together with the string like a bunch of carrots and created a type of hot air balloon out of the paper bag. Using the baling wire, he rigged the candles into place beneath the bag, to act like a burner to make the bag rise.

Later that night, Paw and the boys proceeded to the edge of the lawn overlooking Harvey's territory. He lit the candles, and the heat slowly inflated the bag like a balloon. Soon the hot air began to raise the bag aloft. Being considerably higher than Harvey's house to start with, Paw cautioned the boys not to release too much string, for that would allow the bag to rise out of Harvey's eyesight.

JD was then instructed to aim his shotgun at a trajectory that would rain shot onto Harvey's tin roof. JD let loose with two blasts. The sound and the echo had hardly subsided before they heard the slam of Harvey's door and an exclamation of distress. Then there was silence. Though they could not see him in the darkness, Paw assumed Harvey was looking in their direction. That's when the three of them broke out into loud, harmonious singing. *"It came upon a midnight clear, that glorious song of old, from angels bending near the earth, to touch their harps of gold…"*

They could hear ole Harvey call to his sister and brother-in-law, "Come out here, come out here! There's a sight to behold your eyes! Praise the Lord, I've never seen anything like it!"

JD had told Johnny that they all three muttered and exclaimed surprise. He imagined them standing there on the lawn with upraised arms, in awe and reverence. He also said that based on Paw's singing, he figured Paw had probably had a little nip from the tin box upstairs at the start of the evening.

Mrs. Price thanked Johnny for the explanation, and he thanked her for the water.

JD had thought about that night many times since. It was the only time in his whole life that he was glad someone had taken a drink of whiskey. In the interest of keeping the record straight, JD had always maintained that Harvey was a Christian backslider. He said one thing, did another, but he did in fact believe. Except for an annual contribution made to soothe his conscience, Harvey was recorded as an inactive member on the church roll.

CHAPTER 54

A Picnic and a Debate

After the tree felling, Dr. Price was apt to hire Johnny Abel to do chores around the yard, often performing tasks a grown man would not have stooped to do, though many were unemployed. He did such things as washing the car, bringing in firewood, and raking the leaves. He even became quite helpful inside the house.

JD was also a frequent visitor. He took it upon himself to purchase two galvanized washtubs, primed them with vinegar to keep the paint from peeling off, and painted them with a green paint. Then he filled them with petunias and sat them on the stumps of the trees he and Johnny had cut. He noted that one of the stumps had not been sawed off as level as the other. He considered attempting another slice, but decided to place a two-by-four under the tub to level it instead.

Dr. Price had a plan up his sleeve. For years he had entered into contentious discussions with his pastor pertaining to the understanding of biblical text, and JD's biblical thesis and his understanding of the subject had intrigued him. He decided to bring the two men together, each standing on their respective stumps. Dr. Price felt the Lord had *destined* his fundamentally bent preacher and JD to debate the teachings of the Bible. To what end? The preacher would be exposed and JD tested.

So, the day came when a considerable crowd assembled at the Price home for a picnic and a debate between the two parties. The doctor had persuaded JD to participate under the ruse that the original debater had been called away by an emergency and that it would ruin his picnic if he did not provide a substitute.

After the meal, the preacher, with his Bible clutched to his chest, eagerly approached the stumps. JD had already removed the tubs filled with petunias—as well as the two-by-four, and with outstretched hands beckoned the preacher to take the stump that was level. But the preacher chose the other.

The Reverend Thaddeus Stevens Munger began to propound the merits of a literal translation of the Bible. Although he did not use those terms, he summarily began to do just that. "My friends, I hold in my hand a book of truth, of light unto the world, and of direction. There has never been a book like it, and we can rest assured there will never be another its equal. In these troubled times of want and misery, many try to interpret the Bible to their own satisfaction. They scoff at the teachings of the prophets and of Jesus Christ himself that do not comport to their own worldly or temporal desires. They interpret the Bible to fit their sinful ways and thus do not adhere to the true written word in this book. This is like sticking the knife of deceit into the back of Jesus himself.

"The Bible is the true word of God. It was inspired by him and recorded by the prophets of old. In this holy book it says that God created the heaven and the earth in seven days, and that is good enough for me. How he did it, I do not know; but I know and believe he did. Similarly, he gave Moses the Ten Commandments, and I accept them lock, stock, and barrel."

With an air of euphoria for what he had said so far, the Reverend Munger nevertheless seemed suddenly to become uncomfortable in his position on the stump. Without realizing it, he began to paw the lower side with his foot, yet he never stopped talking, which gave observers the impression of one walking and talking at the same time. Marking time, as a soldier would say.

"Now there is a vocal force running amok in this country that is advocating a governmental cure for all our problems caused by this economic depression. We don't need the government to cure our problems; we need to pray to God for things to change. We need only to submit to His will and pray—humbly pray—for understanding and obedience.

"The book of Revelation is replete with warnings that the time is near. It is time we wake up to the written word and not listen to the platitudes and ramblings of those sinful, uninformed tongues, those nonbelievers who contend otherwise. Brethren, the time is upon us. We must repent before it is too late! God has given us a sign. Only those who are not listening cannot see it. This great depression is not a mere happening without meaning. It is an act of God. We have been unfaithful to His word; therefore, the wrath of God is upon us. The ship may right itself, but only by prayer and faith in God—faith that God rules the earth and all that is in it. We must go on bended knee and ask for his forgiveness."

All the while, JD stared at the pawing foot on the stump feeling a strong urge to fetch the two-by-four block and place it under the reverend's foot. Knowing this to be futile and fearing it would be misinterpreted, he looked for Doctor Price to bring an end to his opponent's sermon by asking with his eyes, *"When do I have my turn?"*

Reverend Munger suddenly tugged at his pants, first one side and then the other, and gave a haughty flip of his shoulders as if to say, *"Let's see you top that!"* It was finally JD's turn to speak.

"I'm sure the Reverend Munger is entitled to his thoughts. His long service to his church is most commendable and deserves the gratitude of all who follow and believe his teachings.

"First, let me say that the reverend would want me to point out that he misspoke when he said that God created the heaven and earth and all that is within it in seven days. It was six days. God ended His work and rested on the seventh day. I point this out only because neither of us would want any one of you to go out from here confused. Also, as a young man not long off the farm, who having witnessed my mother working at her job for six days a week and then ironing on Sunday,

I shall seek to convince our leaders with as much zeal as I possess to support the unions and our government leaders in establishing a five-day workweek."

This statement elicited a mummer of laughter and stirring within the gathering that did not dissuade JD from continuing. "The reverend has been in the trenches and the pulpit long before I became a student here. I not only intend to go on and seek ordination into my brotherhood, but also to proceed further into graduate school. I say this in all humility and respect, not only for those working for the church, but also with the hope of creating an understanding of the character of God and Jesus Christ.

"Though I have gone to church all my life, most of that time was spent without a preacher or priest. Yes, I have attended on rare occasions the Catholic Church. I must tell you that in all that time, I have not observed a man of perfect doctrine. I have not even read of a man whom I believe was perfect in this respect—not even in the Bible, except for Jesus. To some of you, this perhaps sounds confrontational, even heretical, but let me explain.

"First, I separate the Old Testament from the New Testament, as do most Christians, I believe. Second, I go to the part in the New Testament that is printed in red. Even then I am somewhat perplexed at the red print in the book of Revelation that is also purported to be the very utterances of Jesus. I believe that the red print in the Bible is the heart of the soul of the revelation of God. And the Beatitudes are the very spirit of that part. And while I am on that point, ponder the thought that the Ten Commandments were, for all intents and purposes, rendered obsolete and superseded by these same Beatitudes. Did not one man say to Jesus in so many words, 'Master, all these things I have done,' referring to the Ten Commandments? And didn't Jesus respond by giving us the Beatitudes? 'Blessed are they that...'

"Now I will move on to something different that preys on my mind. We consider the Jews to be of one faith and the Christians and their different denominations another, and the Catholics yet another. Nevertheless, all these separate entities of belief have one thing in common. And that one thing is this: they all think they have the true understanding of God. Consequently, much time is wasted trying to convince the other party that their view is correct rather than trying to gain a better understanding of those misunderstandings or bring those with no knowledge into the flock.

"Let's take the Jews. There are those who wear black hats and have curls down the sides of their head. Generally, they adhere to the strict dietary laws and are very conservative in their beliefs. They don't eat ham or fish that do not have scales. However, those who are raised in the confines of a city do not know that catfish, for instance, do not have scales. I tell you from firsthand knowledge that there are many good Jews who eat pork and fish without scales with a smile on their faces. Remember, Jesus said, 'It is not that which enters a man's mouth that defiles him, but that which cometh out.'

"Before I continue, I want to ask you not to accept my interpretations as hard and fast facts but, instead, I want you to ponder what I say. For if you accept them otherwise, you would be accepting them through obedience and not understanding. Or perhaps because of my athletic achievement. The latter I say in deference to the youth here.

"Now let's look at the Catholics—they have their liberals and their conservatives. I think we can all agree that they are divided politically at least. I would be remiss if I did not point out that this demographic is not only a result of their religious beliefs but also, being more recent to this country, the Catholics are more downtrodden. By that I mean that the Catholics are, historically, the brunt of prejudice and are less affluent in this country.

"However, it appears to me that the Protestants are even more divided—even beyond the progeny of the Church of England and the Calvinists. I think it is an accepted fact by most historians that when Americans gained their independence, they became more desirous of religious freedoms of thought. Some observers might even say that they became more isolated and even unruly. As to my particular brotherhood, it was birthed from John Calvin's teachings and taken to Scotland, and from Scotland it was brought to this country. Once here, it broke into additional brotherhoods. Some who are less tolerant of such shenanigans may claim this was all to the detriment of their former faith."

At this point, JD cast an eye first at Reverend Munger who was now squatting on his stump, and then at Doctor Price who was now nodding in accession. Observing that he had his audience in tow, JD continued.

"What I have told you all here today is pretty much common knowledge to most grownups. But the purpose of all this is to lay a foundation for my most important point. In all this fruitless argument, we are practically casting pearls to the swine. We all have different minds, different understandings. Indeed, sometimes we may have the very same understanding and beliefs but are unable to make ourselves understood, or we fail to listen as we should. On the other hand, the very reason we meet in the church and in such fine meetings as this is to exchange our understandings and to teach one another. Also, we must read and reread the Bible while keeping an open mind. One can never finish reading or interpreting the depth and breadth of the Bible."

Reverend Munger began to stand. His back appeared stiff, and he had to push himself up by placing his hands on his knees. Doctor Price motioned for JD to sit down as the reverend began to speak.

"I defy anyone here to show me a place in the Old Testament that is not correct and without merit in our society today. Also, I would be most interested in being shown where the disciples or the early followers, such as the apostle Paul, made a miscalculation or error in their teachings."

Pointing to JD, the reverend said, "As to this young man's positions, I would suggest that he wait a few years until he has experience and more study before he makes such outlandish statements about the validity of biblical teachings. When he has been a follower of God for as long I have, he will see things in an entirely different light.

"Now let me make it perfectly clear that I, of all people, wish him well. However, he himself admits he is a short timer here at college and has never been exposed to even the normal teaching of an ordained minister in an organized church setting. No minister of God taught him! Only laymen! Not much of a portfolio for lecturing one's elders! Do we want to base our understanding of such an important subject on the musing of one so young and inexperienced?"

At this point Dr. Price stood and interjected, "Now just a minute. You're placing this discussion on a personal basis. The young man prefaced his remarks with an explanation as to his experience and studies. Let's not resort to the old technique of ridiculing the opponent. By the way, Reverend, would you like to have answers to your questions and comments, or would you prefer to continue on for a while?"

Reverend Munger conceded with a look of confidence. "Very well. Let him respond."

Looking directly as the audience, JD said, "Let me remind you that from the outset I suggested that you ponder and not accept what I say lock, stock, and barrel. Perhaps I should have also pointed out that I feel we must study the Word of God in a proper context. Prior to the untimely death of our minister, he said on several occasions that the Bible was written *by* the Jews *for* the Jews. Let's just assume he was talking about the Old Testament for the time being.

"The Jews and the Gentiles were separate cultures; they did not even intermingle. Like some other segments of our culture today, one might even go so far as to say they were clannish and stuck to themselves. I am not one to quote chapter and verse when discussing the Bible. However, on this day I have lucked out—at least this one time. If you will consult the fourteenth chapter in the book of Deuteronomy, beginning with verse 21, you will find that it says, 'Ye shall not eat of anything that dieth of itself: thou shalt give it unto the stranger that is in thy gates, that he may eat it; or thou mayest sell it unto the alien: for thou art a holy people unto the Lord thy God.'

"Now there's a little context! Do you believe that any Jew among us today would give or sell an animal or fowl of this sort to a Gentile? Would Jesus have condoned this type of behavior? Of course, not! It's my understanding that edicts such as this are what God sent his Son to change. Not necessarily this specific commercial act, but to convey a spirit of love and respect that would prevent anyone from mistreating their neighbor, whether he were a Jew or a Gentile.

"I hope I don't have to point out to anyone here today that this type of action would be covered or prohibited by our Food and Drug Administration. The evolution of society's method or treatment by one man to another has changed our common laws, and I believe man's spirit has been dragged along and enlightened in the process.

"Now, concerning the statement regarding the perfect teachings of the Apostles and Paul, I would say this: There were times when Paul and Peter did not see eye to eye. In early texts, Paul warned that Jesus was coming soon. Many people, we are given to understand, quit work, sat down, and waited for His coming as if it were imminent in a matter of days. Unable to convince them that they should go back to work since no one knew exactly when Jesus would arrive, Paul finally told them that those who did not work would not eat. Even today there are those among us who say he is coming soon. Others say he came right after his crucifixion. I believe Jesus came then, but I also believe he will come again at a time not of our knowing—nor of Paul's.

"Chapter 14 in the book of John states, 'In my father's house are many mansions; if it were not so, I would have told you. I go to prepare a place for you. And if I go and prepare a place for you, I will come again, and receive you unto myself; that where I am, there ye may be also.' I think this was the greatest promise ever given to us."

There appeared to be no objection to what JD was saying, nor did Reverend Munger appear ready to dispute anything, so JD talked on for a while. Then Reverend Munger had his say. And so it went, back and forth for quite some time. Most of the picnickers sat in awe, but they did not reveal or disclose their true feelings. Mrs. Price was later to remark to her husband, "I must say, that young man seems to have a very fine way of expressing himself. He has a richer vocabulary than one would expect from someone his age."

Less than a month later, Doctor Price complained to JD that neither of the protagonists had explained their position or understanding on the contentious subject of evolution, which he admitted he found somewhat confounding. Therefore, he felt compelled to call for another picnic and debate. JD indicated that he would deal with that subject the next time, even if the Reverend did not broach it first.

JD also got a piece of advice for his next debate from, of all people, Johnny Abel. It came in the form of a simple question when Johnny asked, "Should you use big words when kids like me are listening? We don't always know what you mean. Maybe you should 'splain what you say."

JD thanked Johnny. "That's good to know. I'll watch out for that in the future."

It was a tip he would never forget.

CHAPTER 55

The Second Debate

The second debate began in much the same manner as the first with the two debaters heading toward the stumps. JD carried an air of competition as he stepped forward with that same hint of a smile on his face. To the reverend he said, "Would you be more comfortable on my stump this time?"

The psychological inference was intended. He had not only suggested that the level stump was his but also that the reverend had appeared out of place and uncomfortable on the other stump, or that he had used poor judgment in selecting it on the previous occasion. To the public it was all very gracious, but in reality (had they been more familiar with Mr. Crapper's toilet invention) JD was pulling Reverend Munger's chain.

The reverend accepted JD's offer and stepped up onto the level stump. It was by no coincidence that the reverend immediately broached the subject of evolution. Several weeks prior, Dr. Price had stirred him up about the topic. So, the reverend had studied hard and thought considerably on this during the intervening time between the two debates.

"The Bible tells us that man is made in the image of God. Does anyone here dispute that?" No one batted an eye.

"Pray tell me then, was God at the beginning a monkey?" Now that stumped them all. Even JD was caught unawares by the proposition, the doctor also.

"As they say in court, I rest my case." The pastor said this, but he had no intention of turning the floor—or stump—over to JD. "Do I need to go further?" he asked the host.

"Please do," Dr. Price quickly responded.

"Of course, God is not a monkey! He has never been a monkey! Neither has man. God is not shown in human flesh, not revealed before our very eyes, but Jesus Christ was—right before our very eyes. Was his lineage from God? Or should I ask, was there anywhere in his lineage evidence of a monkey?

"If we are to believe the very utterances of Jesus in the red parts of the Bible…" he said this as he leered at JD, "pray tell me, does he address the monkey there? Jesus said, 'He who has seen me has seen my Father.' Was God a monkey?"

As soon as he said that, he wished he hadn't, though it seemed to stupefy everyone—even JD and the doctor. "The Bible," he continued, "is the word of God as revealed to the prophets and Jesus himself. Once we start cutting and slicing it to our own individual desires, we have violated His commandments and teachings. If we do that, are we not saying that we are more knowing and inspired than even God himself?

"Yes, my friends; this Bible I hold here in my hands is the way to salvation and to faith in Jesus Christ. No act of charity or kindness surpasses our faith in Jesus. Works are indeed desirable, but not as important as faith."

When JD arose to speak, he was somewhat nonplused. He was aware that he was advocating for an important truth: the evolving understanding of Jesus's teachings, but he did not have any idea as to what might come forth from his mouth. It wasn't football and tackling, but debate was competitive nonetheless. He needed time to think. With some trepidation, JD resorted to tell a joke. This, he hoped, would not only change the mood of the audience but also put him more at ease.

"I feel like the old fellow still tightening the girth on his horse and standing at the starting gate after the other horses have left. The reverend has presented me with a challenge that I am not entirely prepared for and, frankly, I'm not so sure of my fortitude or courage to stand up and bare my innermost thoughts. That, in case you may wonder, is meant to indicate that I feel exposed. I fear I might lead someone, especially one of the youngsters here, down the wrong path if it appears that I am trying to interpret the Bible to suit my own behavior.

"I may not have a full array of thoughts, but I hope as a result of the simple teachings of laymen and my short time with an ordained minister that, perhaps, I am not burdened by a vast amount of religious teachings and misconceptions. My brother and I would never have been fooled by the tradition of Santa Claus." He smiled, giving his audience a chance to lighten up.

"In addition to the several points I mentioned the last time, which I do not intend to repeat here, there are things in the Bible that are in conflict with or even in opposition to other parts of the Bible. Men wrote the Bible, and it has been translated more than once. While it is sacred, it is not the same as if Jesus himself had written it in his own hand. It was God inspired, but that is different than saying it was laid out word-by-word, or brick by brick as if a wall was being built.

"Over and above that, there were frequent instances when Jesus's disciples misunderstood what he was saying. Where does that leave us? It should leave us with the impression that we need to listen to each other and not be so quick to assume that we are always right and the other person is always wrong. During my adolescent years, a friend of mine who was not even a believer said that the Old Testament prophets' attempts to describe God were like a person trying to describe a rose to someone who was blind."

"I had hoped that we would be discussing the New Testament and not evolution or creationism; however, if I do not take time to explain my thinking on the matter, I'm afraid I will be left holding the monkey, which is worse than holding the bag."

Laughter ensued. Doctor Price thought to himself that while JD had not dismissed the subject, he had certainly maneuvered it to a less than equal position to the New Testament, and he had done this extemporaneously.

JD opened his Bible to Genesis and read, "'And the earth was without form, and void; and darkness was upon the face of the deep. And the Spirit of God moved upon the face of the waters.' Now, that does not say that God himself moved upon the face of the waters; does it?"

Several people said loudly, "No!"

Feeling more fortified in his position, JD pressed on. "It says the Spirit of God moved upon the face of the waters. As I said the last time, we should think of God in spiritual terms, not in terms of flesh. I ask you here today to go home and ponder this, for I certainly shall. Why are we talking about monkeys? Let the scientists talk about monkeys, zoology, archeology, and anthropology. Let us talk about spiritual matters."

It was difficult for those present to determine whether Reverend Munger was frustrated or perturbed with JD's utterances. As he began again, JD placed the two-by-four onto his slanting stump; then he stood evenly on it while the reverend made his case.

"Notwithstanding this young man's contention, I believe with all my heart that faith in this Holy Bible and faith in Jesus Christ is the first of all the commandments. Every sacred word in this book must be believed, and every word in this Holy Bible is sacred!"

Reverend Munger now turned to where he had placed a marker in his Bible in preparation for the debate. He read from chapter 14 in the book of John.

"Thomas saith unto him, Lord, we know not whither thou goest; and how can we know the way? Jesus saith unto him, I am the way, the truth, and the life: no man cometh unto the Father but by me. If ye had known me, ye should have known my Father also: and from henceforth ye know him, and have seen him. Philip saith unto him, Lord show us the Father, and it sufficeth us. Jesus saith unto him, Have I been so long time with you, and yet hast thou not known me, Philip? He that hath seen me hath seen the Father; and how sayest thou then, Show us the Father? Believest thou not that I am in the Father and the Father in me? The words that I speak unto you I speak not of myself but the Father that dwelleth in me, he doeth the works. Believe me that I am in the Father, and the Father in me, or else believe me for the very works' sake."

He closed his Bible with a look of satisfaction, yet he appeared tired and haggard.

"My friends, unless we accept these words—all as clear as can be—we will not enter the kingdom of God! To some of us these are glorious and reassuring words. To others, these words are despised, considered inferior or worthless. Practically all of what I read to you is in the so-called 'red parts' of the Bible—that is, Jesus's very utterances. For those who profess to be Christians but take offense to these words, I can do nothing but throw up my hands in frustration and dismay. For I believe with my very heart and soul that those who do not accept Jesus Christ as their personal savior or believe that he is the Son of God may not be saved and enter into the kingdom of God!"

He stood for a moment with head bowed before squatting on the stump with an air of one who had carried a heavy load a great distance.

JD spoke. "I want to acknowledge the pastor's wonderful remarks—especially his devotion to his beliefs and his witness to the love and respect he has for the words of Jesus. In no way do I intend to equivocate concerning the full meaning of the scripture that he read. However, when I read the lines where Jesus says, 'I am the way, the truth and the life,' and, 'If ye had known me, ye should have known the father also,' I immediately discard any physical aspect of Jesus or God. Ponder this scene for a moment and think of 'the way, the truth, and the life' as spiritual beings. This may enhance your understanding of the text and render a meaning that is easier to grasp and less judgmental. By judgmental I mean not as hurtful to those of other beliefs.

"So, here we have Jesus who says God is love, and that is the truth. He also says that love is the way to find fulfillment in life. Who can take issue with that? However, there has been a constant change in the Christian religion over the centuries, often depending on who is in charge. What do we do about it? We do not let these differences of opinion or understanding divide us. Instead, we should proceed in striving to attain a better understanding. Keep the faith through understanding and not only obedience."

JD had nothing more to say. "You have been warm and considerate of me, and I appreciate it very much. I end with my warmest regards for all of you, especially the Reverend Munger and Dr. Price."

After an icy handshake with the reverend, Dr. Price cornered JD. "Why did you go polysyllabic and then feel you had to define your words?"

JD responded, "Johnny said that he and the other children didn't know what many of my words meant. I wanted to make sure they understood."

"I am most grateful for your explanation," Dr. Price said. "You certainly had me puzzled."

"But did I let you down?" JD asked.

"No, but I must go and ponder what you offered. I observed great possibilities in what you said."

CHAPTER 56

The Monthly Stipend

Doctor Price and his wife sat down for supper in the dining room of their spacious colonial house. The electric chandelier had been turned off in favor of a coal oil lamp and the ambiance of its dim glow. It served as a stalwart replacement for candles and a reminder of the doctor's earlier and modest upbringing. Mrs. Price no longer questioned her husband's use of the rudimentary devise, which was smelly and ofttimes smoky. She, however, preferred candles because they were more genteel and romantic.

The lighting of the oil lamp always signaled the start of a serious and humble, and perhaps religious, discussion. This night was no exception. Nevertheless, Mrs. Price invoked her right of partnership in their house—Tenants by the Entirety, she would declare. But her "turn the wick down, George" lament was always met with passive silence.

As Dr. Price reached up to turn the wick down to quell the smoke, he said, "My dear, we have no children. Nor do we have nephews or nieces to whom we can leave our assets. So, it is natural for us to consider—before it is too late—where and how we will …"

Before he could finish his sentence, Mrs. Price interjected, "You have finally been thinking of having someone draw us up a will, I see!"

"It's not that so much as the fact that I do not want us to depart from this world leaving money in the bank when we could have put it toward some worthy cause. Why should some trustee at the bank, bloated with false pride, have the honor of giving our hard-earned money away when it is we who earned it? It's only right for us to decide its use instead of some man with a puffed up sense of egotism."

"Well, if you ask me, I don't think it's wise at this point in our life to take on the support of an untrained widow and two small children."

"But my dear," Dr. Price objected, "I have not asked you as yet! Please hear me out. Besides, that is not at all what I had in mind!"

"Well," Mrs. Price continued, "I don't think it is up to you to give them free medical care either."

"I have done none of that!" the doctor countered. "Those miserable locust trees had been ravaged by the wind and storm until they looked like a couple of electric poles, bare as bean poles. Those two boys cut them down, which more than paid for my services!"

"I'm sorry I interrupted you, dear," Mrs. Price apologized. "Go on and finish; I'll keep quiet."

"Well, this is my thinking: If we leave money behind, it will soon be dissipated and leave little or no imprint on society or the community. However…" He paused for effect. "Being around JD has been such a pleasant experience. I've enjoyed just talking to him out there in the yard. And then, to hear him discuss his beliefs in the Bible and see such a difference in his thesis and understanding! Well, I just feel like we owe it to ourselves to try to see to it that his sort of belief prevails over that damned fundamentalist's interpretation of God's word!"

"Not to interrupt," Mrs. Price said as she interrupted, "but this is becoming a very interesting scenario, though I'm having trouble keeping ahead of you!"

"This is intended to include you, my dear," Dr. Price stated. "We have always done things together, and this must not be an exception. One may call it my idea, but I want it to be a joint enterprise with your approval, of course."

The seriousness of the discussion was now manifest by the fact that neither had hardly touched their food. The main thrust of the doctor's suggestion was now apparent. He rested both elbows on the table and with both hands opened in expansive supplication said, "I would like to go down to the bank and set up an account whereby the bank would send JD a monthly stipend to cover his expenses for his graduate studies—even if he went on to Scotland to obtain his doctorate. This would all be done anonymously; he would never know the donor.

"You know I am always with you in these things that give you self-worth and pleasure," Mrs. Price stated, "but don't you think he will someday marry, and shouldn't a wife be able to help support him in his tuition and so forth?"

"That can work its way out in time. He speaks of two girls. One is in his hometown. JD believes Johnny and his family may go to serve her family. The other is, of course, the Parman girl. Their backgrounds and assets are quite different. When, and if, he marries one or the other, we can decide then how to proceed."

Several days later, Dr. Price met with one of the men at the bank.

"I thank God every day that I took my money out of this bank before it was lost in the crash. It bothers me deeply that a man could not count on his banking institution back then for the safekeeping of his savings."

"Oh, you certainly never have to worry about that anymore with this bank, Dr. Price," the clerk responded.

"That's precisely what they said about the stock market!" the doctor moaned. "I'm not leaving anything to chance these days."

"What can we do for you this morning, Dr. Price?" the clerk asked. "The lady of the house is all well and cheerful I hope?"

"Yes, she's well, thank you. As to her cheerfulness…" Dr. Price thought a moment. "You know that always depends on variables, such as the demeanor of the lady's husband."

The clerk gave the doctor an acquiescent glance, and the small talk ended.

"Now, getting down to my reason for arranging this meeting with you; I want the bank to mail a monthly stipend to a certain young man by the name of Joseph Emery Beauchamp Dayne, though he goes by JD. Possibly you have heard of him?"

"Why yes! Why yes, of course! Sure have!" the clerk said with much enthusiasm.

"I can't emphasize this too much; this all has to be in the strictest of confidence. Only you, my wife, and I must know the source of this monthly stipend. I need your solemn promise on that."

The clerk nodded ardently. "You have my assurance on that. Of course, there must be a modest fee. I say this as an officer of the bank, you know. How does ten percent sound to you?"

"Frankly, I would appreciate it if you could be a little more modest than that. Say about five percent annually, with the fee payable up front at the being of each year."

"Okay, okay, Dr. Price," the clerk agreed. "For you, I think the bank directors will accept that. After all, you are a valued customer."

"That's mighty considerate of you. And all this must be done in the strictest of confidence," Dr. Price emphasized. "I don't want JD to ever know where the money comes from as long as I'm alive."

"You can count on it Dr. Price," the clerk assured him. "So, it's a deal?"

The two men shook on it.

Several days later, JD was called into the bank. He was advised of his stipend and told to keep the bank informed of his whereabouts so the checks could be mailed to him on schedule. When he asked about the source of the funds, he was told never to expect to learn the name of his benefactor.

He was hardly out of the door when the thought occurred to him that, with this stipend to augment his modest earnings, perhaps he could think about marriage and graduate school at the same time. Although the girl he pined for knew nothing of the stipend and did not relish the idea of obtaining a job, she was having similar thoughts about him, too.

CHAPTER 57

Matrimony

She had never strayed beyond the realm of the flock, but now with quick, deliberate abandon, Katie set out to unite in matrimony with her would-be mate. For all the years they had known each other, it wasn't till now that she had set her heart on getting her man. It was instinct. Instinct, like the sow gathering leaves before having a litter. Instinct, like the trout going upstream to spawn. Is instinct in a human ungodly, she wondered?

At least she hadn't proposed; JD had done that much. JD had always loved her. It didn't matter about the other girl. But it was Katie who secretly approached the minister and the guest witnesses who had come not expecting there to be over one hundred present for the ceremony. Each person arrived thinking he or she had been the only one invited. They came, saw, and gaped at the proceedings, knowing that there had been no rehearsal for it.

Looking back on the day that they were married, it seemed the occasion was a resounding success as the pair marched to union without hesitation. It rolled in quietly like a fog floating in on silence under cover of darkness. Yet it was also dumbfounding because of its secretiveness.

Katie walked into the church with upraised face and directed the participants to take their places. There was a droning silence in the church as the guests came in from the outside. The few lights at the front, and interspersed at that, struggled to resist the darkness so that no one was completely visible. This was done purposely to make it difficult for the guests to identify each other.

In the narthex, Katie held close to the elder who was to give her away. He was the same man who always read the scripture during baptisms. She nervously giggled while he gripped her back to keep his hands from shaking, all the while thinking of the wrath that would fall upon him the next day.

The organ began to play softly, pianissimo. *Here Comes the Bride*. Associate Pastor William Vernon Markham strode to the altar followed by JD and Babe. Though they had never rehearsed, it seemed as if they had done this before. And then, fortissimo, the nervous giggling abated, and Katie pressed the arm of her escort to signal that it was time to go. She smiled upward as he tried to do likewise.

The bridesmaids got too far ahead. At first, Katie and her escort tried quickly to catch up, but then slowed to their own pace. Unimposing in physical statue, her gate and posture and expression were now imbued with determination. There was an air of saintly awe as the guests watched Katie stride in regal splendor toward JD who was peering over his set jaw.

"Joseph Emery Beauchamp Dayne, wilt thou take this woman to be thy wedded wife, to live together in the holy estate of matrimony? Wilt thou love her and keep her till death do you part?"

"I will."

"Katherine Elizabeth Parman, wilt thou take this man to be thy wedded husband, to live together in the holy estate of matrimony? Wilt thou love him and keep him till death do you part?"

"I will."

Pastor Markam then asked, "Who giveth this woman to be married to this man?"

"I do," answered the elder, as if he were making the pre-hanging oath of regret that he could do but once.

Tears welled up in the pastor's eyes, though they didn't run down his cheeks. And then it was over. The guests departed, and so did the newlyweds.

The next morning the associate pastor conducted the Sunday service and brought the morning message. Reverend Parman and his wife, having just returned from a trip, took a seat in the second row to hear the sermon. When the announcements were given at the end of the service, they wondered who Pastor Markham was referring to when he said that the church was the scene of a "spectacular matrimony" the previous night and that the sublime glory of God was written on the newlywed's faces.

CHAPTER 58

Jim's Spring

The train bearing JD and his new wife clickity-clacked past cow pastures not fully recovered from winter baldness, each enclosed in loosely strung barbed wire that separated one man's poverty from the other's. The wheat fields appeared with their rows of bare lemon-shaped spots where the wheat drill had scratched around the autumn corn shocks. JD looked toward the front of the car and was suddenly fearful that the young mother he saw with her infant child might expose her breast in front of him and his bride. When it had happened on his way to college, it had been a pleasant thing. JD now turned away.

"Will your mother be mad?" Katie asked.

"No," JD said. "She loves you very much."

"I must call Momma when we arrive at Snakeden."

"If we ride that far, we'll have to walk back through the woods because there won't be another train going toward Washington until much later."

"That's all right," Katie said.

Four hours later, she made the call from the station. JD didn't hear what Katie said, but he noticed her wiping her eyes. Nonetheless, she felt relieved of a burden as they began the walk to the Browns' home.

The sun radiated heat up from the cinders and ties on the track. JD stopped and turned sideways facing the swamp, his hands in his pockets. In the same moment, Katie, with her arm intertwined in his and with her head leaning on his shoulder said, "I love you." It sounded almost like an apology. In the next breath, Katie said, "Let's go by the grove, just for a moment."

Somewhat reluctantly, JD agreed. "All right. I don't know what you're expecting. Those days are past; I've told you that."

"I know," Katie said. "I just want to see."

As they approached the fence, JD stopped and sucked his stomach up into his chest. He held his breath for a moment; then he released it as the nostalgia expired from his lungs. Grabbing the middle strand of the barbed wire fence, he lifted it up as his foot pressed down on the bottom wire; this made it easy for Katie to slip through.

She clutched him close as they peered up into the giant decapitated dome—the cathedral. The holy silence was unmitigated, even by the bird that stood in peace on an oak limb.

"I hope no one ever cuts these trees—at least as long as I'm living," JD said. Then he squatted to his hands and knees before Jim's spring to take a drink, his nose lightly touching the cool water. It was cold and clear like perfect glass. Katie did likewise though she felt unsteady, as if she might fall headfirst into the water.

"Why do they call it Jim's spring?" she asked.

"Oh, that's a long story."

"Please tell me, Katie begged.

JD was glad to oblige. "Well, you know I think of this place like a church. It's always been that way to me. Not because Paw told me the story; at least I don't think that's why. But here it is. Paw was about five or six when his Dad got to drinking and gambling downtown and didn't come home for Christmas. This made Paw real mad. In order to make it up to his son, Paw's Dad told Paw that he would give him anything he wanted. Paw kept thinking his Dad would renege the next day, but he assured him he wouldn't. So, Paw got up on a chair and said, "I want Jim!" Jim was no older than Paw, a mere child. But he had been born a slave, and Paw wanted to set him free. Jim still lived with his mother and father up there in the old slave house where he and Paw would play.

"Paw's Dad tried to talk him out of it, but couldn't. Eventually he went up to the courthouse and fixed up the papers so Jim could be set free. Then one day, while they were playing together, they found this spring, which no one ever knew about. It ran underground; still does, you see, except where they dug it out.

"The next summer, Jim died. Paw never understood why someone else who wasn't free hadn't died instead. I still don't believe he understands. Anyway, Paw named this Jim's spring after Jim, and it's been called that ever since."

Katie's heart swelled with love for her husband. "Tell me I didn't steal you, that I didn't coerce you to marry me."

"For heaven's sake, Katie," JD sighed with upraised hand as if pleading for divine words to allay her concern. "I'm going to tell you once more, and then I shall never expect you to bring it up again. You reminded me of Little Bonnie when I first met you; she was my sister—my sister! But once I got to know you, I intended for you to be mine. You are mine now until one of us dies. We will walk through life together—you holding onto my big, fat body, and me holding just as tightly to your spirit of love and peace. You are my rock of kindness, and I will hold you the rest of my life."

Katie smiled at up at him with deep adoration.

"What did your mother say?" JD asked.

Katie took a moment to answer. "She said that she and Daddy had been led to the slaughter like lambs."

JD had no response to this.

"JD," Katie finally said, "I want us to be friendly with Billie."

"That's nice of you to think like that," he replied.

"What did Billie mean when she said that you chose the former and ran with the hounds?'"

JD's head snapped suddenly to look Katie in the eye. "Where did you hear that?"

"Billie and I have talked. She told me you heard Little Bonnie say those words to you. Please tell me what it means; I'm your wife now."

JD shook his head. "I guess it meant that lifting the bit and fighting and playing football were ungodly, yet that's what I chose to do."

"I know your sister's death must have been awful, JD, but why did you come here to this grove and talk to her?"

"At first I believed God would bring Little Bonnie back and take me instead. Then on the day she was to be buried, I went to her coffin, which was in the parlor. I wanted to say goodbye to her. Nobody else was around. When I reached down to kiss her, her face was cold and hard like a stone. That's when I realized she wasn't even there. Somehow this was more of a shock to me than when I carried her body back after the accident."

They sat on a nearby log, facing each other. Katie kissed JD's hand and rubbed it against her cheek. "What did Little Bonnie mean by the hounds?"

JD answered as best he could. "I think that was God asking me when was I going to come to Him and stop running with the hounds."

"I still don't understand," Katie said with frustration. "What are the hounds?"

"The hounds are all those things that keep me from living for God, like fighting with Dillie, and playing football, and lifting the bit. I believe God spoke to me. I don't know how he did it, but he did."

"When did you decide to stop running with the hounds?" Katie asked. "Was it when you were baptized?"

"No," JD answered. "I'm sorry it wasn't when I was baptized. It was the day Little Tote got hurt. I was mad, and I started playing mad. Then, when the game was over and you had cried and left, I went up into the woods behind the college to talk to Little Bonnie. But the longer I sat there, the colder I got, until I made up my mind to do what was right. I would play the remaining games because I had promised I would; then I would be baptized and follow the instructions of the Lord fully. And then I'd marry you."

"You planned it just like that?" Katie asked with surprise. "And you didn't even tell me!"

CHAPTER 59

Unable to Hear

Back in Lynchburg, the church was vacant except for the two preachers and the elder who gave Katie away. People had approached the Parmans after the church service with overwhelming congratulations. Their felicitations were so overwhelming in contrast to their feelings that the Parmans were unable to respond in any other way than to nod, with Mrs. Parman wiping the tears from her eyes with her handkerchief. Immediately after the fellowship, she went directly home, whereas Mr. Parman went directly to his office with Pastor Markham and the elder.

"Where is she?" Reverend Parman demanded. "Why wasn't she here this morning?"

In a quiet but determined voice, Pastor Markham answered, "They have gone to his family's home for a few days."

Beating the back of his opened hands simultaneously on his knees, Reverend Parman fumed, "But why? What have I ever done to you to make you do a thing like this to me? I go out of town for three days, and you plan... no, not plan... you *conspire* to do a thing like this. You and the entire congregation! I suppose the whole town knows about it by now. And what a laugh they must be having on the old preacher!

"I have given my entire life to the church and my children. Do you know what I've sacrificed to send my son, Clark, through school? Not to mention my little girl—my little girl whom I've tried to protect and rear to be an angel in the church. How many daughters go through college and become ordained? How many, I ask you? She had one month to go. That's all! And now this. Married! An innocent, little girl taken in by that ruffian! That brawler! What will he do to make a living? How will he support her?"

Reverend Parman swung his head side to side, his voice contaminating the air. "A drunken ruffian, that's all he'll ever be. And Marge and I are led to the slaughter on a Sunday morning before the entire congregation."

"Sit down," Pastor Markham instructed. "Sit down, Tom, and for once, let me tell you something that you obviously don't know."

Reluctantly, Reverend Parman did as he was told, all the while shaking his head in protest.

"Your daughter is the closest thing we've seen to an angel. And let me say that I don't even feel right calling her *your* daughter because there isn't a person in this church who isn't blindly in love with her, including every jealous old lady in this town. She has always been a daughter to us all; she is *our* own daughter.

"Katie came to me and the elder here. Why did she come to us? Because we are not only her friends, we are spiritual instruments of the church. That's what she said. Then she announced that she wanted to marry JD, whom she says you do not know. And I know exactly what she means because I don't think you know him either! And the elder here agrees. What I'm saying to you Tom comes right from the visceral… right from the visceral …"

"I didn't come here for a lesson in anatomy!" Reverend Parman interjected.

"Now you hear me out, Tom," the associate pastor continued. "Katie is a grown woman, and JD asked her to marry him. He wanted to talk to you, but Katie told JD that there was no use in talking to you because you are blind. That's exactly right! You don't see the real JD.

"I've been joined with you at this church for years, working in your shadow. Now, I'm not saying I regret it. I've actually enjoyed it immensely. I've found a home here with you, but remember: neither of us forced our understanding on the other. We've stood face to face in friendship, just like the disciples did, in pairs. But bear in mind that I, like you, have taken a vow to God and not to man. The elder here did likewise. When Katie came to us, she came as a young lady of the church. What would we do if any young lady came to us under similar circumstances? With her credentials, we not only had to marry her, we had to accept it as a rewarding and joyous occasion.

"I don't suppose this makes any difference, but that man professed to being a follower of Jesus since he was a small boy. I asked him, if that was so, why did he take so long to be baptized? He said that when he decided to be a Christian, he decided to go all the way. He kept thinking that someone from the clergy would ask him to join the church, but no one did. Then I asked him who he had expected to ask him, and he said *you*. When I asked him why he supposed that you hadn't, he said you were probably too busy. I tell you this because it needs to be said.

"I asked him how he finally decided to be baptized. You need to know this about your son-in-law. He said that the baptism meant nothing significant to him because he had already felt the hand of Jesus on his shoulder in the middle of a cornfield on a hot July day when his father came home drunk. The baptism here was only to publicly and symbolically indicate his acceptance of Jesus as his savior.

"He also said that a layman had been the only one to ask him about membership in a church. A layman! And this layman not only asked him, but also gave him tuition money so he could go to school to study for the ministry.

"For many years, Christians have wondered about miracles, and we have wondered no less. And then one came to me when I was talking to JD. Here's what I want to say to you: you will see the miracle. You will see a miracle performed by Jesus Christ. You will see Christ in this man the rest of his life, and it should be cause for all of us to have faith. For this man, roughhewn and with heavy feet and the physical strength of an ox, not to mention the best football player I've ever seen, will be transformed into one of the greatest men of our time. Of our time, Tom! He will become a great minister with a wife and companion who will be an asset beyond the likes we have yet to see."

Though Pastor Markham spoke truth from his heart, Reverend Parman was unable to hear any of it. Soon thereafter, he left that church for good, leaving it in the care of the associate. Reverend Parman went on to become an evangelist and never sought placement in a church of his own again.

CHAPTER 60

Amos Cloud

JD and Katie relocated to Eaton, Oklahoma where he began preaching in a small rural church. His intention was to continue his schooling at the Bible College at Eaton in the fall. Head bowed, JD began his first church service with prayer.

"Almighty God, Father of our savior Jesus Christ, lift our hearts so that we may see the glory of your word. In his name we ask. Amen."

He followed up with an introduction of sorts. "There are those who say we must not do this or that or we will reap the fire of Hell, but I say we should think in terms of what we should do, not what we shouldn't. What we should do is find salvation, which is our purpose in life. Once having found it, we should exploit it to the fullest. We need to recognize that which deters us—that is sin, as we know it—and discard it. Discard it as Christ instructed: "If thy eye offendeth thee, then pluck it out." For you see my friends, Christ meant that we should let no part of our body or any animate object interfere with our search for salvation. Salvation can be found here on earth—it is the fruitful and joyful life; it is not dull and commonplace or filled with restriction, but rather free from sin. And we shall not fear death; for if we can conquer life free from sin, death holds no fear. Come now and stand as we sing *A Mighty Fortress is Our God* on page 155 of your hymnals."

Four discordant hymns later, JD and Katie stood in the narthex smiling upon the members of the congregation as they left. Each time they told him that they believed in him, he winced. He thought to himself, they do not yet see.

As Katie prepared the Sunday dinner, JD shared his thoughts with her.

"They did not understand what I said. They came out speaking of *me* though I told them of *Jesus*. I feel as if I failed him. Why don't they listen to *what* I say?"

"Oh, honey" Katie said comfortingly, "they will understand. People just want to attach themselves to someone tangible, but they are relating to Jesus."

JD was not so sure. "I must find someone to help me with the church services. That last song was especially awful."

JD asked of those in town who he could get to help him. One name kept popping up. Finally, he set out to see Amos Cloud, a small, wiry, and industrious farmer. He said to Amos, "I have come on a matter of great urgency to me. I need your help on Sunday."

Amos assumed JD was politely insisting that he come to church. Amos said, "I'll be glad to come, but I don't think your success will depend on my presence."

"No, no," JD clarified, "I don't mean that. In a small church there must be someone with a strong voice to lead the singing. In a big church, it doesn't really make any difference because of the choir and organ."

Amos asked, "You mean, you want me to sing?"

"That's exactly what I mean," JD answered with a smile.

Amos wasn't sure, so JD made him an offer. "If you do this, I'll clean the manure out of your barn everyday. I must get your help."

"I'm not sold on this," Amos said cautiously. "The last young man they had up at the church… well… I couldn't get along with him."

JD had already heard the story. "I know that, but I don't teach evolution. Frankly, I don't give a hoot about it."

Amos was visibly impressed and pleased, but for only a moment. It was as if he had unburdened himself of one concern only to pick up another. "Would I have to stand in the pulpit when I lead the singing?" he asked.

JD responded, "You sit in the first pew, on the left by the piano. When we stand for each song, you stand, of course—but I'd like you to turn halfway around. Don't face the people, but turn enough so they can hear you well. For the song we sing while sitting, you just try to keep the tempo, and sing loud enough for everyone to hear and follow. Don't worry about the communion hymn; we can all sing that one softly."

Amos thought for a moment before answering, "I guess I can help you out on that."

Then the two men went into the house for tea to seal the deal. While they were there, Mrs. Cloud asked JD if he would pray before he left. "The last preacher didn't pray when he came to visit," she added.

JD said, "I'd be glad to pray, but I'd like to explain something to you first. I was reared on a farm in Virginia, and right from the beginning I was taught to pray on my knees. So when I pray in someone's home, I do likewise."

"I would like that," Mrs. Cloud affirmed.

So, they all bent to their knees, and JD began. "Our Father in Heaven, hear our prayer. We believe that Jesus is our savior. Bless this house, and guide us as we work together to spread the good news of thy Son. Amen."

After JD had gone, Mrs. Cloud said to her husband, "Oh, I like that man. He's not a handsome person, but he has something that makes you love him."

CHAPTER 61

Dear Diary

Babe had given up his coaching job at Lynchburg College in favor of a position in Washington, D.C. with Congressman Fitch from Georgia. He was motivated by either salary or close proximity to Billie who now lived with her parents in nearby Virginia, having dropped out of school. Stonewall promised his daughter that if she finished college he would endow her sufficiently, which would allow her to write without working. Billie had declined the offer and took a job in the Library of Congress instead.

For Billie, school was likened to that of a doctor tending the sick and trying at the same time not to fall victim to the same disease. She feared that college, especially English literature professors, would render her unable to write under her terms. While she had teased JD about the subjectivism of his philosophy, she thought the same way. In fact, she talked the same way, which at times made the listener work as if to decipher a coded message. Figuratively speaking, Billie would start at the base of a tree, more so in her writing than in conversation, and branch out the limbs as she went.

Billie rode the train to and from work every morning. Occasionally when she caught the late train, Billie would witness the painful and drunken conversations between Bonnie and Marcus. The ride to D.C. was much more enjoyable, she noted, when Marcus wasn't on board.

Babe treated Billie to lunch every day, but she would only date him on weekends when she was not preoccupied with her writing. Eventually, she completed a two-hundred-page book and tossed it aside as if it were worthless. Then she immediately started on another one with the appearance of having found the secret to writing itself. She seemed happy and lighthearted on the weekends, though quite introverted and somewhat preoccupied during the week.

Following supper each night, Billie would take a brief ride on horseback before pouring herself a double scotch with a splash of water and retiring to her room to write. When not engaged in writing a book, she would put pen to diary. One night, in a bit of a drunken stupor, she wrote the following:

> *Dear Diary,*
>
> *Last night I knew that I had found the secret, the story—the complete story. It loomed before me as if I had observed it for real. Now I need only to paint it in words as if it were a scene on canvas. The bond I made to write without thought of public acclaim or remuneration still is accepted, but tonight it's all about the beautiful story. As I reread what I wrote the night before, it seems worthless in comparison to what I have written now.*

Billie sat astride the buckskin stallion not more than 70 feet from the gate. He had been shaved except for the legs and where the saddle went. Her father had instructed her to face the horse away from the gate, and she did as instructed in spite of his jerking head and prancing feet, which were induced by grain feed. Then she let the stallion look at the five-foot gate, and before he lost his confidence, Billie banged him with the crop while yelling, "Haaa." Together they went up and over.

"Miss Blacksheare," Babe said with admiration, "I couldn't ever hope to jump a horse like that! However, I believe I can give you a stroke per hole and still beat you in a friendly game of golf—at your club, of course."

Billie and Babe played golf at the Chevy Chase Country Club on Saturday afternoon and attended a dinner dance that night. He drank several cocktails, but she had only two. It was enough to loosen her tongue and make her more affectionate toward him.

"Do you care for me?" Babe asked her directly.

"Yes."

"How much?"

"You are first in my heart."

"I'll be damned!" Babe said with surprise.

"What will you be damned about?"

"Just when I thought you were going to beat around the bush, you come right out and answer directly."

"Ah, directly, yes," Billie acknowledged. "But you are not satisfied, are you?"

He looked her full in the face. "You're right," he said. "There's a good possibility that I may always think that you care for JD more."

Billie took a deep breath. "The feeling one person has for another is an irrational thing. JD always said if a red rose and a white rose are pretty, a green rose should be pretty, too. And, he would say, if you love someone just because you have something in common with them, how can you love your brother or your father when you may have nothing in common with them other than being in the same family?"

"You said I was first in your heart," Babe said. "Now, did that mean I come before him?"

"No, that does not mean that you come before him," Billie stated.

"What does it mean then?"

Billie proceeded to explain. "When I was in college, my sociology professor tried to initiate a little extracurricular activity with me. I told him I had a boyfriend, but he wouldn't give up. So we talked about JD, and it all boiled down to this: he said JD and I would never marry because we were both dominants. I didn't understand him at first, but now I do. JD and I do not believe the same things, you know. I don't believe in God, yet the strongest force in my life for a belief in God is JD himself. I believe in JD. I don't know why I feel as I do towards him, but no matter what may come, he will always be something special to me."

"Oh, damn," Babe said, not in anger or frustration, but because there was no use arguing. What he couldn't say was how he truly felt when her warm and full lips touched his or when her body was pressed against him with his hand beneath her jacket. He knew that what they had was special, too. And thence, love endured.

> *Dear Diary,*
>
> *Babe says I can beat any woman at Chevy Chase if I would practice more, but now I have made up my mind that Babe will be first and my passion for writing will be second. Golf will be third. Of course, the priority of my horse must meld in there with those three!*
>
> *Tonight marks the end of another day. I detest writing a simple, chronological list of events like I did yesterday. Tonight I wish to let the words flow from the ends of my fingers, uninhibitedly tapping off into the forest of idle thought. I wish to envision the scene and paint the picture—all indecipherable or perhaps abstract to the reader, but soothing and blissful to my soul. What soul? I mean, why do I say my soul? I have no soul.*
>
> *When it is finished, it is finished! Thus, I must finish it now. There will not be another chance—no second chance to correct the errors and the omissions. But my passion shall not consume me. I shall flit and play with Babe as I choose, but I shall be true to him.*

Shortly thereafter, Billie and Babe were married in the large Episcopal Church in Middleburg where her father had moved his real estate business. Her parents were elated with the union and invited the newlyweds to live with them. They accepted her parents' offer. As was typical in those days, Babe gained a bride but also had the choice of paying dues at Chevy Chase, which her father had been paying, or giving up golf. He joined the club.

Billie continued to work. She and Babe commuted daily into the city together. Before long, Stonewall and his wife relocated to Middleburg, which left Billie and Babe alone to run the farm.

When JD learned of the marriage, he was saddened.

CHAPTER 62

The Abels

Babe was away on a business trip to Georgia, so Billie sat alone in her room with her passion for writing and a glass of whiskey. Had Babe's bottle of whiskey not been visible, she certainly wouldn't have gone to find it. She had felt in no need of it, but now a warm glow came over her as she drank. It was the third glass that led her to mumble.

Dear Diary,

Tonight, I am with my passion, but it shall not consume me; Babe will be first. However, if Babe so much as bats an eye at another woman, my passion will take first place. There is no problem tonight, for I see it all clearly. I shall write the truth, come what may. Even if no more than three read it, I shall know that I have done the right thing. I cannot suit them all. The critics will only accept my writing when the reader acclaims it, and the reader will like it only if it says what he wants to hear. Of course it must be written in terms and phrases than can be enjoyed without much thought. But I shall write for none of them.

I know now that there will be days when I shall write chronologically and mundanely, but the next day the stream of consciousness will flow through my fingers in beautiful prose that makes me love my passion for writing. A different woman will sit at this typewriter each night. Why? I don't know, but I want to find out. JD would be interested in that; not only do we have to contend with life after death, we must also die each night and be born anew the next morning. I wonder what he would say about that!

Oh, if only I could talk to him. If only I could talk to someone who truly has an interest. I must read the critiques, even if I don't like what they say; no more time for books per se.

Paw was sitting in the yard watching as the train came around the bend like a huge snake crawling around the side of a mountain. It stopped for some time, which meant that there was more than one person getting off. You couldn't see who it was until the train had moved away. But even then, Paw didn't recognize them. And when they came over the top of the hill, right toward the yard, he still didn't know who they were.

First, there was a young boy carrying two suitcases. A woman and small girl followed slightly behind, each carrying packages. They appeared to be shy, but not the boy. He walked right up to Paw and said, "You must be Mr. Brown."

When Paw admitted that he was, the boy introduced himself as Johnny Abel and said, "JD said you would let us sleep here until we found a place."

"Hmmm," was all that Paw said.

Johnny asked, "He did write you, didn't he?"

"Yes, he wrote us," Paw said, except he didn't confirm or deny that JD had written about the travelers and their staying at the house.

Paw motioned for the women to follow him inside, but he directed Johnny to seek lodging at the Blackshears' place. He gave him one of the old workhorses to ride over since it was getting late and the sun was beginning to set. As Paw explained it, the Blackshear house would come into view not long after losing sight of the Browns' house. Johnny listened and went on his way.

When he crossed over the bridge where JD had first seen those mysterious floating heads sticking up from the sand, he caught sight of the big house on the hill, its white board fences and huge red barn almost frightening in appearance. It was not until he had reached the yard that he saw the little house at the bottom and on the other side of the hill. That must be it, he thought. Just as he was about to throw his leg over the horse's neck to dismount, a shattering command came down from the top window of the house.

"Take that horse out of the yard," followed by a more copacetic order, "and tie him to the fence."

Johnny did as he was told, then went to present himself at the front door, which they both reached at the same time. Billie looked down to inspect the face of the intruder.

"You" she said, "must be Johnny Abel."

Johnny nodded.

"Do you remember me?" Billie asked.

"Yes ma'am."

She invited him in, and they sat in the handsome living room. His eyes raced up the walls and then over the fireplace. He realized that this was disrespectful, but it was all so inviting and pleasing to look at that Johnny took the chance of offending her. But Billie seemed amused.

"Do you like it?" she asked.

"Yes ma'am," Johnny responded with a smile, thinking it was nice of her to ask. "Mrs. Linford, did JD…"

"It's Lunsford," Billie interrupted.

"Yes, Ma'am," Johnny said looking down.

"Don't let's start off on the wrong foot," Billie iterated. "Let's be fair and honest in our conversation. JD said in his letter that you would say what you think."

Johnny's eyes twinkled as he wiggled in the chair. "I sure will, Mrs. Lunsford."

"Alright then. JD also said that you knew how to care for horses and could ride yourself. Is that true?"

"Why, yes ma'am," Johnny said truthfully, "and I can jump 'em too."

Billie nodded. "If you will take care of the horses and your mother will do the housekeeping, I'm prepared to offer you thirty dollars a month, during the months that you're in school."

Johnny's eyes opened wide. Thirty dollars was a lot of money, and he had never had a real honest-to-goodness paying job before.

"Now the stalls must be cleaned each night, and there must never be a time when the horses are not watered. They must never be mistreated."

"Good Lord," Johnny exclaimed. "Nobody could mistreat a horse, could they?"

"You would be surprised!" Billie said. "Now you all can live in the little house out back for free, and you may have the general run of the place. JD also said you would expect to hunt some."

Johnny nodded, then asked in an all-important way, "And can I get transportation to church on Sundays?"

"Transportation being a horse and not a car, I assume."

"Yes, ma'am."

And so the deal was made, and the Abels moved in the very next day.

Dear Diary,

Babe saw the tears in my eyes when I came in tonight from riding. He thought I was sad, but that's not so. It's my passion—it changes my personality. I know I can write a novel. They may not like it, but I can do it. I think so much about it. I can't even read books without reeling off into thoughts. How did I ever finish school? The professor was right; people such as I, who struggle to focus, should not go to college. But we usually do because our social position would be affected otherwise.

The boy. Why did JD send the boy? And why do I feel a connection between him and JD? There is a story in there. I'm glad I didn't write about this first, for there will be none better than the story I shall write now.

Sometimes I wish—oh God!—all the time I wish that JD were right! But I see no sign of God. If God created us, who created God?

> *Now I must write. I have never had trouble beginning, like some others I have read about. If I go insane with my passion, I shall have this story I am about to write now to show them how.*

The horse stopped by the tree a few yards from the church door. Little Peggy placed her boot on the top of her brother's instep, as she had been taught to do. With their hands clasped together, Johnny lowered her to the ground, yielding to her weight.

"Wouldn't it be easier if you got off first and then helped me off?" Peggy asked.

In a fatherly manner Johnny responded, "The horse might run off with you and hurt you, like JD's sister."

This was their first Sunday in church together. They both went forward for the call—she for the first time to confess her belief in Jesus Christ as savior, and he to join as a member. Johnny had filled out the cards like JD had done for him when he was baptized. There wasn't any preacher to greet them or perform a baptism; there was only Mr. Ferguson, but he warmly welcomed the siblings into the fold. Afterwards, Johnny and Peggy joined the other children for Sunday school in the choir loft, which was still taught by Mr. Ferguson.

In the ensuing months, they rode the horse to church on Sundays and the train to Herndon for school each day. Mr. Loveless, the train's conductor, took a shine to Johnny and taught him how to use the speed handle. Before long, Johnny was able to drive the train by himself, though Mr. Loveless never left his side.

CHAPTER 63

A Long Way to Go

Word came that JD and Katie were coming home the first of June. This had not been expected, for he had been busy preaching and studying in Oklahoma. But school was over and Katie had bore their first and only child, a daughter. They named her Susanne. She was skinny with golden curls and cherished by her father and mother.

JD had already made quite a name for himself, especially after he debated another clergyman of a different denomination. Everyone knew, by word from those in Washington who kept abreast of the denomination, that JD could have led a church of substantial membership if he wanted.

His arrival coincidentally coincided with a revival meeting that was to be led by an evangelist preacher—Katie's father, the Reverend Parman. There were no longer hard feelings between JD's folks and the reverend; without exception, he liked them all. However, he was holding his opinion of JD in reserve until he could hear him preach and see how well his daughter was faring.

With his new baby daughter curled up in his arms, JD preceded Katie across the foot log, glancing up at the railroad trestle as if he wanted to make sure there was no one crouched to jump as Marcus had done that night long ago. He knew there wouldn't be, but he never crossed the foot log without that memory coming to his mind.

The hill seemed steep to Katie as she held on to JD's free arm, thus accepting the help from his powerful body. Corn grew in checked rows up the hill as if taunting a summer thunderstorm to wash the dirt to the stream below.

Bonnie was beside herself with anticipation of her son's arrival. With a kiss and a smile, JD soothed his mother's joyous pain. Then he passed the baby to her outstretched arms saying, "Don't drop her," and "You can't keep her."

"I just might keep her," Bonnie teased.

JD then bent over to kiss Maw who shook her head in admiration to his finishing school, his ordination, his marriage, and for becoming a father.

"It's good to see you back, son," Paw said. "I'm glad you're finished."

JD and Katie glanced quickly at each other, but said nothing. Then they all took a seat at the big kitchen table. Katie and her mother-in-law engaged in small talk while Paw filled JD in on farm news. Looking at the food before him and the beloved faces around the table, JD simply enjoyed the sight.

"What are your plans?" Bonnie asked, not loud enough for Paw to hear, but Paw missed little. He knew something has been asked, so he leaned forward hoping to discern the question based on the answer.

JD wished to forego the question, but with a sigh he finally said, "An anonymous donor has given me a scholarship to study for my doctorate at Saint Andrews University in Scotland."

Maw laughed nervously and said something to the effect that his sense of humor was still intact after all these many years. Paw heard the answer but misinterpreted its meaning. He thought JD was aiming to study medicine.

"Well, it pays more than preaching," he said.

"No, Paw," JD corrected. "I'm going to study theology."

"JD, you're serious?" his mother asked.

"I'm afraid so."

"What have you been studying all this time?" Paw asked with some confusion.

"Theology," JD answered, "but I now have an opportunity to continue my studies."

Paw interrupted JD to tell him that he wasn't too happy about this. "You're sure going to be the most educated preacher we have ever had around here. I guess that's what you eventually intend to do, isn't it?"

"Yes sir," JD answered, but he had no urge to explain further.

Laying his knife and fork on opposite sides of the plate, JD said, "I didn't mean for this to come up during the first moments we were together, but now that it has, let me explain my intentions in full."

"Go ahead, son," Maw urged.

"There are those in the family, and I don't mean you all, who thought that I should go to law school. And there were others who thought I should dig in the dirt the rest of my life. Then, when I went off to college, the rest of you thought it would be wonderful if I could just finish four years.

"I consigned… I mean, Katie and I have *both* consigned our lives to the church; nothing will change that. We've done this for one reason: for the love of God. We've observed enough to know that there will be no great financial reward forthcoming. You all sent me to the well to drink, and Katie's folks did, too; now I wish to partake of it fully—perhaps too fully for you all?"

JD asked the question with his eyebrows raised to accentuate the irony. No one spoke a word, so he continued.

"The first church I had in Oklahoma was attended by no more than twenty-five people when I arrived. When I left, there was more than 150. Some came from as far as 50 miles away. Everywhere I went, the same thing happened, including the revival I led just before we came home. We are not sacrificing the good life; we have the good life.

"After you think it over, I expect you will be happy and pleased at our good fortune. And for heaven's sake, don't feel sorry for us."

"When will you go?" his mother asked, already feeling the pains of their parting.

"In September."

Quickly Katie added, "We'll have plenty of time to talk about this later. Let's get acquainted with what you have been doing."

But Bonnie and the rest didn't even hear her.

"Oh, that's a long way to go—Scotland," Bonnie stated with trepidation.

There was no denying it. "Yes, it is," JD said.

CHAPTER 64

You My Boy?

On Sunday night, the final night of the revival, Reverend Parman stood before the children seated in the front row intermittently flicking something around in his mouth while clearing his throat.

"Alright children," he said, "let's sing *This Little Light of Mine.*"

Wherever Reverend Parman went, he always had the children come early and sing. Hearing the singing made the people feel that the service had already started and they were late.

With eyes shut and his head cast at an angle as if looking to the sky, the reverend began to pray. "Almighty God, Thou art here, we know that. Let us likewise worship Thee in the spirit of Jesus, thy Son…"

His prayer was followed by more singing, which he led in a strong voice. At the end of the hymn, the reverend stood looking to the top of the ceiling as if looking for inspiration from God. Then he began to address those assembled.

"Brethren, we have had a wonderful meeting here. It does me so much good to see old faces. Think of that one who has gone on before us who is already feeling the glory and strength of the presence of God. Truly, I shall always have as a treasure of strength the memory of Benjamin Cowley. Friends, the old bones tire and the throat weakens. I don't know how much longer I shall be able to meet the heavy schedule forced upon me by my commitment to God and church. So tonight, this old man is going to sit and listen. There is one among us whom I should very much like to hear: my son-in-law. He and his wife—my beautiful baby girl, Katie—are here tonight, but they will be departing the country in September so he may study abroad. Therefore, I shall ask Joe Dayne to bring us the closing message. Would you not like to hear him?"

The crowd nodded affirmatively, and JD smiled as he stepped up to the pulpit. "Had I anticipated this, I might have had second thoughts about coming for a visit." Everyone laughed heartily. "However, the reverend's actions here tonight have merit considering the freewill offering has already been taken before I've spoken one word." Again the audience laughed, Reverend Parman most heartily.

"It is good to be home," JD continued. "As you know, I have been preaching in the Midwest. Yet having been reared in this church, I feel a sense of humility and inadequacy. The question that comes to mind is: am I worthy to speak from this pulpit?

"Katie and I shall spend the summer on my Paw's farm and depart for Scotland in late August. There I shall begin to study toward my Doctorate in Theology. If you think of us and pray for us—and I hope you will pray for us—think of us as the same two people you have known all these years. We shall leave as disciples, disciplined in the simple and sublime principles for which Christ lived and died; we shall return likewise. No school, no church—yea, no being—shall diminish the influence this church and its faithful people have had on us.

"I have no prepared message; yet a Christian should always be prepared to witness for Christ, even at the spur of the moment. He must, however, be careful to stay within the bounds of brevity and edification. So tonight, let me share a small moment of God's power, God's strength, and God's potential influence on us.

"The field next to Paw's house is planted in corn; the stalks vibrantly wave in the breeze. They are nourished by the soil much like our bodies are nourished by the food we eat. The corn is set upon its course of growth from that first day when the dead kernels are placed into the soil and covered with earth. It is not the end, but the beginning. Slowly, a leaf of rich green pokes through. Green, we are told, because of the rays of the sun; that's hard to believe. How can the sun from its lofty perch affect the corn? But we know it is true. Who has not seen the ground beneath a canvas or a board where it has lain on the grass for days? The grass beneath is white. There is no sign of the rich green color. The rays of the sun were blotted out, and the grass is deficient.

"The man who stands outside the church similarly grows, but the spirit of Christ is unable to reach him, and he withers spiritually—just like the grass that is unable to take in the rays of the sun.

"So tonight, my friends, I say to you: do not stand in the shade. Come into the church and let the spirit of Christ permeate your souls, and your growth shall receive the sustenance that Christ spoke of when he said, 'Man shall not live by bread alone, but by every word that proceedeth out of the mouth of God.' The corn needs the spirit of the sun, and man needs the spirit of Christ."

Afterwards, JD and Katie stood in the narthex under the dim, frail light and shook hands with the people as they left. Occasionally they would receive a hug. Reverend Parman was overjoyed by the strength in number of those who came to see his son-in-law. The sparse gatherings of past years seemed like a bad dream from which he was just awakening; tonight, the church had been full. He sucked in a deep breath of happiness as if the joy was in the very air and all he needed to do was inhale.

Johnny and his sister, Peggy, hung back and were the last to congratulate JD.

"Hi Johnny," JD said affectionately as he pulled Peggy in for a hug. "I saw you sitting in the back there. How's your mother?"

Johnny heaved a sigh, which JD recognized as apprehension.

"Wait for me," JD said, "and we'll walk home together."

Johnny led the horse with his sister and Katie sitting astride on a blanket.

JD asked, "How are you getting along with Billie?"

"She's real nice," Johnny answered. "Treats Momma nice, too".

"I think she's a very nice woman," JD confirmed. "You know, she doesn't believe; yet she doesn't resent those of us who do."

"I think she would like to see you. Will you come up sometime?"

"Probably," JD answered without commitment.

Suddenly JD asked Johnny, "You love me?"

Looking up smiling, Johnny answered, "Yes, I do."

"You sure you're my boy?" JD asked teasingly.

Johnny's head nodded up and down in quick succession.

Up ahead the road forked in front of them, and they both took the left branch. It was a familiar route. Had they walked straight ahead, they would have walked right into a house. But the left fork bent around in a U, passing under the big tree where the schoolteacher hung himself right in front of Mr. Ferguson's house.

As they walked, the sun began to set and a cool breeze from Oak Run began to blow. JD defied the darkness by standing erect with his thumbs stuck in the pockets of his vest, drawing the sides of his coat back like tiebacks on drapes. He suddenly stopped walking and looked down over the railroad bank toward the Cowley house and said, "He was the only one who knew."

"Didn't no one else love you?" Johnny asked.

JD pursed his lips. "They all loved me, but he was the only one who thought I'd be a preacher. Even I never figured it out."

When they got to the bridge where they would part ways, Johnny said to JD, "Let's hear you whistle like that whippoorwill again."

The big and aging poplar was in complete darkness now as the sun had slipped beneath the horizon like a child on a cold winter night lowering his head under the covers. JD helped Katie down and threw Johnny astride the horse in front of his sister. Johnny pulled Peggy's hands around his waist in a movement that spoke of urgency, yet he was gentle with her. He had been taught as much, but it was his heart that prevailed. Then he looked away and galloped off toward the house where Billie and Babe lived.

Billie must have been watching out the window because she was there to meet Johnny when he rode the horse into the barn, though she tried to appear casual.

"He says he'll probably come up."

"What do you mean he'll probably come up?" Billie asked.

"I don't know," Johnny answered honestly. "Probably means he'll come up sometime, I guess."

She watched as Johnny led the horse into the stall and removed the bridle and blanket. He hadn't used the saddle to go to church.

"You love me?" Billie asked.

"Yes, ma'am," Johnny answered.

"You my boy?" she asked teasingly.

"I guess," he answered.

"What do you mean?"

Johnny said nothing, so Billie provided one. "You mean you love me, but not as much as you love JD."

She'd been drinking; he could tell by the way she grasped the side of the stall to maintain her balance.

"I can talk to you like I can to JD and nobody else, but I believe what JD says. You and I like JD, but I don't know if JD and I think like you."

Johnny had given her an honest answer, and Billie was visibly impressed, though she didn't really understand what he meant. Johnny continued with more confidence than before. "You are against us."

Now Billie was taken aback. "Johnny, I believe I could become very angry with you. What do you mean by that?"

"JD and I are for Christ, and you are not."

"What has that got to do with anything?"

"JD says anybody that is not for Christ is against him."

The tears came cascading down Billie's cheeks without warning. "Why do you say a mean thing like that? I have the same right to my beliefs as you all."

"Mrs. Lunsford," Johnny said respectfully, "some people believe, and some don't. Then there's others who are spectators; they watch the other two battle. The spectator watches and searches for the meaning of life and death and, before long, she's focusing on death 'til the very reflection of death leads her into the chasm of self-destruction. She despises death, but can't resolve the mystery. In the end, death doesn't even have to do its work because the spectator does it for him."

Intrigued, Billie asked, "Where did you hear that?"

"JD says that," Johnny replied unequivocally and quickly. "Someday the spectator *must* join one side or the other. The longer you wait to join the believers, the better chance the devil has to get his due!"

> *Dear Diary,*
>
> *Tonight I feel a warm and mellow glow from the drink, and I feel a joy—pleasant and firm—in anticipation of my affair tonight with my passion. It all seems worth it—not to indulge myself, but to write the truth as I see it and have no fear of plagiarism. How could a coincidence like this happen? No two people are that much alike. That little intermediary gave me the story. It's almost as if I were talking to JD.*
>
> *I wonder what he tells JD about me? I can see how such thoughts might consume someone else, but not me. If there is a God, I shall find out. There must be something. They are right though; death is bleak.*
>
> *Enough of that! I shall write like cantering into the wind—no requirement of five pages a night; I'll write just what I feel.*

CHAPTER 65

Apprehension and Fear

Billie calmly dressed herself and her baby boy for a trip into Vienna. She did so without knowing that Johnny had taken the train there earlier on an errand for his mother who in need of kerosene had nagged him until his hidden fear took a backseat to duty. By taking the train, Johnny had accepted a chance meeting with a boy who, being considerably larger and older, convinced Johnny that they were of equal size and age and should fight to see who was the better man.

Billie saw the bully knock Johnny to the ground with a push. It would have been a quick defeat, except Johnny wouldn't fight back, by the influence of Christ. The bully, having no one to scuffle with, went in search of another victim.

Billie and her son rode home together on the train with Johnny.

"You were afraid of him and some of the other boys, weren't you?" Billie asked.

"Yes ma'am," Johnny replied.

"Fear in a small boy need not be malignant and debilitating unless a spirit remains submerged within," Billie said. "There is no such thing as bravery or courage—neither exist. What we are actually observing is fearlessness—that is, without fear. We all, at one time or another, experience fear just as we experience having a dirty face. We can only rid ourselves of the dirt by washing."

Johnny listened attentively as Billie continued to talk.

"Apprehension and fear are brothers; there is fear of the bully and apprehension of the future. Remember, that boy was much larger than you, and older—nine months makes a big difference, especially when you are small for your age. You've been eating popcorn while he's been eating meat!"

Johnny hung his head, as if embarrassed.

"What does JD say to you about being afraid?" Billie asked.

"I never told him."

"Why not?"

"'Cause I just can't. He wasn't never 'fraid of nothing."

With eyebrows raised, Billie commented, "Oh, so you can talk to me, but not to JD!"

"Yes, ma'am, at least 'bout that."

"Johnny, you know of course that JD and I have been friends for a long time, do you not?" He nodded his head affirmatively. "Then there is no reason why all three of us cannot be good friends. Is there?"

Johnny wiggled in his seat in an attempt to get his rear-end against the back. Instead of answering her question, he asked one of his own. "Why does JD ask me if I'm his boy?"

Billie, of course, had asked the same thing of him, but Johnny didn't inquire about her reasoning for asking the question. "He likes you," she answered, "and wants to make sure that you feel the same way about him."

> *Dear Diary,*
> *Tonight I have reread what I wrote. Why do I doubt it? It's good, and I know it's good. Anyway, it's me, and that's what I want. The whole story stares me in the face. I could write it all tonight if I had the time; yet, I must not rush. Each day I must have a thinking period. It's better to think more than I write.*

Oh, tonight the tears came to my eyes when I thought about his death—just as if it had happened. Sometimes it takes me away like the wind takes a leaf. I must watch my step; to be blown is one thing, but to be consumed is another. It is my life. I know that. I've found my niche, and nothing can ever change that. Though I may stumble over disappointments, and death to my loved ones always looms, I shall maintain my perch at all costs.

CHAPTER 66

Birth of Fall

JD stood in the pulpit beside the lectern, one thumb stuck in his vest pocket and the other moving in cadence with each booming word he spoke.

"This will be the last time Katie and I shall be with you for some time. The summer has been so short, the corn is laid by and the wood is cut for winter. But who among us can guarantee that winter will come? We've seen it lo these many years, and the annals of science assert its coming. Yes, we stack the wood by the stove, the hay in the barn, and the grain in its bin. Why? Why do we prepare? Because we know that there will be a time when the warm spirit of the sun will merely glance at the earth, and the frigid air will blow from the north. Then the trees and the field shall lay bare. The sap in the trees shall know their time and seep to the roots to escape the cold freeze and chill. And the sow shall gather the leaves to her pen; likewise, the bird shall depart for the southlands. Down through the ages man has seen these things come to pass time and time again.

"These things—all these things—are done in slow, methodical steps, without haste, but done deliberately, without question or doubt. Nor are these things done begrudgingly, for the command goes forth from the spirit of God.

"And now picture three crosses on a hill: the cross of Jesus between the two despised. But we shall not sorrow, for the glory of man beckons us to come in truth and purpose and joy. The Sundays have seemed long when only a few have attended. Yet, if Christ can suffer the cross under the humiliation of the scoffers, then you can maintain this church with or without a preacher. The day will come when a new generation is born of this community, and it will thrive because of those years you kept the fire burning. The spirit of Jesus shall warm their hearts then as he does now. The spirit of Jesus Christ our Lord signals us to come in faith and purpose, not grudgingly nor doubting his word, but knowing we are fulfilling man's destiny—fulfilling God's command that good and love in man shall prevail."

While JD preached, Billie and Babe made their way to the golf course to play a round with another couple. Billie hooked the ball on each of the first nine holes, even when she used her nine-iron. Instead of administering a high, floating drive, the ball went low, hooking and hitting the green before bounding over it. Babe cursed under his breath.

"Why don't you turn your left hand over?"

"I tried that," Billie answered. "I had it over so far that the back of my hand was facing the sky."

"No, that's your right hand," Babe coached.

"Oh," she lamented.

The tenth tee was a par four with a sharp dogleg to the left that overlooked a lake. The two men teed off first. Babe's ball rolled well beyond the corner of the dogleg. Then the ladies stepped down the hill to tee off. Billie swung and hit a screaming hook into the lake.

Frustrated, she turned to Babe and said, "I had my hand over!"

"Okay, okay. I know what you're doing wrong," Babe said, ever the coach. "You're flopping your elbow and swinging your shoulders flat. Go back to your hand facing the target, and be sure to keep your elbow in tight. We want to win this, you know."

On the eleventh hole, they were forced to wait for the foursome in front to move on. The other woman took this time to remark about the beauty of the fall—something about the leaves in color, like someone had wildly cast buckets of yellow, green, and red paint into the air. She also commented on the weather—warm, yet, cool enough to wear a sweater.

"It's the death of summer," Billie commented mystifyingly.

"How can you compare the beauty of this time of year with death?" the woman asked.

"That's the author coming out of me," Billie said wistfully.

"Naw," Babe corrected, "she heard that line from our preacher friend."

Ignoring him, Billie recited, "Then one day I woke to a cold wind with a northern head and geese flying south and all. T'was then I knew for sure that summer was dead and t'was the birth of fall."

"I like it," the woman acknowledged. "Did you just make that up?"

"No," Billie answered. "Someone else wrote that."

CHAPTER 67

Fauquier

Before they left the clubhouse, one of the men said to Billie, "I don't suppose you can all wait for the steeplechase to start."

"Oh, yes," Billie agreed. "We feel Fauquier is at his best this year. Johnny is too young to ride in the races, but he surely spoils that horse!"

"I understand that Fauquier is the best chaser you've ever had, is he not? He's certainly the most talked about."

Billie beamed with pride.

It was late afternoon with just a couple hours of light left when Babe pulled the car into the yard. Glancing toward the run, they saw Peggy racing toward the house.

"Fauquier! Fauquier!" she screamed. "Fauquier!"

Jumping out of the car and running to her, Billie demanded, "What about Fauquier?"

Tears were streaming down Peggy's face. "Fauquier… Fauquier is stuck in the mud, and Johnny and Mr. Dayne can't get him out."

"Get in the car," Billie ordered. Babe raced the car down the dusty lane toward the run.

"What happened?" Billie demanded.

"Johnny and Mr. Dayne just found him stuck in the mud," Peggy cried. "That's all I know."

"But how did he get out of the field?" Billie asked suspiciously. Peggy had no answer to the obvious question. The field, being enclosed by a board fence, had only one possible means of escape: the gate. Fauquier could not open the gate, so someone must have not closed properly it after passing through.

Two hundred feet from the run, Babe stopped the car, and they all raced around the swamp to the railroad track and then down toward the bridge. Billie and Babe had both assumed that the Mr. Dayne Peggy spoke of was JD. Thus, when they saw Marcus and Johnny feverishly sawing at the base of a giant gray sycamore tree, the crest of Billie's frustration exploded forth from her mouth. Amid her ranting, she turned to Peggy and yelled, "Go get JD!"

"Why?" Babe asked.

"Because he'll think of something," she responded without any thought as to how her statement might make Babe feel. He turned toward the sycamore tree and relieved the physically expired Marcus on his end of the saw.

Though Marcus had been the one to find Fauquier, he was also the one responsible for the situation. With a violent thirst for beer or whiskey to quell his hangover, he had headed to the Lunsford home to look for alcohol. He got sidetracked from his original mission when he decided to chase the horses in the field. Fauquier had taken off across the stream where the shallow water ran in ripples, but then he headed upstream in an attempt to skirt the deeper waters. It was there that he became bogged down in the silt and mud, and it was then that Marcus had gone straight away to the house to get help.

Johnny had tried to coax Fauquier free by grabbing the part of his mane that hung over his face. The struggle with the tyrannical mud sapped Fauquier's strength and lowered him deeper into the muck. Thus, he stood mired within six inches of his belly and only ten feet away from six feet of water.

Johnny and Marcus had already retrieved from the barn a pulley, rope, and the harness used to pull hay up into the hayloft. They placed the harness under the horse's belly, as if he were a pile of hay. Then they strung the rope from the harness through the pulley, which was tied to a tree on the other side of the stream and some ten feet up in the air, thence back across the stream to the top of the sycamore, which Marcus and Johnny were now attempting to saw down.

The country club bourbon was burning up Babe's throat with each thrust of the saw. "Who thought of this crazy idea?" he demanded.

It was Johnny, but he was reluctant to claim credit. "We just have a little further to go," he said.

Billie had waded into the water beside her horse. As only a woman would do at a time like this, she kissed Fauquier and spoke to him like a baby, telling him that everything would be all right. About this time, JD and Katie appeared on the bridge. Katie clasped his side in fear that the tree would fall in the wrong direction. Of course, anyone with any experience would know that a tree falls the way the notch is cut. Suddenly, a creaking signal drew all eyes except Johnny's to the tree. His were glued on Fauquier.

First the tree moved slowly, merely tightening the slack on the rope, but then its weight gave way to gravity, and the giant sycamore boomed upon the earth, its limbs creating a wave of swampy mud. Fauquier was jerked half up and half sideways across the stream, his hoofs just missing the opposing bank by inches. Then the centrifugal force swung him past the pulley in the tree, and the return motion propelled him back over the water, whereupon Johnny pulled a secondary rope releasing the harness and dispensing the horse like a bundle of hay into six feet of water.

Fauquier floated downstream toward the shallow ripples where he was able to catch his footing. He stood there perplexed as he shook the water from his hide. Then he trotted back toward the field as if he had done nothing more than take a drink of water from the stream.

Johnny had seen his plan work. But now, sitting on the stump completely deserted by the strength and courage that had propelled the saw, he struggled to keep back the tears. Billie raced to him, fell to her knees, threw her arms around him, and buried her head in his chest.

"Oh, I love you; I love you," she cried in both tone and tears.

Moments later she embraced Katie and JD as if she had not seen them for years. Babe observed it all as if questioning his purpose.

CHAPTER 68

Poor

Dear Diary,

I've never been poor, except when I wanted to be. We always had everything, and I was always able to talk Daddy into anything when I wanted it badly enough. But I would be poor sometimes just because I wanted to be. Like when I was little and at the Browns' house at dinnertime. I could have gone home to eat a nice meal (Momma didn't even have to cook it because she always had someone to cook it for her), but I would just stay and eat with JD, Will, and Little Bonnie.

Most of the time, they would just serve boiled potatoes and side meat, as Maw called it. Others called it fatback. Rednecks would joke that it was sowbelly. I would take my fork and push down on the potatoes until they were flat so you could rake the grease over them as if it were gravy. Sometimes Maw would take all the grease in the pan, add a little flour to it and maybe something else, and make a white gravy. We all liked the white gravy better than just plain grease.

The corn bread cakes I liked very much, but only at certain times with certain foods. I felt the same way about the corn pone, which was baked somewhat like a rectangular pound cake and was only good with black-eyed peas and fish when the herring were running in April.

I don't really remember whether I wanted to be poor or whether I just wanted to be with the Browns more than I wanted to be with my own family. Either way, I just think of all the things I never would have eaten if I hadn't wanted to be poor: squirrels, rabbits, quail, and chitterlings. And polk is so much better in the spring than spinach.

I have so much money now that I will never be able to spend it, but it really means nothing to me. What I know I have to have is my horse; I still must have my horse. I feel so sorry for those who cannot ride off the road and take a short cut through the countryside. I can go to Bonnie's house in less than a mile by horseback, but it's eight miles if I go by car.

When I was a little girl, my horse used the same stall in the Browns' barn until the day the barn burned down. Paw had built what he called a colt shed on the end of his barn, but even when they didn't have enough room in the barn, nobody ever put a horse in my stall. It was my stall.

Now I have found my niche. Perhaps I have written that a hundred times in my diary. Everyday I dream of what I shall write. Then I write it, and then I read it, and then I read it again. It's basically daydreaming about my daydreams.

I have said this before, but I'll say it again. My story has been with me for years, but it's bigger than my ability. I shall finish it though, clamp it, put glue on the back, and place a cover around it. I shall do this several times, and then I will leave several copies to my children for their children and their children's children. If just one of them reads it, it will be worthwhile.

This story has become so real to me. It's as if the characters really existed, and in a way, I guess they have. They're as real to me as life itself. I think of them as having been alive at one time, though some are now deceased. I would never try or even intimate that I was playing God and that my characters were as human as ordinary beings. But to me, they are.

This is all so real and emotional to me. I wonder if I am sentimental to a fault? Babe always tells me, "I'll read it. But I'm waiting until you finish it. Then I'll read it." I wonder if he will.

CHAPTER 69

War

The Great Depression had hardly abated before the rumbles of war could be heard in Europe. The Chinese began scattering ahead of the Japanese like defenseless chickens from a weasel. It all seemed like the development of another thunderhead of devastation, the reopening of a wound not yet healed.

Babe was the first to enlist, even though he was a father. Like so many southerners, his military training in college, along with the thought of a commission and adventure, prevailed. He acted like a young boy trekking off to hunt in the woods.

Babe and Billie's parting was neither a fracturing nor a reinforcement of their marriage vows. Instead, she seemed to accept his decision as the patriotic thing for him to do. However, she made it abundantly clear that she did not think much of going with him to Europe with three children in tow—Bobby, the eldest at age six, and the two younger girls.

The war that eighteen-year-old Johnny assumed would take those of the older set was also to take him. He accepted the government's offer to be paid to shoot all the bullets he could. Johnny's departure made Billie cry more than Babe's. One might assume that she needed Johnny more. He did, after all, feed and care for the horses.

Six months after Johnny's induction into the Army, he came home on furlough before he was to be shipped to Europe. Billie knew what she wanted to say to him, but she had trouble finding the words. She wanted to tell Johnny to be brave, but when she tried to put it delicately, she felt as if she were saying, "Don't be afraid; don't be a coward."

Coward. She couldn't forget the word, though she never actually said it.

Marcus, on the other hand, encouraged Johnny by telling him a World War I story about the beleaguered French troops' plan to break a stalemate and attack the Germans. At the rallying point, General Foch had pulled himself up out of the trench and with raised and clinched fist commanded, "Attaque! Attaque!" According to Marcus, had the French not attacked that day, the Germans were prepared to wipe them out with artillery. One man had been bold enough to lead them out of the deathtrap.

Johnny made two parting requests. First, he asked Billie to teach his mother to read and write. Second, he asked Marcus not to drink anymore. Marcus declared with much sincerity that he was never going to take another drop.

It had taken JD just two years to obtain his Doctoral Degree in Theology from St. Andrews in Scotland. He had hoped to be known as Dr. JD, but Katie demanded otherwise. Thus, his full and complete name of Joseph Emory Beauchamp Dayne was shortened to Dr. J. Emory Beauchamp Dayne. His first assignment was to shepherd a flock of almost 400 in Tacoma, Washington. But after the attack on Pearl Harbor in 1941 and the United States' official entry into the war, JD felt called to return to Europe as an Army Chaplain. He placed Katie and his baby daughter on the farm with his mother so they could all look after one another while he went off to serve.

Three years later, Babe could be found serving with the Air Corps, Johnny the infantry encamped just outside Coventry, and JD as an Army Chaplain near Norwich. All three were in England.

Without notification, JD stepped into the darkened Quonset hut, and there on the right stood a perplexed soldier. A faint smile soon rippled across his face. As they both reached to shake hands, JD instinctively reached for the thumb, but Johnny's hand moved higher, and with a quick flick of his wrist he was able to grab JD's thumb instead. They both laughed.

"How do you do it?" JD asked.

"Can't tell you that Doc. Then you'd best me all the time."

As Johnny introduced JD to the other soldiers, his eyes took in the field packs, the trench knives, and the bayonets. It reminded him of hog killing, though the rifles were nothing like the shotguns or the 22s he knew.

Back outside, Johnny noticed that JD had arrived by vehicle. "They gave you a Jeep?" he asked.

"Can you believe it? I had to get in the U.S. Army to get a car. Funny, this driving on the left-hand side of the road came easier than I thought," JD commented. "You know your way 'round town?"

"In the daytime, yeah," Johnny answered, "but you can't see anything at night in the blackout."

"How do you like the Army?" JD asked as they walked around the camp.

"Some of it's all right, but I don't like all the orders and the waiting. Do you know where we're going to invade?"

"Oh, no. I wouldn't be privy to something like that."

"What do you mean privy? I thought that was an outhouse."

JD laughed. "I guess it is. What I meant was that I would not have access to that information. Very few people would."

"Do you think you'll be going out on the first wave?"

"I don't think so," JD answered. "I should, but I don't think they'll let me. How do you feel about it?"

"I figure I'm going to get it. You don't have much chance going all the way to Germany without getting hit. I guess it's just a matter of how bad I'll get shot up. I worry more about Momma and Peggy than I do about me. You know?"

JD nodded. "It's moments like this when a man in my position wants so badly to say the right thing. Yet, in all such moments, the only hope is God. He's the only answer. This war is a mess—started by a couple of raving maniacs. How could so many people allow them to create a mess like this? If we believe that Thomas put his hand in Jesus's side, then we have nothing to fear."

There was a moment of silence while the two men pondered this thought. Then Johnny spoke. "Mrs. Lunsford used to ask me if I was her boy. What did she mean?'

"I used to ask you that, too."

"Well, what did *you* mean?"

"It's a way of affiliating the spirits of two people. Do you understand?"

"No."

JD sighed. "I don't know what Mrs. Lunsford meant when she asked you, but I know what I meant. Remember my teaching you 'bout Jesus asking Peter three times if he loved him?" Johnny nodded at the memory. "Then you remember that Jesus told Peter to feed his sheep." Johnny nodded again.

"When you were a small boy and I asked you if you were my boy, I didn't think much about what I was asking. But now I believe that I meant this: if you love me, be a Christian."

Johnny thought for a moment before speaking. "Why couldn't you ever make her believe?

JD gave a nervous laugh. "Mrs. Lunsford and I were around each other a lot as kids, and much of the time we were together was spent talking 'bout God and Jesus and the spirit of people. She, as well as many, just doesn't accept Jesus as being anything other than a prophet. Once we equivocate on that, we have no belief. Mrs. Lunsford and I are friends. However, I believe Thomas put his hand in Jesus's side. Even if that were not in the Bible, I now know by experience that the word of Christ is the miracle.

"Besides, I tried and tried to convince her. Do you know, she used to ride her horse up and down every row of corn back home arguing with me, but she wouldn't give herself over. I've always had the feeling that she wanted to believe, but she required a sign. So many want to see a sign," JD said, shaking his head.

"Did you love her when you were young?" Johnny asked.

JD laughed. "Usually you don't fall for the girl next door. We were more like brother and sister. Yet, on the other hand, we had a lot in common. She liked to talk about storytelling and writing, and I did, too—though I probably didn't realize it at the time."

Looking off into the distance, JD said, "There was this day where we were butchering hogs when the Cowley boys came by to start some trouble. They started their little routine with me, but when they saw Billie ride up, they went over and started on her. One grabbed her by the boot, and she started fighting them off with her crop. I thought about going to her aid, but I didn't want to offend Mr. Cowley by getting involved in a fight with his grandsons. But you see, I failed her! I should have thought about justice. Fair play. Billie could have become dangerously entangled with the horse or fallen to the ground. I left her to go it alone. Yet because of her spirit, she did prevail without any help from me. But never a day goes by that I don't wish I could go back and correct that omission."

Turning to face Johnny, JD said, "If such an occasion arises before you, just do the right thing. Your spirit and heart are loaded to see the right thing; you just need to act on it! Billie never threw it up to me, but you can bet your bottom dollar she's never forgotten my disregard."

JD and Johnny sat for a rest along the bank of the park, it being built like a dugout football field where the British sailors, known as Limeys, were dressed in white and playing cricket. The slow monotony of the game was as morbid as the day was damp and cloudy. The benches relieved their feet of the weight, but JD speculated on the grief of the future. From his perspective, there was no future—the ages loomed in the present.

"God is in our presence—the God man, the God of Christ. Do not think that you are fighting another man—a German; think that you are fighting a Nazi, as if a wild animal were attacking you. For you have not asked to be put in this position, you were not given a choice. If you meet a Nazi face-to-face, shoot him before he shoots you. Forget the fear, forget the fact that you can't shoot the Army rifle because it kicks too much and makes you pull off target. Don't even let yourself think about these things. Just do it, and hope you get him first."

Johnny took JD's words to heart.

"Mr. Lunsford is a headquarters colonel. I'm a fat chaplain. Mrs. Lunsford, my wife, your mother and sister, and many more are back home—safe. The whole world is depending on young men like you. *You* are the man of the hour."

JD didn't see Johnny again after that. He saw Babe a couple of times before the invasion—once with a little brunette in a blue coat with a white collar. She was hanging onto his arm as if she were the real Mrs. Lunsford. Babe loved his wife—perhaps so much he couldn't stand to be alone. JD didn't like it, though he didn't say so. Babe might just as well have cheated on JD's sister.

Before the dawn of regal glory, there goes the day of doom when any man who tests it will find his innards knot till he escapes the first moments of the story when guns go pounding and mines go "boom." Johnny's outfit, like so many others, was moved to the southern coast of England.

CHAPTER 70

Shell-Shocked

Johnny Abel, having dozed off in a hospital in southern England, was awakened by the touch of a soft hand and a voice that spoke gently in an English accent.

"I need to get back," Johnny said to her. Shell-shocked, he was grateful for her presence. She let him ramble on while she checked his vital signs.

"For days we sat stuffed in a small area with a high fence, just like the windbreak fence—solid, upright boards. They looked like the fence partly around the barnyard where JD lived. Men were milling around like cows waiting to be led out to pasture, and every now and then a young bull sharpened his horns. Nobody seemed to know where we were going, even the high ranking ones like Lieutenant Colonel. They seemed as curious as we were. This went on for several days. As a matter of fact, the chow lines were so long, 'bout all you had time to do was wash, go to the latrine, and stand in the chow line.

"Then early one morning we're rousted out for a fine meal, which reminded me of the times when JD shipped the hogs. They would feed the hogs so they would weigh more when they got to the slaughterhouse in Baltimore. I ate the fine meal. I had learned by now to like Army coffee, though I had never drunk it at home. You had to be careful of a canteen cup of coffee, 'cause the little catch on the handle would slip up and the cup would dump just like a dump truck while you held the handle. I tried to think of what I'd done to get there. Seemed like maybe I'd been born to work and be fattened up like the hogs so I could finally be butchered.

"Then it occurred to me that if I had known this was going to happen, I would have goofed off a little more at the end of those corn rows. And now I wish I'd shot that turkey gobbler right in the middle of summer—that was after I met JD.

"There was this ole guy in our outfit named Kato. Imagine the looks of a convict who wanted to break out of prison—that'd be Kato. I think Kato felt like a hog, too. He acted like he was penned up. Kato had been around a lot. He was old; I'd say 'bout 32 or 33. And if he was still happy with his wife, I don't believe he trusted her, or he didn't like her. One or the other.

"They said it was a long way across the English Channel, but it couldn't be that far or that woman couldn't have swum it. I wasn't worrying too much 'bout that. If she could swim it, I figured we could get across in the landing craft. It seemed definite—not like the other day when we started across and turned back. Course, I still didn't know where we were going. Maybe we weren't even going to France.

"We waited for what seemed like hours before leaving the shore. Right away the water spanked the sides and bottom of the boat, but we couldn't see over the sides, even though the waves were crashing on our helmets. I tasted the saltwater on my lips and knew I shouldn't swallow any of it.

"God, the waves pushed me right up in the air, and then they let me fall—like riding an elevator down. Then we went right back up and right back down again. This went on and on until one soldier turned to his side, and I thought he was going lose it in his gas mask. I turned quick, 'cause I didn't want to see that. But just as he throws up, there's another one. So, all those fine breakfasts are lying right there on the floor of the boat. What's the point of feeding a prisoner just 'fore he's gonna be electrocuted? What good's it gonna do him if he's gonna be dead in two minutes?

"Just when it looked like I'd be the only one not getting sick, I felt this dizzy whirl in my head, and I commenced to look around for a place to vomit, but I didn't have time. The gushing mess erupted from my innards and heaved out my mouth—even out my nostrils—burning my throat and nose like I was drowning. I started spitting water out of my mouth and nose time and time again, for hours. And I was getting weaker and weaker. The damn stuff was like a piece of spaghetti that clings to the bottom of the pan, except this was coming from my mouth and clinging to the bottom of the boat. I tried to spit it out, but it wouldn't come out. And I tried to puke, but there was nothing coming up. And I'm bent over till my head's practically in it.

"The hogs would get sick on the truck to Baltimore after eating their last supper just so they would weigh more. The hogs' last supper was the same thing as our last breakfast. We were just like those hogs. I used to think how they probably wished they could die before they got to the slaughterhouse where they were hit in the head with a sledgehammer. Oh, God, I wish I could die. That's all I could think. Oh, God, I wish I would die.

"The guns were booming and the dirigibles were hanging in the sky while the cliffs bobbed up and down, in and out of sight. They were probably filled with Germans ready to flush up like a covey of quail and mow us down as soon as we touched the shore. God, I wish they would shoot right now, shoot me now and get it over with!

"Then someone yelled to unload. I looked up and saw Kato—his arm was ripped and his mouth was carved into a contemptible sneer. I'm half kicked to my staggering feet and head toward the ramp, which is sinking into the water maybe ten feet deep. And damn, I can't swim with all this stuff on me! Hell, I don't know how to swim anyway. Kato didn't touch me, but he looked me so close in the eye that I could feel his breath on my face, and he said, 'So long sucker. This is as far as I'm going.'

"I stepped into the water and realized, my God, I'm the first one! I knew I had been in the back of the boat, so how in the world did I get up front to get off first? I knew darn well I would be going down ten or twelve feet into the water. You could see that it was that deep. But, what the hell? I knew I was in the slaughterhouse and wasn't going to get out. I sank to my armpits when I was shocked to feel the sand under my feet. I half fell, half waded to shore. And still, I ain't got hit! They're all behind me yelling, but I'm helping myself first. They're just as confused. They were expecting someone to fire on them by now, I guess.

"I think to myself, if I can just make off the beach to that incline, I'll dig in so deep they'll have to get a well digger to get me out. But then, in what seemed like an eternal moment, it hits me like violent stinging bees or the sickle bar on the mowing machine or like the horses running wild. Damn it! Why did I stand in front of the sickle bar to drag the hay off? Something like JD's sister—the horses were running wild, but I wasn't moving.

"I started to crawl, still trying to make the incline where I'd be safe. But my left eye's gone. Gone! It's gone! The sand burns the bone in my thigh, and it stings and burns like fire. But my eye is gone. Least I'm lying flat on my stomach now and won't be a target. I can't get up 'cause I know my guts are going to fall right down into my shorts. The guys are all just lying there getting hit and hit like rabbits in a bed.

"And then, in my mind, I see ole' Marcus with his fist raised. How in the devil I got to my feet I don't know, but my right fist goes up in the air as hard as a rock, and I hear myself screaming, 'Attaque! Attaque!'

"I didn't even look back at them because I seemed to know that they would get up and go. I'm pushing toward the incline, using the gun for a cane, the barrel sticking hard under my armpit. How long? I don't know. But as each man passes me by, I know from the way they shake their heads that I'm as good as dead. But my soul ain't gone 'cause I can see 'em.

"My stomach is bare and bloody; yet the cut seems to be healing. So I sit, and they pass by me leaning against my incline. There's sympathy and revulsion on their faces 'cause I stink. No dirty, filthy buzzard had better try to eat me, I thought. I'm nothing more than a dead horse—too big to bury. But I don't want to be buried. And I don't want to be burned. And God, I hate the water! I'll never drink another drop. My dead soul won't need water anyway.

"Then Whitey, my buddy, with tears in his eyes, with blond hair and the face of a prince, softly touches the cut on my stomach. I could see he thought I was dead, but then he realized I wasn't. He stared into my face, and said in a soft firm cry, 'My God, my God.'

"For a moment, I thought he thought I was Jesus! Ain't that crazy?"

CHAPTER 71

Patch

The English countryside loomed as agile and productive as the old ladies silently peddling and dismounting their bicycles that were yet in motion, gracefully defying age. As the trucks made their way into town, Johnny took in the high and steep hills, the green grass in the winter, hedges grown down throughout the ages, sheep grazing, and a Limey wearing a tweed suit coat and boots shoveling manure in the barnyard. Parking the trucks in the town square, the riders made their way to the pub.

"Come on, Patch" Horner said, "let's go to the Red Cross Club."

Everyone now called Johnny "Patch" on account of the eye patch he wore to cover the hole where his left eye had been torn from its socket. He had been carried from the beach, his thigh slashed and the stomach muscles torn like a wet paper bag about to deposit its contents. Yet, all this had healed except for the eye, which of course never would.

"I heard Colonel Lunsford was at the pub last night," Johnny stated, "and I want to see if I can find him"

"What the hell you want to find him for? You think he's gonna talk to a private?"

Babe was there, leaning over a table that was so small it hardly separated him from the woman. Her thick blond hair streamed down to her shoulders, perfectly framing her full red lips and her bitchy eyes with thinly penciled brows. So that's what a prostitute looks like, Johnny thought. Just as he was about to turn and leave to save Babe from humiliation, Babe saw him and jumped to his feet.

"Johnny boy!" Babe's paw rose right up out of a clutch with the blond. "You boys come on and sit down with us."

Trying to escape, Johnny said, "It's none of my business."

"Come on, relax," Babe said, pulling Johnny to the table. "We're fighting a war buddy."

Johnny's friend, eager to get to the Red Cross Club, declined a seat. "I gotta be leaving, Patch."

But Babe was not willing to take no for an answer. "Just a minute. You boys gotta have a cup of tea or something. These folks'll think you're mad otherwise."

The folks consisted of a handful of characters. One was casting darts—a game Babe had yet to fathom—while the ashes from his cigarette dropped haphazardly and smoke curled around his face. Several Limeys sat nearby drinking, oblivious to the Yank's conversation. They were, however, aware of Babe. They all knew him.

Then there was the blond who, incidentally, wasn't a prostitute. She was the mother of a six-year-old boy whose husband was in Asia. When they first met, Babe had been dancing with another woman when Tillie cut in. This was quite common in the city of Norwich where the girls outnumbered the men. Later that night, Babe had backed her up to a wall and, in a sudden frenzy, kissed her. She had trembled and moaned, which made him wonder if she was going into a fit, but he was too overwhelmed by the sudden heat to stop. Before he was able to lick his chops she had pushed him back, begging to be let go. He did, and to his own surprise, she whispered, "I love you," then disappeared into the night. During the ensuing months, she never pushed him away again.

Horner finally departed, his uneasiness with the colonel being too much for him to tolerate. Alone with Johnny, Babe attempted innocence. "Now damn, I hope you don't think there's anything going on here. You know what I mean."

"I didn't say..." Johnny said, unable to make eye contact.

"I know," Babe acknowledged, and that was all that needed to be said. "Now look Johnny, damned if I'm not gonna call you Patch, too. Hell, you're a hero! You have the ribbons there to prove it, too."

Brushing the praise aside, Johnny said, "I was just doing what I was supposed…"

"Don't you believe it, buddy. I heard about it."

Babe then turned and looked at his fellow officer, the one playing darts.

"This boy was the only one who would get up off the beach, and he led them all to safety. Saved the whole damn outfit! I always did say the best damn soldiers come from the south."

Johnny squirmed and sighed in protest but was unable to speak a word. Babe was the one to speak. "Johnny—I mean Patch—you're just like Lord Nelson, I tell you. You look just like him. Just like his picture anyway."

Tillie asked, "Is 'e going to 'ave a bitters with us?"

"Hell, no," Babe said, "That boy doesn't drink, but he's gonna have a little sip of lager just to toast his being well again. Ain't nobody gonna refuse to drink a toast."

Johnny sat with the small glass in his hand, first looking at it and then turning it around to feel the moisture that sweat out through the glass. Babe raised his in a toast but Johnny continued to press his glass to the table. Tillie and Babe suggestively beckoned, and before Johnny realized it, he'd done it. He'd taken a sip of the beer. It tasted to him like the wet grain he used to soak for Billie's old mare when her teeth got too sore to eat hard corn.

The two conspirators laughed, and Babe said, "I guess I'm gonna catch it when I get home. Many a marriage has been broken by the war separating a man and his wife. Hell, Johnny—I mean Patch—you lose your name, and I lose a wife."

Johnny felt a pang in in his heart. Something had obviously been going on between Babe and Billie that he didn't know about which suddenly made him feel sorry for Babe, maybe because he was present. And it was because of this feeling that he downed the beer. With each passing moment, the beer worked its wonder; his face became slightly flushed, and he became more relaxed.

Tillie stood and ran her right hand down her stomach. "I'll be right back," she said. Babe seemed to know where she was going but didn't give any indication as to where this might be. He turned to Johnny and admitted, "I'm a no-good bastard; you know that."

"I wouldn't say that, Mr. Lunsford."

"No, it's true," he insisted. "Billie's too good for me, I've always realized that, but hell, I've always been crazy about that woman. I should have let her marry someone who would have been true to her, even if he fought in the war. I'm just not that good a man. But I'm not hiding it from anybody! I wouldn't blame you if you wrote a letter to her tomorrow and told her."

"It's none of my business, Mr. Lunsford," Johnny said, lowering his head.

"You're right, Patch. It isn't."

Johnny raised his head and looked Babe in the eye. "Mr. Lunsford, I must confess that I wish I hadn't stopped in here tonight, but now that I have, I know that if Jesus could forgive the prostitute, I believe Mrs. Lunsford would forgive you."

Filled with chagrin, Babe said, "She's a hell of a woman—ain't no man good enough for her. You know, women and men are different breeds. Hell, they don't come from the same mold. Most men are bastards."

"I think I'm gonna join my outfit again," Johnny interjected.

"Join your outfit? Hell, you've made it boy—a damn silver star to wear home on your chest! And if that ain't enough, you've got that patch to let 'em know that you've really seen some action. Don't you believe those bastards back home won't know what those ribbons stand for?"

"Mr. Lunsford, I believe you cuss more than you used to. I guess the Army does that to everybody."

"Patch, I'm really enjoying this little afternoon conversation. Hell, it's early yet, so we can make a night of it. We'll talk about this for years to come after the war is over."

Johnny nodded appreciatively, his cheeks turning redder. "You're the best damn colonel I've met, Mr. Lunsford. Rest of 'em ain't like you."

Tillie returned then with a little brunette just a step behind her, about five feet tall and freckled. Her coat was freckled, too—yellow with brown spots, though it wasn't leopard skin.

"I 'ope you Yanks won't mind, but I ran into Charlotte here, and I thought it'd be nice if the four of us made a night of it visiting around at the pubs.

Johnny turned to Babe and said, "Damn, Mr. Lunsford she looks just like that bitch you used to have."

"I don't 'ave to take that kind of talk from you," Charlotte railed.

Babe started to laugh. "Aw, now wait a minute, Charlie. He didn't mean anything by that. That's just an old saying."

Unsure of his intent, Charlotte asked, "What's the old saying?"

"A country boy always calls a girl a bitch if he thinks she's pretty. And Patch here was just saying that you're as pretty as a speckled pup."

Charlotte looked at Johnny for confirmation, and he nodded in agreement.

"You see, we always call a girl dog a bitch. Well, I had this ole bird dog, she was the sweetest damn thing you ever saw—liver speckled all over with solid, liver-colored ears."

Charlotte seemed accepting of the explanation and took a seat at the table next to Johnny. The guys excused themselves for the latrine and made their way out the back of the pub. There they stood looking at each other while they relieved themselves.

Johnny asked, "This Charlotte, have you met her before?"

"No. First time. Funny though how Tillie just happened to meet her." Babe laughed. "We're going to have some fun tonight. Just relax and talk about old times. Hell, I don't care if you write home 'bout me, I still like the hell out of you."

"You say hell a lot, Mr. Lunsford."

"But hell, that isn't anything," he replied.

CHAPTER 72

Illicit Love

As the night wore on, the beer had its way with them. Johnny sat mostly with the glass in his hand, reluctant to drink any more, as Charlotte and Tillie tried to sing Yankee songs. Johnny kept insisting that they sing *Carry Me Back too Old Virginny*, while Babe kept saying that the best marching song ever written was *Dixie*. "If *Dixie* didn't inspire you to battle, then you just didn't have it in you!"

When it became obvious that the pub was about to close, Babe quickly ordered a couple of rounds, which they gulped down. Then he purchased two bottles that he stuffed in his overcoat pockets. From Johnny's perspective, there just didn't seem to be anything that Mr. Lunsford could not arrange if he wanted to. And apparently, tonight he just wanted to please Johnny.

The four of them piled into Babe's convertible. Johnny couldn't help but think that even the generals didn't have sports cars in England.

Back at Tillie's place, Johnny and Charlotte had a lie on the couch in front of the fireplace. It was very romantic, but not as functional as the upstairs room where Babe and Tillie were. And then the lights slowly began to dim. Johnny looked first at Charlotte and then up at the lights and said to her, "Darned if you can't arrange everything, but tell me how you arranged that."

"Oh, you silly boy," she said. "Give me a shilling, and I'll put it in the meter."

"Look in my pants pocket over there," Johnny said, pointing to his discarded trousers. Charlotte slowly walked to retrieve the shilling and then sauntered over to the gas meter on the wall. The lights brightened again.

Johnny realized that he really enjoyed watching her move. He didn't even have to pretend that he wasn't looking. She didn't care. She was the first naked woman he had ever seen. He was drawn to her little pot of a stomach, which he guessed all women had.

The next morning, taking care that no one saw his eye socket, Johnny washed his face in a basin. It was much like the wash pan he had used back in the mountains where JD had first met him. Johnny felt like he had moved back in time, especially as he watched Charlotte bend over to put the butter next to the fire so that it would soften and spread easily on the bread. There were no eggs, just a steak, which he was sure had come from Babe.

"I'll wait outside for you, Mr. Lunsford," Johnny stated.

Charlotte walked Johnny to the door. "Why do you call 'em mister? 'E's a colonel, you know."

Johnny stopped to look at her, having to stop completely so he could make eye contact with his one good eye. "You better not come out; the neighbors will see you."

"I don't care! We don't even know them," Charlotte said as she sidestepped Johnny and walked toward the car. Once they were out in the front yard, Johnny realized that the place in which they had spent the night was no bigger really than a good-sized room.

"Will you be back again?" Charlotte asked.

"I don't know. Maybe I'll be able to come back someday."

Babe and Johnny drove back to town hardly talking the whole way. Johnny was lost in his thoughts as he pondered how long it had taken him to grow up. In a few short months, he had been wounded in action *and* made love to a girl for the first time. All in all, it had been a good experience.

Suddenly Babe asked, "I guess Charlie told you she's married?"

"Married?" Johnny exclaimed in shock. "She didn't tell me she was married!"

"She didn't?"

"No, she didn't!"

"Well, forget it boy; guess we're two of a kind. You don't tell on me, and I won't tell on you."

Johnny wasn't sure how he felt about this. "You arranged this whole thing, didn't you Mr. Lunsford?"

With a laugh, Babe said, "I have to protect myself—protect my interest. Besides, you grew up a little last night didn't you, and had a good time in the process? I showed you a good time, didn't I?"

Shaking his head, Johnny answered, "You sure as the devil spoiled it now."

"It isn't sinful, Patch," Babe said in an attempt to justify his actions. "It's one of the things that happens in wartime. It's love. Illicit perhaps. But it's still love. It might be one of the only good things that happen in war—actual human feelings for each other. Don't sweat it. You and I have a future together, Patch. We are both going to look out for Billie, look after her interests—and looking out for her means not letting her know that her damn, rotten husband cheats on her."

CHAPTER 73

Your Little Hand

Dear Katie,

Every time I write that salutation I am reminded of literature; letters such as those F. Scott Fitzgerald wrote to Zelda. I always hope that my "Dear" to you carries the full weight of my feelings for you. I can never make myself go into all that 'dearest, dearest darling' those writers put into their love letters. But you know, I think of you and our little girl every day, throughout the day.

I have stopped here at a pub, as it is the only place to have a bite to eat where I can sit at a table and write with my pencil. No pen today. Everyone is sipping beer of one kind or another, and I am having tea. I would prefer a hot cup of coffee, but there is nothing like that here, except for their chicory, which they call coffee. So, I conform to the British with tea—not by desire, but out of necessity. And with what others are going through, why should I complain?

Our young men are remarkable, but not nearly as remarkable as the genteel natives of this land who must be the most understanding of all people to put up each day with boisterous and rowdy yanks. But they prevail in their show of appreciation for those men coming over to help clean up this mess.

In recent days, I have revised several letters edged in black in an effort to make them have some meaning to those who will receive them. I shall probably never lay eyes on the location or know of their arrival back home. Still, I hope that they will mean something more than death to the recipient. Thankfully, there seems to be fewer casualties here in England now than when I first came.

I can't help but think of how many letters and telegrams must be sent from the continent. Notwithstanding the carnage that took place on D-day, I fear there is more to come now that the forces have reached the German motherland. There is a term here that the soldiers use to refer to those who are avoiding service back home. It is "feather merchant." I feel I likewise deserve the same label and, therefore, carry a certain amount of guilt. But they don't want old men such as myself in this war. For the most part, this war is for the young and innocent, the unknowing who are considered the more pliable for combat.

Now I wish to relate to you my experiences regarding my visits to see Johnny. While I do not intend for you to paint a rosier picture of his condition, I must ask that when you relay this word to his mother, you convey the message exactly as I ask.

Johnny has lost one eye. Let his mother see it for herself, for I feel a woman of her nature would have all sorts of misgivings. His stomach was literally ripped open, but they were able, apparently, to keep it clean and without infection. The doctor described his situation with a negative roll of his head in complete wonderment.

When I sympathized with his wounds, Johnny replied, "At least I got back. I'm going to get to go home." This of course eased my mind, for I feel he will adjust and make a life for himself when this war is over. Just tell *his mother—and Billie as well—that he is coming home walking, of sound mind, and finished with the war! Be joyful around them as much as you can, even if you must do a little acting. Show them a feeling that it will all work out.*

Johnny will be on his way in a few days according to Babe who has made the arrangements, as only he can do. Babe has a friend who was an Olympic diving champion. (Quite a specimen of mind and especially body.) He, incidentally, flies mosquitoes on recognizance missions, but he also flies B-17s, in which Johnny will return.

One additional thing I must tell you: I'm comparatively in little danger over here from the war itself. Believe that! But one sees accidents of all kinds. A week or two ago, I saw two B-24s collide after taking off and routinely circling the field. This precipitated a collision of two or three more planes, which all exploded as they hit the ground. But I will never come into a situation such as that, so do not worry for me. But when one sees so much of this, one comes to think in real terms.

I do not worry, except for you and our little girl. Do you notice that I don't seem to be able to say her name? However, if something were to happen to me in all this traffic, burn my letters and move on with your and Susanne's life.

I pray you smile when you think of our wonderful times together. I think of the time when I picked you and your folks up in the old wagon and you placed your delicate, slim white hand in mine and patted it with your other hand. I was in such despair, out of place and embarrassed, that I had my forty days and forty nights in the wilderness beginning with that point. On the way home that night, I figured that I had not knocked the devil out of Dillie, but that he had knocked the devil into me. For surely, I was tempted at that fork in the road to walk toward the life of a ruffian and away from God until I thought of you and your little hand. Your father may have come closer than he knew when he called me a ruffian, though he could not know the influence you would have on me.

I know your psyche and innermost feelings were hurt when you overheard Billie tell someone that you were a real milksop, but if you are, angels are also. So, you see my dear, you are the one who made my life what it has been—wonderful!

In closing, I do thank your father for the kind words he said about me to those in his realm. I'm sure you are right that he is finally pleased and proud of his son-in-law. I was certainly never upset by his accusations, and I will probably act the same way when Susanne's suitors come forth.

Our day will soon come when we are together again as God intended. Until then, my love and spirit are with you. After all this, I hope you don't expect me to say that I love you, for you should know I do.

JD

CHAPTER 74

Wade Simmons

Billie ended her daily rides with a stop at the mailbox. She always hoped for a letter, especially one from Johnny or Babe. Somehow, Johnny's were more interesting. Babe's were always prefaced by the routine comment that he was taking time away from his important work to write. He never bothered to mention what his important work entailed, and he always hinted that his mail was censored.

Mrs. Abel opened Johnny's letters as if she were expecting something to be enclosed, but she was reluctant to take them into seclusion for fear they would bear bad news. Therefore, Billie usually read them aloud to her with expression, which Mrs. Abel appreciated because though she had been learning to read, she still didn't read well.

The letter found in the mailbox today was addressed to Miss Blacksheare. Since Billie assumed it was from Babe, she simply stuffed it into her waistband. Halfway up the hill, she suddenly realized that the envelope had a CBI address on it. China-Burma-India. This stirred her interest for she knew of no one in the Pacific theater.

Captain Wade Simmons. Could it be? She laid the reins down on her horse's neck and made a straightaway to the barn. There she carefully opened the letter as if she wanted to preserve the envelope for all time.

Dear Miss Blacksheare,

Please allow me to reintroduce myself with the hope that you won't take offense at my writing to a married woman. I am the young man who used to visit you at your school at Radford. You may recall that we used to dance and talk on the verandah about writing. If you are wondering what happened to me, I dropped out of school because my mother died, and my father took to the bottle in the worst kind of way possible and was unable to hold a job thereafter. Having two younger siblings, I had to find work to support us. Anyway, that's why I never came back to school or tried to get in touch with you—as much as I wanted to!

I, too, am married. Although I know it will never work out when, and if, I return home. We do not even correspond. I have been over here for almost a year-and-a-half and have no one to write to, which is the reason why I am writing to you. But even more importantly, I have been journaling about my trials and tribulations and have always, during the process, thought of our discussions.

There is a young man here who maintains our tent and does other chores who is from your area. His name is John Dempsey, though I call him Jack. This is how I found out about you. If you would not object and not think it presumptuous of me, I would like to correspond with you. If I don't hear back from you, your silence will inform me of your desire.
Sincerely,
Wade Simmons

Billie read the letter over and over for the longest kind of time. The horse had arrived in the yard next to the barn and grazed while she still sat in the saddle, pensive.

That night she penned her response. The thought never occurred to her that she might be violating her marriage vows or that anyone in the community coming across her correspondence would think ill of her.

> *Dear Captain Simmons,*
>
> *Of course, I remember you! I am not married to a man who would object to my writing and keeping up the spirits of one who is in that miserable theater of operations—although I am not sure where you are.*
>
> *Please do write, and I will look forward to hearing from you.*
> *Sincerely,*
> *Billie*

And write he did!

> *Dear Billie,*
>
> *I've always hated the word "platonic," so let us agree to carry on an intellectual repartee under the aegis that we are both from the academy. Albeit, I dropped out prematurely. I won't be doing too much of that silliness since I recall you being both seriously and genuinely disposed. That is certainly not to say that you did not have a wonderful sense of humor, too.*
>
> *The young soldier I spoke of says to tell you he lived on the railroad track halfway between Snakeden Station and the town of Herndon. His name is John Dempsey, and he was named after the fighter. He was enamored, as I think you were as well, with a contemporary and neighbor of yours by the name of JD. Also, with a boy whose surname is Abel. Dempsey is not always easy for me to understand, and when I first heard him pronounce the name Abel, I could not make out what he was saying. You may recall that I am originally from Newburgh, New York, and we have—for good or bad—a different way of speaking.*

Finally, he blurted out, "Abel, Abel, like Cain and Abel." Then I understood. I had heard the story of those two brothers somewhere as a small boy.

First, I would like to tell you something about myself. I think I can say (without it being censored) that I am near Karachi, which is in Pakistan. We fly cargo, soldiers, and other materials to places like Burma. This is, you may know by now, over the Himalayan Mountains. The parlance we use over here is 'The Hump.' And it is quite a hump! Quite high, which among other things has a depriving result with respect to oxygen. Our planes do not have oxygen tanks. So much for that.

Now for a confession that may come as a surprise, but I hope that is not offensive to you. When I was with you, I was always happy to just talk to you. We did kiss hello and goodnight, as you may recall, but I never had an impulse to go any farther. I found you warm and terrific to hold when dancing. Such was not the case when I was with other girls. And I mean that without exception. I was hell bent on seducing them. (Obviously, oversexed.) I suppose I might as well reveal it all. Clinically, I'm afraid the word is "womanizer."

I go into all that as my way of explaining my failed marriage. I got my girlfriend of the night pregnant and had to marry her. I suppose I did the right thing there. But it was a damn fool thing I did, and it didn't work out. We had absolutely nothing in common or anything going for us. It was a mutual understanding that I had been a bastard. Drinking was not an excuse, but it certainly did contribute to my other deficiencies. We have agreed to stay married until I return, if for no other reason than because the government augments my pay for her and the child's support. I used to have a teacher who said, "If mammy trots and pappy trots you can't expect the little colt to pace." I've never forgotten that. I suppose I take after my poor weak-kneed father.

Drinking became a problem for me over here. After coming back from a mission, flying all the way with a terrific headache, I walked down to Dempsey's tent for a beer. Well, Dempsey wasn't there, but on the little table was a Bible. I realized suddenly that I did not believe in God and that I had never even read the Bible. I bored through the reading of "so and so begat so and so" and so on. I was ready to fold it closed and put it down, but I flipped to the back to see how it all ended when I was caught up by some part that was printed in red. This intrigued me, and I read on. It was not until Dempsey came back, surprised to find that I had some interest in his Bible, that he informed me as to the purpose of the red print.

I mustered a little willpower and made no mention of the beer. I apologized for my actions and started to hand him the Bible and leave, but he said, "Take it. It is yours. I will get another one." I declined at first, but he insisted and pointed me out of his tent, escorting me by the arm like an officer and a gentleman.

As I exited, he asked me if he could make a suggestion. I agreed, and he told me the following: Johnny Abel had passed on a story to him that originated from your contemporary friend, the preacher. It seems the preacher had told him not to worry about reading the Bible from beginning to end but to just pick it up as if it were a fine violin (though I think he did give him the option of calling it a fiddle if it would make him feel more at home). The idea was to take the Bible and cradle it like a musical instrument, then to choose a particular place or just turn randomly to the pages within and begin to play (read).

I read much of the Old Testament and was blown out of the water by some of the Psalms. (I did remember hearing the 23 Psalm at my mother's funeral.) The red parts of

Bible were another thing. The parables and metaphoric utterances of Jesus were forcefully put, yet they were the ultimate in simplicity. It is beyond my comprehension to describe such simplicity, yet I realized in the final analysis how true to life it all is. Of course, I must confess that the story of the prodigal son is, by grace... How do I say it? A gift? Perhaps it is a pardon of a sort. Can you see it?

I realized I was reduced to a state of self-destruction by my own selfish indulgence. And how had I justified my miserable behavior? By blaming it on the death of my mother and the weak behavior of my father. But I was pardoned! 'Forgiven' is probably a better word.

Well, I have gone on and on, but I thought perhaps you might want to know what your friend and Cain's brother Abel had done to me. I'm grateful. Let me not impose on your graceful generosity.
Sincerely,
Wade

P.S. I completely forgot to ask you if you would be interested in critiquing some of the short stories I've written. I suppose "anecdotes" is the more appropriate term.

Dear Wade,
I would love to read your anecdotes, musings, or short stories. I sense we are somewhat in the same boat—that our interest in writing is not shared by others in our realm. I sit each night and write in a diary of my feelings toward that which I have just written or recently written. There is no one to discuss the influence it has on my psyche, and vice versa. Though I am married, my husband's letters from England are about as romantic as a letter from a governmental entity.

My "contemporary friend," as you call him, was my only outlet when I was stuck out here at Snakeden. What a name! It was a postal address in earlier days and the source of much teasing from the children at school—especially the townies whom I loathed. My friend's name was Joseph Emory Beauchamp Dayne, but everyone called him JD—even his family members. Perhaps we all thought that version was worth settling for after that long moniker. When I used to tell him he was the light of my life, he would simply laugh and say that way out here in the country there are not too many lights to choose from. I was told by more than one at Radford that we would never marry.

JD's grandmother, whom I adore, referred me to the book of Corinthians, which was about marriage between two parties of different faiths. Yes, I have always had a Bible. Though, I suppose you recall, I did not believe. I have enclosed a copy of a paper I wrote in high school about a cow of theirs that died that resulted in my leaving school. I thought perhaps you might be interested in reading it since I'm just prattling on herein.

I was reluctant to say that I do not believe in God, but I had already written it. As you can see, it is at the bottom of the page and I would have had to write the whole page over or cross it out. Please do not let my beliefs influence you in any way.

You may be pleased to know that the prodigal son parable posed a quandary for JD. He always said, LOVE AND REDEMPTION were what it was all about. I believe that also.

Stick with it! Send them on! I will keep your anecdotes and protect them for you.
Good luck,
Billie

P.S. Give our best to Jack Dempsey.

Wade slipped a couple of his anecdotes into an envelope and put it into the mail for Billie.

Dear Billie,

It was great to hear from you. My anecdotes do not necessarily represent my own personal experiences. Some are, some aren't. Jack says hi! He cringed when I called him Jack, preferring to be called John, but then he laughed.
Sincerely,
Wade

CHAPTER 75

Wade's First Anecdote

Saint Valentine's Day

There is a constant dilemma with flying over the Hump. Fly high, and there is no oxygen. Drowsy; makes one want to sack out. Fly low, and one hits the mountains.

I was the pilot, and my "co" was on his first flight. He wasn't being unreasonable when he asked how the Chinese would scrape up the rice when the bags hit the ground and broke open. What he had to have explained to him was that there were two bags. The first bag, which was somewhat tight, was in another larger bag. So, when the bags hit the ground near the Chinese soldiers, the inner bag would in fact burst. However, the loosely fitting outer bag would not.

It probably wasn't an aeronautical engineer who had originally figured this out. I suspect it was an old country boy. Townies, even those with street smarts from New York City or Chicago, wouldn't be up to that sort of thinking.

The crew never discussed the possibilities of recovering from a downed flight. If they were to crash into the Hump, there would be no recovering. The deprivation of oxygen—providing the pilot and the co-pilot did not go at the same time—was a matter of playing it by ear. Perhaps even the crew chief could step in and resort to lowering the C-47. Bailing out though would mean a long and presumably impossible trek through the jungle with no idea of direction once one hit the ground. Little thought was given to the latter option.

Among our crew was a muscle builder who was one of the two who jointly threw the bags out the door. He was constantly trying to impress us with his exploits with the mobsters of Chicago, but he wasn't the most popular soldier among our group. His attempts at intimidation were usually met with laughter, which didn't seem to soothe him. This muscle man had regaled us with his feats of strength, such as the unloading of barrels of beer on his back around the hub city. Stories such as this allowed us to assume that he could easily handle the bags of rice.

On this day, although we were at a low level, we were met with considerable turbulence that seemed to buffet our plane up and down. We had our markers, so there was not a choice as to when we could start dumping the cargo off. We were occupied with trying to keep the plane as level as possible when suddenly it tilted up on the side where the door was. This was not only unusual, it was inconceivable as to what caused it. Then we all heard this loud commotion and swearing of accusations, and the muscle man came rushing up to the cockpit.

"We've got trouble! We've got trouble!" he yelled.

"What's wrong?" I asked.

"One of the bags got stuck on the horizontal stabilizer!" he screamed.

And before the seriousness of the situation settled in my head, I hollered back, "Well, climb out there and see if you can shake it off!" He blurted out an oath and started to turn around, but then I came to my senses and was right behind him.

To this day, I don't know why I did it, but I hollered to the other crewmate to hand me the Thompson Machine Gun. Then I yelled for one of the other men to hold on to me as I leaned toward the door and opened fire on the bottom of the bag. First, there was nothing. Then I remembered that I was dealing with two bags, so I opened fire again until I saw rice trickling out the bottom of the bag.

Acting as if I had planned it, I opened the machine gun up again. I noticed that the lower half of the bag was emptying, but the upper half remained intact. My cockiness started to diminish. Then it occurred to me that, while the lower part of the rice flowed down from gravity, the upper part would not flow upward, no matter how many bullets I put into it.

But I did not need to worry because the weight of the upper half finally pulled the empty part up and it all flew off into the air. Fortunately, my image as a leader did not wane. My ego was intact, and I now acted as if I was never without confidence in my leadership as the commander of the flight. I tossed the gun to the muscle man with aplomb.

He asked, "How in the hell did you think of that so quickly?"

I stopped, turned to look him straight in the face and told him nonchalantly with all the acting ability I could muster, "I was just sitting there in the cockpit assuming you all could handle everything back there. So I was thinking of this broad I know back home, and I saw this big heart come up in my mind. Then I thought of Valentine's Day, which made me think of Al Capone and the St. Valentine's Day Massacre—Chicago and submachine guns."

I looked at him, smiled knowingly, and said, "I guess you can figure out the rest!"

CHAPTER 76

Wade's Second Anecdote

A Drink for the Boys

Two pilots decided to fly to Dallas to get their flight hours in so they could get paid. Three of us decided to tag along because a free ride to Dallas for a few days seemed like a gift from Heaven. We were all stationed in Marfa, an airfield in southwest Texas. About the only thing suggestive of civilization in Marfa was the pool table that we used to break the monotony of endlessly idle hours. The two pilots were mildly sympathetic toward our needs, but not overly so. This was to manifest itself a couple of days later when they left us stranded in Dallas (high and dry as the saying goes) with no way of returning to Marfa.

In the distance was a range of mountains that we were told the homing beam ran right through. It reminded us of the mountain range in the Azore Islands off Portugal. Bummey, Jack (not Dempsey), and I boarded the plane with little more than the clothes on our backs. The U.S. Army had drafted Bummey from a little shack in the side of a hill near East Liverpool, Ohio. Jack was a former football player and had a body odor to prove it. Never showered under his arms, nor did he ever use deodorant. Thus, someone had nicknamed him Jack Armpits. The name, if uncouth, was aptly descriptive of him.

To say these two liked to drink was like saying hogs like slop. Bummey, Jack Armpits, and myself, stranded as we were, started hitchhiking from Dallas to Marfa. The hardest place in the world to start hitchhiking is in a city. Think about it! Faced with this situation, we were completely in search for possibilities when a young lady drove up in a 1941 Ford and asked, "You boys want to have a little fun?"

Jack Armpits jumped up to her window. (He had taken charge just like a senior officer even though after three years in the Army he was still a Private First Class.) Before I knew it, we were heading out of Dallas toward Fort Worth with me in the front seat.

Suddenly I started wondering how this scenario was going to play out, but I didn't even have enough of an awareness of the situation to be confused. All I knew was that Bummey and Jack had both been drinking heavily and were dead broke. I now had nothing but change in my pocket, and nobody, sure as hell, had such a thing as a checkbook. Yet nothing of a monetary nature had even been broached. It all had happened so quickly. Even when we arrived in Fort Worth and the lady turned off the car to go into a little housing development, money did not come up. I was completely inexperienced in these types of shenanigans, even though I had been in the Army for three years. I was, however, not long out of my teens.

Jack said to the lady, "Hold on here a minute, honey. I've got to get out for a second."

She accommodated him without reservation. He walked around the back of the car and stood for a minute as if he was going to make water or something, then he slipped up to the driver's window and said, "Hell, honey, we're going to Marfa. This ain't no fun."

Then he opened the door for us and said, "Come on men, she's trying to take us for a ride."

You talk about cussing! I thought I'd heard every profane word that could come from a man's mouth during my stay in the Army, but this lady knew even more. Some words I didn't know existed. But we both followed Jack Armpit's command, even though I was a sergeant and outranked him.

We tried hitchhiking again and were given a little ride for a few miles to a crossroads. That's where our benefactor had to turn to the north, and we were going south. We stood for what seemed like the longest kind of time until finally an old farmer in a truck stopped. The front seat was all occupied with children and the back was half-filled with chicken crates. There were Plymouth Rocks, Rhode Island Reds, White Leghorns and other chickens that a country boy like myself didn't even know existed. We were thus reduced to checking each feather as it blew across and stuck to our bodies. As we rode along, I explained the different chicken breeds to Bummey and Jack and told them that different hens laid different colored eggs.

All you could say about this trip was that it was better than nothing. At least it lasted for some miles. By the time the ride ended, I had restored my rank and was somewhat in charge—at least I had a feeling of superior knowledge. This being the case, I insisted that I was to sit in the front seat of the next car.

It soon appeared, driven by this handsome man, though a little portly— he may have played a little football himself. I looked first at him and then at his cowboy hat that sat on the seat between us. Now this was a nice man I thought, about the age of my father. He had the hat all right, but I bet he didn't have to go out there riding around herding cattle. He was probably into oil or something like that. Great car, but not top of the line.

He started telling us, "There's a little town down the road a few miles, and if you boys can hold out, I'd like to buy you a drink." It was common talk among soldiers who were at a bar on leave to report having someone who had manned the home front during the war—someone like your dad or your uncles—buy them a drink. You'd go to bar, and first one guy would buy you a drink, and then another guy would do the same thing. This could go on and on for hours. This apparently was what Jack Armpits wanted to hear. Music to his ears! Also, I knew without looking that he wasn't messing up Bummey's itinerary.

The driver and Jack started talking about football, and the way he told it, Jack was the rage of the Ohio State campus. Bummey would help him out statistically from time to time regarding his record. I wasn't that much into football; so as we rode on, I began to think about the upcoming drink.

One thing I had always noticed about the city boys is that they have street smarts. (I don't mean townies, they are usually from a small town.) Like sometimes you go into a bar and someone offers you a drink and you know it's probably going to be just that one because there isn't anyone else in the place to buy you another. So, you start to think to yourself, how can I get the bartender to fix me up with a double shot without the sponsor thinking I'm greedy? Well, these city boys seemed to do this by use of some signal. You'd never hear them say anything, but you could see the bartender shake his head that he had gotten the message. And then you'd see him pour out the double shot without the sponsor noticing. I guess its things like that that I always wanted to find out. How did they do it? And that's what I was thinking about as I sat there riding along.

As you may know, when you are riding down the roads in west Texas and a fellow tells you 'this little town is just a little piece down the road,' he could be talking about a hundred or four hundred miles. Maybe more. And when I started getting thirsty and thirstier and thinking about the dust and chicken feathers on that old farmer's truck, it seemed to me that we weren't going to get to this little town in no hundred miles, or even four hundred, but that it was going to be much more than that.

When I glanced at old Jack, I could see there was more than football now on his mind. He finally inquired, "Is this place much further on? I feel like I'm going have to make water here before long. Guess nobody out here would catch a guy if he got out and peed, would they?"

Well, I knew he didn't have to pee because he hadn't had anything to drink for hours. So, his little question was futile. When the driver offered to stop, Jack declined and said, "No, I don't want to put you out." So, I knew I was right about my suspicion.

Finally, the driver said, "There it is. See right ahead, right down the road!"

Well, down there in west Texas you can see something off in the distance that you figure is a couple of miles off and you can drive for an hour before you get there. We finally arrived at the edge of town with the three of us looking for a sign that would indicate some wild ass saloon like you see in the cowboy movies. But before you know it, he's pulling up in front of a sign that read: Pharmacy. As I looked in amazement, he said, "Perhaps you boys didn't know that when I offered you a drink, I meant a soda."

They all walked in ahead of me. I turned around to look at the car and realized that, had we been a little more observant of the license plate, we would have realized that our driver was a man of the cloth.

CHAPTER 77

In the Vernacular

Billie visited the mailbox every day in anticipation of a letter from Wade. In contrast, she thought very little about one from Babe. When one finally arrived, she did not wait until the horse got back to the barn; she would open the letter and start to read, throwing her right leg over the saddle until she was riding sidesaddle. The horse, unguided with loose reins, would continue on his path, stopping at the barnyard and commencing to circle.

> *Dear Wade,*
>   *What an exciting pleasure to read your literary efforts! You must continue on—you are the real thing!*
>   *At the moment, I am not going to criticize your efforts. Instead I want to tell you of my own experiences and feelings in the hope that it may be of more benefit to you. As I indicated before, I use my diary as a kind of means of communicating with an imaginary other. So, I shall just keep a carbon copy of what I write to you for my diary record also.*
>   *When writing, I have this way of using the vernacular of those in a particular setting. An example of this, if you can imagine, is walking up to a lady pushing a baby*

carriage. Just envision this scenario: When one speaks to the lady, one talks in the normal vernacular, but when one bends over and talks to the baby, one resorts to "coochy-coo" and other baby talk.

I see at least a hint of this in your writing also. Whether it is natural or not, I have no idea. This comes naturally to me, and I neither try to add to it or change it in any way. This has been going on ever since I started writing as a young girl, and I always refer to it in my diary as "in the vernacular of the occasion." I've coined an acronym for it: ITVOTO.

In the last couple of days I have even noticed, while writing something that is more sophisticated in narrative and conversation, that I automatically change my vernacular without thinking. Recently, my writing in this vein has gone on at some length, and I'm wondering if I have just become more sophisticated. (I don't like that descriptive word, but you know what I'm referring to.) Now I'm boring you, I know.

I think you will find it beneficial to have someone read your writing. There are those in the literary world, according to the magazine I read, that think otherwise. But remember in our case, it is a two-way street.

After I married, I would repair to my room upstairs and write. Many times this was after having had a little nip with my husband, which seemed to have an unpleasant effect on my psyche and disposition. I didn't drink for any particular reason that I know of, but I feel better having given it up.

Incidentally, I told Johnny Abel's mother about you and she looked at me rather strangely and said, "Be careful, Miss Blacksheare." But we both know that no harm will come of two people trying to find a little understanding and happiness in their life. In spite of all that, she has fixed *up a package to send to you, but in her name only—and one for Dempsey also.*

I don't know why I bring this up, but one time when I was a little girl and sick at home, my dad bought me a bright yellow yo-yo. The country boys always referred to it as being calf-shit yellow. Well, I don't know whether it was the color or the fact that I was sick and played with it at the time, but I have never been able to stand the color yellow since—or anything that is painted yellow.

These are weird thoughts, I know, but I do not write anymore when I am not feeling well. Take that for what it is worth—perhaps nothing!

Now I am as happy as one could possibly expect to be, except for the fact that we are separated as a family; the children and I miss their father. What I am trying to say is that writing is a satisfying way of life for me. Nothing makes me happier, and there seems to be a new experience in it for me each day. But I must tell you, I do not let commercial thoughts about writing enter my mind. I do, however, think about someday allowing someone else to read my writings and enjoy them.

I have enjoyed your anecdotal efforts and hope you will continue to write them. I will be of any help that I can, even to the extent of recording and copyrighting your stories, if you wish. Let me know.
Until next time,
Billie

Though there was never any hint of an overture of romance in their correspondence, their letters arrived just far enough apart to indicate that neither one wished to make it appear that this was the only thing taking place in their lives. Then a package arrived, all neatly bound in protective wrapping. Gunnysack, actually! Billie thought of rice bags. Cautiously, she opened it. Inside was a manuscript of typed pages with changes replete and not too neat. Good enough, she thought for a person living in a tent in some far-off land. And there was a note inside.

> *Dear Billie,*
>
> *I haven't told you, but this has been a project of some duration, which I started long before I contacted you. Several months ago, my superior officer was looking over my flight record and was apparently amazed at how many hours I had logged. Many of those I had arrived with and hadn't thought too much about. He and the flight surgeon insisted that I be given a test.*
>
> *I was placed in a room and instructed to walk across to the other side. The floor was linoleum, or something like that. It turns out that I could not perform this simple task without scuffing my feet. The word 'incoherent' comes to mind, but I think that applies more to speech than physically walking. I was put on medical leave.*
>
> *I haven't said anything about this before because it gave me an opportunity to relax and write full-time, thus completing the pages you now have before you. By the time you receive this letter, I'll be somewhere between here and the States. Probably Hawaii. An airman coming home on a damn boat! I'll probably wind up on the west coast, but I'm not sure just where.*
>
> *If you can manage the time, read what I've written and dispose of it as you wish, or just keep it for me.*
>
> *Best of luck to you, your family, and the lucky guy.*
> *Sincerely,*
> *Wade*

CHAPTER 78

The Loudoun Limited

Johnny had only seen the ocean from a ship. Now, as he rode pensively in the nose of the B-17, he was mesmerized by the waves on the ocean below. They looked like a giant washboard. He wished to see those places on the eastern shore that he had heard about but had never seen—the coastline and Washington, D.C. Maybe he'd even see JD's childhood home and the Lunsford's place from the air. That would be best of all.

Babe had arranged the flight. *Yeah, Babe,* he thought, *could arrange anything.* Smooth. That was Babe. Even when he asked you for a favor, you felt like a vast door of opportunity had just opened up before you.

Johnny hopped a cab from National Airport to Rosslyn. The once stuccoed white train station where Marcus had bristled with booze was now gone in favor of a Hot Shoppe. Only a small canopy remained where passengers could escape from the elements. The railroad company had for some years now tried in vain to discontinue passenger service. However, the shortage of gas and tires due to the war effort had caused many to rely on the train and trolleys for transportation instead of their automobiles.

Service was different, however. Mr. De Faubus, who had been the stationmaster at the Vienna station when JD had shouldered the bit, was now a conductor. He rode the train collecting tickets, intermittently calling, "Board," and occasionally relaying the stops. "The Loudoun Limited is now leaving for Falls Church, Vienna, Sunset Hills, Herndon, onto Leesburg, and Bluemont. Board!"

At the sign of a soldier approaching, Mr. De Faubus's cadence picked up, as did his interest. He did not recognize Johnny at first.

"That you Johnny?"

"Yes, sir."

Mr. De Faubus was 4-F by age and thus exempted from military service.

Johnny asked, "You still stop at Snakeden?"

"This is the limited, but hell, we'll let you off there this evening anyway."

They stepped up to the center aisle with Mr. De Faubus closing the bottom trap door and then the other, leaving a Dutch door effect so he could either lean out and signal the motorman or spit.

Once the train was up to speed, Mr. De Faubus said, "I saw your mother and Mrs. Lunsford the other evening. Mrs. Lunsford was on that horse. Damned if she didn't carry a crop to the store the other day, just like a general carrying one of those… what do you call them?"

"Swagger sticks?"

"Yeah, that's right."

"She's the best friend I got," Johnny said in earnest.

"She's second best, ain't she?" Mr. De Faubus inquired. "JD's best, right?"

"I mean around here." With JD still in Europe, Johnny was looking forward to seeing Billie.

"You seen some of it, didn't you Johnny?" Mr. De Faubus asked.

"Yeah," Johnny answered, pointing to the patch over his left eye. I didn't get this eye ball knocked out in a dress parade."

Mr. De Faubus nodded consolingly. "What's it like?"

Looking off into the distance, he answered, "As Mrs. Lunsford used to say when all those young ladies from the city would come out to follow the hounds: mostly it's a lot of damn confusion. She used to say lots of people would like to go through the open gate rather than jump the chicken coops. I guess it's a lot like that. It can scare the hell out of you going over the jump, especially when you don't know what's on the other side."

Mr. De Faubus nodded respectfully. "Let's go up front and talk to Kelly."

"When did that ole son-of-a-gun start as motorman?"

"About the time you left. Nobody else to do it."

The train picked up speed, and they swayed back and forth in rhythm, like posting in the saddle. All the passengers could see was their backs as they moved toward the locomotive.

Kelly recognized Johnny immediately, and in a friendly gesture, offered him the speed handle. Johnny took over.

Looking at Mr. De Faubus, Kelly commented, "He hasn't forgotten how to do it. As a kid, he used to drive this thing from that school in Herndon to home. But he's no kid anymore."

Mr. De Faubus shook his head in amazement.

"Ain't nothing to it," Johnny yelled over the noise, "except turning it one way to go faster and the other way to slow down. And blow the whistle every time you see a marker."

They all laughed knowing that there really was more to it than that.

"Have you ever hit a car?" Johnny asked.

Kelly shook his head no.

"How 'bout a cow?"

CHAPTER 79

Home for Good

The steeplechases were long gone from the scene. With no one to care for the place, the white board fences around the property had begun to warp and shed their whitewashed skin. Johnny jumped the fence and cut across the field that had been mowed down by the cows and the summer heat. There was no sign of anyone. No Peggy. No Mom. No Mrs. Lunsford.

As he approached the door, he could hear them talking. They were just rattling back and forth about something to do with the furniture. He knocked respectfully.

"Yes?" his mother muttered.

Johnny pushed the door open and walked in.

"Oh Johnny, oh Johnny," she gasped, grabbing him and smoothing his hair. "Oh, it's so good to have you home, son."

"Guess I'm home for good, Mom."

Seeing his patch, she asked, "Couldn't they give you a glass eye? I mean, so you wouldn't have to wear… that?"

"I don't want an eye right now," Johnny said.

Beyond his mother stood Billie, smiling, though her eyes were filled with tears. She tried to appear aloof, but there was joy between them when their eyes met. Johnny noticed that her nose had grown more prominent—not too much so, but just more than before. It was no matter; she was handsome, not delicately pretty. She wasn't creamy skinned; her skin was tanned and freckled, her cheekbones prominent.

"It's good to see you, Mrs. Lunsford," he said.

"It's wonderful to see you, Johnny," she said with sincerity.

It was hard for either of them to proceed beyond the initial greeting, but then Mrs. Abel said, "Let me go get something for us to drink."

She left the room, leaving Billie and Johnny alone.

"Did you paint the rose yet?" he asked.

"No" she answered, smiling. "I've been writing and writing. I know now what I'm doing, and nothing can stop me. Oh, but that's arrogant, I suppose. Yet, I also suppose what I'm doing is pleasing me, and I don't care about anyone else—that is, as far as writing is concerned."

"I saw Mr. Lunsford before I left," Johnny offered.

"How was he doing?"

"Oh, fine. He talks 'bout you all the time."

"Behaving himself, I suppose." It was more of a statement than a question, and Johnny couldn't detect if he was seeing a half-smile or not.

"Oh, yes ma'am," he answered as nonchalantly as possible. "There isn't much to do over there except shoot darts in the pub. He was hitting a couple of golf balls around the baseball diamond the day before I left. I know he'll be glad to get home to see you and the kids."

"So, he's been behaving himself then?" Billie asked clearly this time.

"Oh, yes," Johnny answered a little too enthusiastically.

"Me thinks thou protesteth too much," Billie quoted with a cynical edge.

Johnny wasn't sure what Billie meant, and later she was glad to realize that he hadn't understood.

"What do you intend to do now that you're home?" she asked.

Johnny laughed uncomfortably. "Heck, I'm only home five minutes and you want to put me to work."

Billie laughed with him. But Johnny had thought about his next move.

"I think I'll go into business for myself," he said finally. "Get a G.I loan and go into business."

CHAPTER 80

Real Estate

Johnny went and saddled Fauquier and rode to the station to wait for Peggy's train. She came off flying, first looking at him and then back at a couple of young ladies on the train, as if to say, "Here he is!"

Johnny didn't dismount, didn't even speak. Smiling, he reached down, clasped Peggy's hand, and extended his foot from the stirrup at the same time for her to use as a step. Pulling her up, Peggy swung her leg over the horse doing her best to keep her rear end from becoming exposed in the process. Hugging Johnny from behind, Peggy placed her cheek lovingly on the back of his khaki shirt.

"Oh, I've missed you so," she managed to say before bawling like a baby.

"Whose gal are you?" Johnny asked sweetly.

"I'm your gal."

"You got a boyfriend?"

"No," Peggy giggled. "It's too far for boys to come out here."

Johnny, Peggy, Mrs. Abel, Billie, and her three children all ate dinner together that night. Mrs. Abel fixed a fine meal while Billie fixed the drinks for Johnny and herself. Afterwards, the children played while Mrs. Abel cleaned up, and Johnny and Billie settled into a discussion as Peggy watched them negotiate. The conversation shifted back and forth like a tennis match.

"Babe will not want to enter into any business arrangement with me," Billie stated. "He will want to go back to his job or to one just like it. Daddy left me a very lucrative situation here. If you're willing, you and I could go into the real estate business together."

Johnny, cocking his head at an angle and feeling mature, asked, "What would we need as capital?"

"Nothing," she answered. "Daddy never invested a cent. You and I could take a cram course in real estate and start right away—perhaps after you have had a little respite. Or whenever you feel like you would like to begin. The war will be over before long, I think before the year is out."

"I'll think about it," Johnny said. Then he changed the subject. "When are you going to try to get something published?"

"I have tried, but I don't want to write for magazines. I want to finish the book I'm working on now and maybe write a few short stories, but I don't want to have them published individually. Babe disagrees. He wrote me that that was self-exaltation. However, if it is, that's that, and that's the way it's going to be."

"Excuse me," Billie said, gathering the tired children to her. The little girls—Lillian age five and Charlotte age four—sat on their mother's lap. The eldest, Bobby, with hair as blue-black as his mother's and serious with every word, seated himself on the arm of her chair.

"Come sit on my lap," Johnny offered as he reached his hand out toward the boy. Bobby responded immediately, as if he had been waiting for an invitation.

"Your daddy and I fought the Nazis," Johnny told him.

Bobby looked at him perplexed, for at age six, he did not remember his father any more than JD had remembered his during the First World War. Yet, there was an air of curiosity, and one could see that he wanted to talk more about his father.

"You been fishing in Difficult Run any?" Johnny asked.

"Uh-uh," Bobby grunted, his head shaking from side to side.

"Maybe we'll dig some worms in the morning and go. Would you like that?"

Bobby's head bobbed up and down with yes, but by the way he wrinkled up his forehead, his apprehension was obvious.

The hour was late. "Say goodnight to Johnny and Peggy and Mrs. Abel," Billie instructed her children. After they had bid their goodnights, Mrs. Abel helped Billie put them to bed while Johnny sat thinking of the future.

Billie and Johnny talked late into the night while Mrs. Abel busied herself in the kitchen, barely able to keep her eyes open. They both knew that it was proper for her to be near them while Babe was away.

"Mrs. Lunsford," Johnny began. "I been thinking 'bout your offer. I suggest that we make an arrangement whereby we get an acre or two with each sale we make as part of our commission. That way we could be holding onto something that would not depreciate."

"You mean it would appreciate—enhance in value as time goes by."

"Yes, ma'am."

"Let's start off by you calling me Billie instead of Mrs. Lunsford. While I may be somewhat older than you now, as the years go by you will tend to catch up. Besides, we're partners now."

Johnny nodded his acceptance of the offer, and Billie continued. "And, when using my name in public, I would prefer to be referred to as Miss Blacksheare."

With that, Billie arose and went to the kitchen to pour them each a drink. She threw a few ice cubes into the glasses of whiskey when she noticed Mrs. Abel watching her.

"It's all right," Billie assured her, "we're kind of celebrating. You don't have to worry about him ever drinking too much."

She didn't give Johnny's mother a chance to respond. Instead, Billie strutted out of the kitchen carrying the two drinks. Handing one to Johnny, she said, "I take it you don't want to talk about your experience over there."

Johnny shrugged. "Everybody calls me Patch now—even Mr. Lunsford."

Billie leaned back in her chair. She did not want to press him, but she yearned to hear all about it. So she waited.

Johnny looked at his feet crossed at the ankles and contemplated his response. "They kept telling me that I'm a hero. I don't feel like that. I just feel like a darn hog without any personality. You know? I didn't do anything."

"You stop that," Billie reprimanded. "Babe told me all about it. Many of those boys would be lying on that beach in bits and pieces right now if you hadn't arisen and hollered 'Attaque!'"

"It's funny you'd say that 'cause this guy, Whitey… well, I think he thought I was Jesus."

"What do you mean?" Billie asked.

"Well, I was laying there…"

"Lying."

"Okay, lying there…"

"I hope you don't mind if I correct your English," Billie stated, "but I think it's appropriate since we're going into business together."

"I don't mind," Johnny acknowledged. "Anyway, I'm *lying* there with my eye knocked out and my stomach all ripped open, and I didn't know what was going on. Didn't even know what had hit me! Anyway, Whitey came up and knelt down, I suppose to see how bad I'd been hurt, and then he put his hand on my stomach. All I could think 'bout was when Thomas wanted to put his hand into Christ's side. I thought I was dead, but I still knew what was going on. Fact is, I kept watching overhead for the buzzards. I always hated those darn things. Whitey told me 'bout it later. We were in the same hospital. He got his leg blown off by a mine."

Johnny paused for a moment, remembering. "There I was, running toward those Germans. Now, I've only told one other person 'bout this—all the time, this hero here didn't even have his gun loaded. That's right. I didn't even have my gun loaded!"

"I've read that's quite common, Johnny," Billie said. "At least lots of men never fire a shot. The important thing is that you kept going forward; you rallied the men. Don't be modest about it! I don't mean that you should brag about it either. However, you did what you were supposed to do, and you did it well. We're all very proud of you. Babe brags. He told me he told all his friends about you."

"JD said I did the right thing, too," Johnny said without looking at Billie. "He said he's glad I didn't have to kill anyone."

Billie waited a moment before asking, "So, you told JD that your gun wasn't loaded?"

"Yes, ma'am," Johnny answered looking her straight in the eye. "You two are the only ones who know."

Without breaking eye contact, Johnny said, "JD says you're gonna paint the rose."

Sentimentally Billie said, "I would love to see him… and Babe."

CHAPTER 81

Fishing

Each time Johnny stuck the shovel into the ground, it went nowhere, even though he would jump on it with his right foot. The dirt seemed to get dryer and dryer the deeper he went. Finally, he gave up.

"You see," Johnny explained to the seven-year-old, "the ground is so dry that the worms have gone down deep to where you can't get 'em with a shovel."

"The shobble won't go deep enough?" Bobby asked.

"It's a shovel, Bobby," Johnny corrected. "You don't mind if I correct your English, do you?"

"No, guess not," he answered kicking the dirt.

"Come on. I know what we can do."

Grabbing Bobby by the hand, Johnny led him toward the hill. "We're going to catch some grasshoppers. They're better than worms anyway. Just run up to 'em and throw your hat over 'em."

The two of them ran all over the hillside gathering the grasshoppers and stuffing them into the can. Then they headed to Difficult Run where they cut two limbs for fishing poles to which they attached some string, impaled the grasshoppers on the fishing hooks, and threw their lines into the water. Johnny was just as attentive as Bobby as they sat there waiting for a bite.

"Did I ever tell you 'bout the time I lived down in the mountains?"

Bobby looked up at Johnny with some apprehension. "I ain't never seen you before, so how could you ever tell me?"

"A fella has to start a story somewhere," Johnny said with a laugh. "I know you think you ain't never seen me before, but I've seen you—before I went into the Army. You were a little tyke then. I thought maybe you might remember me 'cause I remember things from when I was three of four years old. Like, I remember going for the doctor on a horse the night my sister was born. My father was drunk and couldn't do it. I was only three."

"How'd you get on the horse?" Bobby asked.

"I just… you know… just pulled him up to a fencepost and jumped on him."

"I've done that with Fauquier," Bobby said.

"You ain't much for letting a fellow tell a story," Johnny observed in jest.

"Go ahead, I'm sorry," Bobby said, hanging his head.

Johnny tousled his hair before continuing. "Well, what I was gonna say was, I was down in the mountains…"

Bobby interrupted again. "You mean *up* in the mountains. Don't you?"

Johnny laughed. "Well, yes, I suppose I do." Even though the mountains that Johnny was referring to were *down* south, it was easier to just agree with Bobby's assessment. "Anyway, there was this ole turkey I had seen in the cornfield on several frosty mornings. I was in the habit of showing up late for school…"

As the story went on, Johnny pulled out a can of Prince Albert tobacco and started to roll himself a cigarette.

"Roll me one of those, too," Bobby commanded.

Johnny stopped mid roll. "What do you think your mother would say? And how about the colonel? He's a gentleman, and he certainly would not want his son to be smoking."

Bobby wouldn't yield. "I don't want to be a gentleman yet. Roll me one."

Johnny wasn't sure.

"I've smoked corn silk before," Bobby offered. "Besides, Momma wouldn't care."

When Johnny thought about it, he knew he was right. They sat and puffed awhile. Bobby talked in a tone like a man of eighty years, or at least as if he were as experienced. Suddenly he pulled his fishing pole out of the water and announced, "Let's move."

Johnny shook his head. "No, son. You gotta be patient. That's why colored boys catch all the fish. The white boys get impatient, but the colored boys can sit for hours under a tree and wait for the fish to bite. We're gonna wait."

And so the days went by, each one marking a new encounter between Johnny and Bobby. By all appearances, they enjoyed each other's company.

CHAPTER 82

Reacquainted

Billie met Babe at Union Station in D.C. Their reunion was cordial. That evening, after the children had gone to bed, Babe asked, "Why didn't you make love to me this afternoon?"

"Because I wanted you to pay attention to the children. Besides, I want you to court me. I don't want to jump into bed with you after you've been gone for three years just like I'd been waiting all this time for nothing except that. I want us to get acquainted again." Then she added, "Maybe I'm not sure of myself after you've been over there with all those European girls."

"What European girls?" Babe responded a little too quickly and loudly. Laughing, he asked, "You're trying to trap me. Right?"

Calmly, Billie said, "I don't care what's happened as long as you know you're home now and you know what that means. Our children come first—before you, before me, and certainly before the club and our social life. So, we might as well start from the beginning."

"You left one thing out, didn't you?" Babe asked.

"Yes. The children come before my writing, too. So do you. While you've been gone, I've thought of you always and have not given myself completely over to my passion because I knew it would change my personality. For this reason, I put you *and* the children's interests first. We both need to do that now."

As they sat watching a blaring floor show later that night at the Lotus Club, a middle-aged Chinese man with his hands folded before him, walked up to Babe and bowed low.

"How you been, Tom?" Babe asked.

"Very fine, Mr. Lunsford. Except I miss our little pool games."

Babe chuckled. "Glad to hear you haven't forgotten me, Tom."

"It's nice to see you with such a fine lady."

"Well, thank you Tom. This is Mrs. Lunsford. You remember me telling you about her before I went into the Army?"

"Oh, yes," Tom answered.

"Are you taking care of these drinks, Tom, or are you using the statute of limitations to welsh on me?"

"No, no, Mr. Lunsford," Tom replied. "I take care of drinks."

Perplexed, Billie asked, "What was that all about?"

Babe shook his head. "Nothing really. We just been shooting pool for years, and Tom owes me a little. He told me I could collect on the drinks when I got back from overseas. I haven't bought a drink in here since I first met him. His idea. I never asked him to play."

"And that's another thing you promised me from the beginning," Billie said with some disappointment, "that you would quit hustling. I don't like that at all."

"Come on now, honey," Babe cajoled. "Your husband is home for a few hours, and all you can do is chew him out?"

"I don't like those vulgar Army expressions either."

Babe shook his head. "Let's dance and go home."

In the bedroom on the west side of the house, Babe lied facing the window that cast the only shred of moonlight into the room. Billie walked in, her frame silhouetted by the glow. Knowing that he was watching, she began to raise her nightgown over her head with both hands. But just as the outline of her nude body came into view, she passed on from the window, turning slightly. For just a moment, he saw the contour of her thigh and breast. Babe anxiously waited for Billie to move to see whether she'd give him her back or her front.

To himself, he said, *"I love her. She intrigues me. I respect her more than anyone I've ever met. She fascinates me."*

He felt her slip into the bed facing him. With a fling of her hand, she threw the light covers over her back and smoothed her hair behind her ears. Then she pressed herself to him. Like a kid, he couldn't have stood it for one more moment. Nothing was better than her love.

As they became reacquainted, he asked himself, *"Who were those broads? Why did I ever touch one of them?"*

CHAPTER 83

Coming Back Home

"Trite are the words clickity-clack, clickity-clack, clackity-clack that describe the train. But all trains go clickity-clack 'cause each rail has an end. But this train is slower than most. It goes chunka-chunka, weaving from side to side in the wind. It doesn't go clickity-clack until the slow pace ends and the quick pace begins." He whispered these words, mostly to himself, as he walked the aisle punching tickets.

He looked right at JD and didn't even know him. Couldn't he see that he hadn't changed a bit in size? Of course he did have on one of those Army hats that folded flat when you took it off. "Ticket please," he stated.

JD looked up at him, his forehead and eyebrows wrinkled upward. At the same time, he handed him his ticket, he asked "How you been, Mr. De Faubus?"

"For Lord's sake JD! I didn't even recognize you!"

The two men shook hands and exchanged regards.

"Some things never change," Mr. De Faubus commented. "You're still studying, I see. What you writing there? A sermon or something?"

JD smiled. "Oh, no. I'm just writing."

With other tickets to punch, Mr. De Faubus excused himself. JD hoped he would return, but he didn't. It almost seemed as if his old friend was avoiding him. If he was, it probably was on account of Paw whom Mr. De Faubus would have had difficulty talking about.

As the train got farther away from Washington, it seemed like the motorman increased the speed. JD watched out the window as they passed Black Pond. Carp and skating was all Black Pond was good for. Of course it was the only pond around. Then the train moved toward the cut where JD had picked quartz or isinglass, or something that looked like it, as a child.

Suddenly, he felt the presence of Mr. Cowley. He looked up toward his first benefactor's house knowing that he wouldn't see him, but fondly remembering the day they sat on the railroad ties together talking. That was the day Will had joined church.

The train emerged from the cut and at that very moment the sun flashed like a mirror. For a fleeting moment, the flashing light seemed to hold the face of Mr. Cowley. JD had always thought of him and Paw as being different about church, but now he wasn't so sure.

The train bore down on Clark's Crossing, swaying from side to side. The bumping and pulling between the two coaches made JD feel like he was sitting on a wobbly spinning top. And then it was over. He stepped down from the train, his eyes searching for Katie. She didn't know exactly when he would arrive, but he had hoped she would be there waiting.

"That's him, that's him," Katie squealed with excitement as she saw JD's towering frame coming over the hill.

Maw agreed. "Sure's I'm alive, that's him."

Katie grabbed nine-year-old Susanne by the hand, half dragging her off balance. They started down the dirt road, but then took off down the hill knowing that they would either have to jump or wade the branch of Oak Run. Katie and JD saw each other about the same time, but he didn't cross the fence, thinking that when they met there would be no reason to hurry back across the short cut. They could walk back slowly and talk before reaching the house.

Halfway up from the ground, the fence was page wire followed by two strands of barbed wire. This fence had been built to Harvey's instructions. You could hear the stretching of steel post and wire clamps as Katie stepped on the wires and pushed Susanne through first.

"Showing a lot of leg for a preacher's wife, aren't you?" JD teased.

"No one is watching except the preacher," Katie responded.

"You've stretched Harvey's fence." But that was as far as he got. By now Susanne was hugging his neck, and he was kissing the tears from Katie's cheek. Each time his lips touched her skin she flushed with warmth.

"I'm sorry about Paw," Katie sobbed.

JD nodded. "If only he could have lasted until I returned."

"Yes. He would've wanted to talk to you about the war, but each day he grew weaker, and you could tell his heart was forsaking him. For over a year he had to negotiate the stairs by sitting on a step and raising or lowering himself up or down with his arms. I know he tried to hold on for you."

JD did not put Susanne down, but carried her along by one arm, intermittently stopping to embrace and kiss his wife. They took their time.

Maw had repaired to the swing on the porch where she sat waiting, swinging back and forth humming. It wasn't a dirge, but it was close. "Your Grandfather's gone, son."

"Paw hasn't gone," JD responded, leaning over to plant a kiss on his grandmother's forehead. "He's here now. Can't you sense his presence?"

Maw dabbed her eyes with her apron. "He would like to have talked to you—to sit here and talk about the wars."

"I wouldn't have wanted Paw to endure any more pain just for me," JD said. "He's rid of that now. I'll never forget him. Paw was never absorbed with material things. His heart yearned for peace and happiness for others. Paw could say, "hmmm," and mean more than most preachers."

"Will you go back to preaching?" Maw asked.

"I've never stopped." Turning his hands up, JD said, "It has me. I don't have it. You remember Paw saying that?"

Maw nodded. "I'd hate to see you go so far away again."

Katie responded, "Maw, you must remember that we have a lot to be thankful for. Everyone is coming back home, and we won't have another war because there'll never be another Hitler. You must think of us as being here—right here with you all the time."

When it was time for Bonnie to come home from work, JD went to the station alone to meet her. He left early to make sure he would be there when his mother stepped off the train. Whereas Maw had aged, Bonnie looked the same. Her figure was still that of a 20-year-old girl. Her red hair had its natural waves, and she flashed her son an endearing smile, one that was more devilish than adoring. The minute she embraced him, she began to cry.

"You couldn't stop by in D.C. to see your mother first?"

"No. I thought about it, but I have four women I must please. I knew you would understand."

"Yes, I do. I always want you to put Katie first—and your grandmother, too."

"It's not like that. It's not a question of who comes first—you or Maw or Katie or even Susanne. One does not compare grandmothers with mothers, and mothers with wives, and wives with daughters. They're all different relationships. You are my mother. There is no one else like you. I know what you sacrificed for Will and me. But do you know what's always pleased me so much about you? Do you?"

Bonnie looked up at her son and simply said, "No."

JD gave her his answer. "What's pleased me most about you is that you've never become embittered with God because of Little Bonnie or *him*." ("Him" was Marcus, whom JD could not bring himself to call "Dad.")

"I'm so proud of you, JD," his mother beamed.

So engrossed were they in conversation that they did not notice Harvey until he yelled at them from his garden. "By golly, what's going on here?"

Harvey was not one to say "good morning" or "hello." No matter the circumstance, his standard greeting was always, "By golly, what's going on here?"

JD yelled back, "You're planting those beans at the wrong time. Moon's not right."

"Think so boy?" Harvey asked. "When's the right time gonna be?"

"Well, the moon was right last week," JD stated. Then he asked, "You planting those beans with eyes down or just throwing them into the hill?

Harvey stood upright. "Now don't tell me that stuff. You know it doesn't make any difference."

"Oh, but it does," JD insisted. "Actually, if you lay them on their sides they will be lazy in growth and reproduction."

"Did you have to go all the way to Scotland to learn that?" Harvey asked sarcastically.

"I don't mean to knock your undertaking," JD said somewhat apologetically, "'course what you really need is a woman's touch to plant those beans right. When are you going to give in and get married, cousin Harvey?"

Harvey shook his head. "I don't need any women to spend my money." They all had a hearty laugh, including Bonnie.

"Come by and see me sometime," Harvey requested. JD smiled but did not commit to a visit.

As they walked away, Bonnie said, "You ought to stop by and see him; he always liked you boys."

"I have no time for him!" JD responded a little too quickly. His mother gave him a strange look. "I suppose you think that's not Christian of me."

"You're right. That is what I think," Bonnie said. "Harvey's been good to me."

But JD saw things differently. "He bought shirts at a discount from you. I don't hate him; however, I cannot forget that he did not allow Paw to put the electric pole across his land. Harvey is interested in money; and Harvey is interested in Harvey. I don't hate him, but I haven't forgiven him."

Bonnie said nothing while JD's statement percolated in his mind. Then he added, "Perhaps I've been keeping him in a judgmental purgatory."

"I hope you're kidding," Bonnie said.

JD started to laugh. "I am." She looked up at him and started to laugh as well. He may be a preacher, but he was human indeed.

JD blessed the food when they sat down to the dinner table later that night. "Our Father, we thank thee for these moments with friends and family where we may enjoy love and friendship and share our common interests. Help us to hold and cherish these moments like a locket around our necks. Let these moments of sweet memory be manifest in our countenance no matter what sadness and sorrow we endure. Let us see greed and covetousness as what they are: weeds in the fields of thy Son's beatitudes. Now, for this food that sustains our bodies we render thanks. However, for the spirit of Jesus that lights our souls, we are even more grateful. We partake of this food in memory of Jesus, and in His name we pray. Amen."

CHAPTER 84

Give It Time

Maw and Katie were in the kitchen when Billie rode her horse into the yard. JD instinctively helped her off, reminiscent of the times he would help her dismount after she rode into the barn and hung from the door tracks in the days of old. As she slid down into his arms, she planted a kiss on his cheek. He, in turn, put his arm around her shoulder, which was surprising she thought, but welcomed. After tying the horse to the tree, he and Billie sat in the lawn chairs under the gum tree.

"It's so nice to see you home, you big lug," she laughed.

"You're looking great; haven't changed a bit," he replied.

"Maw says it's because some of the tan has gone out of my hide. I didn't know if that was a compliment or a scolding," Billie said, to which they both laughed. "You look swell, too. Looks as if the Army did all right by you with respect to the rations!"

JD then inquired about her children, and before long the conversation turned to Babe. Billie said, "My life, I feel, will change. I don't believe our relationship can be the same as it was before the war."

"Oh, give it a little time," JD encouraged, "and you will work it all out. You'll be happy again."

"I didn't say I wasn't or wouldn't be happy. I said it would change."

"Somehow I feel like you're trying to tell me something! Are you sure you want to go into this with me now? You two have only been back together for a little while."

Billie shook her head and looked away. "No. I don't want to drag you into my problems. I suppose because I've always been so close to you and confided in you, I didn't want to sit just here and not say a thing and have you be surprised later by a lot of talk!"

"You have to give it a little time," JD reiterated.

"Do I?"

"Sure! You owe it to yourself and the children to try to work it out."

"You may rest assured that I have been completely faithful to him," Billie stated with conviction. "But someone else has come back into my life."

Before anymore could be said, Maw and Katie came out of the house and the matter was dropped.

CHAPTER 85

The Call

Before the month was out, JD had been called for a trial sermon at a large church in Dallas, Texas. To be called for such a trial meant that the pulpit committee there had selected him and was now merely presenting him to the congregation as their potential minister. Following the trial sermon, a preliminary vote would be taken from the entire congregation, and a two-thirds majority vote would indicate that JD could be offered the position. He would then have the opportunity to consult God and accept or not.

JD made the trip to Dallas alone to speak before the congregation on a Sunday night.

"Tonight, let us be true to ourselves. You and I both know that I am a man reared on a farm in Virginia. I have studied extensively in various institutions of learning, and equally significant, I have thought of God each day along the way. Some say I am well-spoken, and certainly I'm not going to argue with that." They all laughed.

"I cannot carry a musical note in a bucket, and that's why I prefer a large church so no one can tell the difference." They all laughed again.

"My wife says that sometimes I joke and wrestle like a boy, which is true! Yet, on the other hand, I'm serious about my commission as a disciple of Christ. I believe that I understand the Bible, Jesus, and those who tried to describe God. I have sympathy for the impoverished—both materially and spiritually. And my understanding of God comes through Jesus.

"Last night as I sat in the lobby of the Adolphus Hotel, more money probably passed through the pockets of the guests there than I shall ever see or have. I know nothing of money, and I have no desire for it, for I know what it does to man. There's a lot of money in this church, but I would never be influenced by it. Consider that when you consider me. God can make a man free; money can be enslaving.

"Many outstanding theologians emerged during the short span of years directly before and after I studied abroad. Oddly enough, they emerged from corrupt societies in many instances. Yet, the point I wish to make is this: much of their subsequent efforts have produced philosophies, for the most part, that are indecipherable to one without a degree in advanced religious study.

"Now, I am *different*—mind you, I did not say *better*. While I studied such theses, I do not see them as being my call from God. Jesus's teachings are not complex; they are simple, but not simplistic. They are intriguingly enduring and humble and uncommon. Uncommon in that any man can perceive their truth and observe their validity in day-to-day commerce of fellow men. Thus, a better life here on earth is possible by adhering to these teachings.

"Yet, paradoxically, man judges others and not himself by the criteria Jesus shared. I, therefore, call myself a preacher and teacher of Jesus's message. Not my own, but his. I believe that Jesus conquered death and that heaven is a promise known to Him and God alone.

"In closing, I draw a narrow path that the Christian is to follow, which is this: Man knows that he may ask God for forgiveness at any moment and he will be forgiven. It's the theory of deathbed repentance, you say. Such thinking encourages devilment, you say. For a man may sin all his life and be saved at the last gasp of life. But no! Man may sin and sin again, but the spirit of Jesus shall abound. Yes! Life's true secret may be found by constant plodding for higher ground. Higher ground is forgiveness, compassion, concern, and faith."

Before the week had passed, JD had been called to serve at the church in Dallas and accepted the position.

CHAPTER 86

The Businesswoman

Billie passed the real estate broker's exam with ease. Johnny, having been tutored by her, passed the real estate salesman's examination. It was during this time that Billie came to realize that Johnny could read something once and then quote it verbatim. This accounted for his being able to parrot JD's sermons as a young boy years earlier. She also came to realize that while Johnny could recall information word for word, he did not necessarily understand much of what he had heard or read.

Nonetheless, Johnny successfully showed and sold practically all the property they represented. Billie would review the papers and appear at the settlement, but her work generally consisted of assisting. As entire farms were subdivided and sold, Johnny and Billie emerged from each settlement as the owners of a choice section of the property, which they would later sell for a profit after it appreciated in value.

Difficult Run, as well as Oak Run and other small streams, were marked with four to seven foot pools, which were called holes. A popular hole for fishing or swimming was situated on Harvey's land and would come to be called Harvey's Hole. Other holes were named after the owner or a successful fishing encounter. This naming of holes was necessary to enable the fisherman to identify places within the stream. This practice was pervasive throughout the area, as there were not enough street names yet to indicate a specific location.

Similarly, the hole where Fauquier had become mired at the edge of the stream came to be called Hell's Hole. At the same location, Blummer Beshears and his horse and buggy had been swept away following a torrential rainfall years earlier. The horse, which was halfway across the stream, probably could have made it the remainder of the way, but it panicked and backed into the tongue of the buggy until the water capsized its half-bent body. Blummer had tried to aid the horse by holding the front wheel, but the high water washed the sand away beneath him, sending the buggy over his body. At least, that was the speculation when Blummer's body was found the next morning. It was found weaving aimlessly in the now calm and receded stream amidst the flotsam of the buggy; he was still wearing his white shirt, his skin appearing pink and grotesque.

So it was that the land use corporation formed by the two partners was named Hell's Hole Real Estate with the understanding that the name referenced Fauquier's experience and struggle with death, not Blummer's demise. Billie had seen Johnny's extrication of Fauquier from the mud as second only to the Civil War as an historical event in the area. Because the neighboring county was named Fauquier, and due to personal feelings for her horse, they could not bring themselves to name the corporation Fauquier Land Corporation, though the name was of supreme significance to them.

Many people moved into the suburbs from the city; some of the more affluent bought farms as an investment and a place to spend the weekends; others bought homes in which to raise families. The Hell's Hole Real Estate firm prospered by selling both existing homes and farmland, some of which was subsequently subdivided into even smaller parcels. The firm also listed and sold property in the surrounding counties due in large part to Billie's connection with her father in Loudoun County.

Successful by all accounts, Billie felt empty. It was a cold wintry night on the 10th of April when Billie wrote again in her diary.

Dear Diary,

I have turned back to see that one year to this very day I had written 28 pages. Only 28 pages in one whole year! I have potential, and I know it. Why have I let myself become lazy and apathetic? I think of the words 'spoiled' and 'lazy,' but I don't exalt myself when I say that I am neither. I know I can write; JD knows I can write. Babe is currently on a business trip in Europe. Alone. Without me. But even as I finish that statement, I know it is apocryphal.

Why was JD saddened when I married Babe? I suppose I know now. Writing. What the hell do I know about writing? For over two years I have written practically nothing. Though I suppose because I told the truth in the first part of my novel, now I'm trying to compromise and write something sensational. No, no more! I will write the truth, so help me God.

What God? I do believe the devil possessed me this evening though. I do believe there is a devil. If there's a devil, there's an antithesis. That's a stupid word to use. Why didn't I use God? (Because I might admit something if I did.)

What gets them all is that I'm a businesswoman. All those rich, bastardly businessmen were afraid to outbid me for Miss Beau. They weren't afraid of spending their money; they were afraid of losing to me.

Maybe I'm back to writing again. I will have my passion! I hope I don't go too far with it. Damn! Writing can make you eccentric and a loner. I know I have it back now because I want to write poetry—lyrics actually. I didn't even like poetry until JD recited the 23rd Psalm. But it just seems to erupt from my throat like belching. Anyway, I figure it's a waste to write poetry unless it's put to music. Such a waste.

The spirit moves me! God's a spirit. What's a spirit? What's a soul? The spirit is like a wind—unseen, omnipotent, omnipresent, pervasive, and yes, transcendently functional. What is the difference between the subconscious and the soul?

I'm going to make myself a scotch. This will be the very last time I'm going to take a drink. I am going to start a new life.

CHAPTER 87

The Children

Babe took a couple years worth of law courses, although he did not bother to become a member of the bar until much later in life. Instead, he turned his efforts almost entirely to that of lobbying for various corporations, some as far off as New York and California. Babe's paychecks increased dramatically because defense contractors became more prevalent in the Washington area, or at least their business interests did. Out of the proceeds of this effort, he brought home a biweekly check that he gave to his wife for whatever she desired; he never demanded any type of accounting or control. The remainder of the money he deposited into a personal account known only to himself and the bank.

To those working under him (especially the fledglings), he was quick to point out that the first step for a successful businessman to take was to be up front. And the most important part of that was for the client to be up front with a retainer. This was something he learned well before law school, although many would say that the very introduction to law in school was "retainer." It was noted by others that this important step was known and employed, whenever possible, by every subcontractor in the country.

Those who came to know Babe over the years—even those who had been finagled by him—were appreciative of his experience. One even coined the phrase: "the screwing I got was worth the screwing I got." This was later twisted into different forms, but its intent remained pretty much the same.

Babe wasn't an amateur name-dropper like so many others. It was always the responsibility of an underling, at a discreet time, to drop the names of Babe's connections and acquaintances during the negotiations of a transaction. Also, his former status as a colonel was disclosed to those of a military background at an appropriate time.

There were those who would say that he sought first the quid pro quo arrangement. At times, if he were fond of a particular client, he would provide the quid without the quo. Most of this analysis was not of a critical or gossipy nature, but rather shared by those who were in awe of his lobbying and manipulative skills. They would add that his physical appearance and dress code also lent much to his being admired.

So, it was no great wonder that after years of Billie trying to get published on her own that it was Babe who was able to secure for her a publisher in New York. She had said to Johnny at the time that she felt much as she imagined an old rich man to feel after marrying a young, beautiful woman: Was it all on the up and up? Was she in it for the money?

In the meantime, Billie spent almost every afternoon and sometimes well into the night writing. Finding himself in need of a small place to hang his hat, Babe established a modest residence in D.C. where he could conduct business and entertain clients late into the night. Consequently, they were not together much during the week; however, they did spend weekends golfing in the early spring. In the fall, she took to steeplechasing and fox hunting. And in the winter, he went quail hunting.

Thus, between work and their social life, there was little time left for the children.

CHAPTER 88

Respect

Peggy, who worked for the government in downtown Washington, had arranged for her brother to meet a beautiful, sweet, and intelligent young lady from a farm in Ohio who had come to town to work. In just a few short months, they were married. Sarah Hart became Mrs. John Abel. Meanwhile, Peggy herself married a fine young man and moved into the city.

Johnny added a couple of rooms onto the old tenement house where he and his new wife lived with his mother. Mrs. Abel still did the cooking at the Lunsford home, but others now handled the housecleaning and maintenance.

While Billie had always been able to make a horse respond to any command, she had not been as successful with her own son. She complained that even as a small boy, Bobby would go into a store with her and just run wild. Any command she gave was completely ignored. Then, when he did come to the counter as she was checking out, he would have his pockets filled with items he had no intention to pay for.

Johnny was aware of Bobby's noncompliance when he took him to the store one day. Just as soon as they entered, Bobby took off running. Without even thinking, Johnny hollered, "heel," a command normally applied to a dog. To his surprise, the boy turned and came and stood at his side. Johnny knew he had discovered a deep psychological depth in the inner core of the boy's being, though he never revealed this to anyone else. Not even to wife. What he had discovered was worthy in the realm of knowledge, though it was not patentable or of monetary value. Yet Johnny felt as if he had just invented the electric light bulb.

But this had happened many years ago, when Johnny first returned from war. The children had grown significantly since then. Johnny was able to obtain respect from all three of the Lunsford children, as well as the bird dogs and horses. Perhaps this was because he did not approach them with an authoritative or demanding manner but with a firm and kind voice. He himself wondered at times as to the source of his demeanor, thinking it similar to the relationship he had observed between various children and their grandparents, something he had never experienced personally.

Both Babe and Billie had always insisted that their children use terms of respect, such as "yes, sir" and "yes, ma'am." Good manners went with the southern tradition. Yet, the children silently looked up to Johnny, as did others in the community. His being a war veteran—a hero at that—might have played a part in this.

The Lunsford children spent much of their time with Johnny and his wife, as if they lived there. Every Sunday, with the mutual consent of Babe and Billie, the children accompanied the Abels to church, where Johnny was also held in high esteem.

It had been some years since the church had employed a full-time pastor, so a search was begun. The regional minister of the area was contacted, and he furnished the name of an elderly, retired minister to serve in the interim. This man's kind and gentle demeanor gained him the love and respect of the entire congregation. His historical teachings were new and enlightening to degrees not before recalled by those who had observed such matters in the history of the congregation. Particularly noteworthy was his practice of personalizing biblical characters, such as the confrontations between Peter and Paul.

In the meantime, the process was initiated for selecting and calling a permanent minister forth. The regional minister furnished many folders and resumes, but most of what flourished was his self-acclaim and his doctorate, which had been conferred and not earned through any academic accomplishment.

Considerable effort in writing and calling applicants was extended to no avail. Therefore, it was decided that Johnny (who was now chairman of the pulpit committee and responsible for recommending a new minister to the congregation) and an elder of longstanding would pay the regional minister a call. Their purpose was to demand the name of a capable applicant.

These two representatives of the local church made what they deemed a formal and scheduled visit. However, their timing conflicted with a previously scheduled meeting of some importance. As the regional minister strutted around his office, he informed Johnny and the other elder that he had a very busy schedule and would have to change his clothes while they conferred. Whereupon he lowered his pants revealing red polka dot shorts. At that moment, Johnny turned to his colleague and said, "Let's go." But the elderly elder cautioned otherwise.

In a few short minutes, once the regional minister had dressed properly, he released three more resumes. Two proved worthless, but the man represented by the third was eventually selected.

On the way home, Johnny jokingly said to the elder, "I know you were in the Navy during the first war, but for some reason I've only become rehabilitated to white shorts since my days in the Army. It's quite a shock to see underwear that pretty on a man."

It took over eighteen months to obtain the new minister. During this time, a parsonage was built for him and his family. Construction proceeded slowly so as not to encourage the interim minister to stay on.

The church building itself, situated on State Street, was not located where two roads crossed, but the church was at a crossroads nonetheless. Attendance was up, even though the elderly minister restricted his pastoral efforts to visiting only the shut-ins and the elderly who were unable to attend church services, but membership was about to decrease under the pastoral care of the new preacher. Thus the word 'crossroads' was first used as a euphemism, and later as irony, for the declining church.

CHAPTER 89

Secrets

Although Billie would only let a few pages of the manuscript that Wade Simmons had sent to her out of her sight, she had prevailed upon Peggy to type the handwritten parts of his manuscript into two copies. These, and the old correspondence letters between them, were neatly hidden in her writing room.

Babe had never shown much of an interest in Billie's writing, although he did from time to time feign as if he did. This particular night, he had come home somewhat fortified by a long dinner hour of drinks. It was all business, as he would indicate later.

He sauntered into her writing room expecting her to be there. But she was not. He eased himself down into a soft chair and started looking around as if to familiarize himself with what she was writing. It was then that he came across a few pages of the Simmons manuscript. He could tell that it was not something Billie had written by the notations, which were written by Peggy. Her notes indicated that she hoped she had deciphered the handwritten manuscript properly but warned that she may not have.

This led Babe to search further into the box where he came upon the personal letters, including copies of those she had written to Wade. Over the years, Babe had become surer of his relationship with Billie in respect to her earlier relationship with JD. In fact, other than the visit they had paid the Daynes down on the farm soon after the Second World War ended, there had been little contact with them. But now he read and reread the letters between Billie and Wade and kept coming back to the part where Wade had written how he had enjoyed holding her when they were dancing at Radford. His confessions as to his sexual escapades during the war were of equal concern.

Babe left the room as he found it, unsure of his next step.

It took only a few short weeks for Billie to assemble Wade Simmons's manuscript into a neat bundle. Thinking she would prevail upon Babe with all his powers to find a publisher to accept it, she arranged for the two of them to go to dinner in town at the small and intimate Blue Moon Club where there was dancing and the music was known to be soft and semi-formal. Why she felt it necessary to go to this much effort to ask him for this otherwise small favor was known only within herself.

At a romantic and opportune time, Billie mentioned an old friend who was an aspiring writer as if her interest in him was more of a charitable nature than anything else. Babe went along with what he thought was her little game, never revealing any foreknowledge of the manuscript or the letters, but all the while thinking the very worst. Babe assured Billie that he would do everything he could to see that a publisher would accept the Simmons manuscript, even if his associate had to contact every possible publisher in New York.

"If there is a problem we can go from there," he said with a wry smile.

Babe was unaware that Billie had actually met with the agent who had published her first book while he himself had not, even though he had arranged the connection. He had simply made a phone call, someone had picked up the manuscript from his office, and the book went to print. Billie, however, had dealt with a young lady named Doris Wilson who was not only enamored with Billie's first novel but also grew to admire Billie as a type of folk hero.

Not long after Babe took the Simmons manuscript to be reviewed, Billie received a call from Doris Wilson requesting a meeting with her in Washington, D.C. She insisted that she didn't want to discuss any of the particulars over the phone and cautioned Billie not to discuss their upcoming meeting with anyone, including her husband. Billie, assuming there was good news in the offing, could hardly hold her tongue, but she did.

When they met in the city, Doris told Billie that she had inadvertently overheard her boss state that Babe had put out an edict that he did not want the Simmons manuscript accepted—no matter if it was worthy or not. Doris further revealed that until now she had been unaware that such shenanigans transpired in the publishing community. They both agreed, however, that this knowledge would remain a secret between the two of them, for they feared news of this getting back to Babe or, even worse, Doris's boss.

The weather was especially warm outside, but this night there was a palpable chill in the air as Babe and Billie each tried to act nonchalant with the intention of keeping their respective secrets. There was an unspoken agreement between them that they never would discuss any grievance they had if either of them had been drinking. But the club and alcohol went hand-in-hand. Billie finally realized that this situation could go on forever, with him accomplishing his goal and she being left out. So, this night, over dinner at the club, she initiated a conversation in a most equivocating manner.

"I received the most peculiar phone call this afternoon. It has just perplexed me to no end."

"From whom?" he asked.

"Well, I'm really not sure. You see, he didn't want to leave his name. But he was most sympathetic and courteous. He said that the manuscript we sent in for Wade Simmons had been blackballed. All he would say was that I would be surprised at who had put the hex on it. No matter how much I insisted and begged, he wouldn't reveal the source."

"Perhaps your friend has a faulty reputation. What does this fellow Simmons do anyway?"

"I don't know, the last I ever heard from him he was still in the Army."

"Well, honey, you never know what goes on with these guys who have had a drinking problem."

"Yes, I most certainly do," Billie corrected him, "and I also know weird things can happen as a result of jealousy and paranoia."

"What do you mean by that?" Babe asked, finally engaging his wife head-on.

"I mean, if there's a jealous wife or maybe even a jealous husband, you know..." She let her sentence trail off, raising her shoulders for emphasis.

Babe tried to change the subject, but Billie covertly kept it alive. By the time they arrived home from the club, she had had enough. While still dressed in her skirt and jacket, she suddenly turned toward him, placing her hands on her hips, and demanded in a somewhat belittling voice, "Why? Why?"

She didn't speak his name. She couldn't make herself repeat his hackneyed nickname: Babe, though she had called him this during similar moments of displeasure. And she certainly didn't want to repeat his legal name: Jerome—a joint misadventure of his parents, though this was the name she called her husband when he needed to be brought back to earth.

Angered, he reached out to grab her by the arms, but she clinched her fists and shook him off. Calmly, he urged her to sit on the side of the bed, which she finally did.

"Look," he began, "you're my wife. I was away from home fighting a war and someone was trying to steal you. This Wade guy admits he's a womanizer! He admits he doesn't even like his wife. What do you expect me to think? I'm your husband, and I'm supposed to protect you. Besides, you're mine! I'm trying to hold on to the mother of my children and not let some interloper break up our family."

"Yes, that's it. That's it," Billie sputtered, rising to her feet. "You can't stand to think about some young, sad boy who was struggling to stay in school while his mother died and his father turned into a drunk before his very eyes! You can't stand the thought of him carrying around the moment when he held me in his arms years ago. You can't, can you? It's not that you're afraid of him breaking up our home; it's that you can't stand the thought of him holding me and finding, for once in his life probably, a moment of love and joy. You know, I have not laid eyes on him in all this time! It's been years! There is nothing between us. I'm going to bed alone. You can find an extra blanket in the other room." And she pointed toward the door.

Babe walked out with his head bowed; he didn't need a scoreboard or a sports announcer to tell him that he had just lost the game. To make matters worse, he was the one who had fixed it, and one was not supposed to lose a fixed game. Babe had been wounded, and even if the wound healed in time, he knew a scar would be left.

CHAPTER 90

Separated

As he lay awake that night, Babe realized that his little affairs and escapades overseas had been more than the mere dalliances he had tried to portray them as in his mind. Yes, he thought, he had been called out by a false accusation. Billie had done nothing wrong except show kindness to an old acquaintance—one who had been redeemed (in the biblical sense at least) from a life of despair. Unbeknownst to Babe or Billie, Wade Simmons had earned three Distinguished Flying Crosses as well as several Air Medals for devotion to duty while isolated in foreign lands with suffering all around him.

Babe remained isolated at night in the spare bedroom, though he made certain not to indicate in any way that their separation was anything other than temporary. For the most part, his clothes remained in their bedroom, and he came home more often during the week instead of staying in town. However, their relationship was not the same, and he was at a loss as to what to do about it.

Several years had passed since Billie had first received Wade's stories, and at the time she had given the final manuscript to Babe for publication, she had not heard from him for quite some time. After the argument with Babe, she decided to write him.

Billie related to Wade all that had happened to his manuscript, except for the part about her husband. She had typed out a critique of his work, complimenting him on it and suggesting that she was hopeful of putting him into contact with a publisher. Simmons replied with sincere thanks saying he was appreciative of her efforts. Among other things, Wade also told Billie that he was still in the Army and that his wife had remarried.

Privately, Wade thought fondly about Billie and her letter. He took particular notice of the fact that she separated her final personal note from the critique by writing the former in longhand. This, he thought, was a reflection of her upbringing and her time spent at Radford. He remembered that she was well mannered—always crossing her legs at the ankles and never letting her back rest against the back of a chair. However, he'd also never known of any other girl who brought a crop to a dance. Perhaps, he thought, she had some connection to that portrait he had marveled at of General Lee sitting at a table with General Grant at Appomattox.

Finally the day came when Billie received a call from Doris Wilson. She seemed very excited by the fact that her boss had agreed to publish Simmons' manuscript after all; however, she was not particularly optimistic about its sales potential.

"Miss Blacksheare, while I like the book very much myself, there are dozens and dozens of manuscripts about the war floating around right now. One of particular noteworthiness is a book entitled *God is my Co-pilot*. But you may rest assured that I will do everything in my power to facilitate its sale."

"That will be fine, Doris," Billie said. "Anything you can do will be deeply appreciated by both of us. You have been more than kind, and I know you even took a chance regarding your position at work when you spoke with me awhile back."

Doris replied, "Listen, after what you have told me about this Wade Simmons and the way he writes, I could sure fall in love with him."

Billie said nothing, so Doris added, "Well, you know what I mean."

"Yes, I certainly do," she agreed. "Even though I don't know him that well, he seems to have a sympathetic attraction about him that… well… I don't know what I'm trying to say, but I think you know what I mean."

"Yes, I do. Anyway, we'll see what happens."

For Billie and Babe to be separated at night was one thing, but she knew that the real anguish would be heaped upon the children, which she had hoped to avoid. But then Babe was indicted for tax evasion. Billie was heard to say that Babe "had another burr under his saddle." She supposed this would interject further grief and turmoil on their family. So, Babe's lawyer arranged a mutual separation agreement with Billie that would not become formal until his legal problems were cleared up.

Babe assured Billie that the tax fray was all a mistake. He claimed that a jealous member of the Internal Revenue Service and an ambitious prosecutor had brought forth the unfair accusation against him. Further, Babe led her to believe that even if he received an unfavorable verdict in court, the case would be thrown out on appeal.

After months and months of court debacle, Babe lost the case. This brought great shame on Billie, especially for the sake of the children. Her first reaction was to write to JD in the hope that he would have something to offer in the way of encouragement. Then she decided to just write her way out of it instead. She had learned this tactic from JD, and Billie had always marveled at her ability to place her problems upon a shelf and out of her mind by simply writing about them. But in the end, she did not pursue either avenue of relief. Instead, she wrote to Wade Simmons and invited him to come to Washington to visit her.

Billie did eventually write JD, but only after Wade's visit, which she considered a remarkable turn of events in her life. She addressed the letter to Dr. J. Emery Beauchamp Dayne. Billie didn't know how he would receive the information within, but she assumed Katie would be most favorably impressed.

CHAPTER 91

The Shenandoah River

Dear JD (my best friend),

If the 'my best friend' is no longer operative or amusing and thus presumptuous, please forgive me. But I had to write and inform you of the turn of events in my life, which I hope you will find both informative and, perhaps, a bit amusing. I wish to relate to you (sometimes in graphic terms) what has happened to me recently and in the intervening years since you left.

When you noticed the amount of postage on the envelope, you probably realized that this was more than just a note. And, of course, it is.

As it turns out, you were right in being taken aback when you found out I was to marry Babe. How perceptible you have always been! When Babe returned from the war, I forgave him for all his dalliances while he was away— or at least I thought I had. But in all fairness to him, perhaps I had not. Still, I committed myself to making our marriage work and to proceed in rearing our children in a proper way. But, I might as well acknowledge it because I know it is true and that you are aware of it also, that while the two of us (that is, Babe and myself) have both been self-indulgent in our own careers, the Abels have administered to the everyday needs of our children. This certainly is not a criticism, but rather a simple fact.

Along the way, Babe and I grew apart. Later, he became embroiled in a problem with the IRS and was convicted of tax evasion, but he still contends that he will beat the rap on appeal. When I consider his ways of doing things and the amount of money they tell me he is spending for lawyers, I don't doubt that he is right. In any event, our marriage came down like a house of cards. Trite (the house of cards) I know, but that's what happened. We will divorce as soon as this is over, no matter what the outcome of his case.

Now here is the graphic part. During the War, John Dempsey, the little boy who lived up the track from Snakeden, crossed paths with an Army pilot over in the CBI named Wade Simmons whom I met years ago while attending Radford. Of course, they made the connection when the name Snakeden came up. Wade initiated a correspondence with me, which I agreed to. In one of his letters, he reminded me of a dance we had attended together, and he said—and I quote—that I was "warm and terrific to hold when dancing." I read and reread that phrase over and over. It simply wiped me out. Today it still haunts me and haunts me to no end.

Well, when Babe pulled a dirty trick and found out about my correspondence with Wade, I arranged (yes, I was the instigator) for us to meet in Washington for dinner. It had been years since we had spoken, so I did not know what to expect. But the evening proceeded better than I could have imagined. When we finished with dinner, we realized that it had snowed and the roads were too bad for travel. We wound up at your cousin June's house where she provided two rooms for us. Of course, we had to peruse (her word) all her paintings and listen to each attendant story.

Finally, we kissed good night and went to our separate rooms. Yes—I did say kiss!

June lent me one of her nighties. As you know, she is about five feet tall and I have at least seven inches on her. Wade, who is about six-foot-two, was awarded the honor of wearing June's husband's pajamas. You can let your imagination figure out the rest.

We were in our respective rooms for only a few minutes until I could not stand it any longer. I have never felt like this before in all my life—even in all those years when I thought I was madly in love with you and would have welcomed you to have your way with me. Those words "warm and terrific to hold" kept ringing in my mind.

I slipped out of bed and looked for a robe. I didn't want to turn a light on, so I cracked the door and looked for activity from June, even though she was one floor below. Before I knew it, I was raising the covers on Wade's bed and sliding into his embrace. I don't know whether he had heard me and was waiting for me when I arrived, but his arms were open when I got there.

It probably sounds unbelievable, but we simply kissed and held on in the embrace of my life. I finally asked Wade what he meant by "warm and terrific to hold," and he said that he had found me to be outgoing, interesting, and pleasant to talk to. He said it had nothing to do with my body, though the feel of my crop running down my back intrigued him. What I had wondered or dreamt of since the time I had first read those words "warm and terrific to hold" all came true. He may as well have had cupid shoot an arrow through my heart for I knew I was truly in love.

After a while, when I realized that I was probably driving him crazy, I indicated that though I was satisfied just to be held, he could have his way with me if he needed. He tightened his grip and said, "No, honey. I'm in Heaven already. I don't have to go further."

Shortly after this, Wade returned to his base and we wrote and phoned from time to time while waiting for Babe's tax evasion case to be resolved in court and for our divorce proceeding to be brought to closure. (Actually, closure *for me and* foreclosure *for him.)*

Put your graphic sunglasses on again because here comes a little more graphic disclosure*!! In the early summer or late spring, Wade visited me and we went for a ride up in the Shenandoah Mountains. Our plan was to take a swim in the river; it being in the middle of the week, we assumed no one would be at the new park that was being built.*

As we rode along, we discussed the Bible. It was understood early on that once I was divorced, we would be married by the first resource available (preacher, justice of the peace, whatever). This takes into account that we had taken Maw's advice from years past to read the book of Corinthians before we made any decision. This we had done separately. Now, as we rode along up the road, we read the first book of Corinthians again, this time together. After this, we mutually agreed that we would never take another drink of booze or try any mind-altering drug, no matter what! "No matter what" includes a binding agreement even in death or departure of any kind by either party.

Wade does not believe that I am an atheist at all—not even a nonbeliever. He thinks that in all my years of talking with you, I was simply trying to prove (or have it proven to me) that Jesus was all that you purported him to be. He said that I should have never been named Billie, but rather Thomas and nicknamed Tommie! And then he said, "There is no indication as to what position Thomas occupies in whatever eternal life he enjoys." He said that Thomas should not necessarily expect to sit in the same room that Jesus and the disciples occupy. In fact, he would be satisfied in the fulfillment of Jesus's promise of eternal life. Then he said, "You love Jesus because you have indicated it and confessed it any number of times to me. The way you talk of your contemporary friend (that's you!) and Maw makes it all the more obvious and undeniable!"

Then I held him close (I was practically under the steering wheel) and asked him in the most quizzical and genuine way, "What would hinder me from being baptized when we arrive at the river?"

He replied, "Absolutely nothing if you don't mind getting wet!"

I didn't even mind that he said the word 'getting.' You remember my disdain for get, git, got, I suppose? I then asked him by what authority he could baptize me? He replied, "By the authority vested in John Dempsey."

"And who vested this authority in John Dempsey?" I asked.

He said, "That was vested in him by Johnny Abel."

Naturally, I asked Abel's authority, and he said it came from JD. You! "Why not from Reverend Parman?" I asked.

Wade then changed course in order to establish a predicate that would enable him to answer my question. He cited the second or third verse in the Bible—that would be from Genesis. Even today, nineteen centuries after the birth of Christ, people are still saying things like "God created the earth and the land and the sea." That, as you know is an objective statement. God created everything in six days and took Sunday off. All this is objective. However, if you read five different Bibles from five different Christian faiths, they will all be different in some way but will basically mean the same thing. In other words, they will all say practically the same subjective thing: namely that the wind of the Spirit of God blew across the earth. (I'm paraphrasing here.)

So, we are dealing with a spirit, and that spirit is like the wind. It is not some vest or cloak of authority—it is a spirit. Wade then turned to me and asked, "Is it coming to you now?"

I said, "Yes, but go on." And he did.

Here is what he said to me: "When JD told Johnny Abel the story of the eunuch, he put the Spirit of Jesus in him, as if it were a seed in his heart. And to draw another analogy, his heart was impregnated like the seed in a mother's womb. When Johnny was baptized, that seed became a symbol of the release or activation of that spirit within. It is also a symbol of the seedless heart being washed away or cleansed of sin. My understanding of the matter is not an original thought of mine, but it comes from Dempsey's faith. He says belief should come from understanding and not obedience. That's something both Dempsey and JD picked up. In some faiths, it is either overlooked or not allowed."

"In other words," he went on to say, "the Spirit of God was within Jesus and came down through the ages until it reached that Mr. Cowley, or whatever his name was, and then JD, then Johnny Abel, then Dempsey, and then me. It was not planted in each person by some ordination process or some ecclesiastic entity. It came directly from Jesus to a country clodhopper who could tote the football, to a child living near the mountains of Lynchburg, to the son of an indigent family living a mile and a half west of the town of Snakeden where the trout flourish except when they are waylaid by the indigenous snakes living on the creek."

Then he asked if he could have a kiss. I, of course, obliged. I am sorry, but I messed up again. But I can assure you that the graphic part does really start now!

When we arrived at the Shenandoah River, there was not a soul around. I told Wade I didn't want to go into the river with my clothes on. After all, there was no one there to see me, and he had already slept with me half naked. I told him that we should make believe that we were on a beach in Spain or southern France so I could take my blouse off. He said that was okay thinking that I had a bra on. But I rarely wear a bra. Perhaps I'm being a bit prideful here, but I was very appreciative that Wade couldn't seem to believe that a mother of three children, and at my age, did not have to wear a bra. But there they were, and he could see for himself. Anyway, he made me put his T-shirt on, and he insisted that I keep my panties on, which was the proper thing to do.

As you read this, I bet you are thinking of that little heifer named Duty. If you remember, she had the most perfect and beautiful little bag, but would not come into heat. Well, when I had three children, I certainly came into heat and bred, but I never developed much milk in my breasts. Even when I did try, I could not develop enough milk to nurse any of my children. This always disappointed me, but I tried never to disclose it to anyone. I was simply afraid that the children would not bond with me. Now even as I'm writing this, I'm becoming paranoid about my current relationship with my children!

Let me stop here to say that this letter is directed to both you and Katie. After all these years, I think of you as one. However, I hope you and Katie do not think that I am being vulgar in lumping my body talk with a sacred act like baptism!

Now I will continue. We went into the river with the water up above my waist. Wade placed his arm around my shoulders and his hand over my mouth. Just as he started to lower me into the water, I saw people. I tried to cry out, but Wade had his I hand over my mouth, so I just grabbed him and pulled away. Then I pointed over his shoulder.

The couple came nigh. We learned that the man was a Sunday school teacher and the woman was his wife. (I was certainly glad that Wade had made me put on his T-shirt!) We talked for a minute when the teacher asked if we were about to perform a baptism. When we confirmed that we were, the man and his wife informed us that it would be better if we would validate the event in writing. He said that they would be more than happy to witness the solemn ceremony (as they called it) and sign a paper confirming that it all took place in their presence. He, being an elder in one of the neighboring churches, was indeed authorized to witness and document such a wonderful event. We agreed to his offer, and Wade immersed me.

When it was over, I stayed in the river sitting on my bottom while Wade went to the car to pull out the necessary items for writing a statement of baptism. Once it was signed, the couple went on their way.

As I removed my wet clothes, I noticed that Wade discreetly looked away though I probably would not have objected to him looking at me. This is just another one of those comparisons I make between him and Babe. Babe would have gawked and made some remark alluding to Sally Rand or some other exotic dancer.

When I was fully dressed, Wade looked into my eyes and not at my body. I felt as if I were a virgin. (That's a little stretch though!) Then we sat on the bank for hours and talked. Though we had nothing to eat, I was so much in love and happy and filled with the Spirit of His understanding that I didn't need anything to eat. Then I realized that the food bit was what the church communion service is all about! It symbolizes that bread alone is nourishment for our body while the worship service is nourishment for our spirit.

Oh! When I asked Wade if he thought that I had been 'born again', he just laughed and said, "No! Like a mustard seed that can lay idle and not sprout for years, the water in the Shenandoah River has moistened your heart *like rain on the mustard seed. Your spirit has now been activated and is growing."*

So, precious to me were his words and embrace that I cried the whole way home in spurts of joy. I wiped the tears on my brand new, white skirt and even blew the snot from my nose on it, which I strangely wanted to save to preserve the moment.

A few days after this, I rode up to see my parents. I don't know why, for I should have known what would happen. I suppose I was looking for someone to confirm my beliefs that I had a right to my own life, that I didn't have to sit back on my horse with all my affluence and take what was dealt to me from someone else, namely my husband. If I owe a debt of allegiance to someone who is a taker, I don't intend to pay the bill without a fight for my rights!

As I raced up the road toward Middleburg, I couldn't help but think that I was wasting my time; the gas was of no concern. Babe had always been the southern white knight to them. He could do no wrong in their minds. My shortcomings and idiosyncrasies were always the problem. As expected, Dad would hear none of the divorce talk. And I shall say no more about that. I wiped the tears from my eyes with the back of my hands all the way from their house to your mother's house.

Bonnie was caring and sympathetic, but she still believed marriage was a one-time deal. She said living without the love of a man and rearing his children was a heartrending experience, but once committed there was no turning back or changing course. As she said this, I envisioned a ship in a storm where the helmsman refuses to tack to a more reasonable route in order to avoid disaster. I hugged Bonnie and told her I wanted to speak to Maw alone, if she did not mind. Of course, she understood.

I hate to relate to you that Maw is losing her sight little by little each time I see her. Yet, she seems to see more clearly than most! I sat down beside her and told her everything that I have conveyed in this letter—even the part about crawling into bed with Wade. I bared my soul to her. Momma, and certainly Daddy, would never have ever heard such candor from me!

Maw compared me to the old story of the goose flying around the lake calling its mate, for as you know, geese mate for life. She summed it all up so succinctly. "Honey," she said, "just you assume when you came up out of that water in the Shenandoah that you were a born-again virgin. Both of you keep your pledge of abstinence until you are married. Then you will feel true fulfillment for the rest of your life. I know it. Just as sure as I'm sitting here, you will have true love and fulfillment. For the rest of your life!"

She could have stopped there and I would have been happy, but she continued. She said, "Jesus Christ had to come into this sinful world to give us understanding and allay our ignorance. Then he had to be crucified to save us from our sins. The Civil War, in the final analysis, had to be fought sooner or later to rid the country of the misadventure and the sin of slavery, though tens of thousands had to perish in the effort. Your mother and father are misguided in putting social concerns above what is right and wrong and in the best interest of their daughter. And last of all, Bonnie—my wonderful, faithful daughter—made a horrid mistake with her marriage to Marcus. She didn't need to be a martyr for the rest of her life. That was her choice."

As Wade Simmons pretty much said to me in his first letter, if this offends you or otherwise places a burden on our love and respect for each other, you need not reply. Your silence will inform me of your decision, and I will understand.
Billie

P.S. As for Katie: I have completely forgiven her for stealing you away from me. I held the fabric of her soul up to the purest of sunlight. There was not even one stain! White as bleached snow! And all my hostility is gone.

CHAPTER 92

Go With Maw

Dear Billie (Tommie),

Boy!!! Girl, you don't know what you have done to us here! With the weekend holiday and all, it has been a few days since we could reply. After being away, we found your letter lying on the table near the chair where I always sit. Katie always sits in a chair across the room not particularly close to mine. This we have done all our married life to read. Sunday I sat down to read your letter, and when finished, I gave it to Katie to read. She was in awe. Then she came over, sat in my lap, and said, "Read it to me again," which I did several times.

She has been in my lap every Sunday since. Each night I put my arms around her and hold her and rub her back for the longest time. Like your friend says, the spirit and love are like the wind—no man can grab it from another; no one has control or sway of it. They may bend it or divert it, but it slips around into all nooks and crannies.

By whom and where was Wade Simmons baptized?

This relationship you and Wade have going for you is overwhelming in proportions unknown to us. We thought we had a loving relationship, but yours is not described even by the word love. You demonstrate a deep affection and fondness of indescribable magnitude.

Go with Maw! Fly away with your newfound gander. As far as Babe is concerned, he will make out all right. You have done the right thing by him, but let him up easy and forgive him. Not even a stain is to remain in his fabric.

You have given the word 'love' a new meaning, and you have elevated abstinence to unbelievable heights. Enclosed please find our deepest love and affection and, above all, our thanks for considering us worthy of hearing your story.
JD and Katie

CHAPTER 93

Prenuptial

A long white limousine drew up in front of the K Street office of Babe Lunsford. The driver put his trouble lights on and stepped to the building side of the car. In his time, Babe came out followed by two smiling lawyers and a very attractive paralegal with beautiful blonde hair that took one's breath away until, by closer observation, dark gray roots betrayed her. As it happened, her expertise was more in typing and social affairs than in legal work.

Rube was pretty much bald except for the horseshoe of red hair resting above his ears as if it defied gravity. He considered himself not only Babe's severest critic but also a critic at large. So, when Babe suggested that it was in their best interest to show great concern for their prospects in dealing with these country people, Rube laughingly diverted his concern to the success of the recent tax case.

When the jury had ruled against Babe, his case looked like a four-engine bomber beset with flames and ready to crash. But when, as Rube boasted, he simply tacked it into a steep dive to the court of appeals, the sheer force of the wind blew out the flames of guilt and accusation. It was a show that Rube suspected Babe's estranged wife might even appreciate. He assured Babe that his two lawyers had touched all the bases; they certainly intended no animus or ill will.

"Look," he said, "these country lawyers have probably never even seen a prenuptial until they were faced with this one."

But Babe resisted. "You don't know about these characters! You've been down there in the district court swatting a bunch of flies. These people may look like a bunch of busy little workers, but I can tell you that they can act like a bunch of damn hornets. Do you even know what a hornet is?"

"Not particularly," Rube replied, "but I can surmise that it is a stinging bee of some sort by your alarming reference to it. Hell, I didn't take entomology in pre-law! I didn't see any sense in taking those hard subjects just to become a lawyer. What the hell does this have to do with anything?"

"Well, I hope you're right, but I'm telling you," Babe warned, "Billie's like a piece of spring steel wire. Just when you think you can bend her any way you want, she'll snap back and whop you with that damn crop of hers. Hell, I remember the first time I ever saw her; she sat there in a chair with her steely eyes boring holes through me. I've never been so intimidated by anybody like that before or since. She had me so damned transfixed; I couldn't even find a place to put my hands. I'm telling you, she's spring steel, man!"

Rube took steps to cut the decibels down several notches by patting Babe on the leg and saying, "Just let us handle it, Mr. Lunsford, just like we did in federal court last month."

The limousine came to a complete halt, and the driver was out in a second to open the door for Babe. The others were given similar treatment, but they had unlatched their own doors by the time the driver reached them. So, preeminence was established; even though Babe was with ample counsel, he was to be the main attraction.

As they started toward the big house, Johnny's wife Sarah and one Daniel LeFranc, her counsel, came out and directed them to the tack room. Babe started to resist, but Daniel pointed again with great certainty, and the whole entourage entered the building. Once inside, Babe glanced at a fireplace and then to a picture window on the opposite wall.

"Who put these in?" he asked.

"Johnny," was the reply.

"Am I helping to pay for all this?"

"In a manner of speaking, you might say that," Sarah stated.

After they were all seated around the table, Rube took over the introductions. Rube's partner was named J. Berington Colenger. Such a moniker prohibited anyone from calling him anything other than 'mister' or 'counsel.' The fake-blonde paralegal's name was Monica. It was observed that her knees seemed to have a magnetic attraction to those of Babe's as they sat next to each other.

Rube then said, "We herewith present the prenuptial agreement that was signed by both parties and notarized, which states that each party will in reality retain ownership in their respective properties in the event of a dissolution of their marriage. In other words, Mrs. Lunsford will not be entitled to any of Mr. Lunsford's assets. Notwithstanding any claim of ownership to her property that he may otherwise be entitled to by virtue of his periodic monthly stipends that he has made to your client, he will agree to forego any further claims unless your client, at the suggestion of counsel, proceeds to litigation with the intent to seize any of his assets. If this were to occur, our client will file a claim of interest on all of your client's assets, including any animals and down to the very crop that she has carried on her person and he has admired during these many years of their marriage."

Here Rube conveyed a baneful smile. "My client would very much cherish to hold these items in his possession. Accordingly, we would suggest that your client sign our proposed release, including the mutual divorce papers. Then we may all consider that we have acted in a fair and reasonable manner and be on our way to adjacent pastures."

Rube pushed the papers toward Daniel, but Daniel slid them toward Sarah. This prompted Rube to ask, "Don't you think we lawyers should handle these matters?"

Whereupon Daniel quite emphatically stated, "Sarah is Miss Blacksheare's counsel, lawyer, and trustee. She is also the lead counsel in these proceedings."

Babe shot up out of his chair. "What the hell are you talking about? She's no lawyer!"

Calmly Daniel responded, "I proudly inform you that Mrs. Sarah Abel *is* a member of the Virginia Bar, and I'm even more proud to inform you that I have been her mentor for years in the study of law. Mrs. Abel, you might be interested to know, was the salutatorian and president of her senior class in high school. She worked in the defense industry during the war to help the war effort, acquired money to pursue college thereafter, and finished one year before being swept off her feet by her present husband. She finished her undergraduate degree and acquired her law degree during the first years of her marriage. Now, if you don't object, Mrs. Abel will explain her counteroffer of settlement, including the legal justification for her client's position."

About this time, Johnny Abel and a beautiful stallion appeared in full view through the picture window. Babe did not see Billie until Johnny was steadying her foot in the stirrup. As she mounted, Babe craned his neck to obtain a better view of the whole process. After mumbling, "Still has the prettiest ass in town," which all in attendance heard, his eyes searched slightly upward, and he asked, "Where's her crop? She doesn't have that crop stuck in her jodhpurs."

"She doesn't carry the crop anymore," Sarah responded.

Babe looked perplexed. "How long has that been going on?"

Sarah replied in a faint and haunting voice, "Ever since you read those letters she received from an old acquaintance who was in the CBI."

Babe became visibly perturbed. "Where's that damn crop now? I'd like to have it!"

"I don't think that's possible."

"Why it that?"

Sarah produced a controlled smile. "Perhaps, if we could proceed with the matters here at hand, the disposition of the crop will be disclosed."

Then she paused and looked at Daniel. "And perhaps, since Daniel is more learned and experienced in these matters, I could ask him to explain my husband's and my position in Miss Blacksheare's interests."

Daniel began. "Except for her personal items, that is clothing and such, Miss Blacksheare—a.k.a Mrs. Lunsford—does not own a thing. Interestingly enough, she does not even own her old crop that lays with its broken strap on the mantle behind you, Mr. Lunsford."

Babe and his legal counsel turned to look at the damaged crop. Daniel continued.

"Before she was married, and within days of JD's marriage to a Katherine Parman, she bought the interest in this property from her parents and subsequently filed a quitclaim deed transferring her every possession—excluding her personal items, of course—into a living trust, naming herself the lone trustee. At no time was she ever named as a beneficiary of that trust.

"The so-called Hell's Hole Real Estate holdings are in a separate trust and list Mrs. Abel here as the trustee. Her husband John Abel is the substitute trustee in the event that she cannot serve.

"As to the crop, when John Abel inquired as to whether Miss Blacksheare would like him to have the strap fixed—he thinking she would want to wear it as usual—she informed him that she was going to start a new life and would not be wearing it anymore. You will notice the word I used was *wearing*. The Abel's and myself do not know whether that word is used properly in this instance, but she apparently has said that it wasn't a mere swagger stick and that she wore it in her jodhpurs.

"Anyway, she tried to give it outright to John, but he reckoned it might someday wind up as an important item. Only he knows why. So, Sarah here prepared a bill of sale for a dollar, and it's been up there on the mantle ever since. Of course at John's insistence, Sarah did put a caveat in the bill of sale: that Miss Blacksheare or any of her children could reacquire it for a fair and reasonable price." Myriad glances were shared across the table.

"Now, if we could all turn our attention to that of Mr. Lunsford's assets. Our position on that, and in particular the prenuptial agreement, is after thorough review of the court records that materialized during Mr. Lunsford's debacle with the IRS, and which were so graciously provided to us by the IRS Counsel, we have determined that Mr. Lunsford was not completely forthcoming in listing his assets. As a matter of fact, he was completely *In Fraudem Creditorum*. Consequently, the prenuptial agreement is completely invalid from Miss Blacksheare's point of interest." Under the table, Babe pulled his leg away from Monica's touch.

"Accordingly, gentlemen and lady," Daniel said as he made eye contact with the fraudulent blonde, "we submit these simple documents in counteroffer to your large stack of documents, and we suggest it's all to the benefit of your client, Mr. Lunsford, to sign. We believe you will find them readable—and reasonable—under the circumstances."

While Rube and his partner perused the papers, Babe accepted his fate. The game was over. Though he had two very experienced and expensive guns, they were completely devoid of ammunition. But the mountain hillbilly lawyer was loaded for bear. It's one thing to get your ass kicked, he thought, but it's another to be a sore loser in front of your conqueror.

Babe would be signing a paper that split his assets down the middle, her share unencumbered by any current or future claim. All assets would be going into a trust to be established for the benefit of his children, and they were to be administered by and at the sole discretion of one Sarah Hart Abel, Esquire.

CHAPTER 94

I Told You So

"How did you come to choose the legal profession?" Rube asked Daniel. Babe groaned and waited for a long answer, which he knew would be forthcoming.

"When my Daddy would get drunk, which was at least once a week, he would always say that he held me up by the legs when I first came out of my mother's womb, and when he saw that my legs were the same length, he knew I would never be a mountain man or worth a damn. Damn wasn't the word he used; I'm just cleaning it up here in front of the ladies. This went on and on until I began to believe it. Whenever people told me I would never be worth a damn, I decided to fulfill their expectations. So here I am—a lawyer." In reality, Daniel came from a happy, hardworking, and sober family—at least according to Johnny Abel.

Babe had to crane his neck to see Billie dismount after her ride. She passed the reigns to Johnny and Sarah's son. As she did, she grabbed him around the waist and kissed him on the cheek. Tears came to Babe's eyes and he wondered how things might have turned out differently.

Babe signed the paper and laid the pen down slowly so as not to show any animosity. Then he stood up and made his way toward the house. As he approached the door, a uniformed man from the sheriff's office came out and asked, "May I assist you in some way?"

"No," he said. "I'm Mr. Lunsford; I just want to see my wife."

"I'm sorry, I can't let you in. You see, the lady has a restraining order, and I'm not supposed to let anyone in. Since that book of hers came out there's been all kinds of people posing as imposters—from her husband to the governor. Everybody wants to see her."

Babe didn't push the issue. He turned his back on his former home and joined his entourage in the limousine where he grabbed a drink and slipped into an almost prostrate position.

"I hate to tell you I told you so, Rube, but I sure as hell told you so."

"Funny you would say that, because after you left, I asked Daniel what the heat source was for that little building we were in, and he said, 'It's the same thing that fires most conversations in the legal community.' And when I pushed him further, he said, 'It's nothing more than Mr. Abel putting a tank of water and a lot of copper tubing under that pile of horse manure you see out there, which by spontaneous combustion stays so hot it will burn your hand even in the dead of winter. Then the hot water flows through an old automobile radiator and the fan blows through it just like a car.'"

Babe said, "I knew we were in for a lot of horse shit when you asked your first question."

Then Monica spoke up. "What was that phrase he used? Wait… I've got it written down here." She flipped through her notes and finally announced, "*In Fraudem Creditorum*. What does that mean?"

Rube started to explain, but Babe interrupted, sitting upright in his seat, the alcohol finally taking effect. "That's like when you have to pay a damn lawyer twice what he's worth to split your damn bank accounts in half, split your damn houses on Kalorama Road and Florida in half, and split everything you got in half! If they catch you *In Fraudem Creditorum* and you think you are scot-free and about to reach a climax in your life, they come in and coitus interruptus."

Babe slumped back down in the seat. "Just let it go for now honey, and you can look it up in the legal dictionary when we get back to the office."

Rube cleared his throat and said, "I told that Daniel he ought to come down to K Street and have lunch with us so I could soft-soap him a little, and he said they'd all been down there to eat a couple of nights ago with Mrs. Lunsford. Of course he called her Miss Blacksheare. Have they always called her Miss Blacksheare?"

"Ah hell, I believe so."

"Daniel was really impressed with her. He said Miss Blacksheare let him sit right in your chair at your regular table."

"So, you're calling her Miss Blacksheare now, too, huh?"

"Aw, no. I was just saying that it was funny how Daniel said that it was the first time he ever sat in a wingback chair in front of a fireplace in a restaurant. Everyone else had to sit in captain's chairs."

"For God's sake, Rube," Babe whined. "Do you have to go on and on? Don't I have enough to worry about without you making matters worse?"

"I'm sorry. But you can't help but like those people. And the way they talk about her is so mystic. Sarah said the next time I came out to settle things she'd have a couple slices of fresh ham for me from the farm up in Middleburg."

"Middleburg!" Babe exclaimed. "I didn't even know she had anything up in Middleburg!"

CHAPTER 95

Which Ticket to Buy

A few days later, Wade Simmons—now a civilian—showed up at Snakeden with joy in his heart to embrace an equally joyous Billie Blacksheare. He stayed in her house, in his own room, in love and celibate.

Billie's children, now ages 9, 11 and 13, feigned respect with their pretentious silence. Wade bided his time, contemplating his next move that would dissuade them from considering him an interloper. As he had said to Billie, he would try to show them that their mother and he were participants in an evolving situation where marriage between their father and mother had become sterile and without purpose, even to the extent of rearing their children. The Abels, by all accounts, were the surrogate parents by virtue of a void created by the Lunsfords' benign indifference to their lives.

Wade planned to relate to them indirectly the basketball metaphor that their mother had pondered to him. She had asked in earnest whether he thought she was being a wild 'rim shot' off an unhappy relation with Babe only to be 'slam-dunked' by the first man who came along. He would assure them that he and their mother were originally intended to be mates and had only been deferred from such a union by the untimely death of his mother and the war. It would likely require a leap of faith on their part to accept his interpretation, but he thought it was worth a try.

Wade knocked on the door of the Abel's house and went in when he heard a call to do just that. By the look on Sarah's face and the tears descending from Johnny's one eye, he could tell they were in despair. With his patch lifted on his forehead, Patch rubbed his empty eye socket. Not only was he distraught, he was also in painful physical discomfort.

"I know why you're crying, but does your missing eye hurt, too?"

Sarah answered for him. "Yes. It always hurts, too."

"Where are they now?" Wade, asked.

"Most likely, they're over on Brown's Hill," Sarah answered.

"How far is that from here?"

"A little over a mile."

"If I may take one of the other horses, I'd like to go over and talk to them. I know you probably think I can't say anything constructive, but it may just be the opportunity I need to establish a rapport with them. It may work, especially since you all have just had a confrontation with them."

"Do you want me to saddle up a horse for you?" Johnny asked.

"No, I don't need a saddle. Is there a crop in the barn?"

"There's one hanging on the wall just as you go in the door," Johnny told him.

It would seem as though he had thought it all out before going up the hill because instead of bridling the horse, he untied the knot and slipped the rope that was tied to the halter out of the hole in the wooden board. With the crop and rope in his left hand, he jumped across the horse like a sack of feed and then threw his right leg over and came into an upright position. All of this was done in a purposeful manner, a form of staging an event to look like an Indian—without saddle or halter.

As he rode out toward the precipice of Brown's Hill, Wade spied Oak Run curling below. He imagined an audience sitting on the sides of the hill, much like a Greek amphitheater, with actors on the banks of the run below.

He found the children sitting under a lonely cedar tree that seemed to defy the outcropping of rock from which it grew. He looked down onto five smiling youths, all stoned on what Marcus's cousin June—the artist—called Mary Juana.

"Where you going, Mr. Summons?" Bobby asked sarcastically.

"Just came over here to see if I could find a couple Indians to make buddies with, Booby."

They all giggled, but then stifled their laughter after realizing that hostility and confrontation were the order of the day. Three glassy eyed youngsters rose and said goodbye, leaving Bobby and Lillie Lunsford alone with their mother's love interest who had come into their lives without their invitation. After a period of silence, Bobby finally asked, "Where you running away to?"

His sister added, "Yeah, and when are you coming back?"

"We're going to Pakistan," Wade answered calmly, "and I guess we aren't coming back."

"You gotta come back sometime!" Lillie challenged.

"I guess you're right about that," Wade said. "But, we're not buying round-trip tickets." Wade paused to see their reaction; they exchanged alarmed glances.

"You see, I spent a couple of years over in Pakistan with the Army just as my marriage was going on the rocks. It has its drawbacks, but it does get you away from your troubles and heartaches back here in the states. There's no reason for us to come back if troubles and heartaches persist. I mean, if there's no one back here who needs us or wants us, we probably won't even be missed."

"Well, tell her to go ahead," Bobby said spitefully. "We got Johnny and Sarah to stay with us. We spend most of our time with them anyway."

Wade nodded. "Yeah, that's what they tell me, but we have a little problem there also."

"What's that? Are they going to Pakistan, too?"

"Not exactly. You see, I just came from their place, and Johnny tells me you two have been smoking marijuana again. He said, just when he thought there wasn't going to be any more liquor and dope in his life, you two turned on him. So, though your mother and I are heading to Pakistan, Johnny and Sarah are left with troubles and heartaches. I feel pretty damn sorry for a guy who got the hell shot out of him and lost an eye, only to return home to have his friends hurt him some more."

Bobby and Lillie hung their heads.

"As a matter of fact," Wade continued, "Sarah says he just can't stand to cry anymore. It hurts him. Seems like the tears that come out of his good eye don't hurt too much, but when they try to come out of his bad eye it pains him something awful."

"How can it hurt if he doesn't have an eye to begin with?" Bobby asked.

"That's just what I thought, too. I'm told that it's just like one of those guys who got his leg blown off during the war. The leg ain't there, but it still hurts some of the time. Actually, they say it's even worse when it itches. You know, you can take a pill for pain, but there's nothing you can do for an itch. So, I suppose if an amputated leg can hurt and itch, there's no reason why an empty eye socket can't hurt when you're disappointed in the kids you love like your own."

"But we ain't bothering no one," Bobby asked.

"I don't know about that. I've wanted to tell you that I wasn't going to try to take your father's place and that I hoped you would both stay in contact with him. I want to keep in touch with my little girl, but her mother is bent on keeping us apart. My little girl, who's about your age, knows I'm her real daddy. So, you see, I'm sure it's best for your mother and father to both be kind and forgiving toward each other and above all do the best thing for you three kids."

Too stoned to truly track the conversation, Lillie said, "I bet you've never been up on a high place like this before!"

Wade replied, "Actually, I've been up higher than this before—many times, in fact. You see, I'm a pilot and I've flown the Hump. You know where the Hump is?" They both shook their heads no. "Well, the Hump is what they call the Himalayan Mountains over in India and

Pakistan. And they're so high the devil doesn't even attempt to scale them."

"The devil doesn't come up this high either," Lillie countered. "He's down in the ground and never comes up to high places like this."

"I can't say I agree with that," Wade answered, taking a seat on the ground across from the kids. "The devil goes into a lot of places. People just don't always recognize him. For example, when I was younger, I used to box a little—used to spar with this old pro and make about five or six bucks a day doing it. As I became more experienced, I started boxing in these preliminaries to make a little more money. Anyway, one night I was boxing this kid named Al something, I don't remember his last name. When I started to get the best of him, I heard someone yell in a loud raspy voice, 'Take him out Al, take him out Al.' I knew he was just trying to get into my head. Divert my attention. But I knew what was going on, and I wasn't going to let Al have his way with me.

"When the round ended, I went over to sit on the stool and looked around to see who had been yelling, 'Take him out Al.' When I saw this portly guy all dressed up in a tuxedo, smoking a big cigar, I knew it was him.

"About this time, I started to feel this big oyster sliding down my nasal passage, and I knew it was all bloody, 'cause when you box like that you always have a little blood trickle down your nose. No matter how well you're doing, there's going to be a little trickle of blood. I turned my head to spit it into the bucket that was sitting there on the side of the ring, but I realized that bucket was full of the water they used to sponge off the back of my neck and chest. So, I raised my trajectory a little. The spit came flying out of my mouth like a bullet. It either bounced off the bucket or one of the ropes, and it landed on the right lapel of the portly guy in the tuxedo. He just sat there frozen—a beautiful carnation in his left lapel and a bright red oyster on his right lapel.

"Then I saw the guy reach under his tux coat. The first thing I thought was that he was going to pull a gun out, right there in the arena with all those people sitting around. But he didn't. He pulled out a handkerchief to wipe his lapel. All the while, he kept his eyes fixed on me, trying to stare me down.

"The bell rang, and as I got up to do battle again I noticed that there were a lot of guys sitting there in tuxedos smoking cigars. The words 'oxymoron' and 'contradiction' kept popping up in my head. I guess you know why. If someone wears a tuxedo to a prizefight where there's nothing but spit and blood and gore, I suppose that qualifies as an oxymoron. Anyway, I knew it was quiet a contradiction in terms.

"So, Lillie, you can bet the old devil is not sitting up here on Brown's Hill with some hard-pointed rock sticking in his butt. No, he's probably dressed in some finery, sitting in a wingback chair with a stogie stuck in his mouth. And he's smiling all the while."

"Do you have any more stories like that?" Lillie asked.

"I do," Wade answered, and he proceeded to tell them about his experience with the Iroquois and Choctaw Indians. The Iroquois he had met as a boy growing up in New York, and the Choctaw he had met when he was stationed with the Army in Mississippi. Bobby and Lillie just listened, and Wade kept talking until he could tell the kids had come down from their drug-induced high.

"Here's what I suggest we do," he said. "I'll leave you here to think about things, and you decide what you want to do. If you want to be buddies with me, I'll make sure to call you Bobby and you Lillie and not Booby and Tillie. And I expect you can come up with an appropriate name for me—none of that Summons or Simons stuff. Just something we all will recognize as a name of respect and affection. And don't forget to tell your little sister that she's in on it, too.

"I'm hoping that the next time we run into each other, you'll greet me with a new name. And Lillie, I'm hoping you'll come up and hug me and kiss my cheek while I kiss yours. Bobby, I'm hoping you'll come up and shake hands with me. You'll reach out your right hand, and you'll put your left hand on my shoulder to show it's more than just a routine gesture. Then I'll buy two round-trip tickets to Karachi, Pakistan. But if you do none of this, then I'll know where we stand, and though I'll still wish you the best, I'll be buying two one-way tickets to Karachi."

Wade let this all sink in before standing up and mounting the horse. "What I'd really like is to make a deal with you. If you promise to lay off the marijuana and anything else that might burn your brains up, we'll prick our fingers and swap blood and become buddies for the rest of our lives, just like I did with the Iroquois Indians."

Tears were now streaming down both of the kids' faces. Bobby blurted out, "But I thought we could always count on Mom!"

"I promise you, you can," Wade assured them, "but with your Daddy gone, your Mom has to have someone she can count on. That someone is me. I love your Mom very much, and I want to take care of her so she can take care of you. You see what I mean?"

They both nodded.

"Let me know what you decide," Wade said. "I have to know which tickets to buy."

CHAPTER 96

Judge Not

She came out of the house and walked briskly toward Rube who had just exited the limousine alone. He thought to himself, when a woman comes out of the house to greet a guest, she's either anxious to talk to that person or the house is not clean. He suspected the former.

Billie extended her right arm with the back of her hand up. This presented him with two options: either he could engage in a routine handshake or he could kiss the back of her hand without fear of a protruding thumb entering his eye. He kissed her hand.

"I want to thank you for your fine cooperation and to ask you to relate my very best wishes to my now ex-husband," Billie stated unabashedly. "And please inform him that he may have easy access to the children any time he wishes. Also, I wish for you to make it clear to him that I won't cohabitate in any way with my intended until we are married. It would not be good for the children. And of course, I expect he will do likewise if they visit him at his Kalorama house."

Rube tried to say something, but Billie was not done. "The Abels are in the tack room where we always meet to discuss any business. I can assure you that by meeting in there, no effort is being made to either demean this transaction or personally denigrate you in any way. Thank you again, and now if you will excuse me."

With that, she turned back toward the house leaving Rube to complete business with the Abels. He greeted Johnny and Sarah in the tack room with a "good afternoon" and then blurted out, "Damn, she not only deals the cards with precision and dispatch, she deals them face up. Somehow, I like that, but I'm not used to it in my profession."

Sarah smiled knowingly. "I've assembled all the papers, and Miss Blacksheare has signed her parts. I'm sure you'll find everything in order as we agreed. However, if you want to look them over, I'll go cut a little ham for you to take home. Johnny can wait here with you in case you need anything. It may take me a minute or two."

After Sarah left the room, Rube said to Johnny, "Nice little lady there, your wife!"

"Thanks. She's an awful lot more'n I ever deserved," he replied.

Rube glanced at the papers for a few minutes, and then said, "This preacher I hear so much about—JD, I believe his name is—Babe says he was the best damn running back he ever saw. Says he was built like a draft horse but ran like a deer. Must've been something. What does he think of divorce?"

"Well, I don't want to speak for someone on matters like that," Johnny answered cautiously, "especially someone in authority like a preacher. 'Cept he doesn't push himself around as an authority. He'll always start out by saying something like, 'well this is my understanding of the matter.' He doesn't come across like a know-it-all, you know. And he always seems to be interested in your understanding, even someone like me.

"Anyway, on the divorce question… I think he would ask you to consider this: Jesus, as you probably know, said a married person who remarries and has intercourse with the new spouse is committing adultery. But then he throws in what Sarah is always calling a caveat. And the caveat is this: adultery. In other words, adultery by either party is grounds for divorce. Now I could go into that a little further, but I think you can understand."

Rube chose his words carefully. "That seems very practical, but some gentiles don't think that way unless they have something to gain. You know, like money for instance."

Johnny wasn't sure where the conversation was headed, but he was willing to play along. "JD and Miss Blacksheare both deal their cards up. They don't cover anything that should be brought to clearest light. Like divorce, for instance."

Rube accepted Johnny's answer and then changed the subject. "What about the question of someone not going to Heaven unless they believe in Jesus? Us Jews for instance?"

Johnny was prepared to answer such a question as this. "Well now, JD's take on that requires you to separate material things from those of a spiritual nature. He always says that Jesus talked in the subjective, not the objective. And boy, when I got old enough to understand this, it sure explained a lot to me. I'm not educated, but I know how to look things up. And I've had the benefit of being around JD and Miss Blacksheare where I had the opportunity to overhear some things of importance.

"Now back to your question. I believe the passage you're referring to goes like this: 'Jesus saith unto him, I am the way, the truth and the life; no man cometh unto the Father but by me.' I know you've heard it said that God is the great *I AM*. Jesus, on the other hand is *ME*. And who is *ME*? *ME* is love, forgiveness, truth, charity, faith, and redemption, and that is the life. So, if you don't have those things, which are lumped into one name—Jesus—then you can't come unto the Father. Likewise, you can come unto the Father if you have those attributes.

"So, not to answer your question with a question, but do you have those attributes? I'm not in a position to judge. 'Judge not, that ye be not judged.' I guess you've heard that before. If you haven't, you might want to read the beatitudes in the New Testament.

"You might be interested to know," Johnny continued, "that when I first came up here from down in the mountains, JD had me buy a dozen day-old roses from a store run by Hebrew people for his mother's birthday. Then he had me deliver them to her at work. You probably wonder why he didn't just have the florist deliver them, but that was the whole thing. He said that was too commercial, and his mother would like to have all the people in the store see a nice, young man bring them in. And she would hug and kiss me just like I was her own son. I've never missed a year taking her roses since, 'cept when I was in the war. Then my sister Peggy took them.

"Now, here's the thing. The Hebrew florist knew I was religious and that my friend was a preacher; still, he would to some extent chide me about the Jews going to Heaven. So, that's why I was prepared for your question today."

Rube nodded, and then asked, "What about the pork business? Do you have an explanation for that?"

"I do," Johnny answered proudly. "Seems obvious to me that pork was forbidden way back in biblical times because they didn't have any preservatives. Pork spoils quickly and can make you sick. I'm sure you've heard 'bout trichinosis? So naturally the Jews said 'no pork' in their dietary laws. But you know, if we didn't have pork to eat where I come from, we would probably starve. Luckily, we could salt the pork down and preserve it. Can't hunt and eat rabbits and squirrels in the summertime. Can't eat beef or we wouldn't have any milk. And we couldn't eat the horses 'cause we needed them to pull the wagon and the corn plow."

Johnny was on a roll. "Just in case you're gonna ask me about fish, I might as well answer that also while we're on the subject of what to eat and what not to eat. Most of us gentiles believe that the Jewish folks didn't think too much about eating snakes and eels and things like that during biblical times. But when they placed a prohibition on eating anything that didn't have scales, they may have inadvertently excluded catfish as well. Heck, most orthodox Jews today eat catfish and don't even know that they don't have scales!"

Rube appeared dumbfounded. "From whom in his family did this JD get all his wisdom?"

"Well, according to Miss Blacksheare, his intellectual parts come indirectly from the Daynes, but his understanding and wisdom come from Mrs. Brown, but everyone calls her Maw."

"What's she like?" Rube asked.

"Maw never had a prejudiced thought in her body and loved children. Miss Blacksheare was just like her little girl, and she once told me that she preferred eating boiled potatoes and fatback with the

Browns to eating much nicer food with her own folks who were affluent and could serve whatever they wanted. You know, that always made me wonder. Whenever I go down there on a Saturday morning—and I go down there most every Saturday to buy her groceries—she's always listening to this guy preaching on the radio. And you know what? It's always the same rabbi! She says there doesn't seem to be a difference. I've asked her several times about that, and she just smiles and says, 'He tells the truth, as I see it.' 'Course, he doesn't mention Jesus, but apparently he doesn't run his teachings down either."

About this time, Johnny noticed that Rube appeared to be losing interest in what he was saying. "Guess I've talked your ear off, but just remember—like we tell the Yankees when they want to discuss the Civil War—you brought it up first!"

Rube laughed. Johnny added, "So don't go home and say I talk about Jesus all the time."

"Not a word," Rube agreed. Then he inquired, "How do you like Mr. Simmons?"

"Well, he's a bit different than Mr. Lunsford."

"How's that?"

"Well, the other day he mentioned doing something that I hadn't had time to do on account of my darn stomach hurting for a couple of days. Anyway, I thought, here's another one with a white glove. In the Army, we always kidded about some officer coming around at inspection time with a white glove and raking it across a shelf to check for dust. But as it turned out, he was just inquiring to see if I wanted him to do it.

"And then the kitchen sink in Miss Blacksheare's house stopped up. I went looking for a couple of stillson wrenches but got sidetracked. When I finally remembered, Momma saw me with my wrenches and asked, 'Where you going with those wrenches?'

"When I told her I was going to unstop the sink, she said kinda peevish like, 'Mr. Simmons already done it.' I couldn't imagine where he'd got the wrenches, 'cause nobody up there has any. Momma said he didn't use a wrench. He just asked for an old pan and laid down there on the floor, reached under the sink, and twisted that nut loose with his bare hands. Then he rolled over on his right side and did the same thing to the other nut and emptied the drain. 'I stood there and watched him,' she said. He told her that because there isn't pressure in a drain line like there is in a water line, you just want to hand tighten them.

"I'd never heard that before. I know I had tightened them with a wrench. It's a wonder Mr. Simmons could twist them off with his hands. Anyway, I said to Momma, 'It's 'bout time I have somebody 'round here to help me out a little.' She said she thought so, too. I could see that she's taken a liking to the flyboy. So have I. In all the years I've known Mr. Lunsford, I don't 'member ever seeing him with a tool in his hand."

About this time Sarah returned with the ham. Rube said, "Well, I can't say that things went well for my client, but it's sure been a pleasure otherwise. My wife and I will enjoy the fresh ham."

Rube said something that sounded like "shalom," shook Johnny's hand, thanked Sarah for the ham, and left with Babe's divorce and settlement papers. He was not entirely fulfilled, but he was satisfied that he had done the best he could for his client under the circumstances.

CHAPTER 97

Self-Interest

Babe arranged to meet Rube for dinner that night assuming that there would be no fee for an hour or so of advice, especially if he were to pick up the tab. As he sat there ensconced in his wingback chair, Rube handed him the papers. This is what he read:

WHEREAS Mr. Lunsford (the party of the first part) uses the dogs, namely Queenie and Chalky, solely as working animals to seek, stand, and fetch birds at his sole pleasure; and without any indication of affection or fondness during the entire year other than the hunting season; and,

WHEREAS said dogs are fed, housed, and otherwise maintained by the party of the first part's children and an associate, one JOHN ALTON ABEL (hereinafter referred to as the parties of the second part); and,

WHEREAS the parties of the second part do display and share great love, affection, fondness, and care of said dogs on a daily basis, thereby instilling in their hearts mutual warmth and happiness of great proportions; it is hereby agreed and ordained that the party of the first part shall have full control and use of said dogs during the hunting season, and the parties of the second part shall have control and enjoyment of them during the remainder of the year. Except the party of the first part may have visitation rights at any time he so desires, provided he gives full notice either verbally or in writing in advance.

Babe dropped the paper on the table and raised his hands up in supplication. "What the hell is that all about?"

Rube pursed his eyebrows askance and said, "Now, I don't want to become involved in any personal tete-a-tete between you and the lady. Why don't you just chalk this up to collateral damage that sometimes occurs during these kinds of proceedings?"

"I'm asking you, what do you think she means by this kind of crap?"

Rube answered, "Beats me! I told you I don't care to become involved in this type of personal dialogue. As a matter of fact, I like the lady. So, if you're agreeable to the arrangement, what's the problem?"

"Damn it!" Babe exclaimed. "You're supposed to counsel me in these matters."

"Okay, okay!" Rube placated. "Since you're insisting on having my take on the matter, I'll tell you what I think she's trying to say. She's isolated the word 'love' just as if it were a virus or a strain of bacteria. She's saying your interest in the dogs is purely commercial and for your own self-interest. In other words, you love the dogs for your own pleasure. That's the depth and breadth of your caring. You come up a little short on the fondness and affection portion that is supposed to be included in the complete sense of the word."

Babe was angry, but said nothing. Rube surmised, "If you are experiencing a little pain at the knees like they've been cut off, or you're feeling a sharp pain between your shoulder blades like there's a knife stuck and being twisted in your back, then she accomplished what she probably set out to do—namely to prove that you didn't truly love her. While you were having your fun downtown here, you should have been guarding the plate, as they say in baseball, and appreciating the little ballgame you had at home."

Babe knew Rube was right, but he wasn't about to tell him so.

"To tell you the truth it all fascinates the hell out of me!" Rube admitted. "The way it all happened; it seems to be a different way of life. And you can't—or at least I can't—help but wish that there was a little more of it going around in the world."

When Rube realized Babe had no intention of engaging in conversation, he said, "Look, I don't want to add to your woes.

You're my friend as well as my client, but I just think you ought to accept this and move on. You know, you were never suited for the quiet country life of a squire. You require a little more action in your daily routine!"

CHAPTER 98

The River Indus

Johnny, Sarah, and Billie's three children all gathered outside to say goodbye. A few days earlier, Billie had seen the children go to Wade and make their peace. The girls had put their arms around his waist, he bent down and they swapped kisses on the cheek. Bobby had extended his right hand, and when they shook, they both placed their left hands on each other's shoulders.

"It's a deal?" Simmons had asked.

"It's a deal." Bobby had replied, speaking for his sisters as well.

John Dempsey and his wife Maggie accompanied Wade and Billie to Pakistan. "For old times sake," they had laughed. John insisted that he revise his role as Simmons' attendant, but Wade would not hear of this since neither was in uniform anymore.

Well into the flight, with the armrest between them raised, Billie leaned close to Wade and whispered, "I'm so happy with anticipation. But what if something happened to the pilot and it was all brought to an end?"

"If something happened to him, I'd step into the cockpit and you'd have the best pilot that ever flew in the CBI at the controls." Then, in all seriousness he added, "Don't you ever think like that again. This is for real and will last forever!"

"Oh good! I just wanted you to reassure me!"

Many hours later Billie asked, "Will you know where you're going when we arrive?"

"Me? Sure!" Wade answered confidently. "The River Indus starts from the Himalaya Mountain Range in Tibet. It ends at the Arabian Sea, forming a large delta near Karachi that has a population of over ten million. The River Indus does not pass through the city metropolitan, so we cannot be baptized in the waters anywhere in Karachi. However, the river is about 1,800 miles long and passes through Kashmir, the northwest frontier province, the province of Punjab and Sindh. We can travel to the city of Hyderabad on the east bank of the river. It's an old city with a population of over one-and-a-half million, and the water before entering the city should be pure and free from the metropolitan's pollution.

"The River Indus is regarded as the cradle of the ancient Indus Valley civilization, corresponding to the Bronze Age of about 5000 B.C. Today, rice, wheat, millet, and cotton are the major crops. Small industries like woodcarving, embroidery, and handicrafts are pretty common, and I also remember that hanging chairs were all the rage."

Billie stared at Wade in wonderment. "Gee, all I asked was if you knew your way around. A pure and simple yes-or-no question, and you give me a lesson in geography!" They both laughed.

The four spent several days touring the sites in Karachi before they met up with the Reverend Dr. Faith Call, an older missionary woman and medical doctor who not only preached at the local church but also used the facilities as a clinic. Wade had rented a large vehicle for the journey—one they could all fit into, including Dr. Call's two aides who helped with the baptisms.

John Dempsey had introduced Wade to Dr. Call on their previous tour in Pakistan, and she had been the one to baptize him. She was happy to see both men again and was delighted to meet Billie and Maggie.

"It will always remain a memorable occasion when John brought Wade to me to be baptized. I couldn't believe it. Here was an enlisted man bringing an officer to be baptized in a very solemn and humble way."

During the drive, Dr. Call complimented Wade and Billie on their decision to be baptized again, especially Billie since this would provide her with a more authentically executed document for future use.

"What do you think of Pakistan?" she asked. "Do you folks like it here?"

Billie answered enthusiastically, "Yes, it's been an exciting time for us. The people are so different and the area so quaint, although I've never been one to want to live in a city as large as Karachi. As you probably know, we don't have mountains like these in Virginia."

Dr. Call was from Michigan. Nearing retirement, she planned to return to the states in a matter of months. "I'm financially supported by a little church back home through their missionary offering. I'm what they call their Living Link. They know their money goes directly to me, and I keep them apprised of my activities periodically, even down to the eyes of the person from whom I have removed cataracts and the like. The way things work now, my benefactors are able to see a tangible connection to their financial efforts. It puts things on a more personal level. But this is all to change as soon as I leave, and I consider that to be a mistake. When they change to the new method, they will see only the combined efforts here listed as a nondescript budget item. Everything will be hidden without the identity of a human body and a specific little community that appears on their map."

"Who will pay your retirement when you return home?" Billie asked.

"The United Missionary Fund of Combined Churches, but it will be very little, my dear. About thirty-five dollars a month I believe."

"My goodness! How can you expect to live on that?"

"That's just it, honey, I don't believe I can," Dr. Call answered reflectively. "Nevertheless, I'll make out somehow. God always provides. Not much I can do about it really. All these years over here, Social Security was never available to me."

"Well, there is something *we* can do about it," Billie stated emphatically, looking to Wade. "We will provide for a stipend to be sent to you each month."

"No, no, my dear, I couldn't have you do something like that. You owe me nothing."

"It will be our deep pleasure," Billie insisted. "When Wade and I go back to make a home for ourselves, we will want to join the church right up the road. We will make arrangements with them to send you a check each month from what we designate for that purpose. Besides, it's not such a great sacrifice for us, and we can write it off on our taxes. I know that sounds so commercial to you, but that's the way things work."

Dr. Call was deeply touched, but not convinced. "No, my dear. I couldn't have you do anything like that."

Billie was not one to be derailed. "Don't you of all people—one who has done so much for others—realize the satisfaction this would bring to us? Think about it; it will be wonderful for us. You'll be the Living Link for us and my children!"

As promised, the River Indus north of Hyderabad was not only historic, but also free of pollution and thus suitable for baptism. Each person dressed in a white gown and stood waist deep in the river, encircled by bicycle inner tubes filled with cut flowers of various colors. Dr. Call's congregation turned out in full force to support the ceremony, both adults and children holding hands in union. The words of baptism were recited as Billie was lowered first into the water, one hand on Dr. Call's arm and the other holding Wade's hand, and the two aides supporting Billie's weight under her back. A tender expression was written on her face as she came up out of the water. Then the process was repeated with Wade.

Having renewed their baptismal vows, Wade Simmons and Billie Blacksheare were wed in holy matrimony. John, being a true courtier, had tied each wedding band to their arms with a string so they would not wash away in the river. As each ring was placed on the intended's third fingers, John cut the string with a knife.

Later when Billie and Dr. Call had gone to a separate room to change into dry clothing, she asked Billie with a sort of motherly care how she was able to keep such a youthful figure, to which Billie responded with a laugh that she supposed it was from pulling the reins on those stubborn horses every day.

Billie also shared with Dr. Call the long years she had spent trying to understand and come to grips with the reality of a spiritual being, as she described it. In speaking of JD, she was surprised to learn that Dr. Call knew of him. In fact, she remarked about the strong faith he exuded during his preaching and traveling around to raise money to pay off church debt.

When Billie, somewhat apologetically, referred to JD's efforts to convert her as fruitless in comparison to the strong urge she felt to be baptized in the Shenandoah after hearing Wade speak of God, Dr. Call smiled and said, "My dear, I think both men in their different ways felt a deep and abiding love for you. JD's efforts were certainly not misdirected or of no avail. At least he kept you questioning until Wade wrote and came into your heart."

Billie agreed with this assessment and felt at peace.

"I notice that neither of you are sharp-tongued," Dr. Call shared. "On the other hand, you are not subtle in expressing yourselves. In fact, you are quite alike, even in your choice of words—so straightforward and sincere. I can see why there was an emergence of your love and spirits."

"I was glad that you baptized Wade again, especially standing there with me. Have you ever baptized a couple like us and then married them while they were still in the water?"

"No, I definitely have never done that before!"

"Well, Dr. Call," Billie declared, "I can assure you that this marriage will last. I know this in my heart."

"I'm sure it will, my dear. Very sure! Wade's a fine-hearted man. And you, my dear, in the short time I've known you, you are most unusual—an anomaly, if I ever saw one!"

Billie laughed. "I'll take that as a compliment. The last time I heard that word was when JD's father called me an anomaly after reading a as a pearl and we should not cast it into a hog mire where it would not be appreciated. Now let me finish my thoughts without interruption, and when you think of pearls and diamonds, put yourself right there in the pile with them because that's how precious you are to your mother and me."

Susanne smiled, thus allowing her father to continue.

"I'm very empathetic with women in their quest to lead their own lives, live their own dreams and, above all, flourish, free of a husband's tyranny. Remember, I spent years witnessing and empathizing with my mother's plight."

"Billie was in much the same position," Susanne interjected.

"In some ways, yes," JD acknowledged. "She was never going to let some boy, or even a man, bear hard on her, and she even went a step further in thinking those that tried to be tyrants or masters were themselves lacking in courage or perhaps even decency."

"Did you love her, Daddy?"

"Yes, but like a sister."

"Like Little Bonnie?"

"Somewhat, perhaps," JD responded thoughtfully.

Susanne felt she might need to justify herself in some way, so she said, "I have never put my arms around another boy, except Uncle Will or Paw when he was still alive. While you were in the war, I was always defending myself against some overbearing kid or a drunken handyman."

"I know those summers you spent with your Grandma Bonnie and Maw left an impression on you. Couple that with Miss Blackshearc's ideas, and you had some sorting out to do. Billie spent much of her time trying to figure out those who painted the rose without ever admitting or realizing that Jesus painted it like no one ever could or ever will. Instead of enjoying and appreciating Jesus's painting, she wanted to paint her own—paradoxically, and quite possibly to prove that there was indeed no existence of the rose."

JD stopped and looked at Susanne quizzically. "I assume Billie told you about the rose?"

"O, yes, she did, Daddy. And she told me about the beggar lice also."

"What did she say?"

"She said that you told her she was like beggar lice—the prickly seeds of weeds that cling to the fur of animals or the pants of a man to be carried to a new destination where it would fall and germinate into the soil."

JD laughed. "That's right. That's exactly what told her. Did she also tell you that I partook of the chalice and she of the stirrup cup?"

"Yes," Susanne acknowledged. "She told me that as well."

"Billie is no longer the woman she used to be, Susanne. She has found and accepted Jesus as the rose."

Susanne's eyes widened in question.

"You remember the Shakespeare saying, 'A rose by any other name is still a rose.'" Susanne nodded. "It has always seemed to me that the importance we put on family lineage is parochial at best. Our approach and appreciation of lineage should be of God, not family or country. If we look back at the intellectual gift of the Daynes, we will see that it actually comes from my great-great grandmother on the Baber side of the family and not from the Daynes at all! Coincidentally, I think my spiritual acumen comes from my mother's side of the family, not the Brown side. More accurately, Maw's relations. Now I know Paw's spirituality was equal to many we know, but some of his forbearers were actually of ill repute.

"Thus, if we follow our family lineage, we will see that our intellectual and spiritual acuity veer from family name to family name. You and I are in the here and now. We should not only build on our God-given gifts, but we should also concern ourselves with our neighbor's potential. To name a person Caesar does not make him a ruler."

Susanne finally understood the purpose of her father's little sermon, and she smiled at him knowingly. JD in turn looked her directly in the eye and said, "The endowment of a husband's name at the time of marriage is a symbol of love and commitment, not merit or stature."

"I understand, Daddy."

JD leaned over and gave his daughter a warm hug. She had grown into a lovely young lady, but she would always be his little girl. "The young man you love is a good man," JD stated.

Susanne smiled proudly. "He dropped the touchdown pass in the end zone."

"I know," JD responded with a twinkle in his eye. "But when the referee didn't see it and called it a winning touchdown, the goodness and honesty within Matthew caused him to confess to the referee that he had dropped the ball. Not only was the game lost, Matthew subjected himself to ridicule rather than the acclaim that was his if only he had remained silent. Don't make him jump through hoops on his wedding day, honey."

"Oh, Daddy, you could make a horse cry! But I love you!"

"I love you, too, Susanne. And when you marry, I want the honor of walking you down the aisle as your Dad and not your preacher."